FATAL CONVERGENCE

Books by Bryan Davis

The Time Echoes Trilogy
Time Echoes
Interfinity
Fatal Convergence

The Reapers Trilogy
Reapers
Beyond the Gateway
Reaper Reborn

The Oculus Gate
Heaven Came Down
Invading Hell
My Soul to Take
On Earth as it is in Hell

Dragons in our Midst
Raising Dragons
The Candlestone
Circles of Seven
Tears of a Dragon

Oracles of Fire
Eye of the Oracle
Enoch's Ghost
Last of the Nephilim
The Bones of Makaidos

Children of the Bard
Song of the Ovulum
From the Mouth of Elijah
The Seventh Door
Omega Dragon

To learn more about Bryan's books, go to
www.daviscrossing.com

FATAL CONVERGENCE

BOOK 3 OF
THE TIME ECHOES TRILOGY

BY BRYAN DAVIS

Copyright © 2017 by Bryan Davis

Published by Scrub Jay Journeys

email: info@daviscrossing.com

Print ISBN: 978-1-946253-45-3

Printed in the U.S.A.

Library of Congress Control Number: 2016919006

Cover Design by Rebekah Sather - selfpubbookcovers.com/ RLSather

Fatal Convergence is a rewrite of *Nightmare's Edge*, published in 2009.

CHAPTER ONE

CERULEAN AND I walked through Kelly's dream — a dark cemetery with tombstones protruding from the ground at odd angles. The air grew frigid, making me glad for the gray Iowa sweatshirt I had borrowed from Nathan of Earth Blue. Since he had suffered a tragic death, he no longer needed it.

With Cerulean holding a slender white candle to counter the dimness, we searched for any sign of Jack, the Earth Yellow plane crash survivor who suffered the loss of his eyes to Mictar's fiery hand. We couldn't risk calling for him. Mictar might be lurking somewhere within earshot.

Bones littered the weed-infested ground. Gnarled oak trees with hanging moss painted twisted shadows on the path that coursed through an abandoned yard. As we passed by a bent, leafless tree, draped with long, hanging vines, Cerulean whispered, "Beware of the spider trees. They are one of the few realities in a dreamscape. Stay away from them."

"Good to know."

A large raven perched atop one of the burial markers, staring at me as I passed.

"Read," it croaked, its red eyes shining. "Read. Read."

I stopped and leaned closer. "You mean the tombstone?"

"Read! Read!"

Cerulean grabbed my arm. "It is not wise to heed the words of the dream creatures."

"Just reading the tombstone won't hurt." I took the candle from him and walked to the side of the grave. The raven still leering at me, I held the flame close to the stone and read out loud, "Here lies Kelly Clark, murdered by Nathan Shepherd and unable to rest in the glare of her killer's light."

"What?" I leaned back. "How could a tombstone know I'm here?"

Cerulean stared at the raven. "Three possibilities. First, Kelly sees us in her dream, so she created the inscription even as you drew close. Second, a dream stalker is trying to intimidate you to keep you from proceeding. Third, and perhaps the most dangerous of all, maybe you are becoming part of the dreamscape."

"How is that possible?"

"Patar likely sent Jack here to keep him alive, knowing the poor man would soon become part of the dream world, a living phantom who wanders in people's nightmares. Jack would survive, but only Patar would know how to extract him without killing him. This melding with the dream world eventually happens to all unguarded humans, depending on their ability to resist the temptations they find within."

I pointed at myself. "Will I be able to leave safely? I'm not part of this place yet, am I?"

Fixing his gaze on me, Cerulean shook his head. "You appear solid, so one of the other two options is more likely. I suspect that a stalker is present."

"Who? Mictar?"

"He is powerful enough." Cerulean took a quick step and grabbed the raven by the throat. It choked out a squawk and flailed its wings under the supplicant's grip, vainly trying to claw his arm. "Where is your master?"

"Read!" it croaked again. "Read!"

Cerulean shook its body. "You have a voice. Tell me who sent you."

"Read! Read!" The raven broke free. In a scattering of feathers, it flew into the darkness above.

Cerulean took the candle from me. "Come. We must hurry. The longer we stay, the greater the danger."

"The raven wanted us to read the inscription again. Maybe there's a new one."

Cerulean held the flame high and grasped my arm. "It is of no consequence. If the message has been written by the stalker, it is likely a lie. If it is a product of Kelly's nightmarish fears, it will heighten your own. If you are becoming part of this world, deep emotions will only hasten the process."

"Not knowing will drive me crazy." I squinted at the tombstone, but it was now too dark to read. "Taking a second or two won't hurt."

Cerulean held fast. "The risk is too high. Your unwarranted insistence demonstrates that the effect this place is having on you is escalating rapidly. You are losing your ability to reason."

"But I have to know." As I pulled against Cerulean's grip, the supplicant's blue hair grew fuzzy, like reeds waving under restless waters. "Let me go."

"Nathan!"

The shout sounded like a thunderclap. Ahead on the path, a man stood with his fists set against his hips, his face bent into a deep scowl.

I blinked. "Is it Mictar?"

"No," Cerulean said, loosening his grip. "It is Patar."

Patar walked three steps closer before halting. The candlelight gleamed on a plastic bag in his hand. "I sense conflict. What is the trouble?"

I nodded toward the tombstone. "I have to know what it says. Kelly might be communicating with me."

"As you can see, Cerulean ..." Patar's voice grew distant, warped, as if he were speaking from the midst of a cave. "He is being absorbed." The stalker's slender form now seemed foggy as well, distorted, more like a dream than reality.

Cerulean nodded. "I can see that now. He is showing signs of fading."

"I'm fading?" I pointed at Cerulean, then at Patar. "You two are the ghostly looking ones."

"It's only going to get worse," Patar said. "His mental defenses are withering, and Kelly's nightmare is reaching a climax."

A sudden gust blew away a blanket of clouds. A full moon, at least five times its usual size, hovered in a purple sky. Its glow illuminated the cemetery, allowing a clearer view of the dozens of tombstones.

"Shall I take him out immediately?" Cerulean asked. "Or should I find Jack first?"

A low rumble sounded at my side. At the gravesite where the raven once perched, a hand pushed out of the earth, then a second hand and a head. Finally, an entire female body climbed up and shook dirt from her shoulder-length blonde hair. She looked straight ahead and called, "Nathan? Are you here?"

"Kelly?" I stared at her. "It really *is* you!"

Wearing a knee-length nightshirt, she brushed off the soil, revealing letters on the front that read "Sanity Is Overrated." She staggered toward me, feeling for obstacles in her way. "Nathan? Where are you? I hear your voice."

As Kelly drew closer, her face clarified, revealing vacant sockets — dark holes instead of eyes. I stiffened. Could she be the Earth Blue Kelly, somehow resurrected? Or was she Kelly Red, a new victim of Mictar's cruel, electrified hand?

No, I told myself, *she's only part of a dream.* Yet, she looked so real.

Kelly stopped and touched my cheeks with icy fingers. "There you are. Why didn't you answer me?" She shivered and rubbed her arms. "I'm cold and scared. Will you get me out of here? I can't see a thing."

I reached for her hand, then jerked back. "You're just a mirage. I can't take you anywhere."

"You are correct." Cerulean lifted his candle higher. "Stay in the light, Nathan. Do not be deceived."

"This is no time for joking around," Kelly said as she bounced on the toes of her sock-covered feet. "You can't leave me in this horrible place. It's so cold, so terribly cold. Please take me home." She reached out for me. With missing eyes and a dirty face, she seemed like a pitiful waif as her voice broke into a lament. "Nathan … please … I'm scared."

"I'll get you out." I grabbed her hand. "Just hang on."

The chilled fingers of her other hand wrapped around my upper arm. She was solid, real, without a hint of fading.

"Oh, thank you." She leaned her head against my shoulder. "I told you never to leave me, not even for a minute. I felt so alone. So scared."

For a moment, dizziness flooded my mind, but I shook it off. "Just stay with me. Cerulean will get us out of here."

"Nathan," Cerulean said, "if you continue—"

"Let him go for a moment." Patar's voice faded even further. He poured the contents of his bag into Cerulean's hand. "When I wrestled with my brother, I recovered these from his energy reserves and was able to reconstitute them. You will find Jack approximately one hundred paces ahead. Restore these and get him and Nathan out of here with all speed."

In Cerulean's transparent palm lay two perfectly formed eyeballs with nerves and moist tissue attached.

"Have you found your new charge?" Patar asked.

Cerulean gave him a pensive look. "Not yet."

"Have you not been listening? She calls for help from this dream world. If I can hear her, surely you can."

"I have heard her song, but I was unsure of my responsibilities. Much has changed."

Patar laid a hand on Cerulean's shoulder. "You are still a supplicant to Earth Blue. You must continue your duties."

"Then my work with Nathan is finished," Cerulean said. "I will have to find this new gifted one."

"You will." Patar handed him the empty bag. "Because Nathan broke the portal mirror and lost the camera, he will not be able to travel to my world to play the violin at Sarah's Womb, at least not at this time. You can, however, send him to Earth Yellow to find other options."

"Yes," Cerulean said. "Before we came here, Nathan's mother was playing Foundation's Key to see which mirror is the correct portal. With so many mirrors, it is a grueling task. While she rested, we decided to try to find Jack. I was unsure of how the dreamscape would affect Nathan, so this was a test."

"And he failed, just as he did when he allowed his desire for revenge against my brother to outweigh his wisdom. He had the power to escape with the mirror intact."

"Nathan," Kelly said, her fingers growing warmer on my skin. "Don't let him talk about you like that. You did the best you could. You were under a lot of pressure."

"You're right." I stared at Kelly. Even with dirt smeared across her cheeks, black holes where her blue eyes should be, and grungy, tangled hair, she seemed lovelier than ever. "And I really didn't have much of a choice."

"Then don't listen. We'll find our own way out."

"Go now," Patar said, "before that rotting cadaver becomes more real to him. He will soon bond with it beyond all hope of reason." Patar faded out of sight.

Cerulean put the eyeballs into the bag and stuffed the top into his waistband. Lifting the candle, he pulled my elbow. "Jack is near. Let us retrieve him and flee this place."

Leading Kelly by the arm, I followed Cerulean, now a blue ghost. "Did you hear that, Kelly? We'll be out of here soon."

"Thank you, Nathan." She staggered along, her empty eye sockets still wide. "I knew you wouldn't leave me here."

With the moon shining brightly, the going became easier. It took only a few seconds to find Jack sitting on the ground, leaning against a tombstone. He seemed solid, though Cerulean was now as transparent as thinning fog.

Jack ran his fingers through his thick beard. "Who's there?"

"He is losing his grip on reality as well." Cerulean crouched next to the tombstone. "I will have to work quickly."

"He looks fine. He's not fading at all." I turned to Kelly. I almost said, "Right, Kelly?" forgetting for a moment that she couldn't see anything.

"Take this." Cerulean handed me the candle. "Watch me through the flame."

"Okay." Feeling dizzy again, I held the flame close to my nose and peered through it. Cerulean pulled the eyeballs from the bag. Then, while singing unintelligible words at a high pitch, he laid his palm over Jack's empty sockets and pushed the eyeballs into place.

Blue light seeped around the edges of Cerulean's hand. He appeared to have an ability similar to Mictar's, a powerful light that flashed from his palm. With every second I peered through the candle's flame, Cerulean grew more solid while Jack stayed the same. I looked back at Kelly. Her face seemed fuzzier, distant.

She angled her head as if listening. "What's happening?"

"Everything's okay." As I spoke, her features clarified. "Cerulean is repairing Jack's eyes. We'll leave in a minute."

I turned back to Cerulean, lowering the candle to see him better. Ghostly blue once more, he helped Jack to his feet.

"Can you see?" Cerulean asked.

"Very well, thank you." Jack pulled a rumpled fedora from beneath his jacket and straightened it. "Everything is clear, except for you."

"Your normal sight will be restored soon."

"Excellent! Excellent! The end of a nightmare at last!" He put his hat on and turned toward me, his restored eyes glistening. "Nathan, I'm so glad to see you."

"Same here." I gave the candle back to Cerulean and shook Jack's hand, grimacing at the pressure on my wounds. "Now let's all go to the real world. I have to figure out what happened to Kelly and get some eyes for her, too."

"Nathan." Cerulean pushed the candle closer. "You and Jack will come with me. You must leave Kelly behind."

"What?" I shook my head hard. "I can't leave her here."

Kelly's arm locked around mine. "Of course you can't. I have to stay with you."

Cerulean pulled Jack and me together and held the candle's flame near our eyes. His voice mellowed to a soothing chant. "Stare at the flame. It is the light of reality. The images around you are mere phantoms. Bring what is real into focus, or you will not return to the ones you love."

He blew a puff of sweet-smelling air into my face. "Think of your mother. She waits for you in the Earth Blue bedroom. You have to go back and search for your father. The real Kelly is there as well. We need to awaken her from this nightmare so you and she can go to Earth Yellow and save two world populations from disaster."

The flame's glow spread over Cerulean's face, making his features clearer. He compressed my chin with his hand, forcing me to keep my stare locked on the flame. "You must let this Kelly go, Nathan. She is not real. Night is over and dawn is breaking."

"No, Nathan!" Kelly's voice spiked into a wail. "You promised to stay with me. This place is cold and dark, and I'm scared."

Ever so gently, Cerulean pulled on my chin, drawing me forward, his voice hypnotizing. "Release her, Nathan. All will be well. You will see the real Kelly in mere moments. We will awaken her, and she will escape this torture."

Heaving shallow breaths, I pried Kelly's fingers loose and pulled away.

"Nathan! What are you doing?" Kelly, now ghostly and floating backwards, reached for me with open hands. "I'll be alone again. All alone in this cold, dark place."

"I … I can't leave her. She's—"

Cerulean's voice sharpened again. "She is not real!"

My mind now swimming, I repeated the words in a whisper. "She is not real."

Cerulean blew out the candle. As the light faded, Kelly's voice faded with it. "I'm so cold. So cold."

CHAPTER TWO

L IGHT FLOODED MY vision. I blinked, trying to focus as the Earth Blue bedroom materialized around me. Mom sat on a chair, her violin clutched at her side, while Amber, the Earth Yellow supplicant, held a small square mirror at her waist. Jack stood next to Cerulean, a wide smile on his face as he looked around with his restored eyes.

On the floor, Kelly lay on a mattress, shivering. "So cold," she whimpered. "So cold."

I dropped to my knees, grabbed her arm, and gave her a shake. "Kelly, wake up. It's just a bad dream."

Her eyes shot open, glassy and wild. "Nathan! Don't leave me!"

"I'm here." I wrapped my arms around her. "I won't leave you. I promise."

She returned the embrace. "But you did leave me. I begged you not to, but you left anyway."

Cerulean, his hair and skin glowing blue, crouched at Kelly's opposite side. "Nathan, invaded nightmares are the most vivid of all, and now you understand the danger. When you go to Earth Yellow, it will likely be worse. The nightmare epidemic has proven that the veil between dreams and reality is thinner there, and Mictar will also be watching for you. If you lose your grip on reality, you will fall into his clutches, for he can manipulate the dreams and lead you into a trap."

"But if I think something is real when it's not, how can I ever be sure?"

Cerulean held the extinguished candle in front of my eyes. "You must focus on light from the real world. It will keep you anchored."

I released Kelly. Her glassy eyes gave evidence of her damaged vision, a malevolent reminder of a violent encounter with Mictar. A spot of blood on the white fabric of her Newton High School sweatshirt told the tale of another wound she had suffered during the fight. Seeing her so afraid wrenched my heart. "I'd never really leave you in a graveyard, you know."

Tears now drying on her cheeks, she nodded. "Sorry about my reaction. I was kind of spaced out."

"What exactly happened in there?" Mom asked.

After explaining my journey through Kelly's nightmare, Jack and Cerulean adding a few details I had forgotten, I finished with a sigh. "So that's why Cerulean's worried about what might happen next time."

Amber set the mirror on a pile of matching squares. "I counted forty-one mirrors that we searched before you left. If we are unable to find one leading to Earth Yellow, then surviving the dream world will be the least of our worries."

"I don't want to drive five hours to the observatory," I said, "not with all the crazy problems going on. Even if we could get gas, who knows what the roads will be like?"

I picked up the mirror with my unbandaged hand, still raw from sliding down a rope into Sarah's Womb. Although it was worth the pain to play the chasm's violin strings and temporarily thrust Earth Red away from the threat of the merging worlds, when Daryl Blue plunged into the void while trying to save my life, the effort turned into a catastrophe.

Amber seated herself on the trunk next to the wall. With long blonde hair draped over a simple yellow dress and skin shimmering like gold, she looked like a storybook fairy.

Lifting her head, she gazed upward, her face dreamy and her eyes far away. "While in prison I could watch and pray for my beloved as I listened to the music of her soul, but now the songs are many, and most are dissonant and troubling. If I do not find her soon, I think I will drown in this sea of sorrows."

"We'll get you to her," I said. "The right mirror has to be around here somewhere."

Mom played Foundation's Key, then laid the violin in her lap. "Kelly, what do you see?"

Kelly and I looked at the mirror in my hand. The reflection showed a terrified boy, maybe five years old, standing with a shivering beagle on a snow-covered sheet of ice in the middle of a raging river. Two men wearing military garb threw a rope to the boy. The moment he caught it, I blew a relieved sigh. If not for the men, I would have been sorely tempted to try to save the boy, even though we had no time to rescue every endangered person we might find in the mirrors.

"It's not Earth Yellow," Kelly said. "Too fuzzy."

Mom nodded, her shoulders low. She had played Foundation's Key more than forty times, and we had more than three hundred mirrors to check. I was beginning to regret smashing one across Mictar's face, even though my decision was probably the only reason the stalker hadn't shown up yet. Because that mirror was missing, we weren't able to get the entire mosaic of mirrors operating simultaneously, forcing us to look at them one by one.

Kelly sat on the trunk next to Amber and propped up another mirror. Looking at me, she asked, "If we find the right one, have you decided what to do with the others?"

I shook my head. "Mictar will come here eventually to look for a mirror, but we can't take four hundred of them to Earth Yellow."

"Right, but we have to think of something." Kelly turned the mirror toward Mom. "Ready?"

Mom played the key once more. The mirror displayed a deserted city scene—closely packed multistory buildings, streetlights illuminating empty sidewalks, and vacant newsstands with magazines and papers rippling in the breeze. A young woman, maybe twenty years old, dressed in a long coat, scarf, and ski cap stood at a corner. As windblown snow buffeted her face, she clasped a bundle to her chest.

I drew closer. Could that bundle be a baby? Was she waiting for someone? Maybe a bus or a taxi? With the streets empty and the snow mounting, it looked like she might have to wait a long time.

"It's Earth Yellow," Kelly said as she angled her body to see the image. "It's as clear as crystal."

"But where on Earth Yellow?" I asked. "Can anyone tell?"

Jack peered at the mirror with his newly restored eyes. "That's Michigan Avenue in Chicago. I was a cab driver for years, and I know every corner in the city. Since she's standing outside in the snow with a baby, she's probably waiting for a ride." He ran the brim of his hat through his hands. "Can we go there? Help her out?"

"If we flash a light. At least we would be on the right earth, and then Amber could take us to the dream world. Still pretty far from Francesca Yellow, though."

Kelly held the mirror closer to her eyes. "The snow's making it hard to see her face, but ..."

"But what?"

She grabbed my wrist. "Come with me. I'll need your eyesight."

As she pulled me out of the room and down the hall, I had to jog to keep up. "Where are we going?"

"To my dad's bedroom. I know this house well enough to find it, but I'll need you once we get there."

After hustling through a second corridor, we entered a spacious bedroom. Still holding the mirror, Kelly slowed and blinked in the dimness. I flipped the wall switch, but the twin ceiling-fan lights stayed dark. "I forgot. Still no power."

Kelly tiptoed around a king-sized bed and stopped in front of a dresser sitting against the far wall. Its attached mirror reflected our shadowy forms and the smaller mirror in Kelly's hands. A large leather photo album sat on top of the dresser under a jumble of socks and old receipts.

She laid the mirror next to the album and lifted the cover. Inside, photos filled the pages, each neatly inserted in a protective pocket. "Can you look for a picture that shows a woman holding a baby?"

I flipped a couple of pages and found one. "Here."

She slid the mirror next to the photo. "Does she look like this woman?"

I stared at the two images. The woman in the mirror swayed from side to side much faster than normal, like a movie playing at high speed. "I'm not sure. I think she resembles—"

"Shhh." Kelly raised a finger to her lips. "Let me listen."

I closed my mouth. Although I couldn't hear anything, I knew better than to say so. Kelly's gift of interpreting sounds from other worlds was at work.

After several seconds, her finger hovered over the woman's face. "She's singing to the baby. It's real fast, but I can pick it up." Kelly sang the song in a trembling whisper. "Hush little baby, don't say a word. Mama's gonna buy you a mockingbird. And if that mockingbird won't sing, Mama's gonna buy you a ruby ring."

"Ruby ring? I thought it was a diamond ring."

"My mother always said *ruby*. I know, because she used to help me babysit."

"Your mother?" I pointed at the photo. "So that's you she's carrying?"

Kelly nodded. "We must be ... I mean, they must be freezing. We have to help them."

"Ahem!"

I looked back. Jack stood at the door. "You had better return to the other room," he said. "We have a visitor. No danger, but you'd better come right away."

I enclosed the mirror in the photo album and picked it up. Hand-in-hand, we hurried past Jack. When we reached the bedroom, I slowed and peered in. Mom stood holding the violin at her side while Cerulean and Amber gazed at a mirror square.

I helped Kelly through the door and gave her the photo album. She opened it and slid out the mirror.

"What's up, Mom?" I asked.

She nodded toward the mirror in Cerulean's grip. "See for yourself."

Cerulean turned the square toward me. A narrow, pale face filled the entire image—Patar, his eyes glowing red, though a softer hue than usual. Seeing this stalker meant a tongue lashing was probably on the horizon.

"I'm here." I cleared my throat. "What do you want?"

"It occurred to me," Patar said, his voice more pleasant than usual, "that I gave instructions while you were in a dazed state of mind, and I was concerned that you might not have understood my meaning. Simply put, once you reach Earth Yellow you must find a way to travel back to my world to finish your task."

His eyes shifted from side to side, apparently looking at each of the supplicants in turn. "Because of Scarlet's plunge into Sarah's Womb and your loss of the mirror and camera, the only way to enter my world now is to use the observatory."

I drew a mental picture of the Earth Yellow observatory mirror, anchored in the foundation at the future site of Interfinity Labs. Since we needed piano music, Kelly persuaded a radio station to play Moonlight Sonata to open the portal to Patar's home. Yet, Yellow's time was zooming relative to ours. Things might be a lot different there now. "Any idea how the Interfinity construction is coming along on Earth Yellow?"

Patar's brow bent. "I am not omniscient. I suggest that you go there and investigate."

"We have a portal, but it leads to downtown Chicago. Maybe a different mirror will take us directly to the observatory."

"No," Kelly said, showing me the mirror. "My mother's walking away. We have to go through this one. Now."

I pressed a hand against the side of my head. Once again, the weight of multiple worlds rested on my shoulders, and the wrong decision could mean the deaths of billions. "Okay. Okay. We'll go."

"Do you have a vehicle?" Jack asked. "If so, can it transport with you?"

I looked out the bedroom window. Windblown snow raced across the front yard, blending with yellow leaves that had fallen from the now-naked cottonwood tree next to the empty driveway. "No. We left the Toyota at Tony Yellow's house. So even if we went through this mirror, we'd be stuck—"

"Gunther will show up," Kelly said. "I know he will. Just like he did at the Burger King when he and Francesca dreamed about us."

I looked at the fierce determination in her eyes as her creased brow accentuated a gash across her forehead. No matter how many times these adventures left her bruised and battered, she was always ready for the next one. "You're probably right." I gave Patar a nod. "We'll trust in Gunther and Francesca and their dream prophecies."

Patar's red eyes brightened. "Remember what I told you about how to save the worlds. You have seen it work. Although it is a tragic path, it is the most efficient one."

I sighed. Yes, Scarlet's death did save Earth Red, but the cost was so high. And what right did Patar have to make that kind of call? He wouldn't have to suffer; those supplicants meant nothing to him. I couldn't kill Amber and Cerulean, even if their deaths would save countless lives. I had to find another way.

As Patar's image faded, I snatched a phone from my pocket. "Better let Daryl know." I looked at the phone's screen. "No signal and the battery's almost dead."

Kelly tightened her grip on the mirror's edges. "My mother walked out of sight."

I dropped the phone to the mattress, picked up a flashlight from the floor, and aimed it at the mirror. "Everyone on this side. I'm not sure how many it will transport, but we'll soon find out."

While Mom, Jack, Amber, Kelly, and I positioned ourselves in front of the mirror held by Kelly's extended arms, Cerulean stepped away. "I can be of no help to you there. I will stay and secure the mirrors." He kissed Amber's cheek. "Then I must search the dream world here. My new beloved calls for me, and I must find her."

"Might I be able to help you?" Jack asked. "Although I had no eyes while I was there, I became well acquainted with the sounds and smells of that world."

Cerulean held out a hand. "Perhaps you would be of service."

As Jack joined the supplicant, I gave them a nod and turned on the flashlight. The beam bounced off the mirror and splashed over our bodies. The room crumbled into thousands of tiny shards, replaced by the city corner we had seen in the mirror. Frigid wind tore into our bodies, and snow pelted our faces.

Bouncing on her toes, Kelly rubbed her arms. "Brilliant! We forgot to bring coats."

I untied the sleeves from around my waist and reached the sweatshirt toward Kelly.

She waved a hand. "I'm already wearing the one I borrowed from Kelly Blue."

I looked at Mom. She, too, already wore a sweatshirt, so I pulled my own over my head and scanned the sidewalks, trying not to shiver. The curtain of falling flakes veiled my view of the nearly vacant block. Tall buildings lined both sides of the street, and an "L" train rumbled somewhere out of sight. Only a few pedestrians interrupted the sea of white sidewalks and office buildings.

Mom shielded her eyes with one hand and tucked the violin to her side with the other. Amber, now holding the photo album, stooped and pushed her finger into the six-inch layer of white. As dozens of flakes coated her blonde hair and eyebrows, she looked up at me without a hint of a shiver. "The snow is deep enough. We could follow the woman's tracks."

Someone called out, "Need coats?"

CHAPTER THREE

D ARYL, HER RED hair partially covered by a woolen hood, extended an armful of coats, a wide smile on her face.

I puffed her name in a stream of white vapor. "Daryl!"

"In the flesh." She pushed the coats toward Kelly. "Yours is on top, Kelly-kins."

Kelly lifted the coat and slid her arms through the sleeves. "How did you—"

"Easy. You left the coats in the observatory. I brought them. You know me. Always prepared." She peeled off the second coat and gave it to Mom. "This was Daryl Blue's. I think it'll fit you."

I took the last coat and passed it to Amber, feeling guilty that I hadn't offered her my sweatshirt earlier, but she waved it off. "I am not cold." Her body, now glowing with a pale golden aura, shifted as if swaying to an inaudible tune. Her bare feet rose to tiptoes and lowered with each cycle. She smiled. "Are you perplexed, Nathan?"

"I guess so." I pushed my arms through the coat sleeves. "I'm wondering how you stay warm."

"Now that I am in this world, I hear the music in the air, and it has eased my troubled mind. Once you learn to dance with the heavenly sounds, the corruption of the elements will no longer overwhelm you." She touched my cheek with her warm fingers. "This will be a new journey for you, one that cannot be explained here and now. Yet, at some point, you will have to learn the dance."

Kelly glanced around. "Does anyone see my Earth Yellow mother? She was here a few seconds ago."

Daryl looked at her wristwatch. "More like seven minutes ago. Gunther and I picked her up while we were looking for you guys."

"Did Gunther have a dream?" I asked as I buttoned the coat.

"Yep. He and Francesca locked in on you popping into this world right at this location. He picked me up at the observatory yesterday, which was about an hour ago, Earth Blue time."

"Why did you decide to make the jump?"

She held up a finger. "One, I was on generator power at the observatory, so the equipment couldn't run much longer, and two"—she lifted another finger—"I found out Earth Red's in a heap of trouble, so I came here to see what I could do about it."

"Earth Red? I thought we pushed them away from Interfinity."

"Well … sort of. You see—"

A gunning engine sounded from behind her. As Daryl turned, I looked over her shoulder. A van marked "Stoneman Enterprises" wheeled around a corner, slipping and sliding through the snow. As soon as it straightened, Gunther came into view through the windshield, his face taut.

When the van pulled up to the walkway, I opened the side door, revealing a woman seated on the rear bench holding a bundle in her arms. With shoulder-length blonde hair and blue eyes, she could have passed for Kelly's older sister. "Mrs. Clark?" I asked. "Molly Clark?"

Molly tucked the blanket around her baby and scooted away from the cold air. "I am." An Irish accent flavored her words. "It seems that every stranger in town knows my name."

"Hop in," Gunther said. "Let's get moving before the zone police find us."

Mom stepped up into the van. "The zone police?" she asked as she slid close to Molly.

Gunther pointed at himself with his thumb. "I'm a marked man. It helps to keep moving. That's why I dropped Daryl off to look for you while I drove around. They're cracking down on us travelers."

"As well they should," Molly said, now sitting next to the window. "You people get us all in trouble."

Gunther gave her a thin smile. "And *out* of trouble, it seems."

I reached for Amber's hand, but she drew away and peered inside, angling her head as she scanned the interior.

"It's safe," I said. "It's nothing like your prison dome."

"I have seen such machines in my visions, but I never imagined I would ride in one." She took my hand, stepped up to the bench seat, and settled next to Mom.

I leaned close to Daryl and whispered, "You can ride shotgun up front, and I'll sit with Kelly in the cargo area. I don't want to mention Kelly's name in front of Molly for obvious reasons."

"Gotcha, boss." Daryl jumped into her seat. "But I wish I *had* a shotgun. That could come in handy."

With an eye on her Earth Yellow mother, Kelly hopped up and squeezed into the back. I joined her, whispering, "Is that baby you?"

She nodded, pushed aside an empty Ritz Crackers box, and sat cross-legged on the flat carpet. "Ask her why she's by herself. It's important."

As Gunther began driving away, I cleared my throat. "Uh … Molly. We were wondering why you were standing out in the snow. Was someone supposed to pick you up?"

Molly turned toward me, a worried look crossing her face. "My husband, Tony. We just returned from Europe, and he dropped me off at Neiman Marcus to shop while he picked up a shipment he sent from Scotland. The store closed because of the snowstorm, so I had to watch for him from the sidewalk. I couldn't very well look for other shelter, because he wouldn't be able to find me. I had to keep my baby warm somehow, so when Gunther drove by with Tony's old girlfriend, I decided to ride around with them until Tony came back."

"His old girlfriend?" Daryl let out a huff. "When pigs fly to Pluto."

"Tony is a fine man," Molly said in a sharp tone, "and since he calls you his former flame, it seems that pigs have sprouted wings."

Daryl swung toward Molly. "Speaking of pigs—"

"Cool it," I said. "Let's just concentrate on finding Tony."

Crossing her arms, Daryl glared straight ahead, muttering something unintelligible.

Kelly reached up and touched Molly's shoulder. "Was the shipment a bunch of mirror squares?"

"What?" Molly looked back at her. "How could you know that?"

"It's a long story, but when we find Tony, I'll try to explain. He's at a sports bar just a couple of blocks away."

"A sports bar?" Molly asked. "He wouldn't—"

"He would. Trust me. You'll see." Kelly pointed at a Ford pickup in the distance. "I don't know the name of the bar, but I think it's just past that truck."

Gunther nodded. "We'll be there in a second."

As the van slipped across the snowy pavement, Kelly whispered to me, "My parents have argued about this incident ever since I can remember. I know every detail."

"A turning point in their marriage?"

"A wrecking ball." She fastened her coat's top button and rose to her knees. "Let's see if we can defuse this bomb before it explodes."

"What are you going to do?"

"Find Tony and come up with a story that'll get him off the hook."

"You mean, tell a lie?"

"If I have to." Her whisper turned harsh. "I'll do anything to keep them loving each other."

"But maybe we can—"

"Nathan." Amber's soft, melodic voice came from the seat in front of us. "I sense disharmony." Her brow wrinkling, she continued in a low tone. "Emotional turmoil creates dissonance just as surely as a discordant measure interrupts the flow of a musical masterpiece."

"Yeah. Sorry." I bit my lip. Amber was every bit as insightful as Scarlet had been. I wouldn't be able to hide even the smallest secret from her. "We'll try to harmonize better."

"We're here," Gunther said. The van slid to a stop behind the pickup, a beige Ford F-150.

Molly squinted. "That's our truck."

"Could it be stuck in the snow?" Kelly asked as she squeezed between the seat and the side of the van. "Maybe Tony's just trying to get help somewhere." She opened the side door, climbed out of the van, and high stepped toward the pickup.

"Everyone wait here," I said. "I'll be back in a minute." Shuffling my feet to clear a path through the snow, I followed Kelly to the truck. After brushing a frosty buildup from the small window on the side of the truck's cargo cap, I peered inside. Several boxes lay on the bed with "Glasgow, Scotland" imprinted in bold red letters.

I turned to Kelly. "The mirrors."

"Right." She nodded toward the bar, a small hole-in-the-wall establishment less than half a block away. "He's got to be inside."

A slamming door made us turn. Amber stood on the sidewalk and scanned the area, her eyes narrowing. Hundreds of snowflakes swirled around her head as if attracted to her aura. Her graceful sway now at rest, she shivered, and her voice trembled. "There is much turmoil in the air. The sensation of coldness has penetrated my shield."

"Then maybe you should get back in the van," I said.

She shook her head, making the snowflakes fly. "I sense that you will need my help."

"Who am I to argue with a supplicant?" I took her by the arm. "Let's get you inside before you freeze."

I led Amber and Kelly past the bar's outdoor seating area. Bordered in front by a wooden rail with varnished support slats, it held five snow-covered tables, but no chairs or stools stood in sight.

At the entrance, I stomped my feet to shake off the snow. When I opened the door, a wave of television noise and rumbling conversation flowed from within, followed by the stench of cigar smoke and beer.

Amber wrinkled her nose. "Is this a latrine? It smells of human waste."

"It's called a sports bar." I waved them inside and closed the door. "But you're right. It stinks in here."

"This is a new experience." She looked all around, her eyes unblinking in the smoke-filled room. "I don't think my beloved has ever been to a place like this."

"If you mean Francesca Yellow, you're probably right." I scanned the area, letting my gaze rush past ten or so unfamiliar faces, mostly male, until I spotted Tony sitting on a stool with his back to the bar, his long legs reaching the floor. Clutching a sweating beer bottle, Tony watched a television mounted on a side wall. A cheer erupted from the speaker, and Tony's bellow followed.

"All right! Slam dunk!"

I strode toward him, waving a hand. "Tony! It's me, Nathan."

Tony swiveled my way, a smile on his face. "Future Boy! Glad to see you again." He took a swig from his bottle. "I'd offer you a beer, but you don't look old enough to drink."

"I'm not." As Kelly and Amber joined me, I pointed over my shoulder with a thumb. "We picked up your wife. She was standing out in the snow."

Tony jumped down from the stool. "In the snow?"

"Yeah. She was—"

A roar broke out from several of the men. A few pointed at a screen on the opposite side of the room while one raised both fists into the air.

I winced at the sound. "Why are they so excited? Haven't they already dreamed about who's going to win?"

"Things have changed." Tony guided me toward the exit while Amber and Kelly followed. "Did I ever mention Flash, a friend of mine?"

"Yeah." I paused at the door. "You said I look like him."

"Well, he's got some kind of spiritual connection going on. You know, spooky stuff like in the movies. Anyway, he figured out how to stop the next-day dreaming, and now only travelers get a hint of what's going on, and they're not always right. It's helped a lot. Things are getting back to normal."

The door burst open, and Daryl bustled in, shaking snow out of her hair. "The ice planet Hoth's got nothing on this place."

"Something wrong?" Kelly asked.

Daryl nodded toward the door. "Molly's getting all worked up about Tony leaving her out in the cold, and baby Kelly's got a good temper tantrum going so Molly's in no mood to be mollified."

Tony pointed at her. "Mollify Molly. That's a good one."

"Since I'm the former flame," Daryl said, giving Tony an icy stare, "I took the brunt of her wrath."

He shrugged. "She loves to shop, so I decided to give her some time while I caught part of the game."

"Well," Daryl continued, "to quote Mad Molly"—she pinched her voice into a scratchy, witchlike tone—"I can't believe he would leave me with Kelly for so long. He knows I can't handle her when she gets like this."

Tony's cheeks turned red. He grabbed a coat from a nearby table and shoved his arms through the sleeves. "I'll talk to her."

He jerked the door open and stomped down the stairs to the snowy sidewalk. The storm had eased, leaving only a few straggling snowflakes swirling here and there.

I followed close behind, motioning for the others to keep up. No matter what happened with Tony and Molly, we had to hurry. Two worlds needed saving, and the zone police, whoever they were, might find us at any minute.

Amber rushed ahead and grasped Tony's arm. "There is disharmony in your spirit," she said as she shivered in the cold breeze. "Wait for the music to balance before you speak."

Tony stared at her, his eyes bulging. "Who's the glowing girl?" He looked at me. "One of your friends from the future?"

"Not exactly. She's—"

"She's right." Kelly stepped forward and nodded toward the van parked only a dozen or so paces away. "Molly's probably in no mood to hear how you wanted to let her shop. All she knows is that she was trapped in a snowstorm with a crying baby while you were at a bar watching basketball."

Tony eyed the van. "So what do I tell her?"

Kelly looked at Daryl, Amber, and me, then gazed into Tony's eyes. "Tell her you're sorry. Tell her you won't let it happen again." With snowflakes gathering on Kelly's eyelashes, tears began streaming down her cheeks as she continued in a trembling voice. "Tell her it was a big mistake and that you love her with all your heart, that you'll never let sports come between you and her ever again, and that you'll help her learn to deal with a crying little girl who needs both her mother and her father very, very much."

Tony raised his brow, his eyes darting from Kelly to Amber to me, then back to Kelly. "All right. I can do that."

Amber caressed Tony's shoulder. "Dance with her music, and she will be able to hear yours. Only then can harmony overcome discord."

"Dance with her?" Tony looked at Amber's hand for a moment, then nodded. "I think I know what you mean."

"Tell you what," I said. "Why don't you and Molly ride in your truck and follow us to the Interfinity Labs observatory? When we get there I'll explain everything about us coming from the future. And I'll tell you more about those mirrors in the back of your truck."

Tony glanced at the pickup. "You know about everything, don't you?"

"Being from the future has its advantages."

He touched a phone on his belt. "Can Flash get in on this? He's in town, and he's been talking about this dreaming stuff for weeks."

"Sure. Call him and ask him to meet us at Interfinity Labs with Francesca."

"Interfinity Labs. Gotcha."

I pointed at Tony's phone. "Can I get your number in case I need to call you?"

"You bet." He pulled a wallet from his back pocket and fished out a business card. "It says 'Office Phone,' but that's my cell."

"Thanks."

"Can I see that?" Daryl asked.

"The card?" I gave it to her. "Why?"

Daryl glanced at the information and handed it back to me. "I like to memorize numbers."

"That's all the time you needed?"

"Yep." She winked. "And I love pi. I have it memorized to a thousand places."

"I'll stick to cherry pie." I stuffed the card into my pocket. "Stay close, Tony. It could be tough to follow us in this weather."

"Not a problem. I have four-wheel drive." Tony strode to the van and opened the side door. He helped Molly step down to the sidewalk, careful to keep one of his large hands under baby Kelly. Arching over Molly and whispering into her ear, he guided her across the slippery sidewalk.

I opened the van's front door for Daryl and stood by the back with a hand out for Kelly. "Let's get going. It sounds like my Earth Yellow father's been busy keeping this world from going crazy, but we still have a lot to do."

"I will go with Tony and Molly," Amber said. "Their music is not yet fully in harmony."

I shrugged. "Okay. It looked like there was room in the front for three."

Amber flashed a smile. "The closer she sits to him, the better for the blending of their music."

Once everyone was seated—Daryl in front and Mom, Kelly, and me on the bench seat—Gunther shifted into gear and drove away, keeping his eye on the rearview mirror. "Tony's right behind us, and he's on his phone."

"Perfect," I said. "Now we can talk about what's going on."

Mom touched my knee. "I heard Tony mention Flash. That's your father ... I mean ... well, you know what I mean."

"Right. We're hoping he'll come to the observatory. Apparently he put a stop to the next-day dreaming, at least for a lot of people, so he must have a handle on what's going on." I looked at Gunther. "Tony says pretty much only travelers have prophetic dreams now. I guess we should be grateful you're one of them."

"I'm just glad the weather kept the zone police from tracking us down." Gunther turned onto a narrow back road and accelerated, taking advantage of the lack of traffic as the sun broke through the clouds. "They caught me once and did some tests to determine that I'm a traveler."

He tapped the back of his skull. "They implanted a tracking device, and if I go outside of my zone it sounds an alarm somewhere. Then these police swoop in like a SWAT team. If they catch a wayward traveler, they have the authority to shoot him on the spot, but usually they just use torture to get him in line. They zap you with these sonic rods."

"Sonic rods?" I spread my hands two feet apart. "Are they this long, as thick as a policeman's nightstick, and make a sound that'll split your skull?"

"That's them. How did you know?"

I arched my back, recalling the pain I received from a paralyzing rod. "I got zapped by one."

"Hurts like crazy, doesn't it? Anyway, if you're a traveler who hasn't been implanted, they fingerprint you, register you as a traveler, and send you to a deprogramming camp where they do the surgery. And it's a particularly nasty deal. The chip is booby-trapped with a tiny bomb. If I got my own surgeon to take it out, it could go off, and my brains would be scrambled eggs."

"Ouch," Daryl said. "Brain splatter. No one wants to be zombie food."

"Exactly. The situation stinks for travelers, but everyone else is doing a lot better. Solomon and Francesca worked with the two Dr. Simons to cook up this megacool way to stop the dreams, and just about everyone is participating. People are clueless about the existence of other worlds, but since they're tired of knowing the future, and since it keeps Mictar from sneaking in and dream-snatching their souls, they're going along with Solomon's plan."

"Don't be surprised if Mictar makes a comeback," I said. "He had a sharp run-in with a mirror, so that kept him away for a while."

"I wouldn't mind taking a mirror to that creep myself." Gunther glanced over his shoulder and gestured at a duffle bag lying on the floor. "By the way, I thought you guys might be hungry, so I brought some crackers and stuff. Help yourselves."

I rummaged through the bag and passed around the food. As I handed Daryl an apple, I asked, "So what's going on back home?"

Daryl planted an elbow on her armrest. "Before I lost contact with Dr. Gordon, he said news reports were buzzing about sound waves getting bent out of shape. It started with mid-range musical notes. If someone played a middle C on a piano, it didn't sound right, like the frequency got warped. Then it spread to all sorts of sounds, and finally it killed analog radio and TV broadcasts."

"And then you got cut off from Dr. Gordon."

"Yep. Just before it happened, I asked him to call my father to let him know I'm all right, but I'm not sure he understood. Even his voice sounded weird, like he was doing whale-speak — you know, long, moaning notes, like Dory when she talked to the whale in *Finding Nemo*. I suggested that he switch to digital encoding, but I don't think he heard me."

"So Earth Red people probably can't talk to each other."

"That's my take, unless they all learn whale-speak."

I blew out a sigh. It was like the Tower of Babel all over again. The world would be in chaos soon, if it wasn't already.

I turned toward Kelly, but she showed no sign of concern. Her mind seemed far away, and a sweet smile made her face glow. I smiled back. No doubt defusing the bomb, as she had put it, gave her reason to celebrate. Maybe Kelly Yellow would have a better life than her own.

After we drove out of the city and onto a narrow country lane, Gunther glanced back and forth between the mirror and the road. "We've got trouble."

CHAPTER FOUR

DARYL LOOKED OUT the back window. "The zone police?"

"Yep," Gunther said. "Two of them on my tail."

A pair of red cars with gold racing stripes and flashing lights roared up behind Tony's truck, splashing through the fast-melting snow. One blared a horn as it passed the pickup and pulled within a few feet of Gunther's bumper.

Gunther pressed the gas pedal, making his engine whine. "I can't outrun them, not in this hay baler, but I'm not about to get shot or stunned by those sonic rods." He nodded toward the back. "Nathan, open the hatch. I have a surprise for them."

I climbed to the rear and swung the hatch out and up. "Done."

"Daryl," Gunther said as a breeze swirled throughout the van, "look under your seat and get the first-aid kit."

She bent over and reached under the seat. "For what? To bandage your brain when it explodes?"

"It's a fake kit. I keep a gun in it."

"You're going to shoot them from the driver's seat?" Daryl slid out a white metal box and withdrew a short, fat-barreled pistol. "You'd be better off with a good blaster at your side, kid."

Gunther took it from her. "It's a sound-wave gun Solomon and I invented. It neutralizes a sonic rod, but since there are two zone cops, I can't stop them both if they use different frequencies. I'd let one of you operate it, but it takes some time to learn."

Behind us, one of the police cars shifted to the left lane and eased closer. As it pulled up to our driver's side, its lights flashed and its siren blared. The other car drew close behind. The driver's gaunt face and pale complexion became clear.

"It's a stalker." I looked at the car to our left. The driver and a man in the passenger seat were also stalkers from the misty world.

That car's window zipped down. The passenger, his lips thin and firm, pointed a sonic rod at Gunther. A blue light flashed on at the tip, and an ear-piercing shriek ripped across the rushing air and into the van.

Gunther cringed. Keeping one hand on the wheel, he pointed his gun at the pale-faced officer and pulled the trigger. A loud bass tone roared from the barrel. As it melded with the sonic rod's wall of sound, the combined noise shook the van, rattling the frame, but the painful sound waves eased.

Another shriek blasted through the rear hatch, higher-pitched and louder. I clapped my hands over my ears. Mom and Kelly did the same. Gunther kept his gun trained on the first officer, his jaw trembling as he grunted through his words. "Have to slow down before this tin can breaks into pieces!"

"Want me to close the hatch?" I asked.

"Not yet. I might have to aim back and forth between them and hope for the best."

The van slowed. Tony's truck and the two stalker vehicles matched its pace, maintaining their positions.

"Call Amber," Kelly shouted. "Maybe she can neutralize the other rod."

Daryl unclipped the phone from Gunther's belt and punched in the numbers from memory. With her teeth clenched, she held the phone to her ear and waited.

To the rear, Tony had pulled his pickup alongside the trailing squad car. All three front-seat passengers came into clear view. Amber's expression was serene, while Molly and Tony both looked tense as Tony pressed the phone against his cheek.

"Tony!" Daryl shouted. "Ask Amber if she can cancel the sonic rod in the car next to you."

Tony turned to Molly and Amber, speaking to them while keeping a grip on the wheel. Two seconds later, Amber's head emerged from the passenger window.

"She has to do what?" Daryl yelled. "You've got to be kidding!"

"What?" I asked.

Daryl pulled the phone away from her ear and looked back. "Sounds like she's going to do an Indiana Jones!"

Her bright yellow hair whipping in the wind, Amber climbed out the truck's window and swung herself to the bed cover behind the cab. The officer, still aiming his sonic rod at the van, stared at her with wide eyes.

Amber stood upright and raised her hands. As her hair blew across her face and her dress flapped against her legs, she took in a breath and sang a note as low and loud as a ship's foghorn. Like a battering ram, her song plunged into the rod's wall of sound, counteracting the horrible noise.

The officer pulled back his sonic rod and pointed a pistol at Amber. His hand shaking, he fired a shot. With a deft turn, Amber dodged the bullet.

I reached to the front, grabbed the cell phone from Daryl, and shouted into it. "Tony! Back off! The stalker's shooting at Amber!"

"And leave you to face the zone police?" Tony said. "No way. Besides, she's got it under control."

"Yeah, but—"

"Duck!" Tony pushed Molly's head down. The gun fired again. The window on Tony's side shattered, sending glass flying. The stalker shifted his aim toward the van and shot a third time.

"Arrgh!" Mom clutched her wrist. Blood flowed from her palm and streamed along her arm.

"Mom!"

"Mrs. Shepherd!" Daryl called from the front. "Are you all right?"

Grimacing, Mom pressed her fingers against a gash in the side of her hand. "It's just a flesh wound."

"This is no time for a Monty Python routine!" Daryl searched the area around her seat. "Gunther, do you have a real first-aid kit anywhere?"

"I used to. Somewhere. Maybe."

While Daryl searched, the stalker aimed the gun again, this time at Tony. Amber leaped toward the police car. She seemed to float across the gap, her dress fanning out as she stretched toward the roof.

Landing feet first, she spun 180 degrees on her toes, then fell to her stomach and clutched the window frame just in time to keep from sliding off the passenger side.

While holding the frame with one hand, she grabbed the stalker's wrist with the other. His fingers straightened, and the gun clattered to the road.

The car decelerated and dropped back. Still keeping his sonic gun trained on the officer in the car to the side of the van, Gunther slowed to stay close to the one behind.

As Amber rose to her feet, she jerked the stalker out through the window and planted the tall, thin man upright on the roof. The car, now driverless, rolled on, swaying from side to side. The stalker dropped to his knees in front of Amber and folded his hands as if begging.

Gunther eased the van to a stop, allowing the trailing car to press against his bumper until it stopped as well. The other police car roared away.

Amber set a palm on top of her captive's white hair. As she drilled her stare directly into his eyes, she sang a high-pitched note. His jaw dropped open. His eyes bulged. His cheeks sank, his body withered, and his shirt slipped off his shoulders as he seemed to age at high speed.

Kelly joined me in the cargo area and leaned out the back hatch. "Amber!" I shouted. "No! We can get information from him."

She turned toward me, her eyes ablaze in yellow. The stalker heaved rapid, shallow breaths, spitting out short, pathetic vowel sounds.

"Spare me, O mighty supplicant," Kelly translated. "Forgive me of my many transgressions against you."

Amber moved her hand from his head, sweeping a shower of white hair to the roof of the car. Now smiling, she reached for his hand and sang a burst of notes.

"Will you dance with me?" Kelly said, again translating. "I will provide the music."

With his hands still folded and his chest heaving, the stalker forced out a halting lament. Kelly gave each note its meaning the moment it passed his lips.

"I beg you, holy one. Spare me, and I will fight against my brethren." His eyes bulging within his sunken face, his voice shook wildly. "But I cannot dance with you. One such as I could never be your partner in dance."

She gazed down at him, love bathing her expression as she crooned a musical reply.

Kelly swallowed before translating. "You have always had the ability to dance with me, and I will gladly be your partner, but if you refuse, I will have to kill you."

The stalker closed his eyes and wailed. Amber laid her hand on his head again and reprised her song. His limbs stiffened. His clothes dropped away. Lines etched his skin, creating a patchwork of decaying flesh until it flaked away from his skeleton-like body. Soon, he crumbled into a heap of dust.

As a breeze carried the dust away, Amber's shoulders sagged. After watching the pile dwindle for a moment, she walked down the windshield and jumped to the pavement.

Kelly clutched my hand. "What ..." She swallowed again. "What *is* she?"

"I don't know," I replied, keeping my voice low. "We knew the stalkers were scared of the supplicants. Now we know why."

Daryl let out a long whistle. "I'll tell you one thing. If Amber asks me to dance, I'll be ready to rumba."

Amber walked toward the passenger's side of the truck, her head low, a tear tracking down her cheek. Inside, Molly punched the door lock. Amber halted.

Tony's voice pierced the silence. I lifted the phone to my ear, keeping my stare on Amber. "Sorry, Tony. I couldn't hear you. What did you say?"

"Molly's scared to death." His voice was low and shaky. "Can Amber ride with you?"

"Sure." I waved at Amber. "Hop in the van," I said, speaking through the open hatch. "There's plenty of room."

The shining supplicant nodded and shuffled toward me.

Kelly opened the side door. "I'll get Molly calmed down. I know what usually worked with my mother." She jumped out and hurried toward the truck.

I closed the hatch and climbed to the bench seat, while Mom slid to the side window to make room. When Amber climbed in, she settled onto the bench next to me and stayed quiet.

Mom lifted her bloody fingers away from her ripped hand. The pressure had temporarily closed a gash an inch or two below her little finger, but blood still trickled. "It looks like I won't be able to play violin for a while."

I tried to rip my sweatshirt sleeve, but it was too strong. "Got a knife, Gunther?"

"Yep. It ain't much, but it's sharp."

A small pocketknife landed in my lap. After I cut a wide strip from my sleeve and wrapped Mom's hand, Gunther shifted the van into gear and eased ahead. He and Daryl kept their gazes forward, saying nothing.

Mom broke the silence. "I don't understand, Amber. Why did you insist that he dance with you?"

Amber let out a sad sigh. "All of his race must align with the eternal purpose. When they refuse to do so, it leads to death of innocents. You see, the three earths once danced together in a cosmic waltz, in perfect balance and harmony. When dissonance shattered the harmonic structure, the worlds bent away from the dance and into a collision course, and the stalkers are contributing to the coming disaster. Playing the violin in Sarah's Womb will restore the balance, but since Nathan was unable to finish the song and instead sacrificed Scarlet, only one world broke free from the converging path. Now Earth Red has no dance partner. It spins alone and is suffering because it cannot comprehend the music."

"What exactly is Sarah's Womb?" I asked. "And what does spinning alone do to Earth Red?"

Amber formed her hand into a loose fist and slowly expanded her fingers. "Sarah is the great emptiness, the void that pushes the worlds apart, like a barren womb that is filled with heartache."

"So is it a buffer?" Daryl asked. "Like insulation?"

"In a manner of speaking. Yet she offers more than insulation. Just as when the biblical Sarah's womb was filled with a child of promise, when the cosmic Sarah is filled with perfect song, she gives birth to harmony that pushes the worlds into their proper paths, the paths they must follow to avoid destruction."

"If it's a song Sarah wants," Mom said, "why did Scarlet's sacrifice make any difference at all?"

"We supplicants represent the elements that make up perfect music. Although we all have the gift of song, Cerulean is the master of musical notes, Scarlet is the mistress of words, the lyrics of the psalms, and I" — Amber set a finger on her chest — "I am the mistress of dance, the natural movement that arises from rhythm. When Scarlet fell into the void, Sarah was filled with only part of what makes for perfect song. Perhaps Earth Red is safe from Interfinity's reach, but with no dance partner, she labors without relief."

Daryl turned and set her arms on the top of her seat. "So that must be why sound waves are messed up on Earth Red. They're all going nuts."

"Their world needs to dance," Amber said. "It restores balance and brings light to darkness, which brings me back to the original question. If that stalker had agreed to dance with me, he would have come into harmony with my purpose, which is his sworn duty. This one, like many others, decided to rebel."

As I looked out the rear hatch's window, the image of the pleading stalker came back to mind. "But he said he couldn't. He seemed to think he wasn't worthy."

She nodded. "That is the way of the faithless. They do not believe in perfect dance. You see, whenever someone dances with another in heart, soul, and spirit, the partners move with each other step by step, symbolizing that they will never stray from one another, not even for a moment. They are one in a purpose that is greater than both of them."

"Can two humans dance together like that?"

Amber smiled. "That's what human marriage is all about. Dance is the symbol of submitting to the greater purpose, a humbling of yourselves in order to move in step with the higher music." She looked straight at me. "Eventually you will have to dance to the higher music. This journey you are on is preparing you for that moment."

The phone in my lap chimed, giving me an excuse to turn away from her piercing eyes. I handed the phone to Gunther and settled back in my seat.

"Hello," Gunther said. "Yeah, Tony. I think there's a station in a couple of miles. We can stop."

Heat from Amber's body radiated into mine, sending mixed sensations — the soothing warmth of a protective friend and the chilling ice of the unknown. I glanced at her out of the corner of my eye. She stared straight ahead, her lovely face still exuding a golden glow. A placid hum emanated from within her, a melody that was all too familiar, Foundation's Key, the piece I had tried to play on the strings that spanned Sarah's Womb. The tune fit her perfectly — simple, yet powerful. Lovely, yet frightening.

Yes, this woman was a mystery, a deep, dark mystery.

When we stopped for gas, Kelly hurried to the van and opened the door. "Amber, would you be willing to switch again? Molly wants you to ride with her now. She's sorry for being so scared."

Amber's smile seemed to melt her somber mood away. "I am glad to."

As soon as Amber climbed out, Kelly jumped in and scooted close to me. "This is all so cool," she said, keeping her voice low. "Tony and Molly are like lovebirds right now. He's sweet talking her, and she's eating it up."

I nodded. "That *is* cool."

Letting out a sigh, she slid her hand into my bandaged one and leaned against my shoulder. I glanced at Mom, wondering what she might think about this show of affection, but she just smiled and took my other hand.

I added my own sigh. There was no doubt about it. Dancing in harmony with beloved people was very cool.

Gunther maintained a steady speed and frequently glanced at his rearview mirror, apparently checking Tony's progress and keeping watch for anyone else who might be following.

After another stop for gas and sporadic conversation about recent events, we pulled into the observatory's parking lot. As expected, the set of buildings looked exactly like the observatories on Earths Red and Blue, including bronze block letters on the front brick wall that spelled out "Interfinity Labs."

Gunther pulled into a space in the first row of the nearly empty lot, and Tony parked his pickup alongside. Daryl jumped out first, followed by Kelly, Mom, and me. We joined Amber and Gunther, who were watching Molly lift baby Kelly from her place in the truck's backseat.

Now wearing a gray sweater over her yellow dress, Amber leaned close to me and whispered, "Tony allowed me to use his outer garment, but I have no need of it. Harmony has been restored."

"That's great news." I looked up. With the sun shining through scattered clouds, the temperature had climbed to a comfortable level. The sky looked strange, more purple than blue, and hints of the atmospheric holes I had seen on Earth Blue speckled the canopy.

Kelly strode toward Molly. "May I hold her?" she asked, extending her arms.

"She's almost asleep." Molly passed her bundle to Kelly. "I gave her a bottle, then Tony sang Italian songs. She seemed to like it." Molly meshed her fingers with Tony's and gazed at him lovingly. "He has a soothing voice, you know."

Kelly nodded, tears welling in her eyes. "I remember. I mean, I could tell." She pushed the baby's blanket to the side and stared at her face.

Amber and I joined Kelly and looked at the drowsy little girl in her arms. With delicate pink skin, dainty eyelids, and a button nose, she seemed like a tiny angel, as vulnerable as she was beautiful. I let my gaze wander to Kelly's face and scanned her features—the same nose, to be sure, but her skin had changed, tougher now with peach tones instead of pink. Still, the vulnerability remained, a girl wracked with pain—pain that her own life couldn't reflect the joy of the life she had arranged for the duplicate angel in her arms.

A tear streamed down Kelly's cheek, then another. Soon, she began weeping. Her head bobbed as she clutched baby Kelly to her chest.

"Are you all right?" Molly asked.

"I'm okay." Tears still flowing, Kelly looked at my mother. "Can we talk?"

Mom gave her a smile. "Of course."

"Thank you." Kelly sniffed. "Let me collect myself first."

"Whenever you're ready."

Tony pulled a collapsible pink stroller from the back of his pickup and unfolded it. "Time for baby Kelly to test out her new wheels."

As Kelly laid the baby in the stroller, she looked up at Molly, her voice strained. "Why did you choose the name Kelly?"

"Well, Tony wanted a boy, and I wanted a girl, so we settled on a good Irish name that would work for either one."

"You're right. It does." Kelly buckled the baby in place and took my mother's hand. As the two strolled to another part of the parking lot, a new sound rode the air—a car motor, chugging as if missing a spark plug. A sky blue Volkswagen Beetle lumbered in, a young man at the wheel. When he parked next to the truck, the woman in the passenger's seat came into view — Francesca.

Amber squeezed my arm. "It's my beloved!"

She stepped toward the car, but I grabbed her hand and pulled her back. "She's never met you, has she?"

Amber's brow wrinkled. "We have met in her dreams, but I don't know if she will remember."

"Then maybe it's better to wait until she's settled here. You don't want to startle her." Just as I released her hand, a nervous shiver buzzed along my skin. The driver had to be Solomon Shepherd, the Earth Yellow version of my father. Meeting him would be strange ... maybe too strange.

CHAPTER FIVE

SOLOMON YELLOW, WHO appeared to be in his early twenties, helped Francesca out of the car and nodded at me, as if to say, "I'll talk to you in a minute." He then folded down the front seat and lifted a baby from an infant carrier in the back.

After settling the baby in Francesca's arms, he strode toward me, a big smile on his face. "You must be Nathan, my Earth Red son."

I cleared my throat and extended my bandaged hand. "Yes sir. I mean, yeah. That's me."

"Glad to meet you." Solomon slid his hand past the bandage and grasped my wrist. "We have a lot to talk about."

"Yes, we do."

He bowed his head toward Amber. "I assume you are Francesca's supplicant."

She smiled. "Yes. I am looking forward to meeting her."

"I'm sure you are, but if you don't mind, I would like for you to wait until I introduce you to each other inside. It's important. Just keep your distance from her until then."

"Very well." Looking disappointed, Amber turned and walked toward Tony and Molly.

"Would you like to meet your twin?" Solomon asked, pointing over his shoulder with a thumb.

I glanced at Amber. Now talking to Molly, she seemed all right. "Sure."

"Only for a moment, though." Solomon's brow creased. "We have a considerable amount of work to accomplish. As soon as I heard about your arrival, I arranged for the others to meet us here. We've been waiting for Tony to bring the mirrors from Scotland, so now we can carry out our tests."

Francesca joined us, carrying the blanket-wrapped baby in her arms. "Hello, Nathan. It's so good to see you again."

I tried to hide a nervous swallow. With her raven locks flowing in the cold breeze and her smile as vibrant as it had been when I met her as a precocious ten-year-old, she was as beautiful as ever. "It's good to see you, too."

She placed the baby into my arms. "Nathan Shepherd, meet Nathan Shepherd."

I pushed the corner of the blanket out of the way, revealing little Nathan's face. With wisps of dark hair protruding from the edges of a blue cap, thin lips pursing into a lax pucker, and a tiny nose wrinkling, this little one was as familiar as my own reflection, the living image of dozens of photos that adorned an album Mom always kept on her dresser.

Francesca touched a dimple in the baby's chin and grinned. "He looks just like you, Nathan."

My cheeks warmed. She was right, almost embarrassingly so. Would this child do everything I had done? Even the stupid things? "Yeah. I can see that. At least, I remember the pictures."

The baby squirmed and whimpered. I handed him back to Francesca. "When he turns six, he might give you a hard time about violin lessons, but don't listen to him."

As she laid the baby in a stroller, she winked. "Don't worry, Son. I won't."

Gunther slapped the side of his van. "I'd better get going before the zone police track me down again."

"Where will you go?" I asked.

He shrugged. "Anywhere but here. Maybe I'll find a secluded shady spot to sleep." He climbed into the driver's seat and started the engine. "Just call if you need me." After giving everyone a wave, he drove out of the lot.

Solomon nodded at Tony. "Did you bring the mirrors?"

"Got one right here," Tony said, lifting a sports bag. "The others are locked in the back of my truck."

I looked at the far side of the parking lot. Mom and Kelly were now walking toward us, still hand in hand. "I guess we'd better get going," I said. "It might take a while if we have to figure out the security codes."

"No need for codes," Solomon said as he led the way, walking at a quick pace. "I called ahead. Both Simons are waiting for us, so the security doors should be deactivated."

"How long have you been working with the Simons?" I asked.

"For a while." Solomon opened the front glass door and held it while waiting for everyone to pass through. When we all entered, Amber trailing the pack, Solomon followed, closed the door, and turned his attention back to me. "We have been analyzing the data, and we came up with a theory that might explain what's happening, but we need the supplicant to do something for us before we can test it."

I scanned the lobby, a room I had not yet visited. A polished floor returned a skewed reflection of my body, and a huge crystal chandelier dangled about ten feet overhead. Earth-toned panels covered every wall, with photos of the observatory's groundbreaking ceremony hanging at precise intervals, their wooden frames matching the panels perfectly. Someone had spent a lot of money on this place. "What about Gordon Yellow? Is he around to help?"

Again Solomon led the way, this time along a corridor to the right, another unfamiliar area. "Since Dr. Gordon is the founder of Interfinity Labs, he is here, but we haven't entrusted him with all we know." He stopped in front of an elevator, much bigger than the one in the secure area, and pushed the call button. "Since Gordon Blue chose the path of greed, we can't be sure Gordon Yellow won't do the same. I'm afraid he has a poor temper at times, so I decided to watch him for a while."

When the door opened, everyone piled into the roomy elevator car— Kelly Red, Molly Yellow and Francesca Yellow with their strollers, Tony Yellow, Solomon Yellow, Francesca Red, Daryl Red; Amber, and me. Amber pressed into a back corner, well away from Francesca Yellow.

Solomon pressed the button for the third floor. "Although this observatory will seem familiar," he said, raising his voice to compete with the elevator's humming motor, "the two Simons have worked with Gordon Yellow to make some important enhancements that will come into play soon."

The elevator slowed to a halt, and the doors slid open, revealing a hallway. To our left, another door stood open, the tourist entrance to the telescope room. Directly in front of us on the opposite wall, two restrooms flanked a water fountain.

Solomon nodded at the restrooms. "It would be a good idea for everyone to use the facilities. We have no way to know when our next opportunity will be. But let's hurry. Interfinity won't wait for us."

All but one of the ladies filed into their restroom. Amber stayed behind, her expression again anxious and longing. She still hoped to talk to Francesca Yellow as soon as possible, a desire I couldn't relate to, so I decided to leave her to her thoughts and join the men in our restroom. When everyone returned, Solomon led the way to the tourist entrance. He peered through the doorway before nodding to the rest of us. "It looks like everything is ready."

When we entered, light from the corridor faded. A candelabrum sitting on the floor near the telescope illuminated the room. Flickering candlelight made the chamber seem like an underground cavern or a vestibule in an ancient castle—dark, cool, and mysterious.

I passed by a piano and hard-shell cases for two cellos, three violins, and a viola. Apparently, the scientists here had been experimenting with various instruments.

With the mirrored ceiling reflecting only the flickering flames of six candlewicks, and the mounted telescope barely visible in the dancing orange glow, the place seemed like an odd mix of medieval and modern, as if a caravan of mystified travelers from the modern age had just strolled into King Arthur's court.

The candles stopped flickering. My fellow travelers froze in place, some in awkward positions. Every sound, even the buzz of nearby computers, fell to silence. A sense of heaviness entered my mind—grave and foreboding. Patar was near.

He walked through the doorway we had just entered. He weaved around Tony and Molly, his scowl not quite as deep as usual. "You don't seem surprised to see me, Son of Solomon."

"Not really. When everyone stops moving, I kind of guess you're around somewhere."

With a hint of mirth in his expression, Patar drew within a few feet and stopped. "I come only when you need a gentle push in the right direction."

"A gentle push?" I rolled my eyes. "I'd hate to see one of your forceful shoves."

Patar's white eyebrows bent down. "If you continue ignoring my counsel, you might very well get the opportunity."

"But you said we had to go to the observatory to get to the misty world." I spread my arms. "That's where we are."

"True, but the scientists here will not offer to send you to play the strings over Sarah's Womb. They have other plans, and they will reveal only what they want you to know."

"But what choice do I have? I can't tell them what to do with their own equipment."

"No, but you also do not have to follow their instructions. It is clear that you are in awe of Solomon Yellow. Yet, he is not your father, nor has he attained your father's stature in wisdom and experience. Do not allow him to tell you what to do. It is crucial that you follow my counsel instead." Patar folded his hands behind him and strolled past Solomon, looking at his rigid face for a moment before circling back to the piano. He set his fingers on the keys, played a scale effortlessly, and turned to me with a haughty air. "The fools know so little about real music. They have no idea that passion must enhance precision to open the portals."

"Why don't you just tell them what to do instead of freezing everyone and giving me orders?"

He played an irritating set of chords. "One of them has a mind to kill my people. His hatred for my race is intense, a bigotry that knows no reason. Trying to persuade him to be rational would be impossible."

"Okay. I'll just have to take your word on that."

"These self-proclaimed scientists," Patar continued, "plan to transport you to the world of dreams, which fits well with my plan, because once you are there you may do as I tell you. You must find Cerulean's new charge and give her the Earth Blue mirror you brought. In the gifted one's hands, Cerulean will be able to use it to send you to my domain."

I looked at Kelly, frozen in mid step only a couple of paces behind me. She carried the photo album she had picked up in her parents' bedroom. The edge of the Earth Blue mirror protruded from the top.

"Who is Cerulean's new charge?" I asked. "And will I be able to find her in the dream world?"

"I have not yet learned who she is, and we are not even sure that she is a she. We know only that a high voice calls for help from the dream world, so it could very well be a male child. In any case, Cerulean seeks for her there. If you find her, she could lead you to her real-world form, and you could give her the mirror."

"And if I don't find her, then what?"

Patar began another stroll, this time focusing on Amber. With her arms stiff and her glow dissipated, she looked like a normal girl. As he circled her, his eyes glistened and his lips softened. He looked like an old, sad grandfather. "In the dream world, there is a way to enter Sarah's Womb, though the violin is not within reach from that entry point. Look for a flaw in the wall of the dream world's central core. It will take some effort, but Amber should be able to open it for you. Then …" From behind, he grasped Amber's neck and lightly dragged his pointed nails across her throat. "You must slay this supplicant and cast her into the chasm."

"Coward!" I took a hard step toward him. "I've seen how powerful she is. You wouldn't dare talk about killing her if she wasn't paralyzed."

"Oh, how little you know." He stepped away from Amber. "If she knew there was no other way to save the worlds, she would gladly give her life. This is the lesson that you cannot seem to grasp—true sacrifice, a love that allows no obstacle to prevent its fulfillment, whether in deed or in word."

"I know more about that than you think," I said, but the words seemed to wither in the air. Did I really know what I was talking about? Had I done everything I could in sacrifice?

I gazed into Amber's beautiful golden eyes. Even if I hadn't done all I was supposed to do, I could never kill this amazing girl. It would probably be best to dodge the subject for now. "What about Mictar? Is he still alive? Do I have to watch out for him?"

"He is very much alive, and he is still quite able to kill your friends." Patar reached out and touched my forehead with his finger, as if anointing me. "But you have no reason to fear him yourself. Just leave him to me. After what he did to Abodah, either I or one of our children must see that justice is carried out."

A whispered voice came from behind Patar. "Nathan?"

He spun and backed out of my way, a tic twitching an eyelid.

Amber blinked and moved her limbs stiffly. "There is a strange power here. I have not felt it in quite some time." After blinking again, she stared at Patar. "What are you doing here? Has the time arrived so soon?"

Patar tightened his jaw, squeezing his words into tense bullets. "No, it is not the time. I did not intend for you to see me yet."

Amber's glow returned, casting her once again in a brilliant aura. "I sense great pain within you. Although I am not your supplicant, I will pray for your grieving heart."

He gave her a brief bow. "I am grateful for your kindness."

Amber's brow arched up. "Perhaps when we meet again, harmony will have been restored, and the music in the air will guide your feet into the liberating dance."

"Perhaps." Patar bowed again, backed away three steps, and vanished in a column of mist.

Everyone in the room jerked into motion. Kelly bumped into me, nearly dropping the photo album. "Whoa!" she said as she repositioned her load. "Your brake lights must be out."

I steadied her. "Sorry. We had another Patar stop-action incident."

"We did?" She looked around. "What did he want?"

"Same deadly demand as usual." I glanced at Amber, who was looking at Francesca Yellow but still keeping her distance. "Need I say more?"

Kelly shook her head. "That creep needs a new song."

A shadow passed through the candelabrum's glow, short and hurried. Dr. Simon's voice penetrated the dim air, its familiar British flavor sounding strangely appropriate. "Another intersection will come around in moments. An especially strong dream is within reach." Simon Blue's bespectacled face and nearly bald head appeared as he drew near. "We should prepare everyone immediately. Introductions can wait."

A crease dug into Solomon's forehead. "Shouldn't we take the time to explain what we've learned?"

"That can also wait," Simon Blue said. "This is only an experimental journey to see if we can monitor their activity and use the findings to calibrate the dream viewer. It should be short-lived, and we can explain when they return. We might not get another intersection for hours."

Solomon pressed his lips together. "I understand, but I will have to introduce Francesca to someone."

"Fine. Let's turn on the engine." Dr. Simon waved toward the perimeter and called, "Begin the sequence."

Violin music poured from speakers embedded in the walls — sweet, vibrant, and alive with joy — Vivaldi's "Spring," the arrangement Mom and I had performed so many times.

As the violins played, Solomon reached for Amber's hand. "Francesca, I would like to introduce you to Amber, your supplicant, whom you have met in many lonely dreams."

Francesca turned toward Amber. "But I have never met—" Her eyes suddenly grew wide. As Amber's golden glow strengthened, Francesca stepped closer. "I ... I do know you."

"Emotional energy signatures identified," Dr. Simon said. "The receivers can now track Francesca and Amber."

Amber raised a hand and touched Francesca's cheek, then crooned, her voice soft and lovely. "My beloved, I have guided you through troubled waters, both in dreams and in reality. To finally touch you and feel your love is my dream come true."

A new voice called from near the outer wall. "Reception is excellent. The emotion waves match the predicted amplitude and frequency."

Solomon addressed the others. "That's Dr. Gordon of Earth Yellow. I will explain in a moment."

"I am capturing the energy," Dr. Gordon said.

"It's a dream come true for me as well." Francesca's voice quavered. "Why didn't I remember you until now?"

Amber brushed a tear from Francesca's cheek. "At the dawn of every day, you remembered my face, my song, my love, but the troubles of the waking hours always pushed me into the periphery."

Francesca heaved a short breath. "I called you" — she licked her lips, her voice faltering — "I called you Sarah, my shepherdess."

"You heard that name whispered on the winds, for Sarah is the shepherd of the three worlds. She guides them in the cosmic dance."

"Wave forms are balancing," Dr. Gordon called. "We are nearing perfect harmony."

Solomon touched Amber's shoulder. "Will you open the dream gate for us?"

Her glow now pulsing, Amber glanced around the room. "For how many? I have never taken more than one."

Solomon reached for the candelabrum and withdrew one of the long, slender tapers. "We need six, including you." He handed her the candle and took another.

"How do you know so much about this?" Francesca asked as he gave her the second candle.

Solomon withdrew a small notebook from his back pocket. "You talk in your sleep." He opened it toward the back and squinted at a page. "Now comes the dance, correct?"

Clutching the candle close to her chest, Amber looked at Francesca. "Do you remember the steps, my beloved?"

Francesca glanced at Solomon, then back at Amber. "The circle waltz?"

"Yes." Amber's fingers tightened around her candle as she lifted to tiptoes. "I'm so glad you remembered."

Francesca gave her a hesitant nod. "I think I can do it."

"One for each of you," Solomon said as he gave candles to Kelly and me. He then turned to Amber. "Will you be able to hear the music from the dream world?"

She nodded. "I can hear sounds from both places simultaneously."

"Good. As long as the dream world is in sync with this one, the music will continue playing. When it stops, that will be your signal to return."

"I understand. Our purpose is not to find Solomon Red during this journey but to allow you to gather data."

"Correct." Solomon gave a candle to Daryl. "Now we're ready."

I counted five candles. We needed one more person. "Can Mom come with us?"

"I suppose she can," Solomon said, extending the final candle toward her. "I had thought Gunther would come, but she can be number six."

"It would be better if she did not," Amber said. "There is an old song we supplicants know that says if two people from different worlds see each other in the dream world, the one who is not in her own dream world will die immediately. We call it Convergence."

I whispered, "Convergence. That sounds familiar."

"Perhaps Scarlet mentioned it. She sometimes called it Fatal Convergence. She knew how dangerous it is."

"But how could it be fatal? We're talking about dreams, not reality."

"It can happen in dreams, though it is rare." Amber's expression tightened. "The true danger lies in Convergence's effect on the real worlds where the manifestation and circumstances are quite different. If Interfinity occurs, even if the three worlds survive, one of the worlds would dominate the other two, and Convergence would take place. Perhaps in a matter of hours, every duplicate on two earths would perish."

My heart pounded. "So if Earth Red survives—"

"And that's a big if. It is quite possible that all three earths would be annihilated."

"Right. I understand that. But you're saying if Earth Red survives, then Francesca Yellow would die."

Amber nodded. "As would Nathan and Kelly Yellow, along with billions upon billions of other innocent souls."

CHAPTER SIX

A FEW MOMENTS OF silence passed while everyone contemplated the magnitude of Convergence. I imagined a billion voices silenced all at once — fathers, mothers, children — unable to take another breath.

I inhaled deeply, as if breathing for them. "I'm ready, if everyone else is."

"Good," Solomon Yellow said. "You have to enter the dream world as soon as possible, but you don't have to stay long during this phase. Once we have the data for calibration, we can send you on a longer journey to find your father."

"Does that mean you aren't coming?"

Solomon looked at the candle. As the flame on the wick burned higher, the yellow glow washed over his tense features. "I wasn't expecting to go. I have to consult with the others as the data stream comes in." He gave a nervous laugh. "Besides, you heard what Amber said. Suppose we run into Solomon Red. We wouldn't want to cause Convergence, would we?"

I took a step closer to him and studied his expression. This man who looked so much like my father now seemed different. Dad would never send his wife on a dangerous journey without him.

Setting my bandaged hand on Solomon's shoulder, I added an edge of sarcasm to my voice. "It'll be hard, but I'm sure Amber will get us through okay. She's a brave girl."

He seemed to ignore my tone. "Who will go in Gunther's place?" he asked, lifting his candle. "The group will need a bass voice."

"I'll go." Tony stepped forward and took the last candle. As he caressed it, he nudged Solomon's ribs with an elbow. "Hey, Flash. Remember how all us guys used to serenade the girls back at the dorms? I sang the bass part with you. We weren't half bad."

Solomon laughed. "You're right. We were one hundred percent bad."

Dr. Gordon's voice broke through the violin music. "We're in perfect balance. I'm not sure how long it will last."

Solomon waved his hands. "Everyone who has a candle, make a circle around Amber and Francesca." He kissed Francesca. "Don't worry about little Nathan. I'll take good care of him."

"I'm sure of that." Francesca shed her trench coat, revealing a bright white blouse and a blue daisy-embroidered skirt that fell to her ankles. With a phone clipped to her waistband, she looked like a high-tech flower girl.

While we gathered, Amber and Francesca stood face-to-face about three feet apart, holding their candles at chest level. With the undulating flames flickering in their faces, their gazes locked. A light flashed in Amber's eyes, then in Francesca's, as if one pair of orbs had set the other aflame. Twin beams emerged, thin shafts of light that met at the center and blended, brightening as they touched. As the violins played a crescendo, Amber swayed to her left, dipping first before rising again. Francesca matched with a sway to her right.

As Amber shifted from side to side, her every move reflected by Francesca, she opened her mouth and tilted her head up. Vowel sounds poured forth, warbling and echoing in the vast chamber.

I let out a sigh. This had to be the most beautiful song ever sung. Yet, it was more than a song; it was passion—pure emotion wrapped in a melody, an expression of love so untainted, it was as if Amber poured out her life energy for her beloved Francesca.

Amber's song changed. The vowel sounds transformed into words, clear and resounding.

> My love is pure, my love is wild;
> It longs to dance with heaven's child.
> O let the music flow within,
> The song of love that purges sin.

Amber joined her free hand with Francesca's, palm to palm, and they intertwined their fingers as they continued to sway.

> To dance with me is life from death;
> To dance with me is reborn breath;
> To join our hands, to meld as one,
> Reflects our merging with the Son.

> To supplicate is but a sign,
> A portrait of your savior's mind.
> His love for you, his gift to share,
> Compassion bleeds in souls stripped bare.

> Forgiveness flows in hearts of praise,
> In eyes that choose the forward gaze.
> Let partners lose what love has burned,
> For love sets fire to pages turned.

So dance with me, forget the past,
Re-pour the mold, the die is cast;
The music burns the settled dross;
Our dance restores the deepest loss.

As the song began again, I drank in the words once more, and this time I sang along. Kelly, too, joined in, as did Tony and Daryl. Somehow everyone in the circle knew the lyrics after only one performance.

With candles in hand, and their fingertips touching, the two dancers twirled, rising to tiptoes in time with the song's easy rhythm. As if brushed by loving hands, their hair flowed around them, black and gold fanning out with each graceful turn.

Our surroundings brightened. Above, sunlight shone through a veil of clouds, making our candles seem feeble by comparison. A cold breeze whipped across our clothes, but the flames burned on without a flicker.

The music faded, and the song died away. As the last syllables tripped off my lips, I relaxed my muscles. For some reason, ending the song brought a sense of relief.

Tony patted his trousers pocket. "I have matches. We could blow out the candles and light them later if we need them."

Her smile unabated, Amber ceased her dance and released Francesca's hand. "We must keep the candles burning. Their light is the only connection we have to the real world. Nothing from the dream world will affect the flames, though we are able to extinguish them ourselves."

The golden glow in her eyes dimmed, and her voice lowered. "As you interact with the dreamscape, keep the flame close at hand. It is your anchor. The images here are figments—fabricated manifestations that display the fears of the faithless as well as the hopes of those who eagerly await the dawn. Whether for good or evil, they will draw you in. They will reach for your hearts, even reading your thoughts to see by what means they might capture your compassion." She gazed into each pair of eyes, her voice growing even more somber. "If you give in to their siren call, you could be trapped here forever."

I stared at my candle's flame, conical and unwavering, a steady beacon, like a lighthouse signaling safe haven. I had to be careful. If not for Cerulean, I might still be trapped in the world of dreams.

With the flame's image firmly seated in my mind, I scanned the area, a playground in the middle of a park. Two swing sets, one with a tire swing, lined the right side. Sliced and shredded, the tire wobbled, dangling under rusted chains. Three broken seats hung by frayed ropes in the other set.

On the left side of the park, a wooden carousel spun lazily in the stiffening wind. Skeleton oaks stood here and there, their low-hanging branches dipping toward small tombstones that dotted a meadow of lush green grass.

I shuddered. This wasn't a playground at all. It was a portrait of perdition — a child's nightmare. "I don't see anyone. Is there a way to find out whose dream this is?"

"Odd." Amber looked through the candle's flame, blinking as she turned in a full circle. "It seems that at least two minds have created this playground and cemetery, and its borders are indistinct." She lowered the candle. "A blend of two dreams could be a dangerous place."

Daryl hugged herself and shivered. "Well, if *you* think it's dangerous, then I'm ready to push the panic button."

"No need to panic." Amber lifted her candle. "As long as we hold to our anchors, we should be safe."

"What are you doing here?" someone called in a gruff tone.

At a nearby sandbox, a small boy pushed a plastic shovel into dark sand. Dressed in a miniature business suit, complete with a button-down shirt and a tie, he seemed half man and half child. He poured the sand into a black bucket and glared at us, his short, curly black hair tossed by a foul-smelling breeze.

Amber whispered, "Just you and me, Nathan. The others should wait here. We want to avoid too much interaction."

Walking ahead of me, Amber stepped into the sandbox and sat on the corner board. "What is your name?"

He scowled. "Who wants to know?"

"My name is Amber." She reached for his hand, but he jerked it back. "Do you mind if I ask you some questions?"

Still scowling, the boy raised a pair of fingers. "You already asked two. How many more questions do you have?"

As I edged closer, the stench grew stronger. I crouched, pinched the brown sand, and raised the sample to my nose. It smelled like manure.

Amber laughed gently. "A few more questions. I will not weary you."

"Then out with them." The boy pushed the shovel in for another scoop. "I'm busy."

"I can see that." She touched a finger to her chin. "Again, what is your name?"

He kept his eyes down and answered with a sharp, "Frederick."

"May I call you Fred, or perhaps Freddy?"

His scowl deepened with each punctuated word. "My name is *Frederick*."

"Very well, Frederick. Have you seen a tall, broad-shouldered man?" She pointed at me. "He looks like this young man, only older."

Frederick glared at me, patting the manure in his bucket with hefty slaps. "Ask the others. No one ever stops to play with me, so I wouldn't know."

Amber cast a glance at me, then turned back to Frederick. "Where may I find these others?"

He flipped over his bucket and pulled it up, leaving behind a castle of packed manure. "Hard to say." Keeping his head low, he shrugged, though he glanced at her every few seconds. "Stick around. They'll come by eventually. They always do."

"From which direction?" Amber asked. "The little tombstones?"

He squinted. "What tombstones?"

Amber stared at him for a moment before nodding. "I see."

"If no one plays with you," I said, "what do the others do when they see you?"

Frederick lifted his head, his expression softer. "They spit on me."

"Spit on you? Why?"

"I can't understand it." Frederick reached into a back pocket and pulled out a fat wallet. "No matter how much money I offer, no one will be my friend."

"Money cannot purchase friends," Amber said. "Only sycophants and flatterers would respond to such a call."

He scooped another shovelful of manure and muttered, "Do-gooder."

Amber rose. "I have no further questions."

I helped her step out of the sandbox, whispering, "What's the deal with the tombstones?"

"It's the blended dream. I believe Frederick is one of the sleepers, but the tombstones are not part of his dream. Someone else has conjured the cemetery."

"But no one else is around. Could he or she—"

Kelly's voice stretched out in the breeze. "Nathan. You'd better come and see this."

Backing toward me, the four others stared at the tombstones — six or seven ashen pillars arrayed in a broken circle. Gray mist rose from each, human-shaped, though warped and stunted.

As the mists gathered into small, deformed bodies, Daryl gulped. "Dead children?"

"Well," Frederick said with a snort, "they might remind you of children, but I'd keep my distance if I were you."

The bodies congealed, clarifying their features. A boy, his body bent and his limbs crooked, stood in front of the largest tombstone. Gathering around him in a semicircle, several others solidified. A girl, tall and slender, with deep cuts marring the underside of her forearms stood to his left. Beside her, another girl gripped a crutch on one side of her single-legged frame.

Two other boys, apparently twins, each with pale skin and barely a wisp of hair blown about by the breeze, stood to the first boy's right. Two other girls stood behind him, one with a tattered shawl over her head and shoulders that covered a ratty mop of gray hair, and the other with a long scar that ran across the bridge of her nose. Wearing dark glasses and carrying a walking stick, she grabbed the fringe of the shawl of the girl next to her and shivered.

My throat tightened. These children weren't merely handicapped; they were —

"They're zombies," Daryl whispered. "Somebody's dreaming about zombies."

Tony spread out his arms. "Stay behind me. If they're just kids, maybe I can scare them off."

Frederick snorted again. "Good luck."

A smile spread across the face of the lead boy. Circling Tony, he limped toward me, his arms flopping at his sides. "Excuse me, good sir. Would you please help us?"

"Help you?" I replied. "What do you need?"

The girl with the slashed arms wrung her hands. "Tell him nothing, Thibault," she said with a heavy Irish accent. "He is one of the ghosts."

Thibault nodded. "He's a ghost, all right, but he looks like the man who saved us from the pale one. What was his name?"

"He did not give his name," the girl said. "He was a snob, to be sure."

"Liar!" The girl with dark glasses hobbled forward, tapping her walking stick on the ground. A skull-and-crossbones medallion dangled from a thin cord draped around her neck. She stopped in front of me, sniffing through her blood-tinged nostrils. "Your voice carries Solomon's melody, and you bear his scent as well."

"Solomon?" I reached for the girl but hesitated. "Do you know where he is?"

The girl, barefoot and smiling, groped for my hand and, finding it, latched on. "I am Felicity. Come with me. I'll help you find Solomon."

"Nathan." Amber's call bore a warning tone. "She is a phantasm, a figment who will vanish with the dawn. Do not be taken in. Focus on the light of reality."

I lifted my candle and looked at Amber through the flame. Already she seemed less solid than before. "But she knows my father's name. Maybe she's seen him in her dreams. Shouldn't we at least find out what she knows?"

Frederick pointed at Felicity. "Don't trust her. She's the worst of all, a beggar with the bite of a serpent."

"Oh, Freddy," Thibault said, limping toward him, "you are such a pathetic soul."

Frederick stepped back, holding his shovel like a weapon. "Don't you dare!"

"Or else, what?" Thibault set a foot in the manure. "You should be used to this by now." The boy spat a black and bloody wad. It landed on Frederick's hair and spread across his scalp like reddish tar.

While Felicity hung on to my hand, the other children joined Thibault, spitting viciously. Wads of various colors flew toward Frederick. He flung his pail and shovel at them and covered his head with his arms. "Get away, you monsters! Get away!"

"Leave him alone!" I shouted. I took a step forward, but Amber pulled me back.

"Do not let his cries sway your resolve. You must stay anchored with me."

I stared at Amber's glowing eyes. They transformed into a pair of blurry orbs and then back to normal. "This feeling," I said as I wobbled in place. "It's ... it's something I can't seem to control."

"Your instincts are strong." Amber pushed my wrist, lifting my candle closer to my eyes. "You have been taught to help the suffering and the downtrodden, but you must realize that Frederick is a victim of his own fears. He is punishing himself."

I looked back at the others. Kelly's mouth hung partially open, apparently in a hypnotic state, but she seemed far more solid than Amber.

As the cries grew louder, I cringed. Tony, now fading into a ghostly blur, walked closer. He grasped me from behind and propped me up. "Shake it off. The kid's a creep, some kind of money-obsessed adult who never grew up. He's not worth it."

Amber caressed my cheek and whispered, "On the contrary, my kind-hearted friend, Frederick is worth your sympathy. But have no fear. He will likely wake up soon, and his demons will crumble to ashes."

Felicity tugged on my hand. "I'm real." With dark glasses covering her girlish face, and a cane propped against her narrow chest, she seemed vulnerable, helpless, lost. "You'll stay with me, right?" She sniffed again. "Please don't go away like all the others."

"Don't listen to her, Nathan." Amber's voice seemed distant, foreign. "She has seized your heart and will soon wring it like a sponge."

Holding the candle with a shaking hand, I concentrated on the flame. I had to fight this pull — pity for a little blind girl who begged for rescue from a lonely cemetery. Ignoring her seemed impossible.

Frederick screamed. The manure under him crumbled away, and he and Thibault fell into the void. Air swept into the hole, creating a cyclone that slurped the surroundings into its swirling grip. The swing sets tore from their moorings and flew toward us.

"Hit the deck!" Tony yelled.

Everyone dropped to the ground. I pulled Felicity into my arms and crouched over her, still holding my candle as its undisturbed flame stood tall in the center of my vision.

As debris flew overhead, Daryl called out, "Shades of *Twister*!"

An oak tree sailed past, then the carousel and several tombstones. One by one, the children fell into the sweeping wind and disappeared in the dark vortex.

The vacuum jerked Felicity from underneath me and dragged her toward the void. She fought back, sliding as she dug in with her toes. She reached toward me with spindly arms and bony fingers. "Help me!"

I lunged and grabbed her arm with my bandaged hand. "Hang on! I've got you!"

"Beware!" Amber shouted from her knees. "You can go with her, but I do not know how to bring you back. It is far too dangerous."

"But she knows where my father is!" I looked into the pitiful girl's eyes. The wind had torn her dark glasses away, revealing vacant sockets. Was she one of Mictar's victims?

Kelly crawled toward me, ducking her head to avoid flying branches. "She's just a dream, Nathan!" She held her candle close to mine. Both flames burned steadily in the violent gale. "You have to let her go!"

Ripping pain shot up my arm and into my spine. "If she was just Frederick's dream," I grunted, "she wouldn't have known my father's name!"

Amber shouted again. "She probably knows something, but if she is one of the dreamers, she, too, is waking up. She will be whole in mere moments, and her fears will vanish."

I gritted my teeth. I had to hold on. If Felicity was lucid enough to know Dad's name, she had to be thinking clearly.

Tony braced a foot against a metal rod protruding from the ground while holding Francesca in one arm. "Get a grip!" he shouted. "Your father wouldn't want you to take the risk!"

"To save the world?" I strained to push out each word. "Maybe he would!"

Kelly, Daryl, and I slid closer to the roaring black tornado. Felicity hung sideways like a flag, her feet pointing toward the cyclone and her long dress flapping.

My hand cramped. I couldn't hold on much longer. "Can you take me to my father?"

After hesitating for a second, she closed her sockets and cried out, "I'm not sure! But I have met him!"

I rose to my feet. Pulling Felicity against my chest, I let my body slide toward the void.

Kelly grabbed a fistful of my sleeve and jerked me back. Her eyes flashing, she roared into my ear. "Listen to me! If you can't fight this dream-world delusion, you'll never find your father." She pried my hand away from Felicity's arm and pushed me toward Tony. The release made her stumble backwards, and she fell into the rushing wind.

"Kelly!" I tried to lunge for her, but Tony held me back. As if swimming in a whirlpool, she fought against the cyclone, but it sucked her and Felicity into the black hole along with the remains of the dreamscape. Seconds later, everything vanished.

CHAPTER SEVEN

I FELL TO MY bottom. I couldn't say a word. I could barely breathe. What had Kelly done? How would I ever find her?

I scanned the area—dim, cool, and vague. No sign of anything except my fellow travelers.

A few paces away, Amber stood near Francesca, touching her arm as if checking for injury.

Daryl pushed up to her hands and knees. "I think I just did the twist with the Tasmanian Devil."

Tony stared in the direction Kelly had disappeared. "She's gone. I know she's not my real daughter, but I kind of feel like she is."

"We'll find her," I said, trying to push confidence into my voice. "She has to be somewhere. I'm sure the scientists have a way to track her."

"Right. And Kelly's tough. She'll be fine." He set a hand under my elbow and helped me rise. "You okay?"

"I think so." My cheeks burned. Kelly had sacrificed herself once again. I pivoted toward Amber and spread out my arms. "Will she be all right?"

"I cannot be certain." Amber glided toward me through the dimness, the glow of her candle lighting her way. "Dreams always end," she said, her voice calm and soothing, "but I have never followed one into the mind of its creator."

"So Kelly's trapped in Frederick's mind?" I asked. "How could that be?"

Amber shook her head. "I suspect that Felicity was the second dreamer, and Kelly went with her, but I know not where. Felicity was a strange phenomenon. We supplicants can easily discern the vague profile that the phantoms carry, but Felicity never displayed it."

Francesca took Amber's hand. "I noticed, too. She didn't fade at all."

"Then perhaps she has taken Kelly to a place of safety. We have reason to hope."

I fumed inside. Her disappearance was all my fault. Hope wasn't good enough. I had to do everything possible to find her.

"So where are we now?" Daryl asked. "Someone else's dream?"

"No, but we are still in Earth Yellow's dream world." Amber swept her arm across the darkness. "It is an infinite universe with infinite horizons, and it abounds with countless visions of the night. If we were to walk in most directions, we would soon come upon another dream, but, for now, we are in an area void of the imaginations of mankind."

"Most directions?" Francesca said. "Not all?"

"No, not all. One direction will take you to the barrier that separates the dream world from Sarah's Womb. It is difficult to see it when you are actually within a dream, unless you know what you are looking for."

Daryl's gaze drifted across the expanse. "It's like being on the holodeck in *Star Trek*."

"So what do we do?" I asked, trying to subdue my anger.

"We have no choice but to return to the observatory."

"Return? But — "

"Peace, Nathan. If the scientists are unable to track Kelly, we can come back here." Amber tilted her head as if listening to something in the air. "The music is dying. That's our signal."

A few seconds later, the darkness faded. Light filtered in, brighter with each passing second. Soon, the telescope room appeared around us, still dim and now without the music.

Solomon Yellow stood next to Francesca Red, his finger lifted in a counting pose. "I see only five. Kelly is missing."

"Nathan," Mom called. "Where is she?"

I shuffled toward her, my legs weak and wobbly. "I don't know. She got sucked into a dark hole with a girl named Felicity. I couldn't follow. We're hoping there's some way to track her."

"Maybe there is." Solomon picked up the empty candelabrum and reached for my candle. "Does she have her light?"

I gave him the candle, still burning and now about three-quarters its original size. "I think so."

Solomon blew out the flame and showed me the lower end. Something circular and dark was stuck to the bottom, like a thumbtack driven into the wax.

"A transmitter. All the candles have one." Solomon dug his fingernails around the circle and plucked it out. "As long as she hangs on to the candle, Dr. Gordon should be able to track her."

"Why didn't you tell us about the transmitters before?" I asked.

"Because you didn't need to know."

His reply felt flippant, dismissive. How much more did he know that he wasn't telling us?

"I have a signal," Dr. Gordon called. "It's weak, but it's definitely hers."

Solomon turned toward him. "Can you identify which realm she's in?"

"The computer says the echo signature isn't like any we've encountered, so I can't determine its origin. But she seems to be moving, so I assume she is alive."

I blew out a relieved sigh. "So if you can't find her using the tracking device, can we go back and look for her?"

"That depends." Solomon laid an arm over my shoulders and led me toward a row of desks that abutted an outer wall. "Amber is capable of taking you back to the dream world, but even she would have no idea where in the dreamscape you would go."

I looked at Amber, raising my eyebrows in a questioning way.

"He is right," she said. "If I am physically with a dreamer, I can easily find his or her dream, but if we jump in from a random place, we are more likely to enter a gap than anyone's dream, and gaps can be huge and dangerous to navigate because of their darkness."

"True," Solomon said. "We should wait for another dream to come close enough for the computers to pick up, but unlike planetary orbits, intersections can't be predicted. Just be patient. I think we will be able to show you a new searching option in a minute."

I nodded. I didn't have much choice but to go along. Now that Kelly was gone, our plans seemed to be falling apart. How could we get to the misty world without the Earth Blue mirror she'd been holding? That realm and its healing violin seemed farther away than ever.

Solomon stopped near a desk where Dr. Simon Blue sat in a rolling swivel chair. Next to him, Simon Yellow sat facing an adjacent desk, while a man who looked like a younger, heftier version of Dr. Gordon attended a computer screen on a third desk.

Simon Blue spun toward me. "You have seen Dr. Gordon of Earth Yellow, but allow me to make a formal introduction. Dr. Gordon of Earth Yellow, this is Nathan Shepherd of Earth Red. Nathan Shepherd, Dr. Gordon."

Dr. Gordon gave me a quick nod. "Pleased to meet you." He then turned to his computer screen.

I returned the nod, though he was no longer looking at me. "Pleased to meet you as well."

"After we met," Simon Blue continued, "I was able to combine his technological knowledge with our experience studying the various cross-world phenomena. We have also been in contact with the Earth Red Dr. Gordon through a digital channel that gives us clear transmission, and he added to our understanding, enabling us to deduce how everything works."

"Is Gordon Red okay?" I asked. "Does he know how Clara's doing?"

"They're both well, considering the circumstances there. Clara wanted to join us, but we had to decline. We have been able to receive inanimate objects from Earth Red using the digital channels, but some of them came across rather singed on the edges. Transporting humans is far too risky."

Gordon Yellow pushed back, rose to his feet, and rolled his chair toward Francesca Red. "Please. Rest."

The two Simons followed suit, offering their chairs to Francesca Yellow and Molly.

"Well," Solomon Yellow said, clapping his hands. "Shall we get on with it?"

Dr. Gordon handed Solomon a page of printed data. "The experiment worked perfectly. We captured the energy flow and imported its fingerprint. If we assume that the other dream worlds have the same format, we can shift our instruments to read and reproduce them in three dimensions."

"Then our theory is correct," Solomon said.

"What theory?" I asked. "And what does this have to do with finding Kelly, or stopping Convergence?"

Dr. Gordon nodded at Solomon. "It will take a few minutes to align the telescopes and search for the signals.

Perhaps you should take that time to explain the situation to Nathan."

"Very well. I will start at the beginning." Solomon picked up an iPod on Simon Blue's desk and extended it to me. "Here is the key, perhaps literally in one sense of the word."

"Doesn't it hold the music that opens dimensional portals?"

"Yes, but we added a piece that has a different function." Solomon slid his finger along the iPod. A violin played the simple melody of Foundation's Key, but it was more than a rote recital. The violin sang with majestic fervor, a brilliant rendition that only one person in the world could have created. Even the tinny, built-in speaker couldn't mask the quality.

I looked at Mom. Obviously, she couldn't have recorded it. She had been with me or in Mictar's clutches ever since before Solomon Yellow came onto the scene. As the music continued, I turned to Francesca Yellow, now holding hands with Solomon. She gave me a timid smile.

I nodded. Of course. That Francesca could play like this. No doubt about it.

Solomon turned off the iPod. "After many nights of experimenting, we learned that Francesca's playing of that piece protects sleepers from dreaming about the future and blocks Mictar from entering their dreams. We think it somehow interferes with the open channels that the wounds created, but we have no idea how it works."

"So what did you do?" I asked. "Distribute it on the Internet?"

"It's nineteen ninety-three. The Internet isn't nearly as widespread as it is in your world, and the circumstances we've lived with have delayed its progress, so we sold the recording the old-fashioned way—in Walmart."

"So are the worlds still running in parallel? I mean, with all the disturbances we've caused, I guess nothing is really predictable, is it?"

Simon Blue took the iPod and laid it on his desk. "You are correct. In fact, accurate next-day dreaming would likely have ceased on its own. Fortunately, when Solomon invented the cure, it was still a huge concern, so we sold hundreds of millions of copies and made a fortune."

Prickles ran along my neck. "So is this just a profit-making scheme to you?"

Solomon laughed. "Nathan, every penny went to finance this observatory." He patted me on the back. "Did you see that old wreck I was driving? You'd think I'd keep a few dollars to get a better car."

"Yeah. I saw it." I averted my gaze, warmth surging into my ears, half from anger at the seemingly endless delay and half from embarrassment. "Sorry. I jumped to conclusions."

Simon Blue spread out his arms. "All is forgiven. As you will soon see, this is a vastly improved observatory from the ones you've visited on the other earths. We will find Kelly, and we will stop Interfinity and the tragedy of Convergence."

I looked around. So far this observatory didn't seem much different. In fact, the laptop computers were bulkier, obviously older technology, and the smaller screens forced them to feed the video signal to large stand-alone monitors. Those looked pretty sharp, though they were an old style, not the flat screens that would come out in a few years.

"Here's an interesting innovation." Simon Blue opened a drawer and pulled out a device that looked like a walkie-talkie. "We call this an interworld audio receiver and transmitter unit. It's so new, even Dr. Gordon on Earth Red doesn't have one yet. The only three in existence are here in our lab."

"An interworld what?" I asked.

"Interworld audio receiver and transmitter unit." He set it in my hand. "We call it IWART."

"That should be easy to remember." I looked it over. "What does it do?"

Simon Blue touched a round plastic knob at the center of the IWART's front casing. "This switch has three settings, one for each of the three earths. For example, if you use the Earth Yellow device while you're here and turn the switch to the Earth Blue setting, you will be able to talk to someone holding the Earth Blue device while he is in that world, regardless of the difference in time passage. First, you press the talk button." He pointed at a black button on the side. "Then you say something and let the button go. It transmits the sentence or paragraph or whatever in its entirety, allowing the receiver to play it at a normal rate. The only drawback, of course, would be for the person on the faster world. It would seem to him that the person on the slower world is taking a long time to record his reply."

"Sure," I said. "That makes sense."

Simon pointed at one of the computers on the desk. "We have the same technology in our transmissions between the laboratories, but this allows someone to be mobile; that is, he would be able to use it outside of the lab. You would still, however, have to be stationary for it to make cross-world contact. It doesn't work while you're moving, but since it also has a built-in GPS receiver, it might come in quite handy for many applications, don't you think?"

"Definitely." I eyed the switch on the IWART. The three settings were labeled *Yellow, Blue,* and *Red.* "What happens if the Earth Yellow device is set to the Earth Yellow position?"

"It contacts us here in the observatory, and, as you might expect, the Earth Red device's Red setting would contact Earth Red headquarters, and so on. We will be sending the IWARTs to those worlds soon. But now we must turn to other matters." Simon Blue nodded at Dr. Gordon. "Is the Scotland mirror locked in place?"

"It appears to be." Dr. Gordon tapped on his keyboard. "I can show the local energy emission first. Perhaps by the time they synchronize, we can look deeper." He turned toward the center of the room and pointed upward. "As you watch, I'll explain what you're seeing."

On the ceiling, a curved reflection of everyone in the room looked down at us. The mirror darkened, and pinpoints of white light dotted the purple canopy—stars twinkling in the night sky. The darkness broke apart and scattered, like oil droplets on water. They changed into oddly shaped globules of various colors, much like the patterns at the other observatories.

"What you are seeing," Dr. Gordon said, "is the radio noise generated here on Earth Yellow. As you might expect, our own earth has the strongest signal. The computer will lock on the closest dream and interpret its sound emission. Then we should be able to see a visual representation, the music of the mind, if you will — energy that can be translated between light and sound.

"All the light energy we collect is now being sent through the mirror Tony brought from Scotland. This should allow us to visually search the three realms safely. And I hope we will eventually learn how to open a portal to the stalkers' world. From what I have learned, eliminating those creatures would help our cause greatly."

"Can you play the transmissions out loud?" I asked. "I'd like to hear them."

"I could, but it will be severely garbled until we translate it."

"I'd like to give it a shot, if you don't mind." As I stared at the scene above, static began buzzing from hidden speakers. I concentrated on the noise, trying to pick it apart and decipher the tune as I had once before.

As I caught the notes, I mentally combined them into measures and hummed along. The static began to clear. Just like last time, my physical ears heard what my brain put together.

Dr. Gordon's voice broke through. "Shall I begin the translation? Nothing will happen without the appropriate music."

"No," Francesca Yellow said. "Let Nathan do it."

The interruption jolted my concentration. Static blended with the music. I closed my eyes more tightly. I had to refocus and get the music back.

Soon, the melody flowed again, and it took only seconds to recognize it—Be Thou My Vision—the same piece that had cleared the air during Daryl Blue's nightmare. Yet, this didn't sound like a choir of angelic singers. It was more like a duet—a violin and a piano, beautiful in passion and haunting as each piano note echoed the violin's strokes.

Someone slipped a violin and bow into my hands. "Now play it, son," Mom said. "Play it with all your heart."

"But my hands, they're—"

"Play it anyway." Her voice sharpened. "Let the pain flow. Without pain there is no passion."

I rubbed my fingertip across the violin's smooth wood grain. It felt good ... very good. Maybe Mom was right. Maybe I could still play. "Okay. I'll try."

Keeping my eyes closed, I raised the bow to the strings. Mom's voice smoothed to a poetic cadence. "Only sacrifice draws a holy flow from within, and only a bleeding soul can reach deep enough to find the blazing fire—the God-given inferno that purges every particle of dross that spoils the master's silver."

I pressed down on the fingerboard and pushed the bow across the strings. Pain ripped through my hand. A note screeched, worse than nails on a chalkboard.

I lifted the bow. "I can't. My hands hurt too much."

"Think about healing," she said. "Imagine yourself playing with soft, supple, perfect hands. Let the pain melt away."

I created a mental image of myself and forced the imaginary Nathan to strip off the bandage, but both hands were still raw and oozing blood. I couldn't make the redness go away.

Again I pushed against the strings, and again a horrid screech erupted. Pain shot from the tips of my fingers to my shoulders.

"Let's do it with the computer," I said, opening my eyes and lowering the violin. "We don't have time to —"

"Nathan." Mom's voice stayed calm, yet forceful, "I have told you a hundred times that you have more talent than I do. You just haven't reached into your soul to grasp it. You have to roll away the stone that's keeping your talent from rising into your heart and hands." She pressed a fist against her chest. "Your music has to come from a heart of pure passion. Otherwise, it will be nothing more than a mechanical recital of rigid notes on a page."

I touched my own chest with the butt end of the bow. "But there isn't a stone in the way. There isn't anything blocking my passion."

Mom's brow eased upward. "Isn't there?"

"No." I lifted my bandaged hand. "This isn't pretend. We're dealing with reality."

"I see." She took the bow and pointed it at the violin. "I will need that, please."

As the static continued, I gave her the violin. Her makeshift bandage had loosened, exposing her bloody gash. "Mom. Your hand. There's no reason to—"

"I told you I'd show you some of my old spunk," she said as she set the bow over the strings. "You might want to take notes."

Grimacing as she pressed down on the fingerboard, Mom played the last few notes of the song, apparently matching what she heard in the static. Although she began with a hint of flatness, the melody soon sharpened to the proper pitch. As she glided into the first phrase, cringing with every note, the tune's lyrics came to my mind, as if bidden to rise by the matchless virtuoso.

Be thou my vision, O Lord of my heart;
Naught be all else to me, save that thou art.
Thou my best thought, by day or by night,
Waking or sleeping, thy presence my light.

She took a breath and looked up at the ceiling, tears flowing. Then, raising the bow again, she played the same notes, this time even more beautifully than before. Every push and pull of the bow brought an anguished frown and a weak grunt, but she played on, sweating, crying, and bleeding.

A trickle of blood dripped and streamed down the fingerboard. Francesca Shepherd of Earth Red seemed to pay no mind. Playing on and on, she had lost all awareness of her surroundings.

Above, the globules in the curved mirror burst open, and the colors merged into a scene, blurry but discernable. Little Francesca Shepherd, no more than ten years old, stood in her old bedroom, playing her violin in front of a music stand.

Yet, how could this be? Gordon had said they would pick up the strongest dream signal, but Mom wasn't dreaming. I looked again at her face—eyes closed, breathing steady, body moving in a flowing rhythm — wide awake.

Or was she?

In the scene above, little Francesca stopped playing and crawled under her bed. As if followed by a movie camera, she appeared in the dim shadow of her bed's frame, her eyes peering from under a frilly dust ruffle at shoes rushing past her hiding place. Then, closing her eyes, she folded her hands into a praying clench and moved her lips rapidly.

Deep lines creased Mom's brow. Blood dripped from her hand to the floor, but she played on.

Little Francesca crawled out from under the bed. Kneeling by her mother's body, she wept pitifully, rocking back and forth in time with her sobs. Soon, a large hand came into view. Francesca took it, rose to her feet, and walked away with Nikolai Malenkov hand in hand into a dense fog.

The scene shifted. Now in the backseat of an old car, she gazed out the window, watching her home shrink in the distance. As she held a stuffed bear in her arms, tears streamed down her cheeks.

Breathless, I again looked at Mom. The lines in her forehead had disappeared. Her eyes still closed, a gentle smile graced her lips — soft, pain-free, content.

The final note rose from the strings — stretched out and fading to a whisper. Mom withdrew the violin and dipped her head low, letting her black hair drape the front of her shirt. After taking a deep breath, she looked at me. Her smile was weak and sad, but she said nothing.

I couldn't say anything either. There was nothing to be said. She proved once again that something was wrong inside me. If I really did have her talent, I hadn't yet dug deep enough to let it flow. Somehow, I had to find a way. The fates of three worlds might well be hanging in the balance.

CHAPTER EIGHT

"THAT WAS REMARKABLE," Dr. Gordon Yellow said. "I'm learning something new with every experiment." Solomon Yellow turned toward him. "What was new?"

"Francesca generated her own sphere. Her thoughts penetrated the dream world, and the Earth Yellow telescope picked it up." Dr. Gordon tapped at his keyboard. "I am adjusting the fields to plunge deeper into the dreamscape."

"And what of the other earths?" Solomon asked.

"Francesca's energy surge allowed me to refine the calibrations. I'm pretty sure we can bring the other two in clearly. I'll let the computer generate the music for each world, but I'll keep the volume down. With three different tunes playing simultaneously, it would not be pleasing to our ears."

Above, Mom's dream scene had darkened, replaced by the usual chaotic colors. At the center, however, a circular portion stayed dark, taking up about a tenth of the mirror. With a black hole in the middle, the curved viewing area now looked like a doughnut.

After several seconds, three wedges began to clarify, as if the mirror had been cut into equal pie sections. In one, a snow scene took shape — the same city block where we had picked up Molly and later found Tony. With deepening drifts covering parked cars and sidewalks, no pedestrians braved the wintry storm.

In another section, a static-filled picture took shape. Weather-beaten tombstones rose at crooked angles from a weed-infested lawn. Storm clouds boiled in the sky. Jagged bolts of green lightning crashed to the ground, raising sparks and igniting fires that sent purple smoke and yellow embers into the swirling breeze. Again, no one was in sight.

The third wedge stayed dark.

At the computer desks, Dr. Gordon and the two Simons alternately watched the ceiling and their monitors. "Can someone give me an explanation?" I asked. "What's going on up there?"

Simon Yellow pointed at the snow scene. "That's from the dream world here. Someone has likely fallen asleep recently and is remembering the snowstorm, but he or she has exaggerated its ferocity." He shifted his finger to the cemetery. "That is the Earth Blue dream world. A dreamer has imagined a graveyard nightmare. Perhaps soon we will see that person appear." He walked closer to the center of the room and nodded toward the final section. "The telescope is still searching for a dream from Earth Red."

I stepped closer to the computer screen and eyed the unintelligible digits filling several windows. "Are there any more clues to where Kelly's signal is coming from?"

"It is somewhat stronger," Dr. Gordon said, "but we still have no way to determine its source. There just isn't anything comparable."

Simon Blue raised a finger. "Shall we show the new arrivals the hologram imaging?"

Dr. Gordon studied his screen for a moment. "Since we have good data in two of the realms, I don't see why not."

"If this works," Solomon Yellow said, "we can begin our search for Solomon Red immediately. We already have my energy signature in the computer, so we just have to find an exact copy somewhere in the dream worlds. He may well provide the final pieces to the Interfinity puzzle."

Using his laptop's touchpad, Dr. Gordon adjusted a slider on his screen. Above, dozens of light beams shot out from hidden sources. The beams converged inches above the floor and surrounded the telescope in a wide cylinder of swirling fog and multicolored light, rising from near the floor to about twelve feet in the air.

"Synchronizing the beams," Dr. Gordon announced in a mechanical voice. "Visual clarification commencing."

The fog evaporated, leaving behind recognizable shapes within the hologram's cylindrical stage, the same trio of scenes that had been displayed on the ceiling, but upright in a three-dimensional image. A narrower, black inner cylinder hid the telescope from view, keeping its presence from interrupting the presentation as it continued collecting data.

In the closest of the three sections, a knee-high tombstone stood near the edge of the cylinder, though the surrounding light made it look like an apparition, too vaporous to be seen clearly. Beyond it, the dream in the Earth Yellow world was more difficult to see, somewhat veiled by the Earth Blue dream.

"Reducing background radiant energy," Dr. Gordon said. "In a few seconds we'll see the results of all our efforts."

The laser beams diminished, leaving only the holographic images and the dark central cylinder in view. The nearby tombstone clarified. I walked to it, stooped near the marker, and read the engraving.

Here lies Felicity, an ugly blind girl.
Born—No one knows
Died—No one cares
Doomed to rot in this dark hole for all eternity.

A hard lump grew in my throat. This had to be Felicity's dream. Whoever she was, she generated powerful signals.

A shadow rushed away from the tombstone, then darted back, but the dimness prevented a good view. The shy ghost would stay hidden, at least for now.

"I think the graveyard is Felicity's dream," I said, "and Kelly went to wherever Felicity went. Maybe if I search inside the dream, I can find a clue."

"I hope you will search." Dr. Gordon walked to the hologram and pushed his hand into the field. Like electrified ripples on a pond, the boundary shimmered with warped light waves, but it seemed to offer no resistance. "As you can see, I can interrupt the flow without disturbing the image. You can literally walk through this dream without harming it or yourself."

I pushed a hand into the image. Although a slight tingling sensation crawled along my skin at the entry point, it didn't hurt at all.

Dr. Gordon withdrew a pair of eyeglasses from his shirt pocket. "We made these lenses from the shattered Earth Red mirror. Before our recent calibrations, the dream images were fragmented. Because of these distortions, we were rarely able to figure out what was happening. Dreams might move at ten times normal speed or appear warped. We were unable to sort them out."

I nodded toward the graveyard. "Yeah. I noticed something moving in there. It was too quick to see."

"That's why you need these." Dr. Gordon slid the glasses over my eyes. "Now when you walk inside the hologram you will see a much clearer picture, as if you were actually within the dream world."

Something cold rubbed across my ear. I took off the glasses and found a tiny metallic plate on one of the earpieces. "What's this?"

"An amplification device, one for each ear. Although the mirror transmits sound, the signal is too weak for our instruments to detect outside the hologram. These will amplify the signal, allowing you to listen to the dream, just as if you were actually there."

"But without the danger," Solomon added. "You will be invisible to anyone in the dream world."

I put the glasses back on. "What does Kelly's signal sound like?"

"You won't be able to hear it," Dr. Gordon said. "Her candle's signal can be detected only by the radio telescopes. We will continue to monitor it and let you know if we can pinpoint its location."

I let out a sigh. "Okay. What should I do? Just walk around in there?"

"Yes. Go from one earth dream to the other and study the features. Maybe by the time you get to the Earth Red section, we will have found a dream there. When you come out, you can report your findings."

"Will do." I strode into the hologram and studied the graveyard. Several paces away in front and to each side, the scene blurred, as if a wall of fog blocked my view, maybe boundaries to the next world's dream.

Standing still, I listened. The only noise the earpieces transmitted sounded like the whooshing of a breeze, perhaps created by an occasional wisp of fog that blew slowly past.

I turned left and walked parallel to the outer boundary through crawling vines and weeds that did nothing to slow my progress. When I came to a tombstone that stood in my way, I tried to touch its rough stony top, but my hand passed through it.

I straightened and pressed on. As I walked, I glanced from time to time at the onlookers — hazy but recognizable as they stood at the periphery of the hologram. Daryl stared with her jaw hanging open. Tony and Molly held hands, both watching with transfixed expressions. Amber looked on as well, though she seemed stoic, at peace.

The only others in sight were Dr. Gordon and the two Simons. All three beamed, obviously proud of their technological feat. But could they use this device to locate my father? Or Kelly? Was this venture really the key to stopping Interfinity? And if so, shouldn't I hurry to get the job done? Convergence was a dagger at the door. We had to stop it.

I scanned the graveyard once more but detected no sign of the fleeting shadow. Even if I could find Felicity, she wouldn't be able to tell me anything. It would be best to move on.

Still walking parallel to the hologram's outer boundary, I stepped through the fog and entered the Chicago snow scene. Although nearby objects, such as a fire hydrant next to my shoe, were clear, distant objects, especially tall ones, seemed indistinct. Maybe they stood outside the dreamer's thought range or were veiled by the wind-driven snow. I half expected to feel a chill from the breeze, but the temperature and air movement stayed the same—a bit cold, but not nearly blizzard-like. The whooshing sound continued, louder now as the snowstorm raged.

I marched on, plowing through snow drifts that piled against cars and vans on otherwise deserted city streets. Since my legs left the drifts undisturbed, any telltale footprints from dream-world inhabitants would be easy to spot, but none appeared. Whoever was dreaming this scene hadn't bothered to include any living creatures—no people, no dogs, not even a shivering bird to disturb the pristine layers of white.

I studied the falling snow, each flake just a tiny dot of white— no sign of crystalline uniqueness, more like Styrofoam particles than true snow. With nebulous boundaries all around, I felt like a human ornament in a recently shaken snow globe.

Again I strode ahead until I reached another wall of fog, the wall before the Earth Red dream section. Since that dream was dark when I last looked, it might not do any good to go there.

I turned ninety degrees and looked at the center of the hologram — dark and foreboding. Could that represent the central core Patar had mentioned? If I went into it, would the hologram show what was inside Sarah's Womb? While on the ceiling, that portion had been the doughnut's center hole, the mystery spot that hadn't yet revealed any secrets. Maybe the telescopes hadn't penetrated it and couldn't display its contents.

A gnarled oak stood near the barrier. With bent, twisted branches and long vines hanging from top to bottom, it looked like one of the spider trees Cerulean had said to avoid. I eased close and studied its tough, ridged bark. Harmless as it was in its hologram form, it gave me a shiver all the same.

I plunged through the dark barrier and into the center of the hologram. For a moment, only blackness greeted my eyes, then a flicker of light, like a firefly that glowed red for a brief second, then another light glowed blue, hovering at eye level not more than two steps away. I blinked and looked for the lights again, but they were gone.

I pressed on, feeling my way around the telescope until I exited the blackness, expecting to enter the darkness of the Earth Red dream world, void of an active dream. Yet, light appeared. A piano sat on a hardwood floor, a Model B Victorian like the one in Kelly's living room.

Other furnishings faded in and out of the scene—a chandelier dangling low directly over the piano bench; portraits on the wall of people with contorted faces; and a basketball hoop, complete with a backboard and net hanging from a pole that suspended the orange metal rim within free-throw distance of whoever might play the piano's keys.

Atop the piano sat dozens of glass figurines, each one a little girl in a different pose. Some were dressed in feminine attire, while others donned athletic gear, everything from a racing swimsuit to football pads and helmet to basketball shorts and a tank top.

A little girl, maybe nine years old, appeared next to the piano, glaring at it, her blonde ponytail protruding from the back of a baseball cap.

I swallowed. Could it be? It had to be. Kelly Clark as a young girl.

CHAPTER NINE

ISCANNED THE ROOM, hoping to pick up some clue that might reveal where Kelly was sleeping — nothing obvious. I returned my gaze to her young, dream self. She slid onto the piano bench and turned up the keyboard cover, exposing a set of warped, stained keys, nothing like those on the real piano back at her Iowa farmhouse. With a slap, she opened a music book poised above the keys and let out a huff.

I smiled. That huff was definitely Kelly's. I had heard it plenty of times before.

Squaring her shoulders, she set her fingers on the keys and looked up at the chandelier. It hung so low, the bottoms of the prismatic crystals nearly brushed the top of her cap as they swayed.

Beings of light, colorful and sparkling, danced around her head like wingless fairies in long dresses. Representing every color of the rainbow, each pint-sized pixie shook a tiny conductor's baton at Kelly and shouted chipmunklike commands that were too squeaky to understand.

I knelt at Kelly's side and looked into her eyes — the same ocean-blue eyes the real Kelly had. They seemed so innocent, reflecting the days before she had to face the trials of adolescence, the days when childhood fun held sway over fashion, popularity, and boys.

Flashing an impish grin, Kelly batted the pixies away. A basketball appeared in her hands, and she shot it toward the hoop. It banged against the backboard, swished through the net, and bounced onto the piano top, bowling over the figurines as it dribbled back into her grasp.

The pixies returned and buzzed around her head like a swarm of angry hornets. Kelly sighed and tossed the basketball away. It bounced once and disappeared.

After giving the pixies an angry scowl, Kelly expertly ran her fingers through a scale across the keys. Then, after finishing a second warm-up drill, she flipped through an old music book, its pages like ancient parchment. She looked at the musical score and played with a lovely touch, lifting her fingers and hands in slow, graceful arches.

The notes passed through the transmitters and into my ears, familiar notes that pieced together a haunting tune. I looked at the music book. The title, written in bold black script, seemed to float above the page—Amazing Grace. The music synced with the strokes of her little hands, her finger falls recreating one of the most heartfelt songs in human history.

Kelly swayed in time with the song. Her lips moved, as if she were singing in her mind but not letting the words come out. She now seemed older, maybe twelve or thirteen. Her baseball cap was gone, and she wore a long skirt and a button-up blouse that revealed her blossoming femininity. The pixies had vanished, and new figurines appeared on the piano — young men dressed in white tuxedos, one for each Kelly figurine.

As if preparing to dance, they paired up. When their hands touched, the Kelly statuettes transformed. The old clothes burned away, revealing a long, lacy gown every bit as white as her partner's tuxedo. Then they danced, a waltz of sorts, though slower than most — moodier and more contemplative.

With tears flowing down her cheeks, Kelly played on. Now dressed in the blood-stained safari outfit she had worn when we first traveled to Earth Yellow, she appeared to be sixteen. Even the cut on her head returned, oozing a dark red stream.

Kelly began to sing, her voice sweet, yet tortured, and dirge-like in cadence.

> Amazing grace is lost for me,
> A harlot soiled and stained.
> A wretch I am, a wretch I'll be,
> Till love unlocks my chains.

The figurines continued the slow dance. Each young man drew an image of Kelly into an embrace and waltzed with more energy. The male faces were perfect reproductions of my own.

Kelly continued her song, her voice still wracked with pain.

> Could Nathan ever dance with one
> So foul, unclean, a liar?
> Will grace he plays on strings of ice
> Be wrought in hands of fire?

Kelly's clothes ignited. Fire swept across her sleeves and down her legs, raising showers of sparks that consumed the bloodstains. As dark threads sizzled away, spots of white appeared. Soon, a radiant gown covered her body. Its long sleeves ran to the heels of her hands, and the hem brushed her ankles. Her eyes now sparkling, she played on, her voice louder, less tortured, yet filled with plaintive passion as she stretched out the final words.

The girl I was is crucified,
Impaled with God's dear Lamb.
Can Nathan purge the girl I was
And love the girl I am?

Trembling, I backed away. Thousands of thoughts flooded in, battling each other until no single thought made sense. What could all this mean? Kelly had to be dreaming this, but where was she?

I tried to slow my breathing as thoughts stormed. Did Kelly really think she was a harlot in my eyes? Was she really begging me to show her more grace? Or was this dream just a device she had conjured to torture herself?

I leaped out of the hologram. My eyes burned, yet not as if they had been scorched from the outside. The heat seemed to come from within, more like the scalding touch of ice than fire.

As I rubbed my eyes, Solomon Yellow braced my shoulder. "That dream really shook you up, didn't it?"

"Yeah." My eyes now clear, I looked again at the dream. As it slowly faded, Kelly seemed to stare directly at me, her eyes still sparkling.

I shook my head and looked again. The Earth Red section had fallen dark. "How long was I in the hologram? I … I kind of lost my sense of time in there."

Solomon glanced at his wristwatch. "Not long, maybe two minutes."

"Two minutes?" I stole a peek at Solomon's watch. "It seemed more like ten."

"Your mind adjusted to the time shift. The events in the dreams moved too quickly for us to tell what was going on, so only you can report what happened. We could see that Kelly and a piano were there with you, but little else."

I pointed at the Earth Red sector. "I'm sure it was Kelly's dream. Since she's the interpreter, her signal is probably strong."

"My thinking as well." Solomon turned toward the central core of the hologram and called through it. "Dr. Gordon, any word on Kelly's signal?"

"It's stronger," came the echoing reply. "We're still hunting it down."

I nodded at the hologram. "Since Kelly's dreaming in the Earth Red section, doesn't it mean she's somewhere on Earth Red?"

"Not necessarily. Apparently Felicity is able to dream in both the Yellow and Blue sectors, so the cosmic wounds must be allowing passage."

I pinched Solomon's sleeve and pulled him closer. "Can Dr. Gordon send me to Earth Red? The least I can do is look for her. It's better than staring at dreams—"

"Hey!" Daryl yelled as she stared into the Earth Yellow section. "You'd better get a look at this!"

I turned her way. "What is it?"

"See for yourself." Daryl waved a hand. "Hurry!"

I jogged over to Daryl and squeezed between her and Amber as they watched the Chicago snow scene from the edge of the hologram.

Inside, a lanky, pony-tailed man stalked through the blanketed street. Nearly as pale as the snow, he peeked into each car he passed, his eyes narrowing with every search. A red scar etched his cheek from ear to chin, stitched but still oozing blood.

I whispered, "Mictar?"

"Yes." Amber's whisper sounded like a calm wind. "The stalkers heal quickly when they feed on life energy. I fear that he has killed again."

"Any idea what he's doing?"

"If I am reading his eyes correctly, he is looking to murder the dreamer." Amber's voice turned melancholy. "He has the power to reach through to the dreamer's mind and deliver a mortal shock. Once he finds the dreamer, rarely does he fail to kill."

While Tony, Molly, and Solomon gathered around, I kept my stare riveted on the stalker. With a bare hand, Mictar brushed snow away from a pickup truck's windshield. Obviously he had physically entered the dream world. Even his breath raised clouds of white vapor that were quickly swept away by the wind.

"Can he hear us?" Daryl whispered. "I mean, is he dangerous?"

Solomon joined us and peered into the dream. "He's dangerous but not to anyone here. What we're seeing is like a satellite broadcast of a movie. He has no idea we're watching."

Mictar shifted to a taxicab and looked inside. He yanked open the door, grabbed a man's arm, and dragged him out onto the sidewalk, knocking a hat from his head in the process. He pushed his victim face-first into a snow drift and stepped on his neck. As snow swirled, Mictar appeared to be shouting something, but no sound came out.

"It's Jack!" I leaped into the hologram and knelt at Jack's side. Now aided by the transmitters, I picked up the dream's sounds.

Jack grunted and cried out, but Mictar just laughed and twisted his heel into Jack's neck.

"No more playing with supplicants for you," Mictar said. "If you'll tell me where to find the gifted girl, I'll let you live."

I shouted toward Amber, "Can we stop Mictar from killing him?"

She strode into the hologram, carrying a lit candle. Standing toe to toe with Mictar, she stared at him through the flame. As her glow strengthened into a blinding aura, a deep frown marred her features. "I do not sense a portal. I could enter the dream world, but I have no way of knowing if I will be able to find this particular dream."

Laughing again, Mictar leaned over and laid a hand over Jack's eyes.

I shot to my feet. "We have to do something! Mictar will kill him!"

Solomon ran into the hologram and shouted toward the computer desk. "Dr. Gordon, did you test the transport?"

"I didn't have the mirror until now." Dr. Gordon's voice sounded distant, warped. "It was impossible to conduct a test."

Sparks flew from the sides of Mictar's hands. Jack's body jerked, his arms and legs flailing.

"Do you think it would work?" Solomon yelled.

"So far every prediction has proven true, but transporting someone to the dream world is beyond the scope of predictable science."

I grabbed Solomon's arm. "I'll go. Send me."

"You cannot defeat him," Amber said. "I will go."

Solomon shook his head. "We can't risk either of you. We have to—"

Another figure rushed in among us, also lanky and pale. With a series of gruff pushes, he shoved Solomon, Amber, and me out of the way. "Send me," he shouted. "You can risk my life."

I stood with Amber at the edge of the hologram. "Patar," I called, "I thought you said I was supposed to—"

"Never mind!" Patar looked toward the computer desk. "I demand that you send me immediately."

"A few seconds," Dr. Gordon said. "I have to check the—"

"Now!" Patar screamed. "We have no seconds to spare!"

Light flashed around Patar, veiling the scene for a moment. The dream image returned with Patar standing behind his brother. Patar grabbed Mictar's ponytail and jerked him backwards. Mictar flew away from Jack, fell into a drift at the edge of the sidewalk, and banged his head against a snow-covered car.

While Patar helped Jack to his feet, Mictar opened his mouth and spewed a jagged black bolt. Arching his body over Jack, Patar ducked and launched his own barrage of dark lightning.

Mictar threw himself to the sidewalk. Patar's blast splashed against the car, sending the snow scattering in a mix of black and white droplets.

"I'd better listen," I said, straightening my glasses. "They might say something important." I stepped back into the hologram and stood a few feet away from the struggle.

Patar propped Jack up and barked at Mictar. "Leave now before this dream dissolves. When I awaken this human, you will be left without a light."

Mictar sneered. "I know how to negotiate the dreamless gaps."

"The rifts are many. It is now hazardous to stalk the dreamscape."

Mictar pointed a long finger at him. "You feign concern, dear brother, but I know you all too well. One of the gifted humans hides here, and you are protecting her. You are playing the crippled mother bird that keeps me from locating my prize."

"Crippled mother bird?" Patar furrowed his brow. "Your metaphor eludes me."

"You're holding back. Why aren't you trying to reverse and bleed my energy?"

"That works only when you are taken by surprise."

"Perhaps, but using darkness merely delays me. You are protecting instead of fighting."

Patar heaved a sigh. "A darkened heart is unable to understand nobility."

"Ah, yes, this from the one who would have the boy slay the supplicants." Mictar spat on the snow-covered sidewalk. "Such murderous nobility is beyond my grasp."

"I have no need to explain myself to you." Patar pointed a rigid finger of his own. "Be gone."

"Tell me where to find a mirror used by one of the gifted, and I will gladly go."

"The gateways to Cerulean are out of your reach." In a flurry of swirling snow, Patar lowered his head and muttered, "No thanks to the humans who should have secured them."

My shoulders slumped. Patar's quiet words were obviously meant for me. Cerulean had said he would take care of the mirrors, but he might not have known enough about the real worlds to find a good hiding place.

"So be it," Mictar said as he walked away and looked back with a scowl. "I will leave you and your nobility to die with the rodents you seem to admire."

Patar laid a hand over Jack's eyes and spoke with a gentle voice. "Awake now, my friend. I heard your murmurings."

"Yes," Jack said. "I was tired. Had to sleep."

"How is it that you are dreaming in the Earth Yellow realm? Have you and Cerulean left the Earth Blue dream world?"

"Cerulean found a cosmic wound and thought it best for me to sleep near it, hoping I'd search in other dream realms while I rested. It seems that the rift led me here."

"I see," Patar said. "Is your real self with Cerulean now?"

"I assume so. He was at my side when I went to sleep. He hoped to search here as well."

"You must find him immediately and send him to the dreams of his new charge."

"Where"—Jack squirmed in Patar's grip—"where should he go?"

"Cerulean knows that she dreams on Earth Blue, and I have seen her there, but that is not where she sleeps. If he goes to find her physical body, he will not be able to return. He must devise a way to solve that dilemma." Patar pulled his hand away from Jack's eyes. They were whole, glowing like two phosphorescent marbles.

"I don't understand."

"Cerulean will. Tell him that Mictar is on the prowl and has grown strong again. He must find the gifted one before Mictar does."

I searched the dreamscape. At the boundary of the hologram's central black section, Mictar stood in front of the dark wall. As if widening a flaw in the fabric, he opened it with both hands and slid inside. The gap then sealed itself, hiding him from view.

With three quick steps, I exited the hologram and rejoined the others. "Mictar's still on the move. It looks like he went into a core area at the center of the dream worlds, but I don't know where that leads."

Solomon gave me a somber nod. "And we don't know where Amber went either."

"She's gone?" I looked in every direction. "Where did you see her last?"

"When Patar knocked her out of the hologram." Solomon stooped at the spot where Amber had been crouching. "I saw her right here, but after that I was paying attention to the fight. I didn't keep an eye on her."

"Could she have transported with Patar?"

"That is possible, but I didn't see her in there."

"I'll take a look." I walked back into the snow scene and headed straight for the dark center, passing Patar and Jack without a pause.

When I came within a few paces of the central core's wall, the entire city scene darkened. The dream was coming to an end. Only the old tree was still easily visible, standing like an ancient sentry just a step or two from the wall.

A movement to the right caught my attention. Amber skulked out from behind a car and, after giving the tree a wide berth, halted in front of the barrier. As she stared at the black wall, her candle raised a circular glow on the surface. Although her dress flapped in the breeze, the flame stayed steady while she ran searching fingers along the wall.

A few seconds later, she pushed through a vertical flaw, covering her hand to the heel. The material appeared to be similar to rubber, pliable but still tough. She set her candle down and pulled with both hands to separate the two flaps, straining as if trying to open stubborn jaws.

With a final jerk, she created a narrow slit and stepped into it, leaving half her body visible in the candle's light. Keeping one arm and a leg in the opening, she lunged for something outside of the central core, caught it with one hand, and reeled it toward herself as if she were pulling a rope.

After picking up her candle and looking around once more at the darkened Earth Yellow dream world, she whispered, "Nathan, I hope you are still listening. Although the reasons are a mystery to me, I believe the cosmic wounds have allowed the vision stalker to use Sarah's Womb as a portal to go from one dream world to another. If so, I will learn his secrets and perhaps use them to locate your father and Kelly. When I do, I will try to find a way to contact you. I am very concerned about Mictar's new discovery. It could well mean that your loved ones are in great danger, so I have to follow him."

Her eyes shining with a light of their own, and the wind, fiercer than ever, blowing her hair into the core, she let out a sigh. "Please tell Francesca that I love her, and I hope to be able to supplicate for her through the mirrors of the Yellow world."

Straining again, she pushed farther into the slit, popped through, and disappeared from sight.

I turned and searched for Patar and Jack in the darkness, but they were nowhere in sight. In previous dreams I had experienced, a cyclone sucked everything away. This one just faded into nothingness. Could it be a difference of perspective? Maybe if I had actually been in the dream, the swirling windstorm would have been easy to see.

Now that this sector of the hologram had no dream to display, the observatory again filled my vision, and the echoing noises pounded into my ears. Only one dream sector remained — the dark graveyard in the Earth Blue realm.

"We lost the signal," Dr. Gordon called. "I will have to search for another dream in that realm."

His words fell like a ball and chain on a dungeon floor. What had we accomplished? In reality, nothing at all. We sat in the bleachers watching dreams come and go, hoping that one would reveal what we were searching for. It was worse than looking for a needle in a haystack; it was looking for a tiny impulse in an ocean of overstimulated neurons.

I jerked off the glasses. "We can't just stand around here and watch nightmares all day. I've had enough of singing and dancing and roaming through dream worlds. My father is missing, Kelly got slurped into a manure-filled sandbox, and we're just wasting time waiting for a computer to locate a signal when we're not even sure Kelly's holding the candle." I pushed a finger against Solomon's chest. "Send me into the dream world. I have to look for Kelly and my father."

"But that's exactly what we're doing." Solomon pointed at the floor. "Searching from here is safe."

"Safe?" Clenching a fist, I tilted my head up and looked Solomon in the eye. Every feature was so much like

Dad's—the eyes, the chin, the confident jaw. Yet, something was so different. "Did you see that little blind girl in the graveyard? My father would've risked his life to help her, even if it meant getting sucked into that cyclone. My father would've moved heaven and earth to find me or Mom or Kelly. Instead, we're sitting on our hands while the world is about to end. It's just plain stupid."

Solomon's jaw tensed for a brief moment, then slackened. He laid a hand on my shoulder. "What's the bottom line, Nathan? Exactly where do you want to go?"

I shrugged his hand away. "Send me to the graveyard. Maybe Felicity doesn't know what happened to Kelly, but it's a good place to start. And I don't know if we can believe that she knows where my father is, but it's worth a try." I strode to the hologram and stood at the edge. "Play the music and flash the lights. I'm going in."

CHAPTER TEN

"OKAY. WE'LL SEND you." Solomon strode to the computer desk where Gordon Yellow and the two Simons watched their screens. "Get ready to make the jump," he called back.

"Wait!" Daryl sprinted around the hologram and grabbed my arm. "You ain't jumping to light speed without me, buster." She pointed at herself with a thumb. "You need a cool-headed thinker, and I'm your girl."

"And I'm going, too." Mom walked toward us with the violin and bow. "My husband is in that dream world somewhere, so I'm going in, and I'm not coming back without him. Besides, who else will play when you need music?"

When she joined us, I touched my reflection on the violin's smooth surface. "You showed me how to play through pain. I'm sure I can do it now. But I'll be glad to have you along anyway."

As the others drew closer, I nodded at Tony, Molly, and Francesca Yellow in turn. "Your job is to stay here and raise those babies. And hide all the mirrors. Mictar's sure to come looking for them eventually." I took Francesca Yellow's hand. "Amber gave me a message. She wants you to know that she loves you, and she'll try to supplicate for you through the mirrors."

Francesca wiped a tear from her eye. "Little Nathan and I will be watching for her." She leaned close and kissed my cheek. "And I will pray for you and Kelly."

"Thank you." I peered around Tony. Solomon and the three scientists were busy on the computer, apparently preparing for the next cross-world leap.

With Francesca, Tony, Molly, Daryl, and Mom huddling close, I lowered my voice. "Listen. No offense to anyone, but you guys are the only people on Earth Yellow I trust. Can you keep a secret?"

Tony glanced at Solomon. "Even from Flash?"

"Yeah. Even from Flash."

"Sure. I guess so." Tony smiled and pointed at me. "You're Future Boy, so you know more about this stuff than I do."

Francesca fidgeted, then took in a deep breath before whispering, "Nathan, Solomon is my husband. I know you've been my friend for a longer time, but I made a vow. I can't keep secrets from him."

I pressed my lips together. She was right. Asking her to go against her word was a terrible idea. "Then tell him if you have to. I know I can trust you." I looked at Tony again. "Do you remember how to use Daryl's transmitter?"

"The one that talks to the future? Sure. I have it all figured out."

"Then get a message to Dr. Gordon Red for me."

Daryl touched my arm. "We didn't test it after Earth Red pulled away. I'm not sure he'll be able to contact —"

"We have to try it." I raised a finger. "There's one thing I never figured out. That plastic card I took from the shotgun guy, the one with all the letters and numbers on it. It has to be important."

"Where is it?" Tony asked.

"I left it on the computer desk in the Earth Blue observatory, so Gordon will have to —"

"It's not there," Daryl said. "Gordon Red wanted to see it, so Daryl Blue loaded up the interdimensional teleporter and shot it over to him."

I gave her a thumbs-up. "Even better. Tell him to send it to this observatory so you guys can transport it to me in the Earth Blue dream world."

"And use channel three," Daryl added, showing Tony three fingers. "That'll send a digitally encoded message straight to Dr. Gordon's computer. With all the whale-speak going on there, I doubt that anything else will work."

Tony spread out one of his huge hands. "But it's five hours to Newton. By the time I get there, this cemetery dream will be history. How can anyone find Nathan to give him the card when it gets here?"

"Okay, okay." Daryl heaved a sigh. "I'll take care of it."

"What do you mean?" I asked.

She flicked her thumb toward the computers. "I watched El Gordo work the gizmos. Tony and I will figure out how to get everyone to scoot so we can do the transmissions from here, and maybe I can get the card to you before that dream ends."

"Thanks, Daryl." I patted her shoulder. "I know you wanted to come. I appreciate it."

"Not so fast, Tin Man. If you had a heart, you'd remember that I've already spent too much time in this world." She poked my chest with a finger. "You're not leaving me here again. I'm going to find you and hand deliver the card."

I suppressed a laugh. "You're amazing, Daryl, you know that?"

With a wink and a grin, Daryl tossed her hair back. "As a matter of fact, I do. It's obvious you need me around."

"Definitely." I looped an arm around Mom's. "I guess we're off to see the wizard without the scarecrow."

"Scarecrow?" Daryl shook a finger at me. "Listen, Twister Boy, if you're looking to wrestle with another tornado, I'll be glad to—"

"Time to go!" I pulled Mom into the hologram and put the glasses on. Again, everything slowed to a normal pace—the rain, the windblown fog, and the swaying trees. Music filled the air, something mournful and unfamiliar. "Do you know what that song is?" I leaned close to Mom to let her hear through the transmitters.

After a few seconds, her head bobbed with the tune. "It's a slow version of Danse Macabre."

I shuddered. The Dance of Death was the same piece I had played when boarding Flight 191 in Chicago. At this slow pace, it was creepier than ever.

While waiting for the transporting flash, I glanced around, looking for any sign of Felicity. In the midst of a shroud of fog and windswept rain, her shadow rose in front of the tombstone where I had seen her before. She staggered backwards, her face and frame becoming clear. With her mouth agape and her arms trembling, she seemed terrified of something.

I traced a line in the direction she faced. At the wall that led to the hologram's inner core, a long, pale hand protruded from a gap. A man with a white ponytail emerged, but he seemed to be having trouble pushing all the way through.

"Now!" I yelled. "Send us now!"

Lightning flashed. Thunder boomed. The air felt cold and wet. Raindrops pelted my hair, and mist coated my glasses.

Mom pushed the violin under her sweater. "Looks like we made it."

"Stay there." I yanked off the glasses, ran to Felicity, and took her hand. "It's me, Nathan. Are you okay?"

"I smell death." Shivering, she pointed with her walking stick, her voice thin and frail. "I always smell death among the tombstones, but now it's stronger than ever. He has come to take me."

"Not if I can help it." I slid the glasses into my pocket and stepped between her and Mictar. The stalker shook his leg, trying to free it from the dark wall. "He's stuck. Let's get out of here before he gets loose."

When I pulled on her arm, she resisted. "No need. I smell my new friend. He will protect me."

"You're dreaming. The only real things here are me, my mother, and a crazy murderer named Mictar, and we don't want to mess with him." I scooped her into my arms and hurried back to Mom.

"Did Mictar see you?" she asked.

"Hard to say." I nodded toward a cluster of gnarled trees. "Let's find a place to hide."

Still carrying Felicity, I jogged to the biggest of the trees, a thick leafless oak, bent into the shape of an old, arthritic man who covered his mossy head with crooked arms. We huddled behind the trunk, stooping as we watched.

Mictar finally freed himself from the dream boundary. With rain plastering his ponytail against the back of his shirt, he raised his hands and sang out a pair of vowels that sounded like a long E and a short A.

A puff of gray smoke rose from his palms, cloaking them for a moment. When the air around him cleared, a black violin and white bow lay in his hands. He lifted the violin to his chin and pulled the bow across the strings. A high note sang out, warbling with a birdlike vibrato.

"I hear the song," Felicity said, her voice soft and mysterious. "Death is calling me."

I clamped a hand over her mouth and whispered, "When death calls, don't answer."

Playing more vibrating notes, Mictar walked along a path through the graveyard. As he passed each tombstone, he looked at both sides. He stopped and sniffed the air, turning as he inhaled deeply.

I pushed everyone lower. If that stalker smelled fear, hiding might not help, but it couldn't hurt to try.

Another sniff sounded, this one coming from under my protective arm. Felicity whispered through my fingers, "I smell the clutching wood."

The tree's trunk let out a long creaking sound, and the branches sagged lower, saturated and heavy. If much more rain fell, this might not be a safe place to hide.

Mictar looked our way. His nostrils flared. Shuffling closer, he played three short notes as if calling out, "Where are you?"

I clamped down tighter on Felicity's mouth. Why was Mictar hesitating? He had to know we were nearby. Why hadn't he rushed ahead to find us?

The rain stopped. As the clouds raced away, a strange glow shone in the distance. Mictar halted and tilted his head up. I, too, looked skyward. The canopy had turned from gray to purple with hints of azure and blue spreading from treetop to treetop, but no sun appeared. The light seemed to be coming from over the horizon, as if dawn were about to break, but the sky was brightening too quickly — far too quickly.

Mictar pointed the bow at our hiding place. "I smell your presence, Nathan and Francesca Shepherd. The aroma of the gifted is one you cannot hide."

Felicity struggled, but I kept her locked down. Responding to his taunt would give away our hiding place for sure.

"I see you now." Mictar propped his bow against his shoulder and laughed. "Your inexperience is showing. A spider tree is not the best of hiding places."

I looked up. Although the rain had ended, the branches continued to sag as if reaching down. A knobby-fingered hand grabbed my arm. I jerked free and pulled Mom and Felicity away just in time to avoid two other wooden claws, but as I backpedaled, I tripped over a root and fell on my bottom.

Mictar laughed again. "Watching a clown perform is truly entertaining."

I jumped to my feet and brushed mud from my pants. Felicity groped for me with her thin hands. "Death is near. I hear him, smell him, feel his presence."

I grabbed her wrist and pulled her to my side, while Mom wielded her violin like a club.

"Why were you hunting for Felicity?" I asked. "She's just a dream."

"I will keep my own counsel." Mictar took a step toward us. A new voice, powerful and deep, sang from over a hill in the distance, sending beautiful vowel sounds across the cemetery.

Felicity whispered, "Mictar seeks a gateway to the mind of the new gifted one, the sleeper, the dreamer, my beloved."

As the blue light brightened near the hilltop, Mictar retreated and crouched like a wary cat.

We backed away at the same pace. "Felicity, did you just interpret that song?"

"Yes. He calls me his beloved. I must go to him."

A head appeared at the hilltop, then the body of a young man came into sight as he walked to the crest. An aura of blue light surrounded him, and its glow spread throughout the graveyard. With his silky blue shirt and dark blue hair flowing in the breeze, he seemed more unearthly than ever. Jack walked a step behind, threading his hat through nervous fingers.

I stopped and bent close to Felicity. "His name is Cerulean. And another friend is with him, a man named Jack. They'll keep death from finding you."

Mictar straightened and glared at Cerulean. "Since your doom is certain, cursed supplicant, coming to the graveyard is most appropriate."

As Cerulean approached, tombstones crumbled and weeds shriveled. Lush grass grew in their places. Flowers sprouted near Mictar's feet with yellow, orange, and purple blossoms bursting forth. Flashing a brilliant smile, Cerulean spoke, this time with words instead of vowel sounds. "Graveyards become gardens, darkness becomes daylight, and daisies decorate the feet of death."

Mictar leaped to a bare spot on the path and kept his icy glare trained on Cerulean. "Poetry won't save you from your fate."

Cerulean's glow diminished, but his eyes stayed as bright as his smile. "Sacrifice appears as a curse to those of limited perception. To the beneficiary, it is life itself. To the provider, it is the path to enlightenment and the end of all fear, for perfect love casts out fear."

"Trite moralisms nauseate me. You sound like my fool of a brother."

Slowing his pace, Cerulean pointed at himself. "That is because he has listened to my song, to Amber's song, and to Scarlet's song. He has learned the meaning of sacrifice."

"Bah! Fodder for girlish romance." While keeping his stare locked on Cerulean, Mictar pointed at me. "Did you know that Patar has more than once insisted that this boy kill you along with your sisters? Did you know that this boy and his mother are the reason Scarlet lies dead in Sarah's Womb, never to return to your loving embrace?"

Cerulean's smile wilted. He halted and folded his hands at his waist. "All three of us have asked for the cup of death to pass by, but if the master of the table pours it into my goblet, I will drink it to the very last drop."

Mictar waved a hand. "You can stay at the side of this ugly little blind girl forever, but you can't stop me. You will never be able to protect all three of the gifted Earth Red dwellers. I will eventually find one unguarded and reenergize."

With Jack standing at his side, Cerulean stretched out his hand and called with a deep, commanding voice. "Felicity, my beloved, come to me!"

Felicity pulled against my grip. "I have to go."

"But Mictar's in the way, the guy you call death."

She took off her glasses and looked at me with her vacant sockets. "We all have to suffer the presence of death to enter the arms of our supplicant, but death is merely an odor. It comes and it goes, like breath in our nostrils, and after it passes, only the fragrance of life remains."

I stared at her. How could a blind girl who has seen only darkness, who has suffered through countless nights of fear, speak so beautifully? "I'll lead you to him."

Cerulean shook his head. "Let her go, Nathan. Her fears are many, and she cannot overcome them if you guide her." Again extending a hand of invitation, he called out, "Felicity, come to me. I will lead you across the shadow of death with song."

Clutching her walking stick, she tapped the ground in front of her, now without her dark glasses, though her skull medallion still swayed at her chest. Cerulean stood about a hundred feet down the path. As Felicity drew closer, he crouched and held both hands out as if waiting for a baby to approach with her first toddling steps.

Mictar stood between them, no more than thirty feet away from Cerulean. The stalker glanced back and forth between the two, looking frightened and confused. Obviously, he didn't dare confront Cerulean, but he didn't seem to want to leave. Every time he looked at Felicity, he took on a hungry look, even though the little blind girl had no eyes for him to steal.

Cerulean sang new vowels, each one sounding like a daddy's comforting lullaby. Felicity echoed the translations, her voice strong yet tremulous.

You need no crutch, no hand to hold.
My voice is all you need.
So cast away your fears and cares
And give my words your heed.

Felicity tapped the ground with her stick and, extending a hand in front, walked forward.

The smell of death grows strong and foul.
It permeates the air.
It threatens those who fear the dark;
It kills when souls despair.

As she neared Mictar, Felicity slowed. Cerulean raised his voice, his passion increasing with every note.

But neither height nor depth nor darkest pits
Will separate us hence;
The healing one will find you soon
And mend the cosmic fence.

Felicity came within reach of Mictar, her arm still extended and fingers groping. Mictar lifted his black violin to his chin and played a loud note that muffled Cerulean's voice. Then, sawing across the strings, he created a scratching, buzzing noise that barely resembled music at all.

The path in front of Felicity collapsed. A deep crevice stretched at least twenty yards from side to side, and the crumbling earth's edge crawled to within inches of her feet.

I jumped ahead. "Felicity! Stop! There's a—"

"No!" Again Cerulean held up his hand. "Do not add to her fears!"

Felicity halted at the edge and extended her stick into the crevice. "Is it safe to walk?"

"No!" Mictar lowered the violin. "If you take one step you will fall into endless depths, and you will never be in your supplicant's arms."

"He lies," Cerulean said. "Run to me. This is your dream. You can do whatever your faith allows. No valley will swallow you as long as you believe."

Mictar raised his violin again. While Felicity paused, every limb shaking, I whispered to Mom, "It's time to replace that musical hack. Play something. Anything. As long as it's melodic and loud."

She lifted the violin and played the opening measure of *Finlandia*. I lunged toward Mictar. Like an out-of-control linebacker, I rammed into his lanky body and bulldozed him into the ground. I jerked the violin away and jumped to my feet, careful to avoid his deadly hands.

Standing over him with the violin raised, I growled, "Remember the last time I clubbed you with one of these? If you move or make a sound, you'll get an encore performance."

"Fool!" Mictar sang out a shrill note. A streak of blackness shot from his mouth and splashed across my chest, sending me and the violin flying. I slid on my back, while the violin banged against the turf near Mictar and croaked out a violent stream of twanging notes.

The ground shook as if echoing Mictar's violin. The edge of the crevice collapsed. Felicity toppled into the void and disappeared. Her screams, loud and heart-wrenching, faded away. Still clutching his hat, Jack jumped in after her.

"Nathan!" Cerulean shouted. "Take off your sweatshirt! Francesca! Keep playing!" In a flash of blue light, he dove into the expanding chasm.

I looked down at my chest. A mass of blackness stretched like wiggling fingers toward my face. I grabbed the back of the sweatshirt and peeled it over my head.

Mom hustled to my side and resumed her playing, switching to Danse Macabre. The notes flew toward Mictar in long ribbons of white. He scrambled to his feet and dodged. "I may not be able to overpower both of you while you play," he said as he ducked to avoid more ribbons, "but I have another victim in mind."

He picked up his violin, strode to the dream world's core, and clawed at the dark barrier, searching, groping. Soon, he ripped open a gap and squeezed through until he disappeared and the wall sealed behind him.

Heaving a long breath, Mom lowered her violin. "At least we know how to defend ourselves against him."

I held my soiled sweatshirt at arm's length. "Yeah, but Kelly doesn't, and I'm sure she's his prime target."

CHAPTER ELEVEN

I HUSTLED TO THE chasm and looked down. Only darkness lay below — no sign of Felicity, Cerulean, or Jack. As I shuffled back to Mom, I spread out my arms. "Now what?"

"What choices do we have?" she asked, holding the violin loosely at her side. "We can't go anywhere, can we?"

"Besides diving into that chasm or clawing our way into that place Mictar went, not that I know of."

"Then let's sit and think for a minute." She sat on the ground and patted a spot next to her. "Come. We haven't had time to talk."

"That's true." I dropped the sweatshirt and seated myself next to her, careful to avoid putting weight on my bandaged hand. "But we probably don't have time. We have to find Dad."

"Exactly what we need to talk about, maybe probe our minds for clues."

I took a deep breath. "Well, I was hoping Solomon Yellow could help more. You know, tell us what he would do, where he might go, but in comparison to Dad, he seemed … well …"

"Yellow?" she offered.

I laughed. "I didn't want to say it. It sounds too corny."

"Corny, yes, but we can't deny the truth behind the jest." She drummed her fingers on the violin. "There's a story I don't think you've ever heard."

"I hope it's not a long story. Since Felicity fell, this dream might end soon. When I fall inside a dream, it usually means I'm about to wake up."

"That's happened to me, too." She set the violin in her lap. "If this dream ends, what will happen to us?"

"I'm not sure. Some dreams get swept up in a storm. Others just fade away. If that happens, I think it'll get dark and we'll be in a gap between dreams." I looked around at the former cemetery. It was already too dark to see the newly sprouted flowers.

"Darkness is fine," she said. "I used to tell you stories in the dark quite often. Do you remember?"

"Yeah. I finally made you stop when I was about eight. I said I was too old for bedtime stories."

She touched my knee. "Are you too old now?"

"Too old?" I shook my head. "Maybe I'm finally old enough to start again."

"Well, this is a story about courage." She looked at her wounded hand. Blood still oozed into her palm. "Your father learned courage when he and I were courting. You see, we met when I first started playing for the CSO. During my premiere performance as concertmaster, I played the Tchaikovsky concerto, and your father was in the first row. He was a college student, interning for the summer at an applied sciences company in Chicago. That's where he learned what he knows about physics and light bending, but I never understood enough to make sense of it."

I stared at her, transfixed by her serious expression. "How old were you then?"

"I was all of twenty-one years old, not much more than a girl, really."

I picked up the sweatshirt and ripped a piece from the sleeve I had cut earlier. Whatever the black stuff was, about half of it had disappeared. "So, when Francesca Yellow married," I said as I tied the fresh bandage around her hand, "she was a quite a bit younger."

She smiled as she watched me work. "Yes, and that's why I'm telling you the story. You see, after that performance, your father waited for me at the door, even though I had taken a long time to come out because of a reception in my honor. Apparently, he was mesmerized by my performance and wanted an autograph, so he paced around the area until after midnight. Unfortunately, a group of four other men also seemed overly interested in seeing me. As soon as I stepped out the door, three of them brandished handguns while a fourth opened a cello case and pulled out a shotgun."

"A shotgun? Did he have a gray beard?"

"He had a beard, but it wasn't gray." She squinted at me, darkness now shadowing her features. "Why?"

"Just thinking." I tied the bandage in place. "Maybe I've seen him before."

"Well, at first your father—"

"No. Wait." I lifted the violin from her lap. "Play it. Show it to me."

"What do you mean?"

I tried to see her facial expression, but it was too dark. "We're in the dream world. Show me, like you did when you played the scenes of you in your bedroom when you were younger."

"Can we do that from inside the dream world?"

"There's no dream going on right now. And I have a hunch about those gunmen. I want to see what one of them looked like." I set the violin in her hands. "It won't hurt to try."

She laughed under her breath. "It certainly *will* hurt, but I'll do it."

"Oh, yeah." I reached to take the violin back but grasped empty air.

"Just watch and pay attention. I don't want to do this more than once." She paused for a few seconds, the sound of her tuning the violin breaking the silence. She began humming the opening of the Tchaikovsky piece, the orchestra's introductory measures, then, after a short pause, she played.

The vibrant tones sounded more beautiful than ever. Somehow the darkness enhanced the music. In a way, I felt like Felicity—my eyesight impotent, but my other senses acute. I breathed in deeply. Each note had an aroma, even a taste, as the music-saturated air rushed into my nostrils and then out my mouth, passing over my tongue with a sweet caress.

Soon, dim light illuminated the area—a lamp perched high above a street about twenty paces away. It shone on a set of four wood-and-glass doors, the entrance to a brick building. Lights attached to the façade on both sides of the doors cast their glow on a wide walkway in front.

I rose to my feet and walked to the edge of the dreamscape. I stood across the street from Orchestra Hall, deep enough in the shadows to escape notice if someone in the dream world should walk by.

A raven-haired young woman stepped out of the hall. Dressed in a flowing black gown, she smiled at an older woman who walked at her side, also dressed in black.

Staying low, I hurried across the dark pavement and ducked behind a car parked at the curb. Now that I had stepped fully inside the dream, the sounds of Mom's violin faded, replaced by the voices of young Francesca and her companion.

"Tchaikovsky himself would have asked for your autograph," the older woman said. "It was superb. Magnificent."

Francesca blushed and touched the woman's hand. "Clara, you're too kind, but I'm thankful for your encouragement. I was so nervous I almost got sick right on the conductor, and now I don't remember a single note I played."

A man walked out of the shadows holding an open book and a pen. "Excuse me, Miss Malenkov. May I have your autograph?"

"Oh!" Francesca stepped back, her eyebrows raised. "Well, yes, of course." She held the pen while looking at the man's beaming face. "And to whom shall I sign it?"

"Solomon." His voice trembled, but he quickly brought it under control. "Solomon Shepherd."

Francesca smiled. "I like that name. It carries a pleasant melody."

"I know this young man quite well." Winking, Clara shook a finger at him. "Do you often wait two hours after orchestra performances to get autographs?"

"Uh … no." Solomon shifted his weight from side to side. "This was my first time here. Miss Malenkov's performance mesmerized me. I just had to meet her."

"Well, she really needs her rest." Clara hooked Francesca's arm. "We have to—"

"Oh, Clara." Francesca's eyes sparkled as she gave Solomon his autograph book. "It's all right. I can sleep in tomorrow."

Four men jumped out of the car I was hiding behind. Three ran toward the door, one with a handgun drawn, while the fourth, a bearded man, lagged behind, carrying a cello case.

Clara pulled Solomon in front of her and Francesca. "I hope you don't mind being a shield."

"Shut up, lady," one of the men said, "and step away from Malenkov."

Clara wrapped an arm around Francesca and pulled her close. "Or you'll what?"

The bearded man withdrew a shotgun from the cello case and aimed it at Solomon. "Or we'll have to drag more corpses away than we counted on."

Solomon leaped for the shotgun and wrestled it away. One of the men shot him in the chest. As Solomon backpedaled, he returned fire, dropping the gunman with the first shot and two more men with the second. Blood now soaking his shirt and suit jacket, he glared at the bearded man. "Get on your knees, or you're next."

"You're out of ammo." The man drew a handgun. "Good-bye, hero."

Solomon bashed the man's arm with the shotgun, knocking the gun to the walkway. Gasping and gurgling, Solomon wobbled back and forth before toppling to the concrete. The bearded man dropped low and scrambled toward the gun, but a high-heeled shoe stomped on his wrist.

"That's far enough, cello boy!" Clara scooped up the gun and aimed it at his head.

As a siren wailed, the man looked at her with menacing eyes. "I have friends in high places. I will be back to kill the gifted one."

I crept closer to get a better look. There was no doubt about it. The guy with the shotgun was the same man who had chased Clara and me through the streets of Chicago and then stalked Kelly and me in the observatory.

Francesca cradled Solomon and mopped his brow as they whispered to each other. Two police officers ran onto the scene. One barked into a radio about needing an ambulance while the other shouted commands as he checked the fallen bodies.

My heart beating wildly, I backed away to the street and then out of the dream. With the glow of the streetlight guiding my way, I found Mom, still playing her part of the Tchaikovsky concerto.

She opened her eyes and smiled. Then, easing through a final note, she let out a long sigh. "The bullet missed his heart, but there was quite a bit of damage. He almost died from loss of blood. He was in the hospital for more than a month."

With light from the street beginning to fade, I sat next to Mom and tried to calm my heart. "I saw you whispering, but I couldn't hear what you said."

She gave a gentle laugh. "I'll never forget his words. He said, 'It will never hurt worse than it does now.' So I asked him what he meant, and he said, 'Protecting you. I took a bullet for you. I will gladly take another. Let's just hope I never have to.'"

"That's …" I had to fight off a burst of emotion. "That's really cool."

She nodded. "He told me later that what he did was really an instinctive jump, but since then he's never let fear stop him from doing anything. It's as if he faced death and stared it down, and now he's practically immune to fear. At least he never lets fear paralyze him."

I touched her arm and replied in a whisper. "And Solomon Yellow never had a chance to do that. That's why he's so different."

Mom nodded. "I assume Francesca Yellow is not yet concertmaster of the CSO, so I wonder how they met."

I picked up my sweatshirt, now free of the black stuff. "I guess Kelly and I talked her into marrying him. Since she spent so much time in the other earths, she missed some years on Yellow and lost ground. She was hesitant because she was so young, but they managed to get together."

Mom stroked her violin with a tender hand. "Well, as long as they married and had a baby they named Nathan, I assume it will all work out."

I put the sweatshirt on. "But that Nathan won't learn what I learned from Dad. Solomon Yellow won't be able to teach him to stare down death." I touched my chest. "Dad's the reason I learned not to let fear stop me from doing anything."

She lifted her brow. "Oh, is that so?"

"I think so." I let my hand drop. I was no match for her skeptical stare. "Why do you ask?"

"Because I know what you fear." The slightest of glows still radiating from the dream illuminated her as she wiggled her fingers across imaginary piano keys. "It moved by very quickly, but I recognized what Kelly played in her dream."

My heart thumped faster again. "Are you saying I'm scared to talk to her?"

A gentle smile graced her lips. "She's dying for you to talk to her, Nathan. Begging. Praying. Pleading. She won't ask you herself. You have to be the one to reach out to her."

"But talk about what? She keeps saying she'll wait for me as long as it takes. I thought maybe she wanted ... I don't know ... to be my girlfriend or something. I don't want to go there yet."

"I don't think she wants to go there yet, either. Maybe someday, but that's not what's driving her plea."

"So what *does* she want?"

"She wants to witness real love. Her father protects her, but he also used her. Daryl is loyal, but they are both needy and dependent. In you, Kelly sees something different — spiritual strength and sacrificial love. In short, she sees Christ, and she wants to know that her past is erased in your mind. She wants to feel forgiven."

"But what was in her past?" I cocked my head. "Do you know?"

"Yes, Nathan. She told me." Three deep lines creased her brow. "It was hard to understand everything, because she was crying so much, but she told me."

"So, what did she ..." I let my words trail off. Did I really want to know? After a second or two, I took a deep breath and said, "Was it really all that terrible?"

Her voice cracked. "Yes, Nathan. It was."

"So what do I do?"

As Mom folded my hand into hers, her voice spiked with passion. "Forgive her, Nathan. Forgive her with all your heart. She has never seen down-to-earth forgiveness lived out in reality, certainly not between her father and mother. At least that's what she told me."

Tears welling, she lifted my hand and laid it on my chest. "She needs to know that this brave-hearted young knight will treat her like the fair maiden she longs to be, no matter what she's done to soil that label."

Her tears drew my own. As one trickled to my cheek, she loosened my bandage and unwound it until my palm's bloody wound lay exposed. "Kelly has crucified herself a thousand times for her sins. It's time for you to put an end to her suffering."

I stared at my hand, barely visible in the waning light. A tear fell from Mom's eye and landed on my palm. As it trickled into the wound, the salt stung, but I refused to flinch. Somehow the pain felt appropriate.

"You're right, Mom. I'll do it." I rose and groped for her hand. "But we have to go."

She grabbed my wrist and let me pull her up. "Where?"

"Anywhere but here. We can't keep waiting for Cerulean. If I'm going to talk to Kelly, I have to find her first. I'm not going to let her down again."

A new voice filtered through the darkness. "Man, Nathan, that was beautiful."

I squinted toward the source. "Daryl? Is that you?"

A beam of light appeared, illuminating Daryl Red's face. "Present and accounted for. I got here just in time. That cool shoot-em-up dream was ending, but I caught the end of it."

"You brought a flashlight?"

"Of course. I'm scared stiff of the dark, remember?" She guided the beam toward a canvas bag draped over her shoulder. "And I have fresh Energizer bunnies in there along with three candles and a lighter, so we're good to go."

"Did you get the card?"

"Yeppers." She put it in my hand. "And something else."

The sound of paper wrinkling rose from somewhere underneath the flashlight's beam. "Remember that report folder you picked up in the conference room back what seems like a thousand years ago?"

"Yeah. I never got to look at it."

"Gordon Red did." Daryl handed me a sheet of paper. "Actually, he was supposed to be at the meeting but had to skip it because he was chasing hot-rod Nathan down the highway."

"Let's see it." I guided Daryl's flashlight toward the wrinkled sheet. Several lines of neatly handwritten numbers covered the top half. "Think it's a code?"

Daryl shrugged. "What else could it be?"

"Did Gordon Red try to decipher it?"

"Yep, but it's a brain-buster. He didn't have time to send it to any cryptology experts."

Mom peered at the numbers. "Any idea how many conspirators were on Interfinity's board of directors?"

"No clue," I said, "but this thing goes a lot deeper than I thought. I got a good look at the shotgun guy in your dream. He's the same one who tried to kill Clara and Kelly and me. I guess he's been hunting gifted ones for a long time."

"He was in jail during my CSO career. I didn't keep track of him after that."

"So he got out." I lifted the plastic card into the light. "But he's definitely dead now."

"But which one is dead?" Daryl asked. "Bearded Guy Red or Bearded Guy Blue?"

I shrugged. "I'm not sure. I can't keep everything straight."

"Yeah. You need a scorecard to keep up with all the players."

Mom ran a finger along the card's numbers. "And did he work for Mictar?"

I shook my head. "He wanted me to destroy the mirrors so Mictar couldn't use them. For some reason, he was trying to kill Francesca Yellow before Nathan Yellow was born. I'm guessing that we gifted ones somehow energize the mirrors, and this guy wanted to stop us to keep Interfinity from coming. He just played along with Mictar to get to us."

"Well," Daryl said, "while you two gifted gabbers try to figure it all out, I have something else to show you from my goody bag." She lifted an iPod into the flashlight beam. "Of course I'll return it to Dr. Simon when I'm finished, but I figured we could put it to better use while he's playing with his hologram."

"Excellent!" I took the iPod and showed it to Mom. "This has all the musical pieces that set the mirror up for transport. With this and your violin we can open ..." I sighed. "But we don't have a mirror."

"Au contraire, mon ami." Daryl slid a mirror square up from her bag, then lowered it. "While Tony was unloading the mirrors to hide them, I grabbed a couple out of the stack. I gave one to Francesca Yellow and kept one for us. I was thinking maybe we could use it to contact Amber, and maybe Francesca could, you know, do the supplicating thing with Amber. And I also brought the Earth Blue one in the photo album. Looks like Kelly-kins left it behind before she went into the dream world."

I patted her on the back. "Great thinking, Daryl."

"Like I said, you need a clear thinker." She tapped her head with a finger. "I'm all brains and no brawn, so I'd better put what I've got to work."

I pulled the Earth Yellow mirror from the bag and looked at its reflective surface. "Since Amber's not my supplicant, I wonder how I can use this to call her."

Daryl shrugged. "Music? A flash of light? Dance a jig? The rules of this game aren't exactly the easiest to follow."

I allowed a weak smile to break through. "I can't keep up either, but I hope I don't have to dance. Mom made me take lessons, but I never liked it."

"So what do we do?" Mom asked. "Go back to the observatory and jump into the yellow section of the hologram?"

"Can't," Daryl said. "El Gordo ranted about entering some kind of eclipse phase that would make creating the hologram impossible for the next few hours, so I hopped in just before it happened."

I held the iPod near the flashlight beam and scrolled the selections. "Let's see if there are any dream-jumping options."

"If you mean from one dream world to another, don't waste your time. Simon and Simon said they have no clue what music will open dream-to-dream portals. But I brought it anyway, 'cause I figured we might need it if we make it back to the real world."

"*If* we make it?" I looked at Daryl's mirthful, yet frightened eyes. "We *are* going to make it. I don't know how yet, but we're going to find my father and Kelly, and we're going to save the world."

"Hey, that works for me, but tell it to Interfinity. Dr. Gordon's radio telescopes can track the meshing of the three worlds, and it's getting real bad again. He showed me a map and a computer projection of how long it will take before everything collapses." She held up a pair of fingers. "Two days, Nathan. Unless we can stop the bleeding, that's all we have. Then Interfinity will arrive and bring Convergence with it."

CHAPTER TWELVE

"TWO EARTH YELLOW days?" I asked.

Daryl nodded. "At least that's what the computer simulation says."

"Then we'd better figure out how to use the mirror to get to Earth Yellow. Time passes too fast on the other earths."

Mom pressed the violin under her chin. "I'll try Foundation's Key. That seems to unlock a lot of puzzles. At least it might let us see something we need to know."

I pointed the mirror at her. "Do you remember all of it?"

"I played it about fifty times back on Earth Blue. I'd better know it." After quickly tuning the violin again, she began playing.

I aimed the mirror at Daryl, Mom, and me. In the flashlight's narrow beam, only Mom's face and hands showed in the reflection. Her left hand, still wrapped in a strip of my sweatshirt, trembled.

The image dimmed for a moment before glowing with soft yellow light. Amber's face appeared against a background of darkness. Deep lines ran across her forehead as she spoke in a whisper. "I am nearby. Come to the dark barrier wall. Find a wound and rip it open. I cannot locate one from the inside."

She looked around as if watching for approaching danger. Her voice lowered even further. "I have seen Mictar lurking, so we must be careful. I will tell you more when you let me out. But, whatever you do, do not point the light at the mirror.

If you transport to this place, we will lose our opportunity to create a path between the Earth Blue and Earth Yellow dream worlds."

Daryl flicked off the light and handed it to me. "Okay. It's dark. But you'd better talk me through this."

"It's all right," I said. "We can still use the light. We'll just hide the mirror for a while." I looked again at Amber. "We're going to put the mirror in Daryl's bag while we search for the barrier wall. We'll be there soon."

After securing the mirror, I guessed where the barrier ought to be, aimed the flashlight, and pushed the switch. Like a wide laser, the beam shot through the darkness and cast a circle on a wall of blackness.

"Coolness," Daryl whispered. "Clear sailing."

I waved the beam from side to side. "As long as we don't walk near any of those hungry trees. Cerulean told me they're fixtures in the dream world, one of the few realities we have to deal with."

"And a dangerous reality," Mom added. "One of them tried to grab us."

Daryl covered her head with an arm. "Got it. Avoid carnivorous trees."

"Okay," I whispered. "Stay close." Setting out at a slow pace, I followed the beam's path while drawing a mental picture of the trees I had seen in the cemetery. But which ones were ready to grab lost wanderers with powerful wooden hands? Impossible to remember. Every few seconds, I made a quick global sweep with the light, but nothing appeared.

When we reached the wall, I touched it with a finger. As expected, it felt tough and hard, like a rubber tire. While I guided the beam slowly from left to right, Mom and I studied the smooth black surface. "See anything?" I asked.

Mom squinted. "Only tiny cracks."

"Let's see if we can make them bigger." I dug my nails into one of the longer cracks, but it wouldn't expand, not even a millimeter. The cosmic wounds had apparently weakened the structure, but what would weaken it further? What special powers allowed a supplicant and a vision stalker to break through?

Scarlet came to mind. Surely she could have pierced the wall— but how? With every second her face hovered in my mind's eye, the fragrance of roses strengthened, and a bittersweet film grew on my tongue. A jumble of words flew through my thoughts, like pinballs in an over-juiced arcade machine. When the sensation became overwhelming, I took in a deep breath and let it out slowly. "A song. We need a song."

Mom lifted the violin. "What do you want me to play?"

"Foundation's Key. I'll sing the lyrics."

"It has lyrics?"

"Not yet, but it will soon."

She set the bow to the strings. "I'll start whenever you do."

"Okay." I concentrated on the flying words. Some seemed brighter than others, almost on fire with red light. Maybe if I sang them from brightest to dimmest, the phrases would make sense. I took another deep breath and began.

A wall divides and sets apart
Our bodies, minds, and souls;
It stymies all embracing arms,
Exacting heartache tolls.

The walls we build are merely smoke,
Forgiveness trapped inside;
Release the love, the spirit's wind,
And sweep away your pride.

One breath for me, your supplicant,
One breath for hearts in need;

One breath for you, beloved son,
In threes we gladly bleed.

When I sang the final words, Mom lowered the bow. "From Scarlet?"

I nodded but said nothing.

"I thought so. Your voice seemed touched by heaven."

"So, Elvis," Daryl said, "did your song open a hole?"

"It's not just the song; it's also the breath." I gave Mom the flashlight, then set my mouth over the crack and blew. Wind poured out, growing hotter and hotter, almost scalding my lips. As the fragrance-saturated air met the wall, the cracks glowed cherry red.

Daryl withdrew the mirror from the bag and talked to it. "Hey, Amber. Stand by. I think we're about to break through."

"Shine a light through the breach," Amber said. "I will look for it."

I inhaled and blew again. The fissure widened, making a crackling noise, like dry leaves burning.

Mom aimed the flashlight at the rift. "Keep it up, son. Maybe one more will weaken it enough to tear."

Feeling dizzy now, I inhaled once more and pushed the air out slowly, pursing my lips to focus the flow on the growing crack. Now hotter than ever, the flow dried out the inside of my mouth and stung the tender skin.

With a final push, I emptied my lungs and staggered back. Daryl caught me and propped me up, whispering, "The big bad wolf's hyperventilating."

I shook the mental cobwebs away and stepped back to the wall. Using both hands, I thrust my fingers into the glowing crack. The touch burned my raw skin, but I gritted my teeth and pushed deeper.

As if groaning in pain, the wall creaked and popped. The breach widened to three or four inches and deepened to almost a foot. Soon, a cooling wind rushed by my hands and into the inner core. With my mouth still in pain, I rasped, "We broke through."

Mom pointed the flashlight beam into the hole. "Keep pulling. Maybe Amber can work from that side."

"I'll help." Daryl set her bag and the mirror down and pulled one side while I pulled the other. As the hole widened, rushing air whistled past.

After a few seconds, a weak voice emanated, strained, as if battling the wind. "Nathan? It's Amber. Can you hear me?"

I called back, "I hear you. Can you see us?"

"Grab this." Something that looked like a rope protruded from the hole.

"Mom," I said, still pulling on the rubbery material. "Can you get it?"

She tucked the flashlight under her arm and grabbed the thick line. "Got it."

Amber's hands pushed through, reeling out the rope. "Nathan, take the vine and tie it to one of the spider trees. I will keep the hole open."

"The vine?"

"Yes. It's from a tree in the Earth Yellow dream world." Grunting, she pushed an arm against each side of the hole. "Go now. I have it."

I eased my hands out and took the vine. It vibrated in my grip, wiggling to get free. "Daryl, stay here and help Amber if she needs it. Mom and I are going to look for the tree."

"Watch out," Daryl said. "That thing's bite is probably worse than its bark."

"You'll be okay without the flashlight?"

"Get going." Daryl lifted her bag. "I'll fire up a candle."

While Mom guided our way with the flashlight beam, I pulled the vine, walking a step or two behind her. Alive and aware, the fibrous line curled around my wrist and jerked back, but not with enough force to slow my progress. "I think the tree's just a hair to your left."

After a few seconds, the beam swept across the familiar silhouette of a bent oak. It appeared to jerk, as if awakened by the light.

"Better slow down," I said. "You keep out of its reach while I do the tying." I bent forward and lugged the vine toward the tree. How long was this thing? I had already pulled it at least sixty feet.

Now within reach of the twisted oak, I looked up at its leafless branches. They bent toward me, reaching with their knobby-fingered twigs.

I dashed forward, ducked under the branches, and wrapped the vine halfway around the trunk. The vine stopped. I pulled, but I couldn't gain another inch. "Amber! I need more slack!"

"I have no more, Nathan." Her distant voice sounded strained. "It's the longest vine on the tree."

The branches arched toward me, closer and closer. Following the flashlight's beam, I looked up into the tree's framework. Looping vines sagged from nearly every limb.

A wooden claw snatched at my shirt but missed. Still holding Amber's vine, I leaped up and grabbed a vine from a branch. As I began tying a knot to attach the two vines, the branches again drew closer.

Mom shouted, "Watch behind you, Nathan!"

A sharp claw dug into my back, and a knife-edged finger slid around my arm. Ignoring the pain, I jerked the knot tight just as the claw lifted me off the ground.

"Nathan!" Mom shone the beam on my chest. "Fight!"

I thrashed and kicked but to no avail. Another set of wooden fingers caught my legs and squeezed them together, immobilizing them. Tiny threads shot out from pores in the wood and arced over my limbs, like webbing over a captured fly.

Mom lunged to the trunk, clambered up the lower limbs, and banged a fist against the branches. "Let go of him!"

"Mom! No! It's too dangerous. I'll get out some—" The claw tightened, squeezing my breath away.

"Daryl!" Mom screamed. "Help!"

"Coming!" A bobbing light signaled Daryl's approach, and her voice grew louder with each word. "I have something that'll teach that pile of kindling a lesson."

Holding the candle high, she touched the flame to the lowest branch. The tree shuddered. Its limbs popped and crackled. The branch jerked away from the fire, but Daryl stalked closer to the trunk, keeping the candle lifted. "Let him go, or you'll be ashes!"

"Daryl," I called, squeezing out my words, "if you set it on fire, we'll get—"

"This rotting hunk of driftwood"—she touched the trunk with the flame—"just needs a little persuasion."

A branch swiped at her, scratching her head. She caught the branch and set the flame against a wooden finger. "Eat fire, you Treebeard wannabe!"

Several branches swung wildly, loosening the web. I kicked free and jumped to the ground. As Mom climbed down, I checked the knot in the vines — good and tight. "Let's go!"

The three of us ran to the barrier, following the taut vine, now illuminated by the jiggling flashlight beam.

We found Amber still holding the gap open with both arms. "Come through," she called, grunting. "Bring your candle."

Daryl twisted the lit candle into the ground, stuffed the flashlight, the violin and bow, and the mirror into her bag, then grabbed the candle again. Amber shifted to one side of the hole and tugged with both hands while I held the other side. Although the earlier adrenaline rush had made me forget about my injured palms, now they ached. I couldn't keep a grip on the wall for very long.

Mom pushed into the narrow opening, wiggling to make headway. As soon as she popped through, Daryl climbed in feet first. Bracing her back against one side and her feet against the other, she made a bridge that opened a gap underneath. "I can hold it," she said, extending the bag. "Take this and crawl under me."

I grabbed the bag, ducked under Daryl's legs, and crawled through. When I came out on the other side, I reached for the ground with my foot but found only air.

"Hold the vine," Mom said as she hoisted me up by my elbow.

I found the vine and hung on. Daryl's bag floated at my side, suspended in midair.

Daryl reached the candle to me. "I'm coming through." With a kick and a push, she rolled out and grabbed my leg while retaking the candle. "This is so cool. We're astronauts."

Amber released the barrier. The two sides merged until the gap disappeared. The vine, now locked in place, quivered but held firm.

"Where are we?" I asked.

Amber plucked a lit candle out of the air and let the glow illuminate her tired face. "We are somewhere in the midst of Sarah's Womb, the center of the three earths. It acts as a barrier for the dream realms as well as the worlds that dwell in what you call reality." She wrapped her fingers around the vine. "We have joined Blue and Yellow, so we can travel between them."

I ran a finger along the vine. "I guess no one ever came up with this idea before."

"I am certain it was impossible before. The exterior of the core was impenetrable, but when the celestial wounds began to appear, so did the cracks that allowed passage from the outside to the inside. Yet I found no way to pass through from the inside without help from the outside."

"How big is this place?"

"Infinite in depth, as far as I can tell, but its breadth is only a stone's throw."

I fanned the air. "Why does it have oxygen and no gravity?"

"I am not sure, but I have heard from the stalkers that Sarah's Womb has everything necessary for sustaining life. As to our weightlessness, I was surprised, too. This is a new experience for me."

"Gravity might exist," Daryl said, "but who can say what's physical or metaphysical in a dream world? What has mass and what doesn't? Everything could be perfectly balanced. No force overpowers any other force."

I searched the dimness but found nothing else floating around. "If this is the midst of Sarah's Womb, is this where something would go if it drops from above?"

Daryl pointed at me. "Good thinking. If this is the center of gravitational mass, a falling object would pass through here, rebound up past this point again, and go up and down like a yo-yo until it finally settles here."

"Exactly what I was thinking. So I'm wondering if Daryl Blue might be around."

"I have been here for quite some time," Amber said, "and I have been searching for a way out, but I have not come across anyone. Yet, since it is dark, I could have missed her."

"Or she hasn't settled here yet," Daryl Red added. "For all we know, it could take weeks, months, years."

"True. But at least we have to try calling her." I cupped a hand around my mouth and shouted, "Daryl! Daryl Blue!"

My call echoed several times before fading.

"She hit the wall on the way down," I said, "so she might be dead or unconscious."

Daryl Red peered into the oblivion above. "Or she's out of reach of your voice."

I nodded. "Could be."

"Remember how your music traveled farther in dark places?" Daryl fished through her bag and withdrew the iPod. "What do you think?"

"Great idea."

She turned it on and scrolled with her thumb. "Let's go with the Moonlight Sonata."

Exquisite piano music flowed from the unit and spread throughout the dark chamber. We waited a minute or so, listening for the slightest call, but no one responded. "I guess it was worth a try," I whispered.

"Of course it was," Mom said. "It's a good theory. We can return and try again."

I nodded. "All right. Let's move on."

Daryl turned the iPod off and opened the bag. When she pushed the iPod in, the strap slid off my shoulder. The contents spilled and scattered in a floating array — the mirrors, the photo album, the iPod, and several wrapped snack bars.

We all reached to grasp the items, though the dimness made the effort difficult. When we had put everything back in the bag, Daryl looked inside. "Wait. No iPod."

I scanned the darkness but found nothing. "Are you sure? I don't see it anywhere."

"Nor do I," Mom said.

"Let me check again." Daryl rummaged through the bag while tilting its opening toward the candlelight. "I'm sure."

"We can stay," Amber said, "but I believe the search for your father is more urgent."

I heaved a sigh. "You're right. Let's go."

"Come." Amber pulled herself along the vine, drawing her body away from the barrier.

I followed, Daryl's candle in one hand and the bag hanging by a strap over my shoulder. Mom and Daryl trailed close behind. With no sound but our breathing and with the heaviness of the failed test to find Daryl Blue, the dark chamber felt empty, as vast as space itself.

The two candles cast oddly different glows. Amber's shone bright and undisturbed, while mine flickered as I pulled my body through the black air.

After another minute, Amber stopped and pressed her hand against a new boundary. "This is the wall separating us from the Earth Yellow dream world. Since the vine keeps the hole partially open, we can escape."

"Brilliant, Amber. Truly brilliant." I pushed two fingers between the vine and wall, then, hanging on to the vine, I pulled to the side as hard as I could. Without anything to press my feet against, the job seemed impossible. Everything ached. Grunts erupted unbidden. After several seconds, the gap slowly widened.

When it stretched far enough, Daryl and Amber pressed close to help. Soon, Daryl had once again made a bridge within the hole. Mom and Amber squeezed through first. Then Daryl gave me a nod. "It's now or never, Elvis. Your singing career isn't over yet."

"Just a second. I think we should mark this wall so we know it's the way to Earth Yellow's dream world and not Earth Blue's."

"Mark it with what?"

I looked at my hand, bleeding once again. "Blood is red, not yellow, but it will have to do." I reached to the side of the hole and smeared blood on the black wall. When I finished,

I belly crawled under Daryl's legs, but my bottom wedged against hers. "Give me another inch of clearance if you can."

Daryl grunted as her body lifted. "Good thing you're the skinnier version of Elvis, or you'd never make it."

Once we made it through the barrier, we found ourselves in a dimly lit bedroom, illuminated by a lamp as well as Amber's glow. The vine, still as rigid as a tightrope, ran out a partially open window. A cool breeze wafted in, fresh and moist. Outside, the vine led to a spider tree standing a few feet from the exterior wall. One of its outstretched branches bent with the breeze, and a leafless twig tapped against the pane.

At the opposite side of the room, a boy slept in a bed against a wall near the exit door. Sitting on the mattress next to him, a woman played a violin, gently coaxing the beginning notes of Brahms' Lullaby. With her back turned, her face wasn't visible, but long black tresses draping her flannel pajamas gave her away.

I tugged Mom's sleeve and whispered, "Look. It's you."

She pointed at the sleeping boy. "And that must be you."

I set the bag down and surveyed the scene. No one in this realm would be dreaming this. Neither Francesca Yellow nor Solomon Yellow would know about Francesca Red's habit of playing that tune as a bedtime lullaby.

I pulled my three companions close and whispered, "This has to be my father's dream."

"Then where is he?" Daryl asked.

Amber nodded at Mom. "Music holds the key. Perhaps you could perform a duet with yourself."

"That would be … interesting." Mom pulled the violin and bow from the bag and played along, embellishing the piece with a few intermixed scales.

The other Francesca stopped, stood, and spun toward us. Her eyes wide, she stared, letting her violin dangle limply.

My mouth went dry. She looked exactly like Mom, only ten years younger.

"Do not be frightened," Amber said, gliding closer to her. "I am—" She halted and gazed into the dream-world Francesca's eyes. After a few seconds, she turned to me. "The dreamer is not using this woman as his viewpoint person. Her eyes do not carry the vision of a living spirit."

"What are you talking about?" The dream-world Francesca asked, pointing her bow at no one in particular. "Of course I have a living spirit."

I gazed at this younger version of Mom. She did look kind of vacant. "If my father is the dreamer, how is he seeing this bedroom?"

"He must have created this scene in his mind and then departed," Amber said, "but since he is manipulating this figment's actions, he must hear us. I suspect, however, that he doesn't see us, or this Francesca would have noticed that her virtual twin stands before her." She touched the dream-world Francesca's elbow. "Would you please call your husband?"

"I will be glad to." Francesca marched to the bedroom door, pushing past the vine as if it were a normal fixture in every child's bedroom. "Solomon!" she called. "We have company. Their voices are familiar, but I don't recognize them."

I shuddered. This was all just too creepy for words. And now who was going to walk through that door. Dad? A dream representation of him?

While we waited, Amber pointed at the bag still hanging from my shoulder. "Francesca. Daryl. Please light a candle. You must be sure to stay in touch with reality. The next few minutes could well challenge your sanity."

Daryl reached into the bag and pulled out two candles. She touched the wicks to Amber's, then passed one of the candles to Mom.

A man who looked just like my father appeared at the door, dressed in dark blue sweats. I took a step back. Mom gasped, trembling as she whispered, "Solomon?"

At first, he squinted, closing one eye more than the other. Then, as a flicker of light danced in his eyes, the dream-world Francesca faded to a wisp along with the bed and the sleeping child. His lips quivered, and his voice shook. "Francesca?" He swallowed hard. "Is that you, my darling?"

She stared at him through her candle's light. "Amber?" she called with a quavering voice. "Is he real or a dream?"

Amber gazed at him through her own flame. "He has not faded yet in my sight, but a powerful mind creates stronger images in this world. At the very least, he is the dreamer's vision of himself, so in one sense, he is real. Solomon, your husband, speaks through this man."

"Of course I'm real." The dream-world Solomon marched straight to Mom and set his hands on her shoulders. "Don't you recognize me?"

"You ... you look like ..." Her legs buckled, but he propped her up. "You were wearing Solomon Blue's khakis and a ... and a polo shirt and trench coat."

Solomon looked down at his clothes. "After all I've been through, I had to change. I found these in a drawer, and they fit."

"But this is a dream world," I said, keeping him within the light of my candle. "Any clothes you find here aren't real."

"They're real enough. They fit, and they're warm." He pulled me into a three-way hug with Mom. "It's so good to see you again. Why are you both acting—" His eyebrows shot up, and he pulled back. "Oh, I see. Did Mictar tell you I'm dead?"

I cleared my throat. "Not dead ... uh ... Dad. We're just not sure if you're real or an image in your own dream."

He locked wrists with me. "Does that feel like an image? Can a dream embrace you like I just did?"

"Well … yeah. I think it can. In the dream world, that is." I raised the candle again, but he showed no signs of fading.

Daryl pushed us apart. "Look. It's time to use a little logic. Someone's dreaming up this place." She pointed at Solomon. "If it's not you, then who is it?"

He looked at her, blinking. "I'm not dreaming. I know I'm in a dream world. I figured that out when I fought Mictar, but I'm fully awake."

Mom held up her candle. "He's starting to fade."

"Indeed," Amber said. "He is losing hold of his dream."

Trembling, I trained my stare on Dad … or Solomon, whoever he was, looking at him directly through the flame. Every detail stayed clear—his noble brow, his firm chin, his sparkling eyes. "Are you sure? I don't see any fading."

Daryl looked through her candle's steady fire. "He's a ghost, Nathan. Better get a grip. We all see the fading."

Dad pulled me close. "Do you remember what I told you about having a minority opinion?"

"Yeah." I let my head rest on his shoulder. His embrace felt good. "Strength doesn't lie in numbers. Strength lies in standing up for the truth, even if you're alone in your opinion."

"Nathan," Mom called. "Come back to us. You're fading, too."

Dizzy now, I looked at her. Her outline blurred, and her voice sounded distant. I had lost control in the dream world twice before. In spite of my surging emotions and the comfort of Dad's arms, I couldn't let it happen again.

I shouted, "Dad! Wake up!" I grasped his shoulder and shook him hard. "You're dreaming!"

He jerked away. Staggering, he braced his hand against a wall. The bedroom darkened. The wall disappeared. He fell to the floor, touching his shoulder. "I thought I had found you," he murmured. "I really thought I had found you."

I knelt at his side. "Let's get some more air in here."

Daryl opened the window a notch wider and let in the cool breeze. She joined us on the floor and patted Solomon's cheek. "Mr. Shepherd, wake up. You're almost there."

The room darkened further. Three candles burned steadily while mine flickered in the breeze. Seconds later, Dad's body crumbled and vanished along with the room and everything in it. Only the spider tree remained.

Daryl snatched the candle from me. "I'm so stupid! I lit this one while in the dream world." She blew it out and touched her flame to the wick. After sparking for a second, the new flame grew high and bright. "Now take this," she said, sliding the candle into my hand. "Look at it until you recover."

"Thanks." I stared at the flame, watching the others as they gathered around me. Their number split to six for a moment before congealing back to three.

"The guiding light must originate where truth is born," Amber said. "Concentrating on the false light in this world surely made it worse for Nathan. It is no wonder he almost lost his bearings."

"My bad," Daryl said. "But what do we do now? Where's the real Solomon Shepherd?"

The newly lit candle shone in Amber's eyes. "I have no experience with dreams that come from the dream world itself, but I assume he is close by."

"Since the dream is gone," Mom said, "he must be awake."

Daryl flashed a thumbs-up sign. "Right, but he still wouldn't know we're here. He probably thought we were part of a dream."

Mom called out, "Solomon! Can you hear me? It's Francesca!"

"Mr. Shepherd!" Daryl shouted. "This is Daryl. You don't know me, but that's okay. When you do, you'll like me."

I pointed at Mom's violin, still in her grip. "Call him with that. If this place is anything like it was where I first found you, your music will travel farther than our voices will."

"Something rousing." She raised the violin and played The Star Spangled Banner. The strings sang out clearly, though in the emptiness, the notes failed to echo.

After several seconds, she stopped. I held my breath, straining my ears. Now that my vision had cleared, my hearing also seemed more acute.

"Not a sound," Daryl said. "But if you're right about voices, maybe he's trying to answer and we can't hear him."

"I have an idea." Amber turned toward the spider tree and let her candle illuminate the branches. She angled her head directly toward its trunk and sang a high note. An echo replied and drifted into the darkness.

She then aimed her body toward the barrier leading to Sarah's Womb and sang out again. Her voice rebounded from the dark wall. "I will sing in all directions," she said. "If anyone hears the slightest echo, stop me. That will indicate a physical presence, perhaps Solomon Shepherd."

"Or another spider tree," I said, "but it might work. It's worth a try."

Amber slowly pivoted, repeating her note every few degrees while we all listened. After several seconds, Daryl spoke up. "Wait. I heard something."

Amber stopped and pointed. "That way?"

"I think so. It was really soft, though, so I'm not sure."

Holding her candle high, Amber strode forward, singing once more. After a minute or so, she stopped, turned a degree or two, and sang a short note. A few seconds later, a weak echo sounded.

"I heard it again," Daryl said.

"Follow me." Amber ran straight ahead, her dress flying as her heels kicked up behind her. The rest of us hustled in her path. The dream world's air rushed past, but our candle flames stayed steady.

Soon, Amber stopped and sang out. This time the echo replied loud and clear. She glided forward, extending her candle. "Solomon?" she called. "Are you here?"

"Honey?" Mom hurried ahead, then slowed. "Can you hear me?"

I caught up and walked at Mom's side. Candles raised high, we created spheres of light that bobbed with our gait.

A low, creaking noise sounded from above. I jerked Mom back. A big claw swiped by, barely missing us.

Daryl stamped her foot. "Cursed spider trees!" She stalked toward it and lifted her candle close to the lowest branches. "This'll teach you to pretend to be a human!" She stepped back, still holding her flame high. "What in the name of Arachnophobia is that?"

"What's wrong?" I asked.

"Spider's got a humongous fly."

While watching the creaking branches for any sign of attack, I edged closer. As I joined my light with Daryl's, a web-covered shape appeared in the branches. The spider tree had caught a victim, a human one.

CHAPTER THIRTEEN

I PUSHED MY CANDLE into Daryl's hand. "Hold this."
With a flying leap, I vaulted to the first limb and scrambled
out to the branch that held the webbed captive. As the branch
sagged under our combined weights, I reached for the
captive's closest extremity.

A claw stabbed at me, driving a sharp finger into my
side. I batted it away, but the motion sent me sliding down
the branch. I lunged, grabbed the captive in my arms, and
dropped through a network of thin branches. After landing
feet first, I rolled to the ground with the load still in my arms.

I jumped up and dragged the web-covered mass to a safe
distance. Mom, Daryl, and Amber rushed to my side and
held their candles close.

"Shades of Frodo," Daryl whispered. "He's been
Shelobbed."

I ran my fingers along the webbing until I found a man's
mouth, the only part of the body exposed to the air. Using
both hands, I ripped the tough, sticky strands and widened
the hole.

After a few seconds, I had cleared the stuff from the man's
face. Although he appeared gaunt and pale, his familiar jaw
and cheekbones revealed his identity — my father, Solomon
Shepherd.

I breathed a relieved sigh. "It's Dad."

Mom cleared a few loose strings from his mouth. "Solomon, can you hear us?"

He opened his eyes. He pursed his lips to speak, but only a rasping whisper emerged. "Francesca?"

"Yes!" She brushed a chunk of webbing from the top of his head. "Everyone help!"

While we stripped away the cocoon, Amber set her candle close to Dad's eyes. "Dear Solomon, here is a light from the living world. Focus on it."

"Thank you. I need one." His voice carried a sandpaper grittiness.

Amber brushed dark bangs from his brow. "How did you become a victim of the spider tree?"

As I pulled a sticky strip from Dad's arms, he winced. "While searching for a way out of this place, I walked into a cemetery. A girl ... a blind girl ... called for help from the branches of this tree. Half her body was already covered with webbing. I climbed up to free her, but while I was working, the tree caught me. Of course, I couldn't jump down until she was free, but by the time I pulled the last strands from her, the tree had already bound me. I couldn't free myself. Then, a strange wind pulled the girl into a cyclonic swirl and dragged her away."

"Was her name Felicity?" I asked.

"Yes." His eyes shifted toward me. "How did you know?"

"We've met." I helped Dad rise to a sitting position.

He coughed and spat out a thread. "I walked through a lot of dreams, some better than others, but this is the best one of all."

Amber pushed the candle closer. "Solomon, look through the flame. Soon, you will know the truth, that this is no dream."

Dad blinked again. As his rapid breaths disturbed the flame, he crossed his eyes to focus. After a few moments, his eyes seemed clearer. He took Mom's hand and pulled her into his lap, laughing as he wrapped her in his embrace. "Francesca, my darling! It's you! It's really you!"

After kissing her, he looked up at me with a grin. "You rascal! Did you drag your mother all the way to this dream world to find me?"

"Did you think I'd ever stop looking for you?" I slid my hand into Dad's. "I'd do anything to get my father back."

He stared at my wounds, then kissed the back of my hand. "Son, I am the proudest father in any world. You are a true blessing to me."

Daryl sniffed. "You three stop it, or I'm going to bawl for sure."

"And who is this spunky redhead?" Dad asked as he guided Mom off his lap.

"Daryl Markey, a friend of your amazing son." She extended a hand. "Since you're probably as cool as he is, I'm glad to meet you."

Dad laughed and shook her hand. "I'm glad to meet you as well. And thank you for the compliment, but I merely aspire to Nathan's level of coolness."

"Good enough." Daryl kept a grip on his hand. "Want a boost?"

"Sure." Daryl pulled him to his feet, while I helped Mom rise.

"So," Dad said, brushing web strands from his khakis. "I'll give you a quick update on what I know, and then you can tell me what you've learned."

My smile made my cheeks ache. "Sounds perfect."

"But we should try to find our way out of here while we talk." Dad nodded at the glowing supplicant. "Amber, it's good to see you again, and thank you for guiding my family."

She curtsied. "It is my pleasure."

"Can you get us out of this dream world?"

"I can, but we have another soul we must find here. Kelly of Earth Red is lost somewhere within this realm."

"Tony's daughter? What happened?"

I piped up. "We were in a dream here on Earth Yellow, and she got sucked into a cyclone with Felicity. We haven't seen her since, except in another dream."

"Interesting. It seems that this Felicity, blind though she is, has a habit of getting folks into trouble."

"I saw Kelly in her own dream," I said. "So I know she's alive somewhere. We just have to find her."

"And we will." Dad stroked his chin. "I have watched many dreams disappear, and, as you mentioned, they often get swept into a cyclone that funnels into a hole of some kind. But if dreams go back into the minds of dreamers, where could Kelly have gone?"

Daryl cleared her throat. "This sounds like a job for the logic queen. Look, dreams are color-coded, right? Red people dream in the red zone, Yellow in yellow, and Blue in blue, but this Felicity chick showed up in both the yellow and the blue dream worlds. And now Kelly's showing up on Earth Red, so I'm guessing they're both snoozing where there's access to all three. And there's only one logical place for that."

"Sarah's Womb?" I asked.

"Exactly. Time to search through infinite darkness with a flashlight, a few candles, and nothing to walk on. A perfect assignment for a darkness-phobic geek." She picked up the bag and hung it from her shoulder. "Let's get started."

I looked toward the central-core's dark wall. "Dad, Amber stretched a vine from a spider tree to Sarah's Womb, so all we have to do is find the tree again."

"Right," Daryl said. "And then we follow the yellow-brick … vine, I guess."

Dad narrowed his eyes as he surveyed the area. "Sounds like a good plan. Maybe we can figure out a way to get to the violin that spans the top of the Womb. If we can play it, we might be able to buy a little more time."

"We'll need it," I said. "According to Gordon Yellow we have only two of their days left before Convergence begins."

Dad blinked. "What is Convergence?"

"If Interfinity comes, the three earths will combine, and one will sort of dominate the other two. On those earths, every duplicate of the people on the dominant world will die. And having one surviving earth is only a maybe. It's possible that all three earths will be annihilated."

He took a deep breath. "So if we Earth Red people survive, our other-world counterparts will die. It would be better for them if we sacrificed ourselves."

"I guess I haven't thought about it that way."

"Don't worry, Son, I'm not saying we should kill ourselves. My point is that we should be willing to risk our lives to stop it from happening."

I nodded. "In other words, keep doing what we're doing."

"Exactly right." Dad turned toward Amber and bowed his head. "Does our supplicant know the way to the tree?"

"I do. If you will please follow." Amber lifted her candle and glided forward as if floating above the dark floor.

As we walked, the area brightened. The sun appeared overhead in the midst of a cloudless, deep-blue sky. The black ground brightened to a lush green lawn. A warm breeze freshened the air, and an amusement park materialized, filled with the typical attractions — a merry-go-round, a Ferris wheel, various thrill rides, and carnival barkers yelling from game booths. Dozens of adults and children milled about, some munching cotton candy, others standing in line for the rides. One male teenager, short and bespectacled, carried a calculator. Dressed in throwback schoolboy knickers and a button-down shirt, he stood stiffly and looked at the other children, staying away from the fun.

I called ahead to Amber. "Can you tell whose dream this is? The guy with the calculator?"

"I think so, but it is another blended dream. If you look carefully, you will see that there are tombstones scattered among the amusements."

I scanned the littered fairgrounds. Next to a trash can spilling over with popcorn boxes, soft drink bottles, and hypodermic needles, a small tombstone leaned at a slight angle. "Felicity again? Is she around somewhere?"

Amber nodded. "Without a doubt."

I gave the boy another quick glance. He looked familiar, like a younger version of Dr. Simon. Could this be Simon Blue's or Simon Yellow's dream?

As a hand slid into mine, a feminine voice filtered in. "I thought I smelled the aroma of courage."

Tapping her walking stick, Felicity faced straight ahead, no longer wearing dark glasses over her vacant eye sockets. Something metallic glinted in her other hand, her fingers tightly closed around whatever it was. "May I walk with you a while?" she asked. "I was getting pushed around in the crowds."

I stopped and extended my candle closer to her. "Of course, but I'd like to ask you a few questions, if you don't mind."

A pleasant smile eased across her face, revealing white, yet crooked teeth. "I will answer what I can."

As the others gathered around, I looked into her sockets. A tiny spark of blue light pulsed deep within. "When I first saw you, you were sucked into a sandbox by a swirling wind, and Kelly, a friend of mine, went with you. Have you noticed her presence around you anywhere?"

Felicity shook her head. "I knew she was with me in the wind, but when it settled, I was alone in my usual nightmare."

"When you're alone, what's around you? What do you do when you're in that place?"

"In my nightmare?" She shrugged. "Nothing. Nothing at all. I can't walk, so it's worse than just being blind. I wait until I wake up. Then I try to find someone friendly to talk to."

"So you think you're awake now?"

"Of course I'm awake." Her smile seemed to add a new light to the dream world. "I'm talking to you, aren't I?"

A possibility popped into my head. Could Felicity be the dream representation of Daryl Blue? Might Daryl be dreaming from within Sarah's Womb, maybe still reeling up and down like Daryl Red guessed? It sounded too crazy to mention, but it was worth checking out.

I pointed at her closed hand. "What are you carrying?"

"I'm not sure." She uncurled her fingers, revealing a small, touch-screen mobile phone. "I woke up with it in my hand."

"It's a phone."

"Oh. That's interesting. But I can't see to call anyone."

"If you could call someone, who would it be?"

"I don't know." She slid the phone into her dress's pocket. "Maybe someone will call me."

"Nathan," Dad said. "We need to press on. Let her tag along, and we'll see what we can do to help her when we get each other up to speed."

Felicity tugged on my hand. "I smell him again."

"Who?" I asked.

"Death."

I searched the crowd, but with so many people flitting from place to place, Mictar could be hiding anywhere. "Can you guess how far away he is?"

"Not far, but not close." She blinked her empty eyes. "I will tell you if he comes closer."

Daryl touched Felicity's head. "Cool. A stalker alarm. She'll come in handy."

Amber's glow brightened. With eyes narrowed and piercing, she seemed ready for battle. "Come." Glancing both ways, she pressed through the crowd, and we followed.

Dad gave us a summary of what he knew about the three worlds, facts I had learned along the way. I added a few tidbits of my own, including the improved state of dreaming problems on Earth Yellow.

When I finished, I reached into my pocket and withdrew the card and the report page. "Check these out. I took the card from a guy who tried to kill me. He had connections with a group that wanted to protect the Quattro secrets. The paper was in an Interfinity Labs report I picked up in their conference room."

When Dad took the paper, the wind kicked up. Clouds rolled in and blocked the sun. Baseball-sized raindrops splattered to the grass. One hit my shoulder. Although the drop was cold and wet, my shirt stayed dry.

The dream people scattered and vanished as they ran. The breeze swirled into a cyclone that wrapped around Felicity and began pulling her body. She clutched my arm and called out, "Help me, Nathan! I don't want to go back to my nightmare!"

With a sudden gust, Felicity jerked out of my grasp. Her body spinning wildly, she plunged into a grave and disappeared. A small tombstone, etched with letters too small to read, crumbled and melted in the increasing downpour.

The cyclone slurped the rain and clouds and everything else in sight. Then, like a high-speed corkscrew, it drilled into the ground and vanished.

Silence fell and with it a cold chill. I shivered. That girl needed help. She couldn't even tell the difference between reality and her nightmares. If she really was Daryl, how could I find her in a completely dark, infinitely deep place?

Amber lifted her candle, revealing a nearby tree. "The barrier is near, only a few paces away."

Dad drew close to Amber's candle. "Let me read this before we go on." As his eyes darted back and forth over the page, he nodded. "Hmm. I know about these people. They call themselves Sarah's Covenant, a cult of sorts. They're the ones who funded Dr. Gordon's research after he lost his grant. Then they secretly took some of Interfinity's technology, inciting Dr. Gordon to get in touch with Dr. Simon and me. While Simon worked with Gordon to install security features, Simon became engrossed in the communications with the other worlds. At the same time, I used the mirror technology and a bit of undercover work to track down the cult. I snooped around their headquarters and found a transport room that sent me to a world inhabited by white-haired men and women who made up the worst choir any world has ever known."

I laughed. "You're not kidding. I've heard them."

"Well, you'll have to tell me about that experience. In any case, while I was there, I met Patar, one of the white-haired men, a vision stalker, as he called himself. He was quite sober, and truly frustrating, but he also seemed very wise. After telling me about Mictar's plot to steal a Quattro mirror and kill all the gifted ones, he explained the cosmic environment—the three earths, the dream worlds, and Sarah's Womb—and introduced me to the supplicants. Cerulean, since he watched over Nathan Blue, alerted me to the deaths of Solomon and Francesca Blue. Scarlet suggested that your mother and I should switch places with them in order to put Mictar off our trail."

"So that's why Patar calls me Son of Solomon. He already knew you."

"And my experience with the supplicants is why Dr. Gordon decided to label the three earths by their colors. I suggested it, though I didn't tell him the reason. Since I wasn't sure whom to trust, Dr. Simon Red and I arranged our deaths. You were supposed to come with us, but it didn't work out the way we hoped, so your mother and I hid my camera and her violin in the trunk in order to give you clues to what happened to us. We knew between you, Clara, and Kelly, you'd eventually figure it all out."

"Yeah, we guessed a lot of it. Kind of a team effort." I nodded at the page. "Do you know what the code means?"

Dad pointed at the numbers and letters. "These represent GPS coordinates that give the locations of the latest foundation points of Sarah's Womb in the real worlds. The cult members guard those spots, because they are the most vulnerable places in the cosmos. If Mictar found them, he could place a stalker at each location, and if they sang their foul songs, with the weaknesses already in place, they could rip the cosmic fabric to shreds."

"Then why print them on a piece of paper that someone like me can pick up?" I asked. "That's not secure."

"It's secure. First, you would have to know you're looking for GPS coordinates. Second, they only *represent* the coordinates. They're musical codes, and only an interpreter like Kelly can decode the music."

"How did you know Kelly's an interpreter? Mom mentioned it before Kelly even knew about it herself."

"Cerulean was aware of Kelly Blue's abilities, and Patar passed the information on to me. We assumed Kelly Red had the same gift." He set a hand on my shoulder. "There is much more to explain about what happened on Earth Blue and how events triggered our decisions, but it can wait. We should concentrate on the code, if you don't mind."

I nodded. "Sure. Go ahead."

He pointed at the first line on the page. "Each symbol is a musical note, zero through eleven in a middle C chromatic circle. It's base twelve, so *A* represents the number ten, and

B represents the number eleven. As you can see, there are three lines, one for each earth."

"Can I take a peek?" Daryl asked.

Dad handed her the sheet.

While Daryl studied the numbers, I looked at Dad. "Do you know where those places are?"

"I had a few ideas and visited some possible sites. Your mother and I even conducted experiments. She played her violin at those spots. But if we were off even by a fraction of a minute on those coordinates ..." He shrugged. "A miss is as good as a mile."

"That makes sense," I said, "but how can so few notes do the job? I mean, how does the interpreter figure out that they're coordinate numbers instead of a message in words?"

"That's where the other codes come in." He took the card from me and ran a finger along the embossed symbols on the front. "It's a string of notes that prepares the interpreter. While she listens, the notes shift her brain to a kind of numerical listening mode. This code never changes, but the cosmic shifts can cause Sarah's Womb's location to shift with reference to our worlds, so the cult updates their members with the new coordinates. That's why the updated numbers were in that report."

I nodded. "It's been a while since I picked up the report. Maybe the numbers have changed again."

"It's possible, but this is all we have to work with." Dad squinted at the card. "Strange, though. There's room for another line of code, but it's blank. I'm not sure what to make of that."

Daryl folded the sheet of paper. "No obvious pattern. I'm stumped."

"We'll just have to wait, I guess." I took the page and the card and pushed them into my back pocket. "Right now we need to find Kelly."

As we continued walking, dim light from above illuminated the area. Tombstones materialized in a weed-infested lawn, and a crescent moon appeared in the purple sky. Was Felicity dreaming again? Cemeteries seemed to be her trademark.

A new voice floated in from the darkness. "Someone say my name?" Feminine and frail, the voice was beautifully familiar.

"Kelly-kins!" Daryl shouted.

Kelly stepped into the glow of our four uplifted candles, squinting at the light. "I guess it's about time I showed up, isn't it?"

With her arms spread wide, Daryl lunged ahead and embraced her. "You're a sight for sore eyes."

Kelly patted Daryl's back and smiled, but she looked worn out. "Yeah. You, too."

I squirmed. It would feel so good to leap ahead and hug Kelly, but maybe she wasn't real, and I would be fooled yet again. I held up my candle and looked at her through its flame. She seemed solid, but it was still too early to tell for sure. "Where's your candle?"

Kelly nodded toward the barrier. "I lost it in there when I stretched that stupid hole open. Good thing the vine was there, or I never would've found a way out."

I gazed at her weary face and sagging frame. She looked so sad, so lost.

Taking in a deep breath, she smiled and extended her arms. "Nathan?"

I gulped. The sight of Kelly's open arms made my heart ache. But if I gave in to my impulses and embraced another dream image, especially this one, I would lose my mind completely.

I turned to the others. "Amber? Is she real?"

Extending her candle, Amber walked up to Kelly and looked her in the eye. "I see a spark of life, but she could be a figment of her own dream. Also, with this dreamscape, whoever Felicity really is might well be dreaming that she is now Kelly."

"Why?" I asked. "Because she knows I'm looking for Kelly?"

Amber gave me a sad sort of smile. "Discerning the reason for dreams is something I learned to leave to the prophets."

"What are you talking about?" Kelly cried, spreading her arms. "Look at me! Of course I'm real!"

"Every dreamer thinks she's awake, Kelly-kins." Daryl pulled away and nudged me. "We need some kind of test to prove it. If this is Kelly's dream, we would need a question only the awake Kelly would know."

"What?" Kelly crossed her arms tightly. "How could you possibly ask me something my sleeping self wouldn't know?"

"What difference does it make?" Mom asked. "If we take her with us, and she's not real, she'll just vanish, right?"

I shook my head. "And then we'll have to come back and hunt for Kelly again. We can't waste time." I looked at each face. With furrowed brows and narrowed eyes, everyone seemed stumped. How could we come up with a question that would work? The sleeping Kelly would know everything, except something recent. Our call for Daryl, maybe? "I think I have something."

Kelly tapped her foot, her arms still crossed. Although she sniffed back a sob, she seemed to be getting angrier by the minute. "Go ahead," she grumbled. "Ask me your question."

I pointed at the vine's exit point from the wall. "Did you hear anything while you were in there?"

"I heard you calling for Daryl, but you didn't hear me shout for you. I guess I was too far away."

My heart ready to explode, I rushed to her and wrapped her in my arms, careful to hold the candle away. She, however, kept her arms locked tightly against her chest.

I drew back. "I'm sorry, Kelly, but if you only knew. I've been fooled by so many dreams. I even saw you playing piano, and I wanted to hug you, but I knew it was a dream that time, because these pixie things were flying all around."

Her arms loosened, but her tone remained aloof. "They looked like my mother." She lifted her brow. "What else did you see?"

"I saw you play the piano, and I heard your song."

Her arms slid around me. "All of it?"

I took a deep breath. Her touch felt warm and inviting, but this couldn't go on. I pulled back and held her hand. "Look, we'll have to talk about your song later. We have three worlds to save."

Closing her eyes, she nodded. Her voice cracked. "Whatever you say, Nathan."

After a few seconds of silence, Daryl clapped her hands. "So, now that we're deep in the heart of Awkward City, let's figure out how to escape."

CHAPTER FOURTEEN

I SWALLOWED PAST THE most painful lump in history. I needed to talk everything out with Kelly, but we didn't have time. I looked at Dad. "So, do you have a plan?"

He lifted a pair of fingers. "We have two choices. Either find our way to the top of Sarah's Womb and play the violin strings, or go to the GPS coordinates on each earth and play the music that will heal the wounds from there."

"Foundation's Key?"

"Exactly."

"And coordinate them from three places at once?" I asked. "How can we do that? We don't have time to fly across the world."

"You're right. We should go with the Sarah's Womb option."

Daryl shuddered. "With all those stalkers around?"

A new voice broke in. "Are you forgetting the third option?" Patar walked close enough to tower over me. "Must I remind you again?"

Dad stepped between Patar and me and pushed him back. "Have you been telling my son to kill the supplicants? I told you that wasn't an option."

Patar scowled and pointed at me. "Your own wife lives because your son killed Scarlet and cast her into the womb. He slowed Interfinity's progress, thereby giving billions of souls a chance to avoid Convergence. Has he not told you of his heroic deed?"

Dad glanced at me, but only for a split second. "Patar, I will tell you again, we will save the worlds with the musical harmony that God has ordered in the cosmos, the breath of God as my wife calls it, not by killing innocent supplicants."

A thin smile spread across Patar's face. "Sometimes, Solomon Shepherd, the willing sacrifice of an innocent lamb is the only way to save the world. The true breath of God has already proven the value of shed blood."

"I can't argue with that." Dad inhaled deeply and shook his head. "You heard our plans. If you have something to add, then say it. Otherwise, I think you should just move along."

"Since Mictar is busying himself with trying to find this girl," Patar said, nodding toward Kelly, "I can provide a safe path to the great violin, but only if she stays away. Mictar has tasted her life force, and now that she has escaped from the Womb, he will track her down."

Dad looked at Kelly, then at me. The perplexity in his face spoke volumes.

"You and Mom should go," I said. "Daryl and Kelly and I will figure out the GPS coordinates and get that process started. If you can buy us some time by playing the violin, maybe we can get it done."

Amber set a hand on my elbow. "I will take you three back to the observatory. From there you can transport to any real world. Once you locate the proper foundation point on Earth Yellow, perhaps my beloved will play at that site."

Dad looked at Mom. "Do you think we can play the big violin?"

She nodded. "But it will have to be pizzicato."

"Maybe it'll be enough to give Nathan time." Dad stuffed his hands into his pockets and turned his head slowly, pausing as he looked at each of his fellow dream-world travelers. "Okay. We'll go."

"Remember," Patar said, pointing at Kelly, "do not doubt my warning. Mictar is a dream stalker. If you sleep, you open a door by which he may find you." He leaned close to Amber as if to whisper, but his voice stayed loud enough for everyone to hear. "I will show the observatory personnel how to open their mirror to my world. When I go, I likely will not see you again until this crisis is over, and perhaps not even then."

She nodded. "I understand." A tear welled in her eye. "I am ready to give my life if need be, but I prefer to stay and help my beloved."

"Of course you do. We shall see what transpires."

Amber's chin quivered. "I had no opportunity to say good-bye to Abodah. I am very sorry."

"I am grateful for your compassion." Patar patted her shoulder. "Her sacrifice will not go unnoticed by the one who watches every fallen sparrow."

"Well stated." Amber lifted her candle and strode into the darkness. "Come. Our entry point into the observatory is this way."

"Wait just a second," I called. "I have to say good-bye."

Amber halted and turned, firming her lips as if holding back her emotions.

While still clutching a candle, I hugged Mom. "Soon," I whispered, "I'm going to roll away that stone you mentioned. Nothing will stop the flow."

She trembled as she returned the embrace. "I have seen your gift from afar. I hope I am able to see it played out, face-to-face."

"Let's hope it's before we get to heaven." I pulled back and strode into Dad's waiting arms. "I love you, Dad. I'm so proud to be your son. Thank you for teaching me courage and —" I glanced at Kelly but couldn't keep my gaze on her for more than a second. "And love. Mom can fill you in on what I mean."

With that, I pulled away and caught up with Amber, looking back to make sure Daryl and Kelly were following. "So how do we get out?" I asked as we walked.

"We will get out through a dream." After a minute or so, she stopped, set a hand on her hip, and looked around. "Yes, this is the place."

When Kelly and Daryl joined us, Amber pulled the mirror from Daryl's bag.

"Wait." I touched Amber's hand. "When we passed through that dark core, do you have any idea how far below the violin strings we were?"

She shook her head. "This is all new to me. Why do you ask?"

"I thought maybe we could calculate when Daryl Blue would settle into the no-gravity zone. We need to come back and look for her again."

"I agree, but I cannot help you with the needed information. The next time we see Patar, I will ask him, then we can plan another visit to Sarah's Womb." Amber laid her palm on the mirror's surface. Within seconds, her soft glow strengthened into a brilliant aura. "Francesca, my beloved, are you watching?"

A face appeared under Amber's hand. She slid her fingers away, revealing a bleary-eyed Francesca Yellow. "I'm here. Do you need me to do something?"

Amber's aura dimmed to normal. "Are you still in the observatory?"

"Yes. Solomon and Tony set up a cot and a stand for my mirror in one of the offices."

"Can you go to sleep? I need to follow your dream path as a way of escape from here."

"Sure. Nathan's napping. I was about to join him."

Amber nodded. "Put the mirror somewhere that will allow me to see you while you sleep."

The four of us gathered to watch the scene in the mirror. The heels of Francesca's hands pressed against the sides of our view, then her face bobbed as she walked the mirror square to another location. Soon, the image settled. A baby wrapped in a blanket slept on the floor next to a low cot. Francesca, wearing loose gray sweats, slid into a sleeping bag that lay on the cot. "Can you see me all right?"

"Quite well," Amber said.

"It's kind of hard to go to sleep on demand, but I'll do my best."

"Just close your eyes. I will sing a lullaby. It will calm your mind."

When Francesca's eyes fluttered closed, Amber began a song in a lovely alto, her voice silky and pure.

A gentle wind, a tumbling brook,
A kiss good night, a well-read book,
The blessings of love coming down from above
Are found in simple places,
In places of the heart.

A crackling log, the smell of life,
A candle's flame, a loving wife.
The finest treasures are never measured
By monetary rules,
The treasures of the heart.

The mirror emitted an aura of its own, a yellow glow that surrounded the square. It grew at a rapid rate, enveloping Amber, then Kelly, Daryl, and me. Soon, it took over the environment, illuminating the expanse with a fuzzy yellow glow that quickly morphed into lights on a ceiling, walls on the sides, and a carpeted floor beneath our feet.

Immediately in front of Amber, Francesca slept on a cot with the edge of her sleeping bag tucked under her chin. Next to her on the floor, little Nathan lay curled in his blanket.

I looked at the mirror. Our surroundings had become an exact copy of Francesca's office area. She was dreaming about the room she was sleeping in.

Amber handed Kelly her candle. Still holding the mirror, she sat on the cot and rubbed Francesca's back. "Can you hear me, my beloved?"

Francesca squirmed and let out a "Hmmm," while in the mirror, she stayed motionless and quiet.

"Arise, my love." Amber prodded her shoulder. "We must join you in the waking world."

Francesca sat up and blinked. As if counting, she nodded at each person in turn before breaking into a wide smile. "You found Kelly!"

"We did, and Solomon, too, but he and his Francesca have embarked on a different journey." Amber rose from the cot. "Now, wrap your mind around us and awaken. Although you are weary, you must arouse yourself and take us out of this world of dreams."

While the dream-world Francesca Yellow slid out of the sleeping bag, I kept an eye on the mirror. A shadow crossed the sleeping Francesca's form, growing bigger and darker. "What's that?" I whispered to Kelly.

Kelly grabbed my arm. "I don't know, but I don't like it."

The image now showed a lean pale hand reaching for the baby.

"Amber," I said sharply. "Wake her up! Quick!"

"My beloved!" Amber cried, turning the mirror toward Francesca. "Awaken! Now! Expand your thoughts and wrap us into your dream."

Francesca's eyes widened. Jumping to her feet, she spread out her arms. "Come close, everyone!"

We huddled into a tight group, holding the candles at our chests. The little Nathan in the dream world faded away, as did the cot and the walls.

Francesca clenched her eyes shut and screamed, "I'm trying to wake up! I have to save my baby!"

In the mirror, the pale hand covered the little boy's eyes, and light began to surround the attacker's fingers.

"Why aren't I waking up?" Francesca stamped her foot. "My baby needs me!"

"Okay," Daryl said. "I guess I have to do it."

Francesca jumped. "Ouch! Who pinched me?"

A strong gust wrapped us in a cyclonic funnel and pulled us toward the mirror. Francesca slid into it first, followed by Daryl, then Kelly.

I resisted the pull, more out of instinct than fear.

"Allow it to take you," Amber shouted through the rush. "I must be last."

I relaxed my muscles. As I stretched toward the mirror, everything warped. The funnel's suction pulled my breath away. Now that my body had been fully taken, I flexed my muscles again. I had to be ready for a fight.

One second later, all was clear. Francesca held the baby in her arms and rocked back and forth. Although he whimpered, he seemed fine.

Grunts and screams erupted. I pivoted toward the noise. Kelly and Daryl were sprawled over Mictar, beating him with their fists. A black violin lay on the floor at the stalker's side.

Just as I cocked my arms and made ready to pounce, Mictar flung Daryl away, sending her tumbling across the carpet. She rolled against a wall and sat up, stunned but breathing.

"Stay back!" Mictar shouted, lying on the floor while clutching Kelly around her waist and pinning her arms. "Or I will kill her."

I threw down my candle and ground in its wick with a heel. I had to think fast, act fast. In a splash of radiance, Amber appeared at my side, still holding the mirror.

Dangling Kelly like a rag doll, Mictar leaped to his feet. "Beware, supplicant. You know I will not hesitate to take this wench's life energy."

Amber's eyes flashed like two suns. "And I will dissolve your bones into dust. Now that I have you in my sight, you cannot hide from me."

Kelly twisted and rammed her knee into Mictar's groin. Without even a wince, he spun her back and again wrapped his arm around her waist, squeezing so tightly her eyes bulged. "If you allow me to escape, I will release her unharmed."

I looked for a weapon but saw only the black violin on the floor, too far away to grab quickly enough. "Why should we trust a liar?" I said. "Once you're free, you'll just kill her."

"Then it seems we're at an impasse once again." A crooked grin bent the scar on Mictar's face. "You won the previous battle. What will you do now?"

Amber touched my elbow. "Just say the word. I will kill that monster, and we will have no obstacles to saving the worlds. You, your mother, and my beloved will carry out our plan. If Kelly dies, she will be honored on the three earths for a thousand years."

Mictar loosened his grip on Kelly, allowing her to breathe. "Is that your choice? Shall I take this harlot's eyes and do battle with the supplicant?"

Panting, Kelly choked out, "It's okay, Nathan. Let him take me. You have to save the world."

"Silence!" Mictar squeezed Kelly and shook her hard. Her eyes closed, and her body went limp, but she still appeared to be breathing.

Her words of courage seemed to sizzle through the air and infuse my body. I couldn't let this happen. "Mictar." I extended my wounded hand toward him. "Take me hostage instead."

"What?" Mictar half closed an eye, but he seemed more intrigued than curious. "Why you?"

"I'm a gifted one, too. With Kelly, you get only what you left behind. With me, you get a full dose of life energy."

"Nathan." Amber pulled on my sleeve and whispered, "Without you, we will not have a third violinist."

I showed Amber my bleeding palm, keeping my voice as low as possible. "I can't play anyway. Maybe you can sing the key."

"I do not know if Sarah will respond. I am not one of the gifted."

"Then set up a keyboard at the spot. Kelly can play it." I took a step closer, again extending my hand. "What do you say? Will you let her go and take me hostage?"

"So, allow me to understand you correctly." Mictar loosened his grip on Kelly again. Her body stayed slack as her respirations wheezed. "Are you saying you trust me to let you live once I escape?"

I spoke through clenched teeth. "I trust you less than I trust the Devil himself, but at least Kelly will survive."

"Wait!" Daryl said as she struggled to her feet. "Let me tag along. I'll be kind of like insurance. You know, if Mictar doesn't keep his word, I can ... um ... drag Nathan's corpse away."

I grimaced. That wasn't good insurance, but it was better than nothing. "How about it, Mictar? Can she follow?"

Mictar pointed at Amber. "As long as the supplicant stays here."

Amber sat on the cot. "I will stay with Kelly and my beloved. We must plan the world's escape from Interfinity." She lowered her head. "Without Nathan."

"Very well." Mictar threw Kelly to the floor, picked up his violin and bow, and grabbed my wrist. "Come, fool."

Amber rushed to Kelly, sat next to her, and gathered her limp body into her arms. "I will care for her, Nathan."

Daryl touched Amber's shoulder as she passed by. "I know I'm not your beloved, but I'd appreciate a big helping of supplication. I have no idea what I'm doing."

As Mictar led me toward the office door, I looked back. Blurred by my tears, Kelly nestled in Amber's arms. Now that I would probably die at the hands of this monster, I might not get to tell her what I had to say. The simple message ached to get out, but I never had the courage to release it. Somehow, I had to let her know. "Amber, please tell Kelly—"

"No more chatter!" Mictar jerked the door open and pulled me into a curved hallway. His voice lowered to a whispered growl. "I don't want to alert the fools in the observatory."

Daryl slid through the half-closed door and pressed herself against the wall several paces behind Mictar and me.

"You two lead the way," Mictar said. "I want to keep my eye on you." He raised a hand, showing me a flash of light in his palm. "If you want that girl to live, I advise you to put aside all thoughts of escaping."

While Daryl walked toward us with trembling steps, I scanned the surroundings. We were in the security corridor on the first floor. The smaller elevator was probably a dozen paces in one direction, while the exit door lay about thirty paces in the other. "Which way?"

When Daryl arrived, Mictar shoved both of us forward. "Do you know where the back door is?"

I nodded. "If it's where the ones on the other earths are."

"Good. Move along."

I looked at Daryl as she walked at my side. She looked back at me, her eyes ablaze with fear. Somehow I had to make sure she would survive, but how? Obviously, the closer to Amber we stayed, the better her chances. "If you want to kill me," I said to Mictar, "why not do it inside? At least it's warm in here."

"I want it cold. You will see why in a moment."

While Daryl and I walked three or four steps in front of Mictar, Daryl slowly pulled out her shirttail, exposing a mirror at her waist.

As I watched, I kept my head as motionless as possible. She had said she brought the mirror from Earth Blue. This had to be it.

Daryl stealthily re-tucked her shirt.

I pushed open the security door that led to the main hallway and held it for Daryl. As she exited, Mictar grabbed my collar. Then, when all three of us had emerged into the corridor, he let me go and returned to his position a few steps behind.

As we continued toward the back door, I glanced at Daryl's shirt. How could that mirror help? Since Cerulean wasn't my supplicant, would he respond to our call?

When we reached the exit, I pushed the door open. Again, Mictar hung on to my collar while Daryl walked outside. Still holding me, he half dragged me into the cold breeze. I shivered as we walked together. "How far do you want to go? This is as good a place as any to commit a murder."

"I fully intend to kill you, but that was not my reason for coming out here." Mictar pulled me closer and dug into my back pocket. "Here they are." He threw me to the ground and displayed the card and folded page. "I learned about these coordinates when I tortured one of the cult members. Yet, it was not until I overheard your conversation with your father that I learned where to find them and how to use the codes."

As Daryl helped me to my feet, I glared at Mictar. If he heard the conversation, he had to know he needed an interpreter to understand the codes. Did that mean he would still go after Kelly?

Mictar held the card toward the fading sunlight. "The cultist told me the truth. The cold weather has revealed more codes."

He flipped it around and showed us. A new line of symbols had appeared near the bottom edge. While carefully folding the paper around the card, Mictar smiled, a nauseating sight. "Now, which of you should I kill to satisfy my hunger? I am sure one will escape while I kill the other."

Easing away a step, I whispered to Daryl, "Run."

She set a fist on her hip. "So, Mictar, how are you going to use the information? Even if you figure out what the codes mean, I'll bet you don't even know Foundation's Key."

I whisper-shouted, "Quiet!"

"What kind of simpleton do you think I am?" Mictar waved his violin. "Of course I can play that infernal piece, but I will not be baited into it. I see through your ploy."

"Chicken?" Daryl pushed her thumbs under her armpits, flapped her elbows, and made a horrible clucking noise.

I spoke through clenched teeth. "Daryl! Cut it out!"

"Fool! You will be my sustenance." With a grunt, Mictar reared back and thrust his hand forward, as if throwing a boulder.

Just as a black jagged streak shot from his palm, Daryl jerked out the mirror and deflected the bolt back toward him. It splashed against his shoulder, spreading dark liquid across his chest and arm.

Spewing a barrage of raging sounds, he hurled streak after streak, aiming high and low. Daryl blocked the first two, but the third struck her knee.

I dropped to the ground and swept a leg into Mictar's, toppling him to the gravelly surface. With a quick thrust, I leaped to my feet to attack again with a fist, but he reached out a long arm and grabbed my ankle. I fell face first, scraping my cheek and nose.

When I leaped up, I punched but struck only air. Just a few feet away, Kelly knelt on Mictar's back, yanking his ponytail and clawing at his eyes from behind.

I lunged toward them, but the sight of the black stuff on Mictar made me stop short. It had already spread over half of his torso and was now creeping around toward Kelly.

With a quick snatch of her arm, I pulled her off him. As I backed away with her, I found Daryl standing as if stunned. Her own black splotch expanded up and down her jeans.

I pointed. "That stuff will burn your skin. Or worse."

She shook the cobwebs away. "Enough said." She set the mirror on the ground, kicked off her shoes, and pushed down her jeans, revealing long thermal underwear covered with smiling cartoon bunnies. She dropped to her seat and began kicking off each pant leg. "How about giving me a hand?"

Kelly pulled the cuffs and slung the jeans away. She set her hands on her hips and grinned. "Well, look who came prepared."

"Yep." Daryl's cheeks flushed. "My mother always told me to wear clean underwear. You never know when you might have to show someone your bunnies."

After helping her get up, I looked at Mictar. Now almost completely black, the stalker picked up his violin, struggled to his feet, and shuffled away, slumped and wobbling. "I have the codes, Shepherd," he said weakly. "I will win this war."

I searched for a weapon. Anything — a fallen branch or a metal rod. Finishing that monster off was probably the best option, but nothing suitable came into view.

"C'mon," Daryl said as she scooped up her shoes. "Let's get out of the cold."

Keeping my stare fixed on Mictar as he slinked away, I felt for the mirror and picked it up. It was better not to focus on Daryl. Her thermal underwear covered her modestly enough, but I wasn't sure I could keep from laughing. "You're right. Let's go."

I offered Kelly my elbow. As she curled her arm around mine, I looked her in the eye. "Thanks. You saved me again."

Kelly gave me a tired smile. "Amber said you saved me first."

"Well ..." I paused, searching for the right words. "You're worth it."

Her lower lip trembled. She seemed ready to say something, but Daryl barked, "Cut the schmaltz! I'm freezing!"

While Daryl lifted one foot at a time to slip on her shoes, I hustled to the door and pulled the handle. It wouldn't budge. "It's locked."

Daryl moaned. "Are you telling me I have to parade around to the front of the building in my long johns?"

I punched a string of numbers into the nearby pad, but the lock stayed quiet. "I got some of that black stuff on my sweatshirt, and it eventually disappeared."

Kelly lifted the jeans by a cuff. The black goo continued spreading up and down a leg. "I'm not sure we can wait for it."

Daryl stooped and tied a shoe. "Well, I'm not exactly a modest maiden, but ..." She looked up, tugging the underwear. "Why didn't I wear my camo thermals? At least I wouldn't look like a girly girl."

I tucked the mirror under an arm and held out my hand. "C'mon. If we hurry, we'll be back inside in no time."

After pulling upright, Daryl kissed me on the cheek. "Thanks for rescuing me."

"No problem. I just wish we could've hung on to the codes."

"Oh, we have the codes." Daryl began marching toward the side of the building. "The problem is that he has them, too."

Kelly and I caught up and matched Daryl's quick pace stride for stride. "What do you mean?"

Daryl tapped the side of her head. "I memorized them, both the card and the page."

"You did?" Kelly said. "That's amazing!"

"Yeah." Daryl tossed her head back in mock conceit. "I *am* pretty amazing."

Marching up a slight incline, we followed a gravel-covered path that led around the observatory's building. A few seconds later, we approached a footbridge that spanned a deep ditch leading to a pipeline protruding from the lab's basement. As we crossed it, a memory flowed — driving a Camry across this bridge in another world while Kelly literally rode shotgun.

I smiled at her. She smiled back. We were on the same wavelength. As we continued walking, I looked at her out of the corner of my eye. The shoulder of her sweatshirt again displayed a dark splotch — blood from her wound. And her eyes were certain to go bad again when or if we ever returned home.

She had suffered much more than I had. And maybe more suffering lay in store. I just had to make sure that I took the brunt of it, no matter what.

CHAPTER FIFTEEN

I RAN TO A tall, leafless tree, crouched behind its forked trunk, and peered through the gap, scanning the path leading to the portico-covered entry. Gunther's van zoomed out of the lot, while someone holding a phone to his ear exited the building in a dash.

When the girls joined me, I whispered, "Is that who I think it is?"

Daryl pressed close to my side and squinted. "Solomon Yellow?"

"That's what I thought. Maybe he's running to his car to get first aid or something."

"Not for me," Kelly said as she huddled with us. "I just fainted because I couldn't breathe."

"How about the others?" I asked. "Did you see them when you revived?"

Kelly nodded. "Tony showed up with Molly, and they took Francesca and the babies out. They said it was getting too dangerous for the little ones."

"So they must have called Gunther to come and get them. I just saw his van leave."

"Tony seemed real nervous," Kelly said, "and annoyed. He mentioned something about Flash staying behind to help with the equipment."

I rolled my eyes. Dad wouldn't leave Mom under such dangerous conditions, especially in a room by herself where Mictar could attack her in her sleep. This version of Flash was getting on my nerves.

I laid a hand on each girl's shoulder. "Let's try to catch him before he gets out of the parking lot."

"The way I'm dressed?" Daryl shook her head. "No way, buster. Not in my long johns."

I focused on her tired green eyes and frazzled red hair. She had stretched herself to the limit. "Okay, we'll wait here till he's gone."

Solomon jumped into his old Volkswagen, started its noisy engine, and puttered out of the parking lot. Seconds later, he had driven out of sight.

"Coast is clear," I said. "Remember, Mictar is still lurking somewhere, and the fact that everyone is leaving in a hurry is a sign that something bad happened inside. We have to be careful and quiet."

Kelly and Daryl nodded.

We hurried toward the building and stopped on a walkway that ran under the portico. As a cold breeze buffeted us, I listened for footsteps or the sounds of approaching vehicles.

Daryl bounced in place. "Let's go! I'm freezing my bunnies off!"

Still carrying the mirror, I jogged to the front door and held it open for the girls.

Once inside the lobby, Daryl halted, her teeth chattering. "So, after Tony and company left, where did Amber go?"

"I don't know," Kelly said. "She told me to stay in that room. Then she took off."

I looked toward the ceiling and the floors above. "Let's visit the telescope room. That's always been the center of activity." I nodded toward a stairway. "Quietly, now."

Daryl shivered again. "As they say in *Star Wars*, I have a bad feeling about this."

I tucked the mirror under my arm and led the way up the stairs. When we reached a closed door at the landing, I peeked out the small, eye-level window. "No one in sight."

As I opened the door, the hinges creaked, but it couldn't be helped. I pushed myself through the expanding gap and waited for Daryl and Kelly to squeeze through.

I looked down the curved corridor. The entry to the telescope room wasn't in sight, but it had to be only twenty or so steps away. I skulked toward the door. After a few steps, it came into view. I glanced back to check on Kelly and Daryl. They tiptoed behind me without a sound.

Once at the door, I turned the knob, pulled it an inch or so, and peeked through the tiny gap. Inside, the lights had been dimmed. Opening the door any further would brighten the inner room, giving away my presence. I whispered, "We need to douse the lights here."

Daryl ran to a bank of switches and turned off the hallway lights. When she returned, I whispered again. "Watch from here. Wait for a signal."

I opened the door just enough to slide through. Walking on the balls of my feet, I headed for the computer desk where a solitary man sat staring at a screen. Shorter than most men and wearing ovular glasses, he looked like one of the Simons, probably the younger of the two.

I crept closer, watching for any sign that Dr. Simon had seen me. It would be perfect if I could just read the screen, figure out what was going on, and then leave without anyone knowing I had been here.

Holding my breath, I took a step. My shoe slid in something wet. I lifted it, eased to a crouch, and touched a dark puddle. I squinted at the splotch on my finger. Blood?

I rose, lunged toward Dr. Simon, and grabbed his chair. His glasses slid down his nose, revealing a bullet hole between his closed eyes. The desk lamp highlighted his face, pale and motionless.

My body shook. I backed away and glanced from side to side. Who could have done this? And where were the others—Simon Blue and Gordon Yellow? Were they safe?

Again I looked at the limp body, now a perforated shell. Simon Yellow had devoted his career to stopping catastrophes in his world, saving the lives of people who had perished on Earths Red and Blue, and now he had been repaid with a bullet.

I averted my eyes. I couldn't stand to look at his face any longer. With nausea churning my stomach, I might vomit at any second.

I turned toward the door. Calling Kelly and Daryl might give me away to a lurking murderer. But maybe Daryl could check all the computer settings and see what was going on at the time of the shooting.

"Hello?"

I jerked toward the voice. It came from the computer.

Still queasy, I tiptoed around the puddle and searched for a microphone, but none of the many pieces of equipment resembled one. Clearing my throat as quietly as possible, I whispered, "Did someone call me?"

The computer's hard disk whirred. Meter readings, both numerical and graphical, pulsed with constant change. When I leaned closer to try again, a speaker let out a sputter, then a voice.

"This is Dr. Gordon of Earth Red. Is that you, Nathan?" Static interrupted the transmission but quickly died away. The voice seemed mechanical, but it still sounded like Dr. Gordon.

"Yes. This is Nathan Red. Your speech is normal speed. Are the two worlds traveling through time at the same rate now?"

Again, a long pause ensued. As I waited, I drummed my fingers quietly on the desk. After another twenty seconds or so, the speakers came alive.

"No. The computers are buffering our transmissions and replaying them at the right speeds. Since I'm much slower, you have to wait to hear me, so after this I will make my communications as short as possible, perhaps even terse."

I scanned the readouts on the computer screen until I found a loudness meter, a vertical line that bounced with the fluctuations in static. Above the meter, a graphical switch was set to digital instead of analog. "Dr. Gordon, Simon Yellow has been shot. He's dead. Were you listening in? Do you know who did this or where he went? Do you know where the other Simon is, or the other Gordon?"

Avoiding another look at Simon Yellow, I sat on the desk and watched the meter rise and fall. When it stopped moving, a horizontal white bar appeared beside it and filled with blue from left to right, apparently indicating the buffering procedure.

When the blue struck the right-hand side of the bar, it disappeared, and the speakers clicked on. "I heard male voices, then a female voice, then a gunshot. Silence after that."

"Solomon Yellow left in a hurry," I said, "but I didn't see a gun."

The voice meter rose and fell several times, then the buffer bar reappeared, filling with blue a little faster this time.

"Do you think your father's double is a murderer?" Dr. Gordon asked. "That doesn't seem likely."

"Your double helped Mictar kill quite a few people, didn't he?"

This time, the delay was much shorter.

"Touché."

I shook my head. This conversation was taking too long, and we weren't getting anywhere. "I'll be back in a minute. I have to do something." I crossed Dr. Simon's arms over his chest and rolled him and his chair near the wall. After finding a panel of switches, I turned them on, flooding the room with light. "Daryl. Kelly. Come on in."

They hustled through the doorway, Kelly with the mirror in hand.

"Someone murdered Simon Yellow," I said.

Kelly covered her mouth. "That's awful!"

"Ewww!" Daryl lifted her foot, grimacing at the blood dripping from her shoe. "A messy murder, too."

"Yeah. I pushed his body out of the way. It's pretty gruesome. Dr. Gordon Red's on the audio link, but he doesn't know who did it or who went where, so I thought maybe we could check the computer to see if we can find some kind of log."

"I'm on it." Daryl rolled another chair to the desk and pecked at the keyboard. "Dr. Gordon? You listening?"

After a few seconds, his mechanically altered voice snapped on. "I am here, Daryl."

She huffed. "Stupid translator. He sounds more like R2-D2 than Dr. Gordon." As she slid her finger across the touchpad, she scanned the screen. "Would the data log be in the system maintenance directory?"

The voice meter rose again. After a few seconds, Daryl clicked on something, apparently halting Dr. Gordon's transmission. "Never mind. I found it." Her eyes shifted back and forth. "I'm going to run the stream through demo mode and see what happened."

"What's demo mode?" I asked.

Her fingers flew along the keys. "If the recorders captured all the images, the system will use the mirror to display everything that took place here, and the monitor will show me every command that anyone entered through the computer. But since it's demo mode, it won't actually create portals or zap anyone to another world."

After tapping a final key, she slid her finger down the touchpad, dimming the overhead lights. She rolled the chair away from the desk. "Okay, let's see what happened."

The mirror above flashed once, darkened for a few seconds, then displayed the telescope room. Dr. Gordon Yellow and one of the Simons stood next to the computer while the other Simon sat in one of the rolling chairs with his elbow on the desk. Gordon seemed to be shouting, apparently angry, while Solomon stood with his arms crossed, staring at him with a stern expression.

"Can you turn on the sound?" I asked. "Looks like they're arguing, but it's kind of hard to tell from here."

"Let's see what we can do about that." Daryl searched the screen while moving her finger around on the touchpad. "Ah! Hologram mode."

When she tapped on the pad, the mirror flashed again. The hologram lights shot multicolored beams into the room. Images appeared around us. Simon Yellow sat in his chair, and Gordon Yellow and Simon Blue stood next to Solomon Yellow near the telescope. All four seemed to be physically present in the room.

I passed a hand through Solomon Yellow's body. He was nothing more than a realistic ghost.

"Got the sound," Daryl said. "Here goes."

The speakers erupted with Dr. Gordon's shout. "So you just sent them without consulting me? I wanted to see that place, maybe even go there. At least give me the secret to why The Moonlight Sonata doesn't work, even on the piano."

Solomon tightened his crossed arms. "Patar's instructions were clear. Only he and the Red Shepherds were allowed to go, and no one may follow."

"He's a stalker!" Dr. Gordon's face blazed crimson. "Those fiends have been terrorizing our world, and now we have a chance to strike. Next you'll be siding with Mictar himself!"

"I am no ally of Mictar." Solomon's jaw quivered, but he kept his cool. "Patar told me his evil twin is near. We should stop bickering and get ready."

"Ready?" Gordon slid out a desk drawer and withdrew a revolver. "I have this ready for any stalker." He paused and glared at Solomon. "Or any stalker's friend."

Simon Blue touched Gordon's shoulder. "Please, if you will just—"

With a quick elbow thrust, Gordon knocked Simon Blue to the floor. "I am finished with you so-called scientists who want to sit around and wait for your deliverance concert to begin." As his finger slid over the trigger, his face flushed again. "Interfinity will collapse the cosmos in days, not weeks or months. If you'd just tell me how to open the portal, we could send the Navy Seals into the stalkers' world and clear them out. We can't hope that three musicians will somehow enchant the powers that be by sawing their fiddles at random points that we don't even know yet."

"They're not random," Solomon said, his voice sharp. "They're the foundation points, the anchor loci that brace the triad structure."

"That's irrelevant." Dr. Gordon pulled the gun's hammer back and pressed the barrel against Solomon's forehead. "I want the musical key to their world, and I want it now."

Keeping his head perfectly still, Solomon swallowed. "If you murder me, you'll never get it."

"True." Dr. Gordon turned and aimed the gun at Simon Yellow. "First him, then the other Simon."

Simon Yellow grabbed his chair arms and trembled.

"I find it quite rational," Dr. Gordon continued, "even virtuous, to sacrifice a couple of hesitant scientists in order to save billions of innocent lives."

"I am on your side," Simon Yellow said. "I just want to save lives."

"And we will." Dr. Gordon pushed the barrel against the bridge of Simon's nose, bending his glasses. "What do you say, Solomon Shepherd?"

Solomon uncrossed his arms. "Look, if I give you the right music ..." As his voice trailed off, his gaze wandered toward the far side of the room.

"What?" Dr. Gordon looked around. "What's wrong?"

"We have company." Solomon folded his hands behind his back. "Very important company."

Amber's image walked into the room. As she glided toward Dr. Gordon she raised a hand, and her voice thundered. "Put down your weapon!"

Dr. Gordon staggered backwards. The gun fired. Simon Yellow flailed, spun toward the desk, and slumped. Simon Blue pushed Dr. Gordon to the floor, kicked the gun away, and ran toward the exit. His image disappeared in the darkness.

As Dr. Gordon crawled toward the gun, Solomon grabbed a phone from his belt and hurried away, shouting into the mouthpiece, "Francesca! Where are you?" He, too, vanished.

When Dr. Gordon neared the gun, Amber picked it up and emptied the cylinder. Without a word, she turned and walked away, dropping a bullet behind her.

Dr. Gordon climbed to his feet and shook his fist. "I know who you really are!" he screamed. "You're one of the stalkers! The apple doesn't fall far from the tree, and your fruit is just as rotten as your father's!"

After taking a few deep breaths, Gordon staggered to Simon Yellow and checked his pulse. He patted the corpse's hand and spoke softly. "I am truly sorry. I know you had our best interests in mind, and I never intended to shoot you. It was only a ploy."

He let out a deep sigh and walked away. Soon, all was quiet.

Daryl studied the computer screen. "Looks like there's not much else until we show up."

"So," Kelly said to me, "this all happened when Patar came here with your parents. He wanted to take them to the misty world so they could play the violin in Sarah's Womb, right?"

I nodded. "But he needed help to transport them. He couldn't do it himself. So Solomon Yellow arranged it without telling Gordon Yellow."

Daryl chimed in. "Solomon Yellow suspected all along that Gordon Yellow wanted to kill everyone in the misty world. That's why he helped Patar on the sly."

"If everything's in the log file," I said, "why didn't Gordon Yellow play it back and find out how my parents transported?"

"He couldn't." Daryl nodded at the screen. "I started from the beginning. Everything before that's been erased."

Kelly bent over Daryl's shoulder and looked on. "So Solomon Yellow covered Patar's tracks."

"Pretty much." Daryl turned off the hologram. "But we have an auxiliary backup."

"A hidden log file?" I asked.

"No." Daryl touched one of the computer speakers. "A hidden eavesdropper. Dr. Gordon Red was probably listening in."

"He already told me he heard a gunshot. Nothing after that. But it might help if we could talk to him more."

"I'll see if I can put him on the ceiling." Daryl pulled the keyboard close and squinted at the monitor. "I haven't done this in digital mode before."

While Daryl worked on the computer, Kelly lifted herself onto the edge of the desk, her shoulders low. "Too many delays. At this rate, we'll never get to the foundation points in time."

"Right," I said, "and we still have to translate the code."

Kelly pressed her finger against the desk's surface. "Translate it here? Even though Mictar might be lurking? And what about Gordon Yellow? We don't know where he went."

"I think we're as safe here as anywhere else." I leaned over the desk and spoke to the computer. "Dr. Gordon, we're going to try to get you on our ceiling mirror. In the meantime, do you know what's up with the music they played to transport Patar and my parents to the stalkers' world? Was it The Moonlight Sonata?"

After the usual delay, Dr. Gordon replied. "Yes. I'm quite certain I heard it. Someone played it on the piano."

"Do you know if it was live or a recording?"

I drummed my fingers again, this time more loudly. I glanced at Kelly and Daryl. Both girls rolled their eyes, apparently sharing my frustration at the delay.

Finally, the speakers came on. "I couldn't tell from here. All I know is that I have never heard it played with greater passion."

I looked at the piano near the wall and imagined Patar sitting at the bench, playing the keys with his long, narrow fingers. From what I could tell from the recorded conversation, Dr. Gordon had tried to play The Moonlight Sonata, but, being a violist, he probably wasn't adept enough on the piano to perform it with the passion Patar had mentioned back when we first entered the telescope room. Yet, why didn't he play it from a recording? Maybe because we had the iPod, and they didn't have the recording available on any other device.

"I found the converter," Daryl said. "Ready to see Gordon?"

"Don't bother. I think I figured out what we need to know."

Dr. Gordon's voice came through the speakers again. "Daryl, your father asked me to send his love. He's not here right now, but he will return soon."

"Soon?" Daryl's ears turned redder than her hair, and her voice cracked. "That might not be soon here."

"No," Dr. Gordon said.

Pulling in her lip, Daryl nodded. "I haven't seen him in years." She opened her mouth as if to continue, then lifted her fist and bit it.

Kelly rubbed her back. "Don't worry. This will all be over soon."

Daryl buried her face in her hands, nodding as she wept.

"What's next?" Kelly asked, now looking at me.

"Two options. We can either check on my parents in the misty world, or we can figure out the foundation points from the card and that report page."

Kelly raised a hand. "I vote for figuring out the points. Let's trust your parents to do their job while we do ours."

Daryl wiped her reddened eyes. "I can monitor the Interfinity simulation forecast. If your parents pull it off, I'll be able to tell."

"Good idea." I nodded toward the piano. "Could you play the sonata if you had to, Kelly?"

"I should be able to. I've played the first movement a thousand times, like I once told you, whenever I was sad."

Daryl tapped at the keyboard. "Nathan, if you'll help me, I should be able to translate the codes into notes—that is, if I remember what Mictar showed us."

I gave her a hard stare. "*If* you remember?"

She turned and winked. "Just kidding. I remember."

"Okay, let's try to get this done quickly." I looked at the screen. Daryl had already typed several strings of base twelve numbers into a word processor. I pointed at a zero, the first character. "Those should all be middle C."

"Right." She switched to the computer's music generator program and entered the note. "I knew that one."

I moved my finger from the zero to a numeral one farther down the line, then to a two, and so on as I spoke. "Then it goes C-sharp, D, D-sharp, E, F, F-sharp, G, G-sharp, A, A-sharp, and B."

"Okay. Makes sense." Daryl continued typing, her gaze locked on the screen. "Just tell the interpreter to get ready. I'll play a violin synthesizer over the speakers in a few seconds; first the notes from the card, then from the report."

"Great." I peered at the doorway. No sign of Mictar or Gordon Yellow yet.

Daryl turned toward me, narrowing one eye. "Whole notes, you think?"

"Probably. Where will the music play? From the desktop speakers or from the wall units?"

"I'll pipe it to the big ones. If El Gordo comes back, this might be our only shot."

I walked with Kelly to the center of the room near the telescope. "Ready to give it a try?"

"Sure. But what exactly am I doing?"

I grasped her wrists and looked into her eyes. "Just concentrate on the music and use your gift, just like when you could pick words out of music when the stalkers' choir sang. This time, it might not be words, so just say whatever comes to you, and we'll record it."

"Right," Daryl called. "I'll be the transcriptionist."

Kelly closed her eyes. "Okay. Ready when you are."

"One minute," Daryl said, raising a finger. "Last line."

As the keys continued to click, I looked back and forth between the two amazing young ladies, both exercising their extraordinary talents — Daryl, a spunky techno-wizard who always seemed to dance to an offbeat rhythm, and Kelly, a pensive, quiet artist. With her eyes closed and her head tilted slightly upward, she seemed to be in prayer, ready to communicate with the music — the breath of God, as Mom called it.

I pushed a hand into my pocket. Again my palm stung. If only I, too, could dig deep into my soul to unearth my gift. But with my hand so maimed, it might be weeks before that could happen.

"Here we go." Daryl tapped a key. Notes played from a synthesized violin, mechanical at best. It sounded like my own playing when I was about six years old.

For a few seconds, Kelly said nothing. Her brow wrinkled, but she showed no other reaction. The early codes were designed to program Kelly's mind, preparing her for the coordinates, so her silence made sense.

After several more seconds, Kelly took in a deep breath and spoke, loud and clear, each word separated from the next by a pause as if guided by a rhythm. "Red … north … five … one … five … zero … zero … west … zero … one … four … six … yellow … north … two … seven … one … seven … four … east … seven … eight … zero … four … two … blue … north … four … two … four … four … four … west … eight … eight … eight … eight."

With a click, the music ended. Kelly opened her eyes and blew out a long sigh. "And one more eight."

"That's five eights in a row," Daryl said. "Are you sure?"

"That's what I heard. It sounded kind of strange to me, too."

I walked with Kelly back to the desk. "Do those look like GPS coordinates?"

"You tell me." Daryl rolled away from the desk and nodded at the screen. "I'm not a travel geek like you."

I pointed at the first number. "If they're all three decimal places, then that one could be fifty-one-point-five degrees north of the equator, and zero-point-one-four-six west of the prime meridian."

"Got it." Daryl rolled back to the desk. "I'll put in the decimal points for all three worlds."

"Does that computer have a way to look up GPS coordinates?"

"It's easy at home," Daryl said, "but I don't think Google Maps exists here yet."

I nodded toward the ceiling. "Can you send them to Dr. Gordon? Maybe he can do it."

"Good idea." Daryl typed rapidly for a moment, then turned back to me. "Let's hope they still have Internet there."

"Right. And even if they do, it could be a long wait."

Kelly scanned the floor. "In the meantime, I'll look for that bullet Amber dropped."

I joined her search. "What are you thinking? She left a trail?"

"Exactly." Holding her hair back as she looked down, Kelly took slow baby steps. After a few minutes, she pointed. "There it is."

I stooped and picked up the brass-colored bullet. "In the hologram, it looked like she was heading for the elevator."

"Then maybe we'll find another one where she got off."

"Incoming email," Daryl called.

I slid the bullet into my pocket. "Did he find the locations?"

"Yeah. Kind of strange, that's for sure." She read the message out loud. "The Earth Yellow point is on the front walkway to the Taj Mahal. Blue is near the radio telescope site on that world, which should be only a few miles from where you're standing now, if you were on Earth Blue, that is, and Red is the lawn at Buckingham Palace."

"Buckingham Palace? That was one of the photos we developed back when—"

"I know," Kelly said. "So was the Taj Mahal."

"My father said he experimented at some sites. He must have been close when he went to London. He just didn't have the exact coordinates."

"So what now, boss?" Daryl asked. "Are you heading home for a world-saving performance at the palace?"

"Eventually, but since this is the fastest-moving world, we'd better coordinate from here first. We have to get Francesca Yellow to India. She'll be our Earth Yellow player. I guess we should call Tony, since she took off with him."

"And your mom has to go to the telescope site on Earth Blue," Kelly said. "That could take a while. We don't even know where they are."

"Maybe if she and Dad did a good job in Sarah's Womb, we'll have some extra time."

"I'll check the collision status." Daryl's fingers flew into action once again. A graphical representation of the three worlds appeared on the screen, each moving along a color-coded line. Earth Red had pulled well in front of Earth Blue, and Earth Yellow seemed to be catching up with both at a rapid pace.

"That's the relative time speed," Daryl said. "I'll switch it to a multidimensional view."

The graph warped, gaining depth and shading. Now the three planets traveled on curved lines, two of which merged at the far right side of the screen.

Daryl pressed a finger on the intersecting point. "That's the big kabloowie for Earth Yellow and Earth Blue. Interfinity is about five days away."

"Five is better than two." I bent closer to the screen. "Mom and Dad bought a little more time."

"I can run the simulator through the projected path. It'll give us a graphical representation of what will happen."

"Sure. If it's quick. We need to get going."

"Right. Old Scarface still wants Kelly's eyes." Daryl tapped a few keys and pressed her finger near the center of the monitor. "That's the impact point, an hour or so less than five days from now. Although the movement on the horizontal scale is based on Earth Yellow time, the distances between the spheres aren't based on time differences. What you're seeing is a representation of metaphysical proximity, so the collision doesn't mean their calendar dates have come together."

Three rotating spheres drifted toward Daryl's finger, each one seeming to float on an undulating surface. The sphere farthest away in the screen's perspective, shaded blue, and the closest sphere, shaded yellow, pulled ahead of the third earth. They arced toward each other and melded together directly in front of Earth Red, then disintegrated into a scattering of green pixels that slowly expanded from the collision point. Earth Red continued on its course and passed through the debris.

Daryl lowered her finger. "I suppose that splash at the end is just animation. I don't think anyone really knows what will physically happen to the planets once they collide metaphysically."

"Earth Red passed right through the collision point," I said. "What does it mean?"

Daryl shrugged. "Hard to say. It's just a simulator. I've never seen a three-world metaphysical collision before, so I can't help you there."

"Maybe it's showing a model of Convergence. Earth Red people survive, and all the copies die."

"Could be," Daryl said. "But since we can't test it in a ginormous cosmic lab, we'd better assume the worst."

I nodded. "Whatever happens, we have less than five Earth Yellow days to stop it, so the first priority is to contact the players."

"Do you think your parents will come back here?" Kelly asked.

"If they're able. My guess is Patar will see to that. But we can't wait around. We have too much to do, like hopping a flight to England and hoping we can get there in time."

Daryl opened the drawer containing the IWART devices and picked up one of two lying inside. "If you're going to play a concerto, you'll need this to conduct your orchestra."

I took it from her and clipped it on my belt. "One's missing."

"I'll bet Solomon Yellow took it for Francesca," Kelly said. "I noticed he had two devices hanging from his belt."

Daryl grabbed the last IWART. "After I send you and Kelly home, I'll wait here for your parents and zap them over to Earth Blue. Then I'll see if I can find Amber. She can contact Francesca Yellow."

"If Francesca took her mirror with her." I glanced at the office chair deep in the shadows. "What do we do about Simon Yellow's body?"

Daryl looked in that direction. "If I get in touch with Solomon, I'll ask him. It's not that I'm unsympathetic or anything, but the farther away I stay from dead bodies, the better I like it."

"So you don't mind waiting here?" Kelly asked. "I mean, you were stuck in this world for so long before."

Daryl pressed a hand against her chest. "Hey, I'm as altruistic as the next girl, but we haven't proven that a digital transport to Earth Red won't fry your circuits, if you know what I mean. If it works, I'll be right behind you."

"Well, if it doesn't work," I said, "our gooses are as good as cooked anyway."

"You need a violin," Kelly said as she jogged to the musical instrument area. Seconds later, she returned with a violin and bow. "How's this one?"

I took them and held the violin close to my ear as I plucked each string. "Needs tuning, but it should be fine."

"No time like the present." Kelly hooked her arm around mine and led me to the center of the room. "We'll either fly together or fry together."

"That's not exactly comforting."

Kelly swatted me playfully on the shoulder. "Buck up, young man! Where's that motorcycle-racing bravado when we need it?"

"I think it sprung a leak when I found Simon Yellow dead."

"You'd better plug the hole, then. You're going to need all the bravado you can get."

"Right." After taking a deep breath, I raised the bow and waved it as if conducting an orchestra. "Don't worry about a thing, Kelly. This is going to be a multi-world command performance. Just take a seat and enjoy the show."

"All right. I like it, but don't lay it on too thick." She nodded at Daryl. "Let's do it."

CHAPTER SIXTEEN

D ARYL SET HER fingers on the computer's keyboard.
"I'm dialing in Earth Red. Say your prayers."

I tried to laugh, but my lungs seemed to freeze. Above, the ceiling mirror brightened to a copy of our own room, displaying Dr. Gordon and at least two other people in the shadows—too late to try to guess who they were. Lights flashed on. Wide beams shot down from somewhere above, making a laser cage around Kelly and me.

As we had experienced multiple times before, the scene in the mirror melted and descended as if ready to swallow us. But this time, the lights collapsed around us, sending a buzzing shock through my body. My teeth clenched. My fingers strangled the violin's neck, and my arm locked tightly with Kelly's. It felt like my bones were cracking. Kelly closed her eyes, and her head rocked back and forth, sending her hair into a static-driven frenzy.

The Earth Red observatory took shape slowly ... too slowly. Pain shot from head to toe and hand to hand. My heart fluttered. My vision dimmed. I couldn't take it for another second. I would pass out for sure.

A pair of figures ran close, too fuzzy to make out. Something slammed into us from the side, knocking us both down. I sprawled over Kelly, stunned. She moaned under my weight, lying on her stomach with her limbs splayed.

Strong arms lifted me to my feet. I wobbled, blinking as I tried to focus on the blurry faces staring at me.

"Are you all right?" a woman asked.

"I'm not sure. I think so." I stared at the violin, still wrapped tightly in my fingers. Whoever that was sounded familiar. "Is Kelly all right?"

"She's a little frayed, but she'll be fine. You both took quite a jolt."

I blinked and looked at the tall, gray-haired woman. With bent brow and taut cheeks, she looked as stern as ever. "Clara?"

"Of course." A wide smile cracked her harsh façade. "I'm glad you still know me."

I shook my head hard and looked again. This time, everything clarified—my tutor, the telescope room, and three other people standing nearby. "What happened?"

"You and Kelly looked like you were trapped in an electrical field, so I tackled you." Clara brushed dust from the front of her sweater and slacks. "Not bad for an old lady, huh?"

I let out a laugh, but it hurt my chest muscles. "You should have been a linebacker." I turned in a slow circle. "Where's Kelly?"

"I've got her." Dr. Gordon walked Kelly toward me. With her hair thrown every which way and her legs wobbling, she looked as dazed as I felt.

"You okay?" I asked.

She pushed her hair out of her eyes, now glassy and bloodshot. "I think so, but I'm half blind again."

When I took her hand, her fingers quivered in my grasp. Since her vision had been restored for several hours, it had to be a huge letdown to lose it again. As I inhaled, the odor of burnt clothes and hair assaulted my senses. Kelly's hair looked scorched on the ends, so my own had probably been cooked as well.

Now that my brain seemed to function normally again, memories of our mission flooded to mind. "Okay, that wasn't the best cross-world jump in history, but we survived. We have to get going." I turned to Dr. Gordon, who now stood next to an unfamiliar man. Both were looking at a phone in Dr. Gordon's hand.

"Did you check flights to London?" I asked.

"We were just doing that." Dr. Gordon showed me the phone's screen. "Nothing is available. Our communications here have been inoperable for quite a while, so all flights have been cancelled."

"Oh, yeah. The whale-speak."

Dr. Gordon drew his head back. "Whale-speak?"

"Daryl's term for how you talked. But you sound fine now."

"I see. Yes, whale-speak would be a good description, but everything snapped back into place only moments ago. Analog communications are again operational. That's why we decided to look at the airline schedule, but it's doubtful that they will return to normal capacity anytime soon."

I ran a thumb along one of the violin strings. Mom and Dad's success on the huge violin must have restored Earth Red's communications, but how long would it take to get flights back on line? A few days? Maybe several Earth Yellow weeks or months? That would be too late. "So if all analog communications are on track, can you get Daryl over here?"

"I just checked to see what she was doing." Dr. Gordon nodded toward the ceiling, which showed the empty Earth Yellow telescope room. "She's not in the Earth Yellow lab, but I sent her an email letting her know that we can switch back to analog. The transport should be much safer now."

"She must still be searching for Amber," Kelly said as she looked at the image above. Her eyes moved from left to right, scanning the mirror. As usual, she was able to view Earth Yellow clearly, even from other worlds.

"Nathan," Dr. Gordon said, nodding toward the unfamiliar man, "have you met Daryl's father?"

"I don't think so." I extended a hand. "Nathan Shepherd."

"Victor Markey." Tall and red-headed, he reached past my hand and patted my shoulder. "No sense inflicting more pain, son."

Dr. Gordon pushed his phone into his pocket. "Victor has a plan that I think is worthy of consideration."

"You mean you know how we can get to London?" I asked.

Victor pointed at a lapel pin, a set of wings. "I don't know if Daryl told you, but I'm a pilot, and I know how to fly the big jets."

"She did, but where can you get one?"

"Well, considering all the problems with schedules, there are plenty sitting on the ground at O'Hare. Some are probably fueled and ready to go."

I furrowed my brow. "You want to steal a jet?"

"Not steal. Borrow. I think the airline company would beg us to take one if they knew what was going on."

"I can't argue with that. But what about security? Even with no flights, O'Hare's got to be battened down. We'd never even get to sniff jet fuel, much less climb aboard and take off."

Victor smiled. "No problem. I flew in to a small airport in the suburbs. The security people know me, so getting through won't be a problem. We'll fly from there to Chicago. With no air traffic, landing will be a breeze. Then just stick with me. I called someone I know with the Feds. He'll take care of the rest."

I looked Victor over. Daryl said he had lost his nerve after his brother died. He'd have to get some of it back to make our plan work. "So, when do we leave?"

"As soon as our airport transportation arrives." Victor withdrew a phone from his pocket and scrolled through the directory. "I asked Kelly's father if he knew anyone in this area who had a vehicle that might not raise suspicion if we stowed away inside, like a florist's delivery truck." He pushed a button and held the phone against his ear. "Yeah, Tony. Did you get hold of him? ... Great." Victor looked at his watch. "Did you give him my number? ... Perfect." The phone beeped. "Wait. That must be him now. Call you later."

Victor looked at his phone, pushed a button, and again put it to his ear. "This is Victor Markey ... Yeah. We're ready ... A van? What color? ... Okay. Drive around back. We'll meet you there." He slid the phone away. "Okay. Everything's set. Let's get this show on the road."

Clara pulled a wallet from her purse. "I withdrew some money from your trust fund and put it in this. If we ever find your parents, we'll just—"

"My parents?" I almost choked on my words. "No one told you?"

"Told me what?"

I took in a deep breath and spoke rapid-fire. "We found them. I thought Daryl might've told you about Mom, because that was a while ago, but we just found Dad recently. He was trapped in a cocoon in a spider tree, so we had to tear him out of it. And Mom was all but dead, so Scarlet gave her life energy—"

A light flashed at the center of the room, interrupting my report. A female human figure appeared with a bag dangling from her shoulder. Now wearing loose jeans over her bunny thermals, Daryl shook out her red locks and grinned at Kelly and me. "Good thing analog's working again. I saw what happened to you two." She pulled a phone from her pocket and turned it on. "Anyone got the time? It might take a few minutes for this to sync up."

Dr. Gordon checked his watch. "Four eighteen in the afternoon."

"Daryl?" Victor's eyes lit up. "Is it really you?"

Daryl gasped, then swallowed hard. "Yeah," she said, pushing back her hair. "Do I look that much older?"

"Yes. I mean, no. I mean …" He drew close and squinted at her. "What happened?"

"Oh, Daddy!" She leaped and threw her arms around his neck. "I missed you and Mom so much!"

Victor returned the hug, laughing. "You've been gone only a few days. Science camp was a lot longer than that."

"I was gone for years!" She pulled back. "Earth Yellow moves a lot faster than—"

"Better explain later," I said. "We'll have time on the way to the airport."

"We're all flying to London?" Daryl asked as she looked in her bag. "And I didn't bring a power converter."

"Yeah, we're all going, but first we're flying from a smaller airport to O'Hare. I'll tell you all about it in a minute."

Dr. Gordon sat in a swivel chair. "I'll stay here in case we need some kind of cross-world transport." He looked at Clara. "You?"

She nodded toward me. "I'm going to London. My knowledge of the city will likely come in handy. And I have friends there. Good friends who might help us."

Victor and Clara led the way out the tourist entry door, while I guided Kelly by the hand. Daryl followed, fishing through her bag. "I have the Earth Blue mirror, candles, and batteries for your IWART. Simon said that thing has GPS mapping built in. We could have looked up the points on that instead of emailing Dr. Gordon. Anyway, I played with it and figured out how it works. Then Patar showed up with your parents, and I gave an IWART to them. I sent them to Earth Blue fully equipped, including a new violin. Patar just vanished, but that was fine. Talking to him is like having a conversation with a snarling dog."

"Did you find Amber?" Kelly asked as we piled into the elevator.

"I followed her bullet trail out to the parking lot. She was trying to hotwire Tony's truck. She was so determined to find Francesca Yellow, I think she almost figured it out. So I just went back inside, used an office phone, and called Gunther. Good thing I memorized his number, too. Anyway, they all came back and picked her up, so Amber's going to help Francesca and Solomon Yellow at their foundation point." Daryl pulled up her oversized jeans and tightened an extension cord she had threaded through the loops. "Thank goodness for Gunther. That guy's like a Boy Scout. Always prepared. He packed an extra pair of jeans along with all that food. Boy, was I glad. I was tired of showing my bunnies to everyone."

"So they're on their way to India now?" I asked. "Flights are still running there?"

"Yep. I gave them the coordinates. They know what to do, but they'll arrive long before we get to London."

As soon as the elevator door opened, I guided Kelly out, and we hustled down the hall. Although she winced with every few steps and favored her wounded shoulder, she kept up with our quick pace.

When we arrived at the rear entry door, I stopped and peeked through the embedded window. An old white van had backed up to the steps, and one of its rusted double doors was open, as if welcoming us aboard.

"That must be our ride," I said.

Victor opened the exit door. "Let me talk to him first." He walked to the driver's side window and spoke to the owner of a burly arm resting on the frame. After a moment of conversation, Victor waved for us to get in.

I helped Kelly into the back, a cargo area with an old carpet covering the floor. Shelves attached to the side panels sat empty except for a few old newspaper pages, folded or wadded into balls. After Daryl jumped in, Victor followed, while Clara hurried around to the passenger side and sat up front with the driver.

As soon as everyone had settled, the driver started the engine and looked back. "Hey, kid," he bellowed. "I see you survived. That witness-protection program must've worked out okay."

I looked at the man. Even with the graying hair sticking out from under his Chicago Bears cap, it didn't take long to figure out who he was. "Gunther?"

He shifted the van into gear and drove away from the building. "I don't remember telling you my first name, but that'll do."

"How did you get in touch with Tony?"

Gunther took off his cap and scratched his head through his thinning hair. "On one of my deliveries to the Newton Walmart, I started wondering what happened to you. I remembered the house you went to, so I stopped by and asked the guy who lives there. He told me a pretty wild story. I'm still not sure how much I believe, but I gave him my card, and today he called me saying he needed a driver, someone who had a delivery truck. I was in the area, so I asked if this old van would do. I used to haul newspapers in it years ago. It's old, but it runs."

I picked up one of the newspaper pages and read the date: July 29, 1978. "Nothing wrong with this van," I said, smiling. "Nothing at all."

"Well, I hear you're in need of speed, so I'll do the best I can."

Once we had traveled well away from the observatory, Kelly and I stretched out as much as we could, while Daryl leaned against her father's shoulder.

I pulled the IWART from my belt, switched it to Earth Blue, and pushed the talk button. "Anyone there? Dad? Mom?"

I released the button. No one answered.

"Maybe the metal in the van is interfering," Kelly said.

"No. I just remembered. We have to be stationary." I called toward the front, "Gunther, can you find a safe place to stop, just for a minute?"

"No problem. There's a stop sign ahead, and no one's around."

As soon as the van halted, I turned the dial to Earth Yellow and tried again. "Francesca?" After waiting a few seconds, I whispered, "Solomon?"

In the midst of light static, a quiet female voice came through. "Nathan?"

I pressed the button. "Francesca, I'm just checking on you. Are you in India?"

"Yes, we're at a hotel. I thought I'd try calling you in the morning."

"How's the delay? Do you have to wait very long?"

"Oh, sorry. I fell asleep. What did you say?"

I held the unit close to my lips, hesitating for a moment before pressing the button again. "I guess the delay's pretty bad. We're just leaving for London, so you'll have to wait awhile."

"I understand. We're prepared. My father … Nikolai, I mean, came with us, so he'll watch little Nathan. But it has already been a day and a half since we left. Time is running out."

"We'll get there as fast as we can. I'll give you an update soon." After reclipping the IWART, I turned to the front. Gunther Red propped his arm on the seat and nodded in my direction. "Ready to go?"

"Yeah. Let's hurry."

While we rattled along, I explained everything I could remember from our adventures. Although Clara asked a hundred questions, and Victor added several more, Gunther never said a word. He laughed from time to time when I described Gunther Yellow's actions, especially when he took out the murderer in Francesca's room and wielded a tire iron when he thought I was a kidnapper.

I had barely finished the story when we pulled into the nearly empty airport parking lot. Daryl's father opened the rear door and helped her and Kelly get out.

"I'll drive around until I see a plane take off," Gunther said. "You have my number if you need me."

I reached over the back of the seat and shook Gunther's hand. Although the muscular driver's grip hurt like crazy, it was worth it. "Thanks for everything. For what you did in this world and in the other one."

Gunther smiled. "My pleasure. If it wasn't for all the crazy stuff going on, I wouldn't have believed a word of it. But it actually all kind of makes sense."

Again leading Kelly by the hand, I followed Victor into the terminal building, while Clara and Daryl tagged along behind me. Victor spoke to a uniformed man, who let us pass, and soon we were walking toward a small Cessna parked inside a hangar.

"My brother's old hangar," Victor explained. "That's why I use this airport. He rented it until he died, and I kept up the payments. He was my best friend, so it's sort of a sacred place for me. I can almost feel his presence when I'm here."

"Daddy." Daryl caught up and slid an arm around his back. "Nathan forgot to tell that part of the story."

He stopped near the plane and turned toward her. "What part?"

"On Earth Yellow I saved Uncle Harry's life."

Victor's mouth dropped open, but he quickly closed it and cleared his throat. "You saved his life? How?"

Daryl grinned and pointed at the plane. "Let's get airborne, and I'll tell you all about it."

"Okay," I said. "I'm going to check up on the other worlds while you get the plane ready." I grabbed the IWART again and pressed the button. "Francesca, we're at an airport, and we'll be heading toward London soon. Just checking on your time status there."

Francesca Yellow replied, her voice now more lively. "Hello, Nathan. It's nearly noon the same day."

"Okay. That's pretty fast, but not too bad. Any sign of Mictar?"

"No, but we brought Amber with us, so he isn't likely to come by while she's around."

"Amber? How did you get her through security?"

"We're living in the days before your nine-eleven, so it wasn't too hard. Solomon was able to get a passport with a girl's photo that looks similar to her, so we managed."

"Perfect. That should help."

"I'll try calling you this evening to let you know where we are on the timeline."

"Cool. Thanks." I switched the IWART's channel to Earth Blue. "Dad? Are you there?"

After a few seconds of silence, a crackling sound buzzed through the speakers, then a voice. "Yes, son. Thank God you made it safely to Earth Red."

"How's Mom?"

"She's fine. We managed to play a few notes at Sarah's Womb, but the ground shook too hard. We couldn't continue. At least twenty stalkers showed up, and Patar helped us escape through a hidden door in the alcove where the strings are anchored."

"A hidden door?" I glanced at Kelly and Daryl. Daryl rolled her eyes, while Kelly just stared blankly. "I wish I had known about that."

"Patar isn't one to dispense much information. Anyway, we went back to Earth Yellow, and Daryl gave us the GPS coordinates and the IWART. Before she sent us off to Earth Blue, she showed me the collision simulator. It appears we had some success with the violin, but those few days might not be enough."

"Any idea what Earth Red's delay in colliding means?"

"Maybe, but just a theory. The other two earths get destroyed and Earth Red survives, only to be taken over by Mictar and the stalkers when the collision breaks the barriers that are keeping them out. I think that's been Mictar's plan all along."

"Yeah. Probably. Anyway, we're leaving now for O'Hare. Kelly, Clara, Daryl, and me. And Daryl's dad. He's our pilot. I'll check in again when we get there."

"Good. We're camping in some woods close to the telescope site. If need be, we can be at the exact spot in less than a minute."

"Sounds like a plan. Talk to you soon." After I clipped the unit on my hip, I helped Kelly climb the airstair and showed her to a comfortable seat behind the pilot's. I slid in next to her while Clara sat across the aisle.

Daryl jumped into the copilot's seat and grabbed the yoke. "Let's get this bird in the air."

"Patience," Victor said as he grabbed a headset. "You know the drill. One step at a time."

She gave him a mock glare. "I thought you said this thing was fast."

Victor slid on the headset and shot her a stern look in return. "Traveling through hyperspace ain't like dusting crops, boy!"

While Daryl and her father continued to exchange *Star Wars* quotes, we pulled out of the hangar and onto the short runway. Soon we took off and climbed at a steep angle. When we leveled out, I tried the IWART again, but, as expected, it didn't work. I wouldn't be able to give or receive updates until we reached O'Hare.

After a short flight, we landed on a much longer and wider airstrip. Victor guided the plane toward one of the terminals where at least fifteen airliners sat at jetways. A few others were parked nearby. Not a soul stirred—no mechanics, no food service personnel, no baggage handlers.

Our plane stopped near one of the larger jets, which sat by itself well away from the terminal. As Victor walked down the aisle toward the back, hunched over to keep from hitting the ceiling, he said, "Be ready to go as soon as I give the word. We will be dealing with men who will be in no mood for anything but quick compliance." He pulled a garment bag from a shallow closet, withdrew a hat and dark jacket, and put them on, completing his pilot's uniform. He then opened the back door and descended the airstair.

Daryl climbed out of her seat and joined us. "Good time to check on the others," she said, pointing at the IWART.

"Gotcha." I pressed the talk button. "Dad? You got your ears on?"

"Right here, wild man."

"Any problems?"

"No. Just waiting for you. We had some concerns that Mictar might be around, but the cavalry showed up.

Cerulean's standing by in case Mr. Ponytail rears his ugly head."

"Perfect. Say hi to Mom for me. I'll call again when we get to London."

"Roger that."

"I'll check on the other Francesca now." I switched to Earth Yellow. "Francesca? Are you there?"

"Yes, Nathan. It's evening now of the same day. Solomon and I are having dinner at a restaurant in Agra."

"Have you gone to the Taj Mahal yet? You know, to check on the coordinates?"

"We found the precise location. If the coordinates haven't moved, we shouldn't have any trouble."

"Right. If there's been any shift, this could all be for nothing." After taking a deep breath, I continued. "I won't be able to call you till I get to London, so ..." I looked around at the three beautiful ladies, both young and old, staring at me. "So pray for us. We're going to need it."

"I will, Nathan." She paused. Then, her voice flush with emotion, she added, "With all my heart."

I re-clipped the IWART and reached a hand to Kelly and another to Daryl. Then Clara joined in, completing a circle, with Kelly and Clara in their seats and Daryl and me stooping in the aisle. "Things could get more dangerous than ever from here on out," I said. "The lives of billions of people are at stake, we have no idea if this plan will even work, and with those cultists probably guarding the spot and with Mictar around, our chances of survival are pretty much zero. So I just wanted to let you three know ..."

As I looked at the teary eyes all around, my throat tightened. "I just wanted to let you know that I love you all. Each one of you has saved my life more than once, even at the risk of your own. And now I'm asking you to risk your lives again. We don't have a supplicant watching over us this time. Amber is with Francesca, Cerulean is with my parents, and Scarlet ..." My tongue felt numb. I had to force it to continue. "Scarlet is dead. But we're not on our own. God has gotten us this far. I'm not going to lose faith now."

Clara gave me a firm nod. "That's right, Nathan. I'm sure I speak for everyone when I say that we're frightened, but that won't stop us."

As each of the others echoed her nod, I looked again at their faces — loyal, courageous, and passionate. I couldn't ask for a better team. "Are you ready?"

"Ready." Daryl extended her hand. Clara laid hers over it, then Kelly added hers, and I covered them all with my still-bloody hand.

Daryl shouted, "Let's kick that self-worshiping, pony-tailed, sanity-challenged freak show in the butt and save the universe."

CHAPTER SEVENTEEN

AFTER STANDING AND helping the others rise, I nodded toward the back exit. "Let's gather over there. We want to be ready."

Less than a minute later, Victor bounded into the plane. His face grim, he waved toward the airstair. "Time to get moving."

I led the way, violin in hand. When I reached the bottom, I looked ahead. About fifty paces away, four men stood next to a larger airstair that led up to a passenger jet entry door. Dour expressions complemented their dark suits, and open jackets revealed shoulder holsters. One of the men, a guy with a headset over his short gray hair, broke rank and marched our way.

Once we had all disembarked from the smaller plane, Victor drew close to me and whispered, "His name is Barker. Just stay cool. It's all under control. I told him what he needs to know, but nothing more."

As Barker approached, he pointed at me while looking at Victor. "Is he the one?"

Victor nodded. "He is."

Barker shifted his finger to Kelly. "I want her as well, but not the other two."

"They come together or not at all," Victor said. "I don't think the extra weight will bother our transport."

Barker frowned but said no more. He turned and waved for us to follow, talking into his microphone as he marched.

Victor waved at us. "Go. I'll be right behind you."

I led the way as we followed Barker. When he reached the other three men, he stopped and pulled a small plastic box from his pocket. "One of you has dog breath. Take a mint." He tipped a small piece of orange candy into each man's palm, then strode on.

As I passed the trio, I tried to read their faces, but they wouldn't make eye contact. The short-haired, clean-shaven men looked ready to chew me up and spit me out, more like marine sergeants than FBI types.

After climbing the stairway and entering the empty airliner, Barker stepped into the cockpit and grabbed a clipboard and its attached pen. While he jotted down something on the top page, I guided the others inside. "Just sit anywhere?" I asked.

Barker replied with a grunt, sat in the copilot's seat, and stared straight ahead.

When Victor climbed aboard, he whispered, "Anywhere near the front will be fine." Without another word, he entered the cockpit and closed the door.

I sat in the first left-hand aisle seat and faced the front of the plane, while Daryl took the window seat and Kelly the middle. Clara sat across the aisle and said, "Maybe you should practice something. This is all for nothing if you can't play your instrument."

With the violin and bow in my lap, I stared at the palm of my bow hand, still swollen and oozing blood, then at my left, also red and raw, though not quite as bad. Could I really play? Could I follow Mom's lead and call for that impossibly powerful passion that would overcome such excruciating pain?

I shook my head. "Not now. I shouldn't aggravate my hands."

Clara gave me a doubtful stare and turned to the front, muttering something about preparedness.

When two other agents entered, I looked out the window. The fourth agent pulled away the airstair while one closed the door from the inside with a thud. Without bothering to look at the passengers, the two agents sat in flight attendant seats up front and buckled in.

"Psst!" Daryl lifted her shoulder bag, slid out a mirror, then pushed it back in place.

I glanced at the agents. A half partition stood between them and our passenger seats, obstructing their view of Daryl.

Giving her a nod, I settled in my seat. Would the Earth Blue mirror do us any good? Could it give glimpses of the future or transport us somewhere if need be? Scarlet did that for us, but Cerulean might not be able to reach into Earth Red.

A click sounded from the plane's PA system, followed by Victor's voice. "We'll be taking off in a minute. You might want to use the facilities. You'll find one in the front and one in the back."

While the ladies took turns in the lavatory up front, I journeyed to the back. I used the toilet, washed my face, and looked in the mirror. With mussed hair, bags under my eyes, and whiskers emerging in the usual places, I looked pretty bad.

As soon as I sat down and we had all buckled in, Kelly lifted the armrest between us and leaned against my shoulder. "Better get some sleep," she said. "It's going to be a long flight, and you'll need your strength."

Daryl had already snuggled up to Kelly from the other side. Her steady breathing indicated that she had fallen asleep.

Settling back, I took in a long breath. The odor of sweat and dirt hovered in the air. Whether it was mine or Kelly's didn't matter. We were both a mess, and that was all right. After toiling, fighting, and sweating together day after day, we could stink together without concern.

I closed my eyes. As I eased toward sleep, I tried to remember the last time I dozed off. The crazy time changes, wild adventures, and constant shots of adrenaline had kept me going for countless hours. Now it felt like my brain was sinking and spinning in a slow whirlpool. Images of Kelly, Daryl, Scarlet, and so many others swirled and blended, then broke apart again.

After a few minutes, I opened my eyes. Although everyone was still seated, something was different—a presence, a touch, a smell. I inhaled. Yes, it was roses.

I looked at the aisle. A young woman in a red dress knelt there, her cheek against my arm. Her hair, redder than Daryl's, smooth and silky, gave off the scent of gardenias, mixing with the roses to create a garden paradise of aromas.

My heart thumped. How could Scarlet be here? She was dead. Or was this a dream, another realistic phantasm? Could I really tell the difference anymore?

I leaned toward her and whispered, "Scarlet?"

She jerked her head up and looked at me, her eyes widening with her smile. "My beloved awakes."

"You mean ..." I could barely squeeze the words through my throat. "You mean, this isn't a dream?"

"It is a dream, my love, and you have awakened within the dream." Still on her knees, she turned my hand over and showed me my palm—smooth, pink, and clean. "You see? This is not reality."

I opened and closed my hand without pain. "Okay. That's good evidence."

"Yes, and I have searched and searched for you in the dream world. At last I have found you."

"But you died. I threw your body into Sarah's Womb."

She lowered her head along with her voice. "I did die, Nathan. I gave my life energy to your mother and the power of my physical presence to you. You now carry my eloquence and my voice, though your gift of music has always been your own."

"So you're like a spirit? You can still visit me in my dreams?"

Looking at me again, she nodded. "I wanted to visit you earlier, but either you have not slept or you have been in other worlds."

"Both, I think."

She patted my arm. "But now you are here, and I can help you."

"Help me? Do you know what's going on?"

"Oh, yes. Now that my physical body is dead, I am much freer to view whatever I wish. I once could see your world only through a mirror, dark and limited, but now I can see anything in this domain."

"This domain? You mean Earth Red?"

"Yes, but I am no longer your supplicant. Although I once lived and breathed to serve you, now you are left with only memories and dreams. I can no longer show you potential futures through mirrors or transport you while you are driving on the highway or ..." She covered a grin with her hand. "Or change you and Kelly into safari clothes and send you into another world."

I smiled with her. "So no more transports of any kind?"

She shook her head. "Not unless I can work in concert with a living supplicant. We would need two mirrors, one on the origination side, and one on the destination side. That wouldn't be practical at all, certainly not for the split-second escapes you have needed."

"True."

"Yet, I can offer you wisdom." She straightened her body and unbuttoned the top of her dress, revealing a dark void. "I have already given you my heart."

I looked at Kelly. She slept soundly with Daryl still nestled at her side. Up front, the two agents stared straight ahead, apparently unaware of Scarlet's presence.

Scarlet laughed. "They won't bother us. They are merely part of your dream. Yet, when you awaken, you must be wary. These men are not what they appear to be."

"Then who are they?" I lowered my voice. "Why are they going with us?"

Scarlet looked at them. "I have not learned all I need to know, but if they are officers of your government, their words do not match what I would expect. One spoke to the other about Sarah and the foundation points, so I think they are well aware of the worlds invisible to this one."

"Cult members? Part of Sarah's Covenant?"

"I am not familiar with this covenant of which you speak, but I am certain these men have not been straightforward with you about what they know. I advise caution. You must learn if these agents are here to help you or hinder you."

"If they want to stop me, then why go through all this trouble to fly us to London?"

"An excellent question. And I would add another." She looked away for a moment as if pondering how to frame her question. Then she refocused on me, her eyes sharp and sincere. "Nathan, why would a friend stay silent when he purports to convey good news? Would he not speak of it gladly and not hide behind a mask?"

I met her piercing gaze. "I get it. If these agents are really on my side and trying to save the world, they wouldn't be so quiet and secretive. Something's definitely wrong."

"Do you really get it?" She took my hand and enfolded it into hers. "Wisdom often has many facets and many applications, my love. Remember what I have told you. You may well need these words again."

"So what do I do about those guys? They have guns. Even if I could take both of them out, there's still Barker to deal with. He's in the cockpit."

"The man you call Barker dreamed for a short while, and I peeked in to take a look. He was dressed in a grim reaper's black cloak. He saw himself as a savior, someone who benefited others by reaping their souls and taking them out of their corrupted world."

"A reaper?" I shuddered. "So he's twisted. A maniac."

"True, but not because he believes a reaper can be a friend of departed souls. A ferryman to paradise is like a rescuing angel. His dream version, however, cackled with glee as if enjoying the deaths of the innocent. He shields his conscience by talking about the greater good, but he merely feeds a god complex that enjoys wielding a scythe to shed a gallon of blood in order to preserve an ocean." She scrunched her brow. "I found it rather melodramatic, but he took himself quite seriously."

"Not to add to the drama, but this is my biggest concern." I ran a finger along my right palm. "Like you said, this isn't reality. If I'm supposed to play music that will set the cosmos in order, how can I do it when I can barely bend my fingers?"

Scarlet kissed the center of my palm. As she lifted her head, she brushed a tear from her cheek with her finger and let it fall on the spot she kissed. "I do not know, my love, but from watching you for so long, I have learned something about you, a beautiful quality in your character that you might not even recognize yourself." Her eyes wide and sparkling, she paused, apparently waiting for the obvious question.

I obliged. "What quality is that?"

She spoke the words with reverence. "You are willing to change your mind."

As her sweet breath caressed my face, I let her words sink in. I did change my mind sometimes, but it usually took a lot of persuading. "Well, maybe, but how's that supposed to heal my wounds?"

"Such willingness heals many wounds. It reaches out to everyone you touch and helps them see what real love means. Love has little to do with emotions, but everything to do with sacrificing yourself for the sake of another."

"How is that supposed to—"

"Speak no more." She covered my mouth with her hand. "For now, you must rest. I feel that danger awaits you when you arrive. London will be inhospitable, and the winds of chaos will surely bring you face-to-face with the pale beast who would destroy Sarah and the worlds that depend on her harmonizing presence."

Her skin felt soft and cool, raising again the aroma of flowers. As the images around us darkened, I whispered, "When will I see you again?"

Her voice sounded like a song. "Whenever weariness overwhelms your mind, whenever fatigue drains your body, whenever sorrows weigh down your heart, come into my world, and I will catch you in my embrace."

Darkness flooded my vision. A few seconds later, I blinked open my eyes. Jet engines hummed, and the aroma of coffee replaced the scent of wildflowers. I swiveled my head toward the window. Kelly and Daryl were gone.

I rose, set the violin on my seat, and looked around. Clara was also gone, as were the two agents up front.

Daryl's laughter drifted from the back of the plane. I walked that way, trying to steady my nearly numb legs as I rubbed my bleary eyes.

Near the lavatory, a curtain had been drawn across the aisle, blocking my view. I slowed my pace and looked out the windows. Fingers of orange invaded the purplish canopy.

The moon, veiled by an odd white mist, appeared to be twice its usual size as it glided along with the airplane.

As I approached the back, the curtain snapped open, revealing Clara. Her brow lifted, and she called out, "Nathan's coming."

Daryl peeked past her, grinning. "Sorry for being so loud. My dad and I are trading *Back to the Future* quotes."

"Your father's with you?" I gave Clara a hug and looked around the flight attendant's food-preparation area. Kelly stood at a counter pouring coffee into a large Styrofoam cup. "Who's flying the plane?"

"Dad is." Daryl pointed toward a phone handset attached to the wall by a cord. "He hasn't flown trans-Atlantic in years, but since he doesn't trust the three stooges, he refuses to take a nap, so we're making him some high-octane coffee."

Clara moved back and allowed Kelly to come through. "One cup of wake-up juice on its way," Kelly said as she squeezed past me and walked toward the front.

"Can you see all right?" I asked.

She glanced back, smiling. "No problem. It's kind of hard to make a wrong turn."

"Where are the stooges? In the cockpit?"

"Two are," Clara said. "The third is in the front lavatory. He's been there a while. I learned their names while you were asleep. You met Mr. Barker. The other one in the cockpit is Dobbins, and the guy in the john is MacKinnon."

"Dobbins and MacKinnon. Got it." I stretched into a yawn and rubbed my eyes again. "How long was I asleep?"

Clara looked at her watch. "About five or six hours."

"That long?" I laid a hand on my stomach. "I guess the growling should have given me a clue."

"We have food," she said. "Nothing real appetizing, but it'll do in a pinch."

I looked at my watch out of habit, but since I couldn't remember which world I was on when I last set it, the 6:15 reading probably meant nothing. "How long till we get to London?"

"Victor said it normally takes about seven or eight hours, but he's flooring it, so we have only about an hour remaining. Since we're heading east, we're gaining time fast. It will be morning when we arrive."

"I guess I'd better eat here. We won't have time to stop anywhere." I looked toward the front of the plane. Kelly had already delivered the coffee and was starting back, but she stopped at the lavatory and set her ear close to the door.

I turned to Clara. "How long has MacKinnon been in there?"

"Maybe an hour," she said. "We think he's sleeping. He looked really tired when he went in."

"Odd. He's supposed to be on duty."

"I told my father," Daryl said, "but he acted kind of weird about it, so I dropped the subject."

"I'll check on him." I strode toward the front.

"I can't hear a sound," Kelly whispered as I drew near. "Not even breathing."

I tapped on the door three times. No answer.

Kelly pointed at the "Occupied" sign. "It's not lit, so it's probably unlocked."

I pushed the door open a crack. Inside, the agent sat on the toilet, fully clothed. He leaned against the back wall, his head tilted and his mouth hanging open.

I stepped in, grabbed his wrist, and checked for a pulse. Nothing. His blue lips and motionless chest confirmed the truth. He was dead.

Trying to stay calm, I looked at Kelly. "Better get Daryl's father on the horn. MacKinnon's dead."

"Are you sure?"

"I'm sure."

She tried to look past me. "Are there any wounds?"

I opened the agent's jacket and checked his shirt for bloodstains. "Nothing obvious."

When I stepped out and closed the door, Kelly hurried toward the rear of the plane, touching the seats on each side along the way.

I looked at the cockpit entry. Should I knock? How could I alert Victor without letting the other two goons know what was going on?

Daryl jogged toward the front, while Clara and Kelly followed at a slower pace.

"Let's call from the phone up here," Daryl said.

Breathless, she picked up the handset and punched a button. A second later, her brow shot up. After clearing her throat, she put on a nonchalant expression and added a matching voice. "Well, hello there, Mr. Barker. May I speak to my dad? ... No, I just wanted to ask him a question." She leaned against the cockpit door and rolled her eyes. "Do you mind if I ask him myself? ... Yeah, it's personal. ... Thanks." Tapping her foot, she looked at me. "He said Dad was talking to Heathrow. He'll be with me in a minute."

The cockpit door opened, pushing Daryl to the side. Dobbins, his jacket off and his white sleeves rolled up to his elbows, stepped out and reached for the lavatory door.

I slid in front of the handle, blocking his way. "Your partner's in there."

"You sure?" Dobbins looked pale and weak as he glanced at the darkened "Occupied" sign.

"Yeah. I already looked. I guess he didn't lock it."

"I'll go to the back." Dobbins staggered down the aisle, bracing himself on a seat every few rows.

"Dad?" Daryl peeked into the cockpit. Inside, Victor and Barker both wore headsets as they adjusted dashboard instruments. "You got a second?"

"Not really," Victor said without looking back. He pointed out the front windshield. "See what we have to deal with?"

At the horizon, bright streaks of light shot up from two sources. To the left, at about eleven o'clock in my field of vision, the top arc of the sun appeared. At about one o'clock, another sunlike sphere rose. Moving faster than its twin, the second sun revealed its entire disk before the first had shown its top half, but it drifted off course to the left.

"Two suns?" I asked.

Victor took off his headset. "Apparently, but if it were true in reality, I don't see how our planet could survive either the gravitational imbalance or the radiational shock. In any case, Heathrow is reporting widespread panic in London. We don't have to worry about air traffic, but getting to Buckingham Palace could be a nightmare."

Daryl stepped farther into the cockpit. "Are we looking through a portal? Like, we can see the other sun, but it's not really there?"

"Precisely," Barker said. He pointed toward the left-hand window. "And we can see one of the other earths."

I squeezed in with Daryl and looked through the window. A huge sphere hovered in the brightening sky. Clouds partially covered blue oceans and continents of green and brown. "So is that Earth Blue or Yellow?" I asked.

"Judging from the rapid sunrise," Barker said, "my guess is Yellow. Our most recent analysis calculated a time-passage ratio of four-point-seven-to-one compared to that of our earth. Still, it's difficult to know. The other earth is not spinning at the same rate as ours, so our perception of their relative positions is confusing and perhaps skewed."

"How do you know so much about this?" I asked. "If you're a government agent, then—"

"Nathan." Daryl nudged my ribs. "MacKinnon?"

"Right. MacKinnon." I cleared my throat. "We have something to tell you."

Victor slid his headset back on. "Is it important?"

"Well," Daryl said, "it's a matter of life and death." She looked at the lavatory. "Or I guess it's just a matter of death."

Victor nodded at Barker. "I think you'd better see to that."

"Agreed." As Barker took off his headset, Daryl and I backed out of the way, joining Clara and Kelly in the aisle.

Daryl pointed at the lavatory. "He's in there. But he's no longer with us, if you get my meaning."

"Not unexpected." Barker opened the door, peered inside, and closed it. "Dobbins will soon join him. If you need to use the facilities before we land, I can move one of them." He pulled the box of mints from his pocket and shook it. "They're slow-release, but they always work."

CHAPTER EIGHTEEN

I BLINKED. "WHY DID you kill your own partners?"

"I don't need them anymore. Working with them was the only way to get this flight off the ground." He withdrew a wallet from his jacket and flipped it open, revealing an FBI badge. "Looks real enough to the unpracticed eye."

Clara pushed me aside and stood toe to toe with Barker, her hands firmly planted on her hips. "Enough of this twaddle. Exactly who are you?"

He rubbed his cheeks and chin with his hand. "I'll let you figure it out."

"Better cool it, Clara." I pulled her back and glared at Barker, mentally adding a gray beard to his face. Yes, he had to be the gunman who stalked us so many times, the Earth Red version. Although the police nabbed him at the Chicago drawbridge, somehow he got out of jail. "So what's this all about? Why did you try to kill me, but now you're helping me get to London?"

"This isn't about you, Shepherd. Never has been. It's to protect Sarah from an assault by Mictar."

"But we were trying to stop him, too. Why try to kill us?"

"You're one of the gifted who can contact the supplicants through the mirrors. If Mictar had obtained one of the mirrors you used, he would have reached through it to one of the supplicants, and the power he would have gained would have made him unstoppable. Killing you would have foiled his plan, but since you have successfully eluded him, and since Interfinity is at hand, it's crucial that we help you heal the womb from the foundation points."

"But why kill the agents? Weren't they helping, too?"

"Like I said, I don't need them anymore. And I cannot allow anyone to know where the points are. No one here is excluded." He withdrew his gun. "No one. Understand?"

I stared at the barrel. After we stopped Interfinity, Barker planned to kill us all. But what could I do? I had to cooperate. Otherwise billions of people would die. And he might kill Clara and Daryl at any moment since he didn't need them, or he could use them to put pressure on me later. "There's one problem," I said. "Mictar probably knows the coordinates. I took your Earth Blue twin's encoded card and a page from the Interfinity Labs report that had the points, and now Mictar has them. I'm sure he'll figure it all out."

Barker's expression stayed stoic. "With the cosmic fabric nearly shredded, those points are probably obsolete by now. That's why we brought the interpreter along." He waved his gun toward the passenger seats. "Strap in. We'll be arriving soon." He ducked into the cockpit and closed the door.

I picked up the violin, sat down, and laid it on my lap. The others settled into the same seats they had chosen before. The moment we buckled our belts, the plane tipped forward, signaling its descent. Victor's voice sounded over the PA system. "We'll be landing in about ten minutes, and we'll hit some rough air. Make sure your seat belts are good and tight."

I checked my belt again. Kelly gripped her strap and pulled. She seemed tired, lethargic. Ever since our return to Earth Red, she had stayed fairly quiet, lacking her usual spunk. The loss of her vision must have drained her emotional energy.

Kelly leaned close and whispered, "So after we save the worlds, he'll kill us."

I nodded. "No doubt about it. And maybe Victor, too."

"Do you have a plan to stop him?"

"Not yet." I looked at the cockpit door. Since we outnumbered Barker five to one, he had to have something up his sleeve, some card he hadn't revealed yet. "From here on out, we're playing it by ear."

The plane's descent steepened. After a few seconds, it dropped, then caught the air again and bounced. Daryl and Kelly grabbed an armrest and held on, while Clara lowered her head, her hands tightly clenched.

I looked out the window. The other earth had dimmed somewhat in the brightening dawn, but it had grown larger, now four times the size of the moon. Below, cars and trucks jammed roads and highways. But where could they go? Did they think the countryside would provide protection from the looming planet in the sky?

The plane began bucking wildly. It banked to one side, then the other, as if slapped by a furious hand.

"Where's the barf bag?" Daryl yelled. "I'm going to be sick!"

I reached around my seat, yanked one from the pocket in back, and threw it onto her lap. "Hang on!"

Victor's voice pierced the roar and rattle. "We have opposing weather patterns, and they're stirring up some violent clouds that seem to be converging on London. Odds are it's only going to get rougher."

"Never tell me the odds!" Daryl shouted. The fear in her eyes said she hoped for her father to answer with another *Star Wars* quote, but he failed to respond.

My teeth clacking with every word, I spat out her hoped-for reply, "You said you wanted to be around when I made a mistake. Well, this could be it, sweetheart."

Daryl forced a trembling smile. "I take it back."

Kelly's fingers tightened on my arm. "We made it through a worse flight," she said, her voice calmer than her grip. "We can make it through this one."

I looked into her eyes. Although still glazed, they seemed at peace. "You're right." As the violin bounced on my lap, I stretched my thumb to hold it down. "But I can't play Amazing Grace this time."

"Maybe not, but I can sing it." She tilted her head up and began to sing, "Amazing gr—"

The plane bucked hard to the side, thrusting her body against mine. I pushed back, trying to get upright, but the force was too strong.

As if recoiling, the plane rocked again and angled just as far to the other side.

Daryl coughed into her bag with heaving spasms.

"I'll sing it in my head," Kelly whispered.

"Great." I grunted out my words. "We'll need it."

Outside, dark clouds swirled, eerie and unearthly, almost alive in their frenzied dance. The ground drew close. The airport runway raced underneath. A wingtip scraped the pavement, shooting sparks into the air. The wheels banged down. Everyone bounced. When the plane's brakes engaged, we jerked forward. I clutched the violin with one hand and my stomach with the other.

When the plane slowed, Kelly flopped back in her seat, while Daryl crumpled the top of her bag. "Don't ever talk me into one of these adventures again," Daryl said. "If we survive, I'm taking up Scrabble. That's all the excitement I need."

As the plane taxied toward the terminal, rain pelted the windows. Barker stalked out of the cockpit, fishing for something in his pocket. "Word is that all roads are too jammed for travel. We'll have to go by chopper."

A gust pushed the plane to the right, lifting the wing. Barker braced against the lavatory door while still digging in his pocket. When the plane settled, he withdrew a small computer chip and pulled his phone from another pocket.

"This chip," he said as he slid the back panel off his phone, "contains the codes for the musical notes that program our interpreter. Although the foundation-point coordinates you acquired are recent, we have to be sure they're accurate."

After inserting the chip, Barker put the phone back together and slid it into his pocket. When we stopped, the engines died away. The plane rocked in place, pounded by the storm.

Barker opened the side door. Wind and rain swept in, whistling and swirling. He backed away and retrieved a large blue-and-white umbrella from the cockpit. "Time to go."

"I need something to protect the violin," I said.

"Check the overhead bin."

I popped open the compartment, pulled out a dark blue blanket, and peered through the window as I wrapped the violin. Two men pushed a stairway toward the plane. Nearby, a large helicopter sat on the tarmac, its blades slowly turning above its camouflage-coated frame. "C'mon," I said, reaching for Kelly's hand. "We're in for another rough ride, but we don't have much choice."

Daryl grabbed two more barf bags from the backs of other seats. "I might need these."

Barker handed me the umbrella. "One at a time. The guy down there will bring it back when you get in the chopper. No use hurrying. I have to make some calls."

As I took the umbrella, I looked at Kelly. "I'll see you in a minute."

She gave me a tight-lipped smile and nodded.

Tucking the covered violin under my arm, I stepped onto the staircase and opened the umbrella. Cold wind beat against it with wet slaps and knifed through my sweatshirt. I hustled down the stairs and toward the helicopter. As I ducked under the blades, they slung water and stirred the wet air into swirling mist.

I handed the umbrella to a tall, skinny man wearing fatigues and climbed aboard. A helmeted pilot sat up front, staying quiet as he jotted something on a clipboard.

I snatched the IWART from my belt, tuned it to Earth Yellow, and ducked out of the pilot's sight, whispering, "Francesca, are you there?"

"Yes, Nathan. Oh, thank God you called. It's the final day, and we can see another earth in the sky. Everyone is panicking."

"Same here. I'm in London, but I still have to take a helicopter to Buckingham Palace. A storm's howling, so we might get delayed."

"I will pray for safety and speed."

"And to get us out of a jam. We're kind of at the mercy of an assassin who plans to kill us when the job's done."

Francesca said nothing for a moment, then whispered, "Amber wants to speak to you."

"Amber?" I cleared my throat and tried to calm my nerves. Whatever Amber had to say would probably rattle me again. "Okay. Put her on."

A quiet voice lilted from the tiny speaker. "Nathan?"

"Yes, Amber. I'm here."

"Nathan, I heard what you said about the assassin. This healing of the cosmos might well cost the lives of a number of sacrificial souls. Do not fear the path of martyrdom. Many great men and women have died to save countless others. That is what heroes do." A pause ensued, then her voice returned, firm and steady. "And that is what you are."

Her words felt like pure warmth, a source of strength that simmered deep within. I held down the button for a few seconds as I fought off a choking sob. "Thank you, Amber. Your faith in me means a whole lot."

I released the button. After another moment of silence, Francesca spoke again. "I will talk to you soon. Take care."

Again fighting tears, I pressed the button once more. "I love you, Francesca."

This time when I released the button, the pause seemed interminable. Had she heard me? Finally, her sweet voice came through loud and clear. "I love you, too, Nathan. If I don't see you again on one of these earths, I will see you in heaven."

Kelly climbed aboard, brushing water off her pants as she sat next to me. "Good thing this helicopter's big," she said as she buckled her belt. "In the rain, my eyesight is worse than ever."

Trying to shove down my emotions, I switched to the Earth Blue setting. "Yeah. Good thing."

She touched my shoulder. "You okay?"

"Not really, but I'll be all right." I buckled my belt and pressed the IWART's talk button, again keeping it out of the pilot's view. "Dad, are you there?"

I waited through a few seconds of silence before trying again. "Dad? Mom? Either of you there?"

No one replied. I left the IWART on the blue channel and reclipped it. "I don't get it. They wouldn't leave their unit with no one listening."

"You're right," Kelly said.

"Brrr!" Daryl hopped into the helicopter, sat on a bench opposite Kelly and me, and buckled up. She shook her hair out, slinging droplets all around. As she pulled her wet, oversized pant legs away from her skin, she nodded toward the door. "Clara's on her way. I figured this operation was taking too long, so I bolted for the chopper without the umbrella."

Soon, Clara joined us, along with Barker, who sat up front with the pilot while Clara slid onto the bench next to Daryl. The blades whipped against the wind, and the engine raised a racket, making it impossible to converse.

The helicopter lifted off and immediately surged to the side. Daryl reached across the gap between the benches and took my hand. "Not to be forward or anything," she shouted, "but I could use a little old-fashioned comfort right now."

I patted the bench at my side. "We have more seatbelts." I had to yell just to hear my own voice. "Wait for a lull in the turbulence and jump across."

"Cancel the waiting." She unlatched her belt, leaped to my bench, and buckled in, then hooked her arm around mine and pressed close. "My father has to stay in the airplane," she said directly into my ear. "I saw him for only a couple of seconds. He said not to worry about him, but …" Her voice took on a tremor. "Nathan, I don't know what I would do without him."

I tightened my arm around Daryl's and whispered into her ear. "Your father did what heroes do. I think he'll be fine, though. No one told him where the foundation points are."

"You're right. That helps." Daryl kissed my cheek. "You're amazing, Nathan. That's all I have to say."

Kelly grasped my arm from the other side and leaned her head against my shoulder. The warmth of both girls' bodies felt good—soothing and filled with love. Clara looked on from the opposite bench and gave me a firm nod.

I nodded in return. We had each other. And we had Mom, Dad, and Francesca Yellow on our side, as well as the supplicants, both living and dead. That was enough. We could do this.

After several more minutes of rough flying, the helicopter descended toward a green lawn. The rain had stopped, but bending trees at the lawn's border gave notice that the wind still howled outside.

Familiar buildings stood in view, including Big Ben and Parliament. I had visited London twice with Clara and enjoyed the sights, but as the buildings sank out of view, my own sinking feeling set in, as if the weight of this city and three worlds sat on my shoulders. My confidence took a nosedive.

When we landed, Barker jumped out and opened the passenger door. "Get out," he said over the wind. "The London police are cooperating by cordoning off the area, but I don't know how long they'll believe that a boy with a violin is going to save the world."

"I'm not sure I believe it myself." Carrying the violin, I jumped from the helicopter into a ferocious gale. Above, the clouds had cleared, revealing again the earth hovering in the northern sky, now at least twenty times bigger than the moon.

Kelly and Daryl leaped out and splashed to the grass beside me. Daryl pointed southward. "Looks like the squeeze is on."

In that direction, another earth loomed over the horizon, not quite as big. "We're on Earth Red," I said. "The other earths are supposed to miss us."

Barker pulled out his cell phone and looked at it. "What makes you think that?"

"I watched a simulation at Interfinity Labs on Earth Yellow. It showed Blue and Yellow colliding and Red skipping past them."

"Don't count on it. The paths shift all the time. There's plenty of dissonance going on to bring Earth Red back into a collision course."

While I helped Clara get off the helicopter, Barker punched in a few numbers and put the phone to his ear. After a few seconds, he shouted, "We're here. Have you detected any shifts? ... All right. We'll use the girl to update the points."

"Who are you talking to?" I asked.

Barker pressed a button on his phone. "A member of my group."

"Are you going to kill him, too?"

"He will be the one survivor who carries on our work."

I pulled the blanket off the violin. "So you're planning to die?"

Barker sneered. "I see that logic is one of your specialties. Now shut up a minute while I get my phone ready to translate the codes into notes."

A fresh blast of air signaled the helicopter's departure as it lifted and rose into the gale. Kelly and Daryl pushed back their whipping hair, and Clara turned away from the gusts. Soon, the five of us stood alone.

While Barker tapped on his phone's screen, I turned slowly in place. Buckingham Palace sat at the far end of the pristine lawn, and a pond bordered the grass on the opposite side. A few trees stood about, all thrashing in the cold wind.

In the distance, ropes spanned the streets, and uniformed officers stood guard at intervals along the boundary. Hundreds of people bent over the lines, trying to catch a view of the happenings on the palace lawn.

Above, the two earths continued to rise, growing larger by the second. It seemed that if they kept the same heading, they would collide at the top of the sky. Not physically, of course, or the gravitational pull would have already forced all three worlds to zoom together at breakneck speed. This collision would be different. But how?

A chill crawled across my body along with a foreboding heaviness. I searched the trees for Mictar but found no signs of him. I pulled the IWART from my belt and gestured for my three companions to come together. When they gathered,

I lifted the device and showed Daryl the coordinates. "Are these right for the Earth Red foundation point?"

Holding her hair back again, she squinted at the numbers. "North, fifty-one point five zero zero; west, zero point one four six." She looked up at me. "Yep. He deposited us right on the money."

In the sky, the two earths moved ever closer together. The distance separating them was now less than the diameter of either one. "Okay. Let's get on with it." My own words sounded hollow. This was like taking a final exam I hadn't studied for. How could I possibly pull this off with wounded hands?

Clara withdrew a notepad and pen from her purse. "I'm ready to record the new coordinates."

Barker extended the phone toward Kelly. The speaker played a string of notes, the musical key that had programmed her brain earlier.

She bent closer to it, but after a few seconds she shook her head. "It's too windy," she shouted. "I'll have to hold it up to my ear."

Just as Barker laid the phone in Kelly's hand, he jerked it back and drew his gun, his eyes wary.

"What's wrong?" I asked.

"I saw something." A black streak splashed against his chest, and a second struck his forehead. About a hundred feet away, Mictar stalked toward us, one hand carrying his black violin and bow, the other poised to strike again.

CHAPTER NINETEEN

BARKER FIRED HIS gun—once, twice, a third time. With each bullet's impact, Mictar grimaced. Dark blood dampened one sleeve and a pant leg, and a red streak marred his cheek. Still, he marched on.

With steam rising from the blackness cooking his skin, Barker fired more rounds. Mictar doubled over and thrust out an arm. A new bolt shot from his palm, smaller and slower. It splashed into Barker's face and covered his eyes.

Like a furious bull, Barker charged blindly, tackled Mictar, and sent them both sliding across the grass. When their momentum stopped, Mictar wrapped his legs around Barker's head and twisted his body, making Barker's neck snap. Mictar then crawled on hands and knees until he collapsed several feet away.

I ran to Barker, knelt at his side, and whispered, "Can you hear me?"

He rasped, "Take the phone. Push ... star seven seven seven ... to get the music."

I pried the phone from underneath his hand. "Anything else?"

He panted, "Save the world ... Shepherd ... I failed." He let out a long breath and said no more.

I checked his pulse. He was dead. I glanced at Mictar. He lay on his stomach, apparently breathing but out of commission for now. I had to get to work while I had the chance.

I hurried to Kelly, pressed the code sequence on the phone, and pushed it into her hands. "I dialed star seven seven seven to start the music. Barker's dead. Mictar's wounded. I don't think he can attack with that black stuff. He has to heal and recharge. But I'll stand guard while you listen."

"Okay. Keep me up to date." Kelly lifted the phone to her ear. Clara and Daryl stood close to her, Clara poised to write in her notebook.

A gun lay on the ground near my feet. I set the violin and bow down and picked it up — Barker's semiautomatic. I walked closer to Mictar and stood between him and the ladies. Now on his knees, he glared at me but stayed silent. I checked the gun's chamber — empty. Mictar wasn't the only one out of ammo, but he didn't know that.

Keeping the gun trained on him, I grabbed the IWART, pressed the button, and shouted into it. "Dad, Mom, are you there?"

A stream of static buzzed through the speaker along with a garbled voice. "I'm here, son. Your mother is at the foundation point."

I shouted again, still competing with the roaring wind. "We're getting new numbers. Hang on."

"Understood. I'll stand by for your instructions."

I switched to Earth Yellow. "Francesca, can you hear me?" I waited while looking up at the converging planets. Mom stood on one of the spinning spheres, her twin on the other, both with violin and bow at the ready. Would anyone on those worlds ever believe that two women with violins were their only hope for survival?

Francesca Yellow's voice came through the IWART's speaker. "Nathan, I'm sorry I couldn't answer right away.

Solomon is hurt. He had to fight off some local guards, and one of them shot him."

I cringed. "How bad is it?"

"I don't know. It's a chest wound. The bleeding's pretty bad, but he's conscious. When the guards saw the earths in the sky, they panicked and ran, so they won't bother us anymore, but we have no way to call for help."

"Give him the IWART. You have to play, and I'll pass along the new coordinates when we get them."

"That's exactly what Solomon said." Francesca's voice faltered. "He's willing to die to protect me."

My throat pinched my voice into a squeak. "That's what heroes do, Francesca."

A moment later, Solomon Yellow spoke, his voice strained and shaky. "Nathan, Francesca's ready to play the key. I'll await your instructions."

In the sky, a jagged green streak ran between the two earths, its endpoints hovering just above the surfaces. An orange streak materialized over our heads and extended from our earth to the one in the sky to our right. Then a purple streak did the same between us and the earth to our left, creating a triangle, one corner pointing at each world, though the two sides that converged at Earth Red didn't quite meet. A gap of about fifty feet separated the two endpoints, both hovering about a hundred feet over our heads.

At the center of the triangle, a black mass appeared and expanded toward the sides. The wind calmed. The air felt eerily alive, as if every particle carried an electrostatic charge. As the sky darkened, screams erupted. The crowd broke through the blockade and scattered. A cacophony of police whistles and car horns filled the air.

When Kelly finished interpreting, Daryl grabbed the notebook from Clara and called out, "We have the coordinates. We're close, but I'm not sure how close."

Again keeping the gun aimed at Mictar, I backed up to Daryl and gave her the IWART. "Find the spot. Tell the others their coordinates, and make sure they start playing. I'll stay here to keep Mictar where he is. I'll join you as soon as I can."

"Gotcha, boss."

Daryl and Clara walked around the lawn, alternately looking at the IWART and Clara's notes while Kelly stayed at my side.

Mictar struggled to his feet. The wound on his face had cleared, though blood oozed through his shirt near his waist. Since he was strengthening, he might soon use his power again. Bullets didn't seem able to kill him, but they did slow him down. My bluff had to continue.

Kelly blinked. "I see colors. Orange and purple. And something black."

"You see streaks in the sky." The endpoints of the triangle's two sides descended, now no more than fifty feet in the air and a few feet apart as they hovered over a section of the lawn closer to the palace. The central black mass had expanded to the lines, filling the triangle. "I'm guessing Sarah's trying to find the foundation point, like she has to set an anchor to keep the earths apart."

Holding a hand over his stomach, Mictar sneered. "Pitiful! Sarah calls for healing from a quack who doesn't even know her illness." He straightened and pointed his violin bow at me. "Go ahead and try, fiddle boy. Play the magic song and see if your bloody hands can heal Sarah's wounds."

I looked at my palms again. They were more blistered and raw than ever, incapable of playing even a simple tune, much less my part in a world-saving performance.

"And don't forget," Mictar continued as he waved his black violin, "I will be here to corrupt every note you play."

I extended the gun. "Leave the area. Now."

"Go ahead. Shoot. Even if you empty that gun into me, I will recover. You cannot kill one of my kind with a weapon like that."

I pushed the gun into my pocket, picked up the violin and bow, and looped my arm through Kelly's. "Let's catch up with Daryl and Clara." We turned and ran.

When we reached Daryl and Clara, Daryl pointed at the ground. "I think this is the spot. Earth Blue's numbers changed a bit, so your parents are hiking to the right location, and Earth Yellow's changed but not as much. I couldn't get hold of Solomon Yellow to let him know."

I looked up. We stood directly under the triangle's corner, the sides' endpoints still not touching each other. "Keep trying."

I lifted the violin and bow into playing position, but even curling my hand around the bow sent horrific pain up my arm, and pressing my fingers against the strings did the same. I couldn't play this thing. It was impossible.

After turning the switch to the Earth Yellow position, Daryl raised the IWART to her lips. "Yo! Solomon! Got your ears on?"

The unit emitted low static and nothing else.

Kelly pointed at it. "Call the observatory and see if anyone's heard from them."

"Good idea, Miss Interpreter." Daryl set the switch to Earth Red. "Dr. Gordon. Can you hear me?"

After a few seconds, a breathless man replied. "Yes, Daryl. I'm glad you called. Tony of Earth Yellow has been in contact with Solomon Yellow by mobile phone. Solomon's IWART stopped transmitting and receiving. He says a black triangle appeared in the sky and blocked out all light. The only thing they can see is the glow from the IWART's screen. Francesca is already playing Foundation's Key, but it appears to be making no difference."

"Do their GPS functions work?" Daryl asked.

"They do. Solomon mentioned that specifically. The satellite signals are coming through."

"Are you still in contact with Tony?"

"Yes. The transmitter you and he put together is operational."

"Perfect. Get these new changes to them, pronto." Daryl looked at the notes Clara had written. "Add point zero zero one to the north coordinates and subtract point zero zero two from the west coordinates. That should put them directly under their triangle's corner. Never mind what that means. Just tell them to head toward the triangle."

"Hold on."

While we waited, Clara nudged me. "Better start playing, or Mictar will beat you to the punch."

"I'll try." I gave her the gun. "It's empty, but he doesn't know that."

She nodded. "Understood."

At the opposite side of the field, Mictar strode toward us, his violin in one hand and his bow in the other. No longer bleeding, he looked as strong as ever. Whether or not he could launch his black streaks at us was impossible to know.

I took a deep breath. I had to go for it, no matter how much my hands hurt.

With a light touch, I pushed the bow against the strings and played the first note. It wasn't quite right, but it was close. My hands hurt like crazy, but maybe I could go on. Just as I pulled the bow back, the IWART interrupted, making me stop.

"Tony is passing the information along," Dr. Gordon said through the speaker. "And the earths seem perfectly in sync with time passage now, as if they've been linked together."

"Yeah," Daryl said into the IWART. "It looks like Sarah sent branches out to the three earths. It's almost like she's making a last ditch effort to get them to dance together."

The sky grew even darker. The triangle contracted, compressed by the force of the converging worlds.

Mictar, now just a dark silhouette in the deepening shroud, stopped and lifted the black violin. With his bow held high, he looked like a ghost, a havoc-seeking phantom of an orchestral opera.

Clara stood behind me and laid a hand on my shoulder. "You can do this," she said as she massaged my muscles. "Release these people from their prisons. Give Sarah the melody she needs to heal the wounds and call the worlds into their dance. Make that triangle strong."

Gritting my teeth, I tried again. This time the first three notes sounded fine. As they rose from the strings, they seemed to pop like tiny firecrackers ignited by the supercharged air. An electric shock surged up my arms, stiffening them. Pain roared across my palms, but I couldn't stop now.

The fourth note spewed flat, and the fifth died before I could finish the stroke. My heart thumping, I looked at Clara. "It's just not right. I have to start over."

Mictar's shadowed arms flew into action. The shrieks from his violin pierced the calm — angry, dissonant, hate-filled. As if set on fire by the mysterious air, strings of white sparks flew from the black violin and rose into the triangle. The sparks ate away at the blackness, making the triangle contract and the worlds drift closer together.

Daryl shuddered. "I'd better go now, Doc. We have a Devil-Went-Down-to-Georgia fiddle duel going on, and the Devil's kicking butt so far." She slid the IWART into her bag and withdrew candles and a lighter.

As she lit one of the candles, Mictar eased closer to us, now only ten feet away. The strokes on his violin raised screeching notes that flew upward like discordant demons with wings of fire, carrying new sparks into the triangle.

Kelly stood directly in front of me and gestured with her hands as she spoke. "Nathan, listen to me. God has given you your talent. You can do this. You can play through pain." She brushed away a tear and continued in a quavering voice, "Even if you don't believe in me, I will always believe in you."

Like a lightning bolt, her words shot straight to my heart. Heat boiled from within and surged through my limbs—pain, sheer pain. Lifting my head, I let out a guttural cry. Then, I bent toward my violin and played.

Again the first three notes sounded perfect. Sparks flew, red and sizzling. A swirling wind ushered them up into the orange and purple streaks, making them brighten. Above, the two endpoints drew closer to each other and to the ground, now almost within reach. Yet, the side endpoints on the other two earths stayed in place, as if unaffected by anyone playing the key on those worlds. The two Francescas had not yet arrived at the new foundation points.

I labored through several more notes. Each shot pain into my hands. Kelly stepped closer and spoke again, new fervor in her voice. "Roll the stone away, Nathan. Reach down deep and call forth the passion, the breath of God that heals the wounds."

Kelly's words were like magic, profound, penetrating. Was she interpreting my music? Was she reading my mind, plunging deeper into my thoughts than I could myself?

When I played a high C, the triangle's two sides converged into a point, knifed through me, and stabbed the ground in a radiant splash. A jolt throttled my body. Total darkness flooded the area, making the triangle's sides vanish.

Daryl's candle interrupted the blackness, illuminating her face, taut and wide-eyed. A moment later, our two sides of the triangle flickered back to life, both more reddish than before, lacking an infusion of yellow and blue.

Mictar's violin squealed somewhere nearby, but how far away? And what did this new development mean? Although our corner of the triangle had planted itself in place, how could I know if the other two had reached their foundation points? I had to keep the music going, push more energy into the triangle's framework, and hope for the best.

As I continued playing, the aroma of roses filled my senses, and the bite of cinnamon and vanilla laced my tongue. My sparkling notes cast an intermittent red glow over my hands before lifting toward the triangle, still barely visible in the darkness.

With pain scourging my mind, I stroked the strings with every ounce of passion I had. Mictar responded. Sparks shot upward, red from my violin, which strengthened the triangle's framework, and a jumble of red, blue, and yellow from Mictar's, which weakened the interior, furthering the contraction. The sparks gave away his position. He was close, almost within reach. He could easily attack me now.

High above, two streams of radiance appeared, bright enough to pierce the darkness. They poured into the triangle's sides, blue on one side and yellow on the other, intermixing with my red streams to brighten the framework.

Daryl pumped her fist. "Rock on, Francescas!"

Goose bumps crawled along my skin. Mom had arrived at the Earth Blue foundation point with her greatest weapon, and little Francesca, my darling from the Yellow world, had taken up her bow. The battle was on. Mictar didn't stand a chance.

I bent my body and dug deep. Heat flowed from my gut and ripped through my limbs. My hands felt like they were on fire, but I didn't care. Let the fire burn. Let the blood flow. Let the worlds dance to the unbridled music.

Red flames burst from my strings and shot into the triangle's sides. A massive streak of blue fire roared to join it on one side and a yellow blaze cascaded on the other. Darkness scattered. The lawn lit up in a frenzy of flickering, multicolored fireworks.

Within the triangle, the blackness spread and pushed against the sides, enlarging the space between the worlds. It was working. Sarah's Womb was healing. A new dance had begun.

Mictar's violin silenced. Something black splashed against my chest. Hot liquid covered my arms and hands and burned exposed skin. I dropped my violin. As if drawn by the light, the blackness lifted from my body and oozed into the sides of the triangle. Energy drained from my muscles, and dizziness washed through my mind.

Breathless, I fell to my knees. Mictar stood a few paces away, his palm aimed at me as if ready to shoot another barrage of blackness, but nothing came out. Daryl and Kelly ran at him and slammed him to the ground.

As they fought, I tried to rise, but the remaining black stuff anchored me. Clara grabbed my arm, then let go and slung the goo from her hands. "It's scalding!"

"Gotta help them." After pushing to a standing position, I shook my arms and stomped my feet. Most of the black stuff scattered, but instead of falling, it flew up into the triangle, adding more darkness to the closer two sides.

The dizziness fading, I spun toward Mictar. He held Kelly from behind, a hand over her eyes. As she struggled, he called out, "You will play no more, or I will burn her eyes out of their sockets."

"Kelly!" I searched the area. Daryl lay motionless nearby, but nothing I could use as a weapon came into view. While Clara rushed over to check on her, I glanced at the violin on the lawn. The goo had vanished. I could play it again if

I had the chance, or maybe use it as a club. Somehow I had to buy time.

Clara helped Daryl rise to a sitting position. As she stared at the IWART in her lap, she seemed dazed, her face marred by deep scratches and her hair matted by blood.

I heaved a sigh. "I stopped playing. Let her go."

"Stomp on the violin," Mictar said with a growl. "Shatter it."

"If I do, how do I know you'll let her go?"

"You don't." Light spilled from behind Mictar's hands. Kelly screamed and thrashed. He held on tight, his body seeming to radiate light of its own. "Do it now or she dies!"

I shouted, "But either way, she'll die!"

"She suffers more this way, and I will get stronger."

My only hope was to save Kelly and try to find another music source. Singing was still possible if I could keep her alive. I stomped on the violin. The wood cracked, and two strings broke loose. "Now let her go!"

"I will ... soon." More light flashed from his hand, and smoke seeped from around the edges.

I charged, grabbed Kelly around the waist, and pulled, but Mictar held fast. I shouted, "Give her to me!"

Mictar's face grew brighter. "She is no good to you now. She will be blind and helpless, an invalid you will have to feed and dress. She's as good as dead."

I peeled back Mictar's lethal hand, revealing Kelly's charred sockets, but I couldn't wrestle her away. "She's more valuable blind than I am with sight."

"That is saying very little." Mictar planted a foot on my chest and shoved me backwards. With my arm still around Kelly, we flew away together and tumbled across the wet grass. When we stopped, she pulled free from my grasp and curled into a fetal position, writhing and moaning.

Mictar's skin glowed white, and his eyes shone red. "The battle is over, little man. Sarah is now guiding the worlds into a deathtrap, thanks to your silence." He picked up his violin and walked away.

Above, the triangle leg between Earth Blue and Earth Yellow lengthened, pushing them farther apart, while the sides shooting out from Earth Red shortened, drawing us closer to the other worlds, or perhaps to a midpoint between them.

Clara dashed to Kelly and gathered her into her arms. Kelly ran her fingers across her charred eye sockets. "My eyes!" she screamed. "They're on fire!"

Daryl scooted closer on hands and knees. She grabbed Kelly's wrists and forced them against her chest. "Just relax, honey," Daryl said through a sob. "Don't touch your burns. Just breathe. We'll take care of you."

Kelly's torture stabbed my heart, but I couldn't help her now. I had to figure out how to save the worlds. "Daryl, call Dr. Gordon. We need a new simulation to predict the timing of Interfinity."

Tears streaming, she picked up the IWART and made the call. "Doc, it's me."

Dr. Gordon's voice broke through a wave of static. "Daryl, what's going on? The worlds are going nuts."

"I know. I know. Did you run a new simulation?"

"Seconds ago. Earths Blue and Yellow are rapidly diverging, and Earth Red will soon come between them. The simulation says that Earth Red will break the connection and thrust the other two away at a rate that would probably destroy them both. If, however, the connection doesn't break, Earth Red might draw the other two earths together and cause them to collide. Either way, only Earth Red will survive.

"Daryl," I said, "call my father. Get Gordon to call Tony Yellow. Both Francescas need to keep playing. We can't let our earth break the connection between them."

"You got it." She wiped blood from her forehead to her sleeve and turned the IWART's switch to Earth Blue. "I hope we can still communicate."

While Daryl relayed the message to my parents and to Dr. Gordon, I helped Clara lay Kelly flat on the ground and crouched next to her. She let out a soft moan with each gasping breath. "Is there anything we can do?" I asked Clara.

In the fading light of the dying fireworks, Clara looked at me with a mournful expression. "I don't think so. Her eyes are gone, but since Mictar's fire cauterized the wounds, she's not bleeding. She has burns that must feel like hell on earth."

"Yeah." I lowered my head. "It's my fault."

"Nonsense. Mictar would have done this no matter how quickly you broke the violin. He wanted to draw energy from her for his next evil act. You saw how he glows now, didn't you?"

I nodded. "So he's still plotting something."

"He couldn't have expected this development. This new dance. I assume he has to prepare for what might happen next."

Daryl called out, "The Francescas got the word. They're still playing."

I looked up once more. The triangle shimmered in the sky. The sides attached to Earth Red fizzled, and the two other worlds remained in sight with a bright connection between them. They drifted slowly apart, one angling to the left and the other to the right, while we approached the gap between them. "Can we get an updated simulation?"

"Dr. Gordon's running it now."

I sat next to Kelly and slid my hand into hers. She gripped it tightly, still gasping, still moaning. "Kelly ..." My throat caught, making my voice pitch higher. "I ... I'm so sorry."

She grasped both of my hands and pulled them close to her chest. "Nathan." She licked her lips, her empty eyes clenched shut. "Nathan, nothing has ... has ever hurt this bad. It's ... it's like fire in my eyes."

I searched the area for a police officer, but everyone had run away. "Maybe I can find a hospital. Get you a painkiller."

She shook her head. "Not you. I heard what's happening. You have to stop Interfinity."

"Then Clara can go. Or Daryl."

Kelly nodded. "Th ... thank you."

"You poor girl." Clara ran a gentle hand along Kelly's hair. "My guess is that the hospitals are overrun or not operating at all, but I have friends in the area. I'll see what I can find."

"Is it possible to get another violin?" I asked.

"Maybe. We'll see." Clara marched toward the edge of the lawn, calling back. "Don't go anywhere until I return."

"We'll do our best."

Daryl turned the IWART toward me. "We have an update."

Dr. Gordon's voice came through the speaker. "Earth Red will pass between Earths Blue and Yellow in mere moments. The connection between those two worlds has not strengthened, I assume because the foundation points have shifted. When Earth Red impacts the connection, I predict that a shock wave will strike our world. It will first hit North America before traveling around the globe and exiting on the other side. I have no idea what damage it will do, but it could be devastating."

My heart thumped, rattling my voice. "What can we do?"

"Daryl told me you don't have a violin, so I have no advice."

"What could I do if I had one?"

"You could play the key again to strengthen the triangle, but your foundation point might have moved so Kelly would have to get us new numbers."

I shook my head. "There's no way. She's ... well ... badly injured. I couldn't ask her to — "

"I can do it." Kelly pushed to a standing position and reached into her pocket. "I think ... the phone is ..." She tipped to the side and staggered.

I leaped up and steadied her. Daryl rose and helped from the other side. As we held her in place, she withdrew Barker's phone and ran her fingers along the screen. "I can't ... see to ... star seven ... something."

"Let me." I took the phone, pulled up the dialer, and punched in the numbers. When the music began, Kelly took the phone and pressed it to her ear, her hands shaking. As she listened, her quivering lips moved, and a bare whisper emerged.

Daryl pulled out the notepad and pen and set her ear close to Kelly's mouth. "Okay. Slow and easy, sweetheart. I can hear you."

Kelly gasped after each grunted number. At about the halfway point, she wheezed, shuddered, and coughed.

"I have Earth Blue now," Daryl said as she pushed Kelly's hair back. "Just one more set of points, babe. You can do it."

A sob pushed up from my gut, but I swallowed it back. Kelly was in so much pain, but that didn't matter to her. She was fighting through the torture to try to save the other two worlds, even though the Francescas had only the slimmest chance of getting to the foundation points in time. Without a doubt, Kelly Clark was my hero.

After another few seconds, Kelly breathed out the final number. Daryl grabbed the IWART and began relaying the numbers to Dr. Gordon rapid fire.

Kelly dropped the phone and fell into my arms. "Oh, Nathan! I'm … I'm blind. … This … this isn't a dream."

I lowered her to the ground and held her in my lap. What could I say? This was worse than any nightmare. It was reality with no way to wake up. I had no cure, no good news at all.

Daryl cleared her throat. "Dr. Gordon wants to tell us something."

I gave her a nod.

She held the IWART toward me. "We're listening, Doc."

"Nathan, Daryl, Kelly. Good news and bad news. First the good news. We managed to get the coordinates to both Francescas. The locations aren't far at all. Good thing for Francesca Yellow. She has to half carry Solomon to the spot. Anyway, both Francescas should be at their positions soon. The bad news is that we have now lost all contact with both Earth Blue and Earth Yellow. No more updates. And no transports. Nathan, your parents can still save Earth Blue, but they will be stranded there."

"Stranded? Can't we fix that? Eventually, I mean? Once the Francescas get to the new points?"

"I don't think so. You see—"

Static emanated from the speaker.

Daryl pressed the transmit button. "Dr. Gordon? Are you there?"

She released the button. Again only static crackled.

Something rumbled in the distance. Buildings toppled, falling into each other like dominoes as the noise rampaged closer to us.

I whispered, "The shock wave."

CHAPTER TWENTY

I GRABBED DARYL, pushed her down next to Kelly, and threw myself over them. Something thumped on me, like a ten-ton weight. Blackness flooded my vision.

A floating sensation took over. I opened my eyes. Light dawned to my right, though no sun appeared on the nebulous horizon. As the sky brightened, the palace lawn materialized around me. I lay sprawled over Kelly and Daryl, both of them motionless.

As I pushed to rise, my body stayed in place. Once I stood upright, I patted my torso. It felt solid, but what did that mean? Was I a risen spirit, or was I dreaming?

Daryl rolled out of her body, climbed to her feet, and stood next to me, blinking. "Are we dead, or what?"

"I'm not sure." I knelt and looked at each body. Everyone was breathing. "We're all alive ... I think."

"Maybe we're doing that dream-together thing you told me about." Daryl prodded my shoulder. "And if I'm dreaming, you might just be a figment of my dream."

"I can't prove anything until we wake up and talk about what we saw."

"Fair enough." Daryl looked at Kelly. "I guess being knocked out is the best thing for her. No pain."

"True." I surveyed the London skyline — normal, undamaged. My dreaming brain must have been unable or unwilling to create a picture of the devastated city. The thought of a toppling building crushing Clara made me wince. "I wonder if Clara survived."

"All we can do is hope." Daryl crossed her arms and scanned the city. "We're not very imaginative. Couldn't we at least conjure a tropical island? Or a ski resort?"

"Maybe our dreaming brains competed and settled on this as a compromise." I shrugged. "It's a mystery we'll have to deal with."

Daryl tightened the cord around her waist. "I'm still wearing Gunther's jeans, but that beats how I'm dressed in some dreams."

"I know what you mean." I looked again at our bodies. "As long as we're dreaming, maybe we can make use of it."

"How?"

"Remember I told you that Daryl Blue banged her head when she fell?"

"I remember. I'm kind of hoping it knocked her out. Can you imagine constantly falling or maybe being suspended in limbo? Since she's phobic about heights, it would be a living nightmare."

I raised a finger. "Exactly. A living nightmare. She couldn't hear us in Sarah's Womb, but she can hear us in her nightmare, a nightmare filled with tombstones."

Daryl's mouth dropped open. "Felicity?"

I nodded. "Think about it. When Kelly disappeared at the end of Felicity's nightmare, Kelly ended up in Sarah's Womb where we think Daryl Blue is."

"Brilliant deduction." Daryl half closed an eye. "Did you just now match Felicity to Daryl Blue?"

"No, I thought about it earlier, but I didn't know how to explain it to Felicity. It sounded pretty farfetched."

"It still is, but now's the best time to test the theory. Since we're in the dream world, we don't have much else to do."

"Right. We can find Felicity and talk to her, maybe somehow get through to Daryl Blue and help her wake up."

"And what about world saving?" Daryl asked. "Do we just forget about it?"

"Unless you have an idea about how we can stop Interfinity while we're sleeping, our world-saving options are kind of limited."

"True. And finding my twin could help. She's just as smart as I am, and that's saying a lot."

"Your humility is so inspirational."

She winked. "I've always thought so."

I crossed my arms and scanned the city again, looking for any sign of a boundary. "Since Daryl Blue is in the core, Felicity might show up anywhere, but our best bet is to go to Earth Blue's dream world."

"Through the black wall?"

"Beats wandering aimlessly."

"I guess we won't need candles to keep our focus on the real world."

I nodded. "We're dreamers now. We belong here."

Kelly sat up straight through the bodies lying over her. She looked at us, blinking her intact eyes. "What's going on?"

"We got knocked out. We're dreaming together." I grasped her wrist and helped her stand. "How's the pain?"

She blinked again. "Pretty bad, but I can handle it."

I gave her a quick summary of my Felicity theory and explained my hope to search the dreamscape to find her.

Showing no emotion, Kelly gestured with her head. "Then let's go."

"Do you know which way?"

She narrowed her eyes. "I see the black wall. Don't you?"

"No, just London."

"I guess you'll have to trust me. I had better eyesight in the misty world, too."

"Wait," Daryl said to Kelly. "What was the last name of our third grade teacher?"

Kelly squinted. "Harley. Why?"

Daryl looked at me. "She got it right."

"Oh, I get it." Kelly turned to me with a furrowed brow. "And your middle name is Paul. Do I pass the real-Kelly test?"

"Yeah. Sure." Although neither of her answers proved anything, I didn't want to push her. "Lead the way."

Kelly strode toward the edge of the lawn. When Daryl and I caught up, the city scene transformed into a grassy field with a solitary spider tree about a hundred feet away and an expanse of darkness beyond it.

We walked past the tree, careful to give it plenty of space, and arrived at the central core's wall. I searched the surface until I located a long, vertical crack. I pushed my fingers through it. The wall seemed far softer and more pliable than the material we opened in the other dream worlds. Maybe being dream people ourselves helped, or maybe Sarah's weakened state explained the difference.

After we wrestled the crack wider, I made a bridge, setting my back on one side of the fracture and my feet against the other. "Once we get inside," I said, "we'll push off the wall and float toward the middle. When we find Amber's vine, we'll follow it to the Earth Blue dream world."

"Which way along the vine?" Daryl asked.

"Not sure. If we get to the end and see blood on the wall, that's Earth Yellow. We'll head the other way."

Daryl set a hand on her hip. "Okay, let me get this straight. We're just phantoms, part of a dream, but we can break through that wall just like when we were physical. We're affected by gravity, but then we'll float inside that core like we're weightless just like when we really had weight. And to top it off, we can grab a physical vine with our non-physical hands and move our non-physical bodies by pulling on it."

I nodded. "That about sums it up. Dreamers seem to be able to manipulate things here and in the stalkers' world."

"Well, if that's the case ..." Daryl ran to the spider tree and returned holding the end of a vine. "To make sure we can get back."

"Good thinking."

Still clutching the vine, Daryl crawled under my bridge, followed by Kelly. Once they passed through, I squeezed myself out of the hole and joined them. As the opening closed around the vine, light from the Earth Red dream world narrowed into a thin shaft, now providing only a glimpse of Amber's vine in the distance as well as something long and narrow floating next to it.

After mentally anchoring my sight on the location, I whispered, "Let's go."

Hand in hand, with Kelly in the middle, we pushed off the wall and sailed toward the center. By the time we arrived, total darkness had enveloped us. I caught Amber's vine with my free hand and halted our momentum. "Do you have the vine?"

"Got it," Kelly and Daryl said at the same time.

Daryl added, "Give me a second to tie the vines together."

"I saw something else from back there," I said. "Now I'm wishing we had a candle or some kind of light."

"If wishes were wardrobes, we'd all be in Narnia." Daryl grunted. "There. It's tied."

I waved my hand through the darkness until it bumped against an object. Weightless, it bounced out of my reach.

"Hey," Daryl said. "Something hit me."

"Try to catch it."

"Got it."

"Can you tell what it is?"

"Wait a second ... Yep. It's the big bow Tony Yellow made."

Kelly sucked in a breath. "It fell into Sarah's Womb, just like Daryl Blue did."

"And now she thinks she's a helpless blind girl," Daryl said, "because she's helpless and blind in this place when she's conscious."

Kelly called out, "Daryl Blue! Can you hear me?"

Her words echoed, but no one answered.

"If she's unconscious at the moment," I said, "Felicity is probably active in the dream world. Now's the perfect time to find her."

We pulled on the vine and floated along until we reached the core's wall again. When I pried the hole open, enough light poured through to allow a scan of the inner surface. No blood. "This is the place."

Again making a bridge with my body, I helped Kelly and Daryl through. As soon as I pushed into the Earth Blue dream world, the opening contracted and closed around the vine once more.

Clouds rolled overhead. Rain fell in penny-sized drops that splattered across our shoulders and heads, dampening our hair. A dense forest of trees lay in front and at both sides with their gnarled roots erupting from the moist dirt. The moonlit sky gave us only a little illumination, though enough to get around.

Daryl pointed. "Tombstones, dead ahead."

"Interesting choice of words." A tilted stone stood about five steps away, several other stones behind it. A cemetery. Felicity's trademark. She had to be around here somewhere.

"Everyone quiet now." I led the way along a path of twisted roots. When I passed the closest tombstone, I checked the other side before moving to the next. Several oaks with low-hanging limbs and dangling gray moss cast humanlike shadows over the gravesites. As a soft breeze swayed the branches, it seemed that dark ghosts waltzed across their resting places.

"Shouldn't we call her?" Daryl whispered. "I don't think we have to worry about waking the dead."

I stopped and looked back at her and Kelly. "It's not the dead I'm concerned about. Mictar is still on the hunt for a gifted one."

"And Cerulean's looking for her, too," Kelly said. "We could use his help."

"I am here." Cerulean stepped out from behind a tree. Holding a candle close to his face, he stared at us with piercing eyes. "I waited in hiding until I was sure of your identities."

I gave him a welcoming nod. "We're looking for Felicity."

"As am I." Cerulean kept the candle raised. The flame burned steadily between his eyes. "You are not real. Each of you is dreaming. What help can you offer Felicity in this state?"

"Advice on how to help her escape from Sarah's Womb." I gave Cerulean a quick explanation about our situation as well as our Daryl-Blue theory. I finished with, "So talking to Felicity is the only way to talk to Daryl Blue."

Cerulean nodded. "We will search for her together."

"Do you have any news on my parents?"

"They are alive, though not in the best of situations. Your mother played at the new foundation point for as long as she could, but an odd bolt of light from the sky struck her and rendered her unconscious. Then complete darkness fell. Your father and I were unable to discern the meaning of the bolt or the darkness, so I suggested that he rest with her while I search for answers. I trust that the cover of darkness will protect them while I am away."

"Do you think finding Daryl Blue will give us any answers?"

"Yes. She is my world's gifted one. She has to restore the balance."

I nodded. Asking the meaning of his cryptic words could wait. "Then lead the way."

With Cerulean a step or two in front and the rain falling more heavily, we continued on the winding path, again checking both sides of every grave marker. Soon, a human form appeared leaning against a tombstone, female, but too dark to identify. Cerulean stopped several feet away from her and extended his candle.

"Can you tell who she is?" I asked as I joined him.

"Felicity. She is sorely frightened." He spoke through the curtain of rain. "Felicity, do you fear our approach?"

A weak voice drifted our way. "I smell death."

I stepped closer and crouched within reach. Her form became more visible in the dim moonlight. Her wet hair and dress plastered to her thin body, and her eye sockets still vacant, she looked as pitiful as ever. "Felicity, listen carefully. You are a dream representation. We believe your real self is named Daryl, and you are floating unconscious in darkness."

Felicity said nothing. She just crossed her arms over her skull-and-crossbones medallion and shivered.

Kelly and Daryl crouched with me, one at each side. Rainwater dripped from their matted hair. "Don't be scared," Kelly whispered. "We're friends. We're here to take you home."

Felicity sniffed. "Your voice is familiar."

I took Felicity's hand. "She's Kelly, your best friend. And you're Daryl. Haven't you heard that name?"

"I dream about being a girl named Daryl." She drew back her hand. "But it's just a dream."

Cerulean pushed his candle closer to her. "Trust me, Felicity, it's not a dream. In reality, you are dreaming now."

"I recognize that voice, too." Her face bent into a scowl. "The last time I trusted you, I fell. When I woke up, I was by myself again."

"That is because you allowed fear to overwhelm you," Cerulean said. "Now you have another opportunity to respond with courage."

"Why should I believe you? You think I'm in a dream, but that's ridiculous." She tapped a finger on the side of her head. "I know when I'm dreaming. I'm always floating alone."

I mopped my wet face with an equally wet sleeve. "Do your dreams ever change?"

She nodded in my direction, her stare vacant. "Now that you mention it, my most recent dream was different. I felt something weird with my walking stick, a tight rope. When I swatted it, my stick flew out of my hands. Then I woke up here without it."

Daryl tugged on my sleeve. "The bow. Tony's bow is her walking stick."

"So she's close to where we were," I said.

Daryl sat in the mud next to Felicity and hugged her from the side. "Listen, sweetheart, I need you to pay attention to my words very carefully."

Felicity blinked her empty sockets. A weak smile appeared, fragile but hopeful. "Go ahead."

"Pretend that you're sleeping. Getting ready to dream."

"Okay." She closed her sockets.

Cerulean began humming a gentle tune that sounded like a lullaby. As the song continued, Felicity faded until nearly transparent.

"Now," Daryl said, her voice soft, "feel your body. What are you wearing?"

Felicity touched her hip. "Jeans." Her hand moved to her chest. "Something silky on top."

"A camisole?" Kelly asked.

"I think so." Now feeling with both hands, Felicity caressed the skull medallion as water dripped from her hair to her fingers. "What's this?"

"You tell me," Daryl said.

"It feels like … a camera?"

"She found it," I whispered. "Daryl Blue found the camera. It can transport her if she has the right music."

Daryl nodded at me. "Then teach her how to use it."

"Right." I knelt directly in front of Felicity. "Can you feel something on top of the camera?"

"I think …" She fumbled with her medallion. "It's a flash unit."

"Can you find the switch to turn it on?"

"Here it is." Felicity touched the back of the medallion. "Something's humming."

"Perfect. Do you still have the phone you found?"

She touched her dress. "In my pocket."

"Daryl Blue found the iPod," I said as I looked at Kelly. "Do you remember which music transports to the Earth Red observatory?"

Kelly shook her head. "It's different depending on where you are. And I got the impression that the camera lens is like a Quattro mirror. It wasn't programmed by Gordon and Simon."

"But the Moonlight Sonata is consistent. It always sends people to the misty world. Daryl could go there first. It's already set to play it. All she has to do is turn it on. Then a flash of the camera, and she's there."

"But that place is dangerous, especially if she's only semi-conscious."

"Then we'll have to go there somehow and help her."

"I'm awake now." Felicity's opaqueness returned. She sniffed and whispered, "I smell death again."

CHAPTER TWENTY-ONE

"WHICH WAY?" I asked.

Felicity pointed toward her right.

Dozens of tombstones loomed in that direction, some small, barely more than a foot high, others tall and ornate, rising higher than my head. Anyone or anything could be hiding behind them.

I gave Cerulean a nod. "Stay here and guard them. I'll check it out." I stalked closer to one of the larger monuments, a head-high obelisk with a marble cross on top. Rain pelted the gray stone, making every drop sound like a breaking twig or the unguarded footstep of an approaching enemy.

Something moved ahead, a shadow on the other side of the stone. I crouched and skulked closer, glad now for the rain's concealing clatter. Pressing my back against the tall marker, I peeked around the edge. A humanlike figure stood nearby, holding a short stick in his hand.

I flexed my muscles. A surprise attack with a swift kick in a vulnerable spot would probably take him out, unless, of course, he was Mictar, but this man was too short to be the deadly stalker. Either way, I couldn't try to hurt someone without first finding out who he was.

Bending low, I crept around the stone and squinted through the curtain of rain. Now a few steps away, the man's white hair came into focus. In one hand he held a sonic paralyzer, and in the other, a small book.

I gulped. Tsayad!

The paralyzer flashed on. A red light pulsed at the top, and an ear-splitting wail rocked my brain. He let out a shrill whistle. Two more figures emerged from the shadows, each holding a paralyzer. The rods flashed on. Twin squeals ripped the air and drove horrific pain through my skull.

Another loud noise erupted to my rear, a deep bass that made the ground shake. Cerulean strode toward me, his mouth open in song. The notes varied, but they stayed deep, rich, and resonant.

The sound waves bowled the stalkers over. When Cerulean reached their prone bodies, he laid a hand on each of them in turn. As his song continued, they shrank into shriveled masses and crumbled to dust.

A stiff breeze swirled. One of the smaller tombstones lifted from the ground, followed by another. Weeds and turf flew into the growing cyclone, along with several trees.

Kelly ran to my side and shouted, "Daryl Blue is waking up!"

"I know!" I shouted back. "Where's Felicity?"

"Behind me. Next to Daryl."

Back at the tombstone where I left Felicity, she and Daryl held hands, both shivering in the cold monsoon. A powerful gust picked Felicity up. Daryl dug both heels into the mud and hung on. The ferocious pull dragged both Felicity and Daryl toward the central core.

I ran to them, grabbed Felicity's other hand, and yelled, "Listen carefully. When you go back to your dream, turn on the phone in your pocket, point the camera at yourself, and take a picture. Do you understand?"

She nodded, her eye sockets tightly shut as the needlelike rain pelted her face.

"Then, you'll find yourself in a misty world. You've been there before. You'll be on a walkway with colored mist at each side. Grab some blue mist, touch it to your forehead, and jump over the edge of the walkway. It will take you home."

"That scary jump?" Felicity's face stretched wild with fright. "I can't. Not by myself."

"Yes, you can. You're brave. You've already proven that. You saved my life, remember?"

"I think I remember." She bit her lip hard. "All right. I'll try."

"No. Try not. Do. Or do not. There is no try." I let go and nodded at Daryl. "She's ready to wake up now."

"Right, boss. The Star Wars quote was perfect." Daryl released Felicity's hand. Her mouth agape in a silent scream, she flew into the wind and rode the wet flow in a wide circle. The cyclone pulled in broken tombstones and shattered trees. Seconds later, the wind compressed into a tight funnel and spun toward the central core. Like a corkscrew, it drilled through the wall and disappeared.

With the dream at an end, the wind calmed. The rain ceased, and darkness flooded the area. Cerulean walked toward us, his candle revealing his location. "We should go. Other stalkers could be nearby. They fear me, but they might summon enough courage to strike from the cover of darkness."

"Right," I said. "Let's get out of here. Maybe we'll get a glimpse of Daryl Blue inside the core."

Cerulean turned in a slow circle, the candle dimly lighting his worried expression.

"What's wrong?" I asked.

"Do you feel the breeze?"

An increasing wind blew across my saturated hair and clothes. "Is a new dream starting?"

"Perhaps. We will know soon." Cerulean waved a hand. "Come. Stay close to me."

Cerulean led the way, while Kelly and Daryl followed. I trailed the group, keeping watch for any sign of a white-haired head. With every step, the breeze grew, though no new lights illuminated the area, and no fresh images rose from the mind of a sleeper in the real world.

Soon, we reached the core. A bluish-white glow dawned on a far horizon, making everything clearer.

Cerulean whispered, "Dreamers approach. They are friendly."

The ground transformed to crystal that expanded as far as the eye could see — no stalkers in sight. The breeze grew warm, drying our hair and clothes and chasing away our shivers. In the distance, a man and a woman walked toward us, both dressed in shimmering white.

As they drew closer, their faces clarified. Mom and Dad were coming, likely dreaming together on Earth Blue. When they saw us, they stopped several paces away and stared. Mom raised a hand to her mouth and spoke between her fingers. "Nathan?"

"Mom!" I ran and pulled them into a three-way embrace.

When we separated, Dad ran a hand through my still-damp hair. "Nathan, I wish you were more than a dream image. We never got to say good-bye."

"Dad, I am more. Kelly, Daryl, and I are part of a combined dream."

Cerulean lifted his candle, the flame undisturbed by the breeze. "I vouch for Nathan, Solomon Shepherd. He speaks the truth."

Tears trickled down Mom's cheeks as she hugged me again. Dad waved to Kelly and Daryl. When they joined us, our group hug expanded to five.

As we stayed in a tight huddle, Dad spoke with a somber tone. "Listen. In reality, Interfinity has arrived, and it's possible that Convergence has already begun. The three earths are in chaos. I have no idea what's keeping them from flying away from each other or colliding and shattering completely, but as long as we have even a thread holding us together, we have hope. I believe Mictar knows he has lost, and he is willing to let every world perish out of spite. But we can still stop him and Convergence."

"How?" I asked.

Dad's lips firmed. "Patar's solution."

"You mean ..." I couldn't say it.

Dad nodded. "But you don't have to do it. You have already sacrificed Scarlet. If we can get the other two supplicants and gifted ones to Sarah, they can fill her womb with the supplicants' bodies."

"So Daryl Blue throws Cerulean in, and Francesca Yellow throws Amber?"

"Right."

"But what if we can't get Daryl or Francesca there?"

Dad set a firm hand on my shoulder. "Then another gifted one will have to do it."

"No." I backed away from his touch. "No, I can't. When Scarlet died, I ... I ..." The words flew away. I had no idea how to finish.

"Nathan." Cerulean stood next to me, his candle again near his eyes. "Do not fear. The greatest of all sacrifices came from a willing lamb. Amber and I are ready to follow in his footsteps."

My legs grew weak. "I ... I suppose that's good, but we ... Kelly, Daryl, and I ... are unconscious in London. We can't possibly get to Sarah's Womb —"

A new voice boomed. "Yes, you can!"

Patar stood at the central core wall, his arms crossed in front.

A sense of futility deflated me. Yet another tongue lashing was sure to come. "How?"

"Your redheaded friend has a mirror, and you know the song that will carry you to my world."

"But we don't have a piano or an iPod or anything else that'll play it."

"You have your voices."

I gave him a skeptical look. "Our voices? I thought it required a piano."

"Not if it is done correctly."

"Correctly? The younger Francesca played it on her violin, and she's a virtuoso."

"Son of Solomon, it is not the perfection of the performance that matters. It is the passion that is birthed by the pathos. The Supplicant's Sonata requires the privation of solitude, the melancholy of loneliness, and the torture of betrayal. Beethoven experienced these trials, but young Francesca did not, at least not until moments ago."

"Moments ago? What happened to her?"

"Let us focus on your situation, not hers. She is out of your reach."

"All right, but who here has experienced those trials?"

"Certainly not you, son of Solomon."

I rolled my eyes. "You couldn't resist another insult. That's fine. Just tell me who."

"The one my fool of a brother labeled a harlot, the blind lamb who never leaves your side, though her faithfulness and loyalty extend far beyond what you deserve."

Dad lunged at Patar and pushed him against the black wall, a forearm pressed to his chest. "Listen, you arrogant cockroach. My son has suffered and sacrificed to a bloody pulp, while you just appear out of nowhere to stab him with insults, demanding that he do the dirty work you're too squeamish to do yourself. You talk about suffering, but you don't know squat about it."

"Silence!" Patar shoved Dad away. While Dad backpedaled, Patar raised a hand as if ready to shoot from his palm. "Solomon Shepherd, I resist the urge to strike you down because I know your heart is noble and that you are ignorant of my sacrifices. My stabs, as you have put them, were spurs to incite your stubborn son toward the right path."

Dad took a hard step toward Patar, but Mom grabbed his arm and pulled him back.

Patar looked at me again. "You have one last chance to do what is necessary to save all three worlds." He touched the taut vine, still attached to the nearby spider tree. "Even now only this bare invention uniting the dream worlds, which Amber and your friend concocted on a whim, has kept the earths from flying apart. It is strained to the breaking point and will fail at any moment. You must come to my world with all speed. Mictar will be waiting, so you will be in peril, but if you fail to heed my counsel, your deaths are a near certainty."

I gave him a defeated nod. "All right. I'll come. I'll do my part." I shot him a hot glare. "Since you're too squeamish to do it yourself, like my father said."

"How little you know." A tear sparkling in his eye, Patar set a hand on Cerulean's shoulder. "You know where to go. I will summon Amber to join us, and she will tell Francesca of our need for her to come as well. Time is of the essence."

I spread out my hands. "So we're in a huge hurry, but I'm unconscious. All three of us are."

Patar looked up as if scanning the skies. "Assistance to rouse you will soon arrive. I fear, however, that Convergence has already begun. We shall see."

I glanced at Mom and Dad. They were on Earth Blue. Younger Francesca and Solomon were on Earth Yellow. Convergence would kill at least one pair. Since Earth Red might be the only place that could hold survivors, maybe all of them would die.

The wind kicked up. Rain again fell, more like water pouring than individual drops. The dream world was fading, and I had to say goodbye. When I reached for my parents, a gust picked me up into a cyclonic spin. I stretched to grab Kelly and Daryl, but my hand merely slapped theirs as I swept past.

The vortex tightened and pushed me into the central core, then out again into the Earth Red dream world where it threw me to the ground. More water splashed on my face, and a voice penetrated my mind.

"Nathan, can you hear me? We have to leave immediately."

I opened my eyes. Clara knelt next to me. Scratches and smudges marred her face, and her gray hair flew in disarray. She held a large soft drink cup at an angle, water at the edge. I murmured, "Why do we have to leave?"

"To find shelter, if there's any left. I barely escaped a collapsing building a few minutes ago." She pointed upward. The two earths nearly filled the sky, separated by about half an earth's radius. Hundreds of fiery streaks shot between them, as if they were attacking each other with lightning. "They're converging. My guess is ten minutes. We're getting bombarded by fire bolts."

A streak burst from one of the earths and blasted the ground nearby. Flames erupted at the point of impact. The ground rumbled and shook.

I scrambled to my knees. Half a step away, Kelly and Daryl still lay on the wet grass, their arms looped together. I lunged to them and shook Kelly, "Wake up! We have to go!"

"I thought you might carry her," Clara said. "If she wakes up, she'll be in terrible pain."

"She has to wake up. She has to sing us to the misty world."

Clara blinked. "What? Sing you to the misty — "

"No time to explain. Do you know where the mirror is?"

"In Daryl's bag." Clara lifted a strap. "I have it right here."

Another fire bolt blasted only ten steps from us, scorching the grass. The boom rattled the ground. Daryl shot up, her eyes wide. "I'm awake!"

I pointed at the bag. "Get the mirror. I'll keep trying to wake Kelly."

"All I have for a flash of light is a candle," she said as she took the bag from Clara and opened it.

"We'll hope it's enough."

Still on her knees, Clara handed me the cup of water. "I was able to get painkilling medication, but it will make Kelly drowsy."

"Save it for later." I shielded Kelly's eyes and poured water on her face. As it trickled down her dirty skin, I looked at Clara. "Did you find a violin?"

"I did." She lifted a beat-up violin case. "It's poor quality, though. I doubt that it will sound — "

"Doesn't matter." When the water ran out, I patted Kelly's cheek. "Come on, Kelly! You have to wake up!"

Daryl scooted closer with the mirror in hand. "Kelly-kins. It's life or death. We'll all die without you."

Twin bolts boomed nearby. A third blasted into the palace, setting it on fire. Above, the gap between the two earths narrowed to almost nothing. The bolts shooting between them became a constant barrage of blinding flashes.

"Daryl, keep trying." I grabbed the case, opened it, and withdrew the bow and violin, a learner's model with scuffs and dents. When I curled my fingers around the bow, pain shot into my hand. As before, I had to ignore it.

With a light touch, I began the first movement of the Moonlight Sonata. The notes sounded flat and scratchy, but I played on. Since I had so recently heard the piece, the measures flowed to memory easily.

"She's awake," Daryl said as she pulled Kelly to a sitting position.

Kelly moaned, blinking her empty sockets. "Nathan, is that you?"

"Yes." I stopped playing and held her hand. "Are you ready to sing?"

"Sing what? I don't know what words —" She gasped. Her face twisted as she wrung my hand with hers. "Oh ... oh, Nathan, it hurts so much!"

Pain tore into my arm and across my skull, but I swallowed back a yelp. "Sing about it. Just follow the melody."

Heaving shallow breaths, Kelly nodded. "I'll ... try."

I pulled back my hand and began the sonata again, whispering, "Scarlet, if you can hear me, please help Kelly find her song."

With Daryl sitting at one side and me at the other, Kelly took a deep breath and sang. Each word rattled as if strangled and tortured.

The veils that blind our hearts and minds
Are symbolized by mists on earth.
When darkness shields our fleshly eyes,
It paints a portrait, dark and dearth.

Kelly gasped, then wailed, as if lamenting. She inhaled again and continued.

The blinders force our steps askew;
We bump and bruise our hands and eyes.
And shedding blood reveals our need
To beg for stripping false disguise.

More fire bolts crashed. Flames erupted all around. The ground trembled, now without ceasing as bolt after bolt pummeled Earth Red.

To heal our injured eyes and hands,
We step in time with borrowed song.

A song of heaven, sung in threes;
Uproot what blinds, the anchored wrong.

So dance in time with healing verse
And peel away the blinding doubt;
Your partner thirsts, forgive the past,
And let it rain to end the drought.

Flames encircled us, crawling closer across the lawn, now dry and parched, but we couldn't move, not yet.

To all who dance forgiveness steps,
The reaching hand, the tear-stained face,
Release the captives from their bonds.
Let love erase the past disgrace.

Kelly took in a pain-streaked breath. The sky turned purple. Wind swirled and howled. Above, the two earths collided. A massive plume of fire erupted at the impact point and began spreading slowly across the surfaces.

I sucked in a silent breath. Daryl stared at me, wide eyed, but we said nothing. I stopped playing. Were we too late? It wasn't supposed to end this way.

After taking another breath, Kelly continued, alternating between sobbing and laughing as she sang.

Ascend on high, O captive ones,
And rise above the solemn sound;
Your joy will make the angels laugh
And lift your souls to higher ground.

The mirror flashed in Daryl's grasp. The image showed the usual walkway, bordered on each side by colorful mist, though now someone lay motionless on the path.

Kelly fell limp into my lap. While I held her with one arm, I reached toward Daryl. "The mirror's ready. Give me the candle. You light it."

"Right here." The mirror on her lap, she pushed the candle into my hand and flicked a lighter. A flame sprouted, bending in the gusts as she set it against the wick. The little fire wouldn't catch hold.

"Keep flicking the lighter," Clara said. "Maybe it will be enough by itself."

Daryl did so, reigniting the flame again and again.

"Let me try." I grabbed the lighter with my free hand. Before I could flick it, a fire bolt blasted into the ground inches away. The explosion sent us all flying. We landed on a glass surface and slid several feet on the misty world's walkway.

With Kelly still in my arms, I climbed to my feet and propped her up. She wobbled, her head low and her eye sockets closed. I pushed the lighter into my pocket. "Are you with me, Kelly?"

She grimaced. "I think so."

Daryl slid the mirror back to her bag and knelt next to the body we had seen — a girl wearing jeans and a camisole. "It's Daryl Blue."

"Is she conscious?" I asked.

"I think so." Daryl waved to Clara. "Help me get her up."

Daryl Red and Clara each grabbed an arm and lifted Daryl Blue to her feet. She blinked at us. "What's going on?"

"We'll explain in a minute." I stripped off my sweatshirt and handed it to Daryl Red. "Here. Help her put this on."

"You got it."

I reached over the edge of the walkway and gathered red mist in one hand and blue in the other. After Daryl Blue put the sweatshirt on, I spread the blue mist on her forehead and red mist on Clara's, Daryl Red's, Kelly's, and mine.

The foundation shook, making us slide toward the edge of the walkway. When we scrambled back to the middle, the glass cracked. Ten feet behind us, the walkway began collapsing. I shouted, "Run!"

I scooped Kelly into my arms and leaped into a hobbling jog. Daryl Red and Clara ran with Daryl Blue between them, half dragging her. Surrounded by a riotous clatter of rumbles and shattering glass, we dashed through the fog.

My arms cramped. My lungs felt like fire. At any second the collapsing walkway might catch up and send us plummeting. With each footfall, Kelly grunted and winced. Her torture had to be excruciating. If only I could take her place, give her my own eyes in exchange for her pain. But I couldn't. All I could give her was my strength. To get through this. To survive.

We burst out of the mist and into the stalkers' central circle. The walkway behind us collapsed and crumbled, leaving us no way to escape.

Ahead, Francesca Yellow stood at the spot where the doorway in the floor led down into Sarah's Womb. Wearing jeans and a black T-shirt, she held a violin, ready to play. "Come," she called. "We must hurry."

The floor still shaking and pitching, we staggered toward her. On the perimeter walls, two of the earths had fractured into pieces, while deep cracks filled the third. When we arrived, Francesca played the first set of notes to open the door. Tears streamed down her cheeks as she looked at us. Between the first and second sequence, she paused and whispered, "Amber told me to come. My husband ... is dead."

The words blasted into my brain. My throat caught. No words could escape.

"Oh, my God," Daryl Red whispered. "Lord, help us, please."

Francesca began the next sequence, but her hand slipped. The note warped, and the lights reset. She dropped to her knees and wept. Her head bobbed as she moaned, "I ... I have to start over."

Kelly patted my cheek. "Nathan ... let me down. You ... you have to do it."

I let her slide to the tilting floor and guided her to Daryl Red. She and Clara steadied Kelly and Daryl Blue, while I shuffled to Francesca. I crouched and set a hand on her back. "The burden is too great," I whispered. "Let me share it."

Looking at me with tortured eyes, she transferred the violin and bow from her trembling hands to my bleeding ones as she whispered, "I think you're the only person who can."

I turned to Clara. "See if you can find some yellow mist for Francesca. It's her ticket home."

"Will do." Clara hurried back to the entrance, knelt over the gap where the walkway used to be, and scooped a handful of yellow mist. "Got it."

I lifted the violin and played the three sequences while Clara anointed Francesca. When the floor's panel altered to allow entry to the stairway, I returned to Kelly. Now able to walk, she held her own as I guided her to the opening, the violin and bow tucked under my arm. "Let's go."

We strode down the stairway in pairs, Kelly and me first, then the two Daryls, followed by Clara and Francesca. Light from below guided our path. Kelly and Daryl Blue seemed to strengthen, able to keep a quick pace, though they stayed quiet.

The end of the stairs appeared, now a bare, ragged opening that led to a straight-down plunge into Sarah's Womb. Almost a quarter of the steps had collapsed and fallen into the void.

I signaled a halt. The rope swayed nearby, its pulley apparently still attached somewhere above. The end of the rope dangled far below with no attached basket. Red light emanated from the depths, making the void look like a volcano crater.

I turned to the others. "It's a dead end."

Daryl Red pointed. "Our stubborn stalker is down there. Maybe he can help us."

On the ledge surrounding the huge violin's strings, Patar stood with Amber and Cerulean. They looked up at us, wearing somber expressions.

As the shaking continued, I braced myself against the side wall and shouted, "How do we get down there?"

Patar's voice boomed. "Hold to the rope, and we will lower you. We are able to handle two at a time. Someone will have to jump to grab the rope."

"I heard you have a secret passage. Can we use that?"

"The quakes collapsed it." He and the two supplicants grasped their end of the pull line. "You have no time to hesitate. Jump now."

I guided Kelly to the last step, inches from the precipice, and set the violin and bow in her shaking hands. "Hold these and stand still."

When she nodded, I leaped and caught the rope. My momentum made it swing out, and the backswing brought me within reach of Kelly. One arm holding the rope, I looped the other around her waist and pulled her from the stairway.

She let out a yelp and wrapped an arm around my neck. "Hang on," I whispered. "We'll make it."

As Patar, Cerulean, and Amber lowered us toward their level, I made the rope swing in a wider arc. When we arrived, the swing took Kelly and me to the ledge. I landed, transferred Kelly to Cerulean, and kept my hold on the rope. Once again, my hands felt like fire. I had to ignore the pain.

The ground still trembling, I set my feet. "Do we need Francesca Yellow and Daryl Blue?"

He gave me a solemn nod. "The gifted ones must be involved in the sacrifice."

"Why?"

"Scarlet's death saved Earth Red from destruction." He nodded toward the alcove where the violin strings were anchored. Scarlet's body lay there, her ghostly white face in view.

Bile erupted into my throat. Cringing, I swallowed it and spoke past the pain. "Okay. I get that part. But why can't I do it? I'm a gifted one."

"Convergence has already begun. Duplicates on Earths Blue and Yellow are dying and disintegrating. Daryl of Earth Blue and Francesca of Earth Yellow are in imminent danger, but they can provide for their own escape by being part of the sacrifices themselves. The sooner the deed is done, the fewer people will die."

"Okay. But Daryl Blue's in no shape to hold on. Can you pull me up to her?"

"We can. But beware. I sense my brother's presence. I have taken steps to obstruct his path to us, but he will not be slowed for long."

"Haul me up." I regripped the rope and swung out. I rose in quick bursts that took me to the stairway level in a hurry. Once there, I swung to the steps and explained the situation to the others with as few words as possible. "So that means," I concluded, "I'll take you down one at a time."

"Too slow." Daryl Red looped her bag's strap over Daryl Blue's shoulder and guided her into my arms. "Go. But stay down there. The rest of us can make it on our own."

I blinked. "Are you sure?"

Daryl Red patted my cheek. "Give us some credit, hero boy. We can hold on for dear life as well as anyone." She opened my hand, revealing my lacerated, bloody palm. "Actually, probably better than you can."

"All right. Let's do it."

I held Daryl Blue around the waist. She wrapped both arms around my neck and said in a weak voice, "I'm ready."

I pushed off the stairwell and sailed over the void. As we descended, I whispered into her ear. "How do you feel?"

"Pretty terrible. Like I'm going to pass out."

"Can I do anything to help you?"

She shuddered. "Just ... just talk me through this."

"Okay. I do have something to tell you." Trying not to grunt as my palms burned, I kept my voice steady. "I misjudged you, Daryl, and I said some pretty bad things about you to Kelly. About you being too scared to be with us."

Deep lines etched her brow, but she stayed quiet.

"I apologize for my stupidity. You're a true hero, and I hope you'll forgive me and help me finish what we started."

A breeze in the chamber brushed Daryl's bangs back. The lines in her forehead slackened. She set her cheek against mine and whispered, "Of course I forgive you. I was worried you wouldn't forgive me for being such a coward."

"You're no coward, Daryl. You faced your biggest phobia and defeated it. I really owe you everything."

Daryl hugged me closer and kissed my cheek. "Paid in full."

When we arrived, we swung to the ledge and stepped to solid ground. Above, Francesca held her hand out. I whipped the rope, sending a wave up to her level. She grabbed it and waited for Patar and the supplicants to reel the lower portion of the rope up to her. When they were ready, she swung out into the open.

While Patar, Cerulean, and Amber lowered Francesca, I helped Daryl Blue sit on the ledge next to Kelly, her back to the wall, all the while avoiding glancing at Scarlet's body. When Daryl settled, she closed her eyes and tipped to the side.

I caught her and laid her on the ground. "Daryl, are you all right?"

"Yeah. Just dizzy."

I set a hand on her forehead — cold and clammy. Concussion symptoms? Or maybe worse.

Francesca landed on the ledge, gasping. "Someone's playing a violin to open the door. He doesn't know the code, but when I left, he was close to figuring it out."

Her legs buckled. She collapsed and sprawled on the ground, her face up and her eyes closed. I lunged to her side and set a hand on her cheek, cool and moist. "She's breathing, but her skin's clammy. Same with Daryl Blue."

"It is Convergence," Patar said. "They are dying." He released the rope. "We must carry out the sacrifices immediately."

I shook my head hard. "We can't leave Daryl and Clara up there with —"

Someone shouted above. Daryl Red jumped from the stairwell and grabbed the rope. Clara leaped behind her, slammed into Daryl, and threw her arms around her. As they swung, Clara slid down Daryl's body and grabbed her ankles to keep from falling.

Mictar appeared at the bottom step, the black violin in his grip. With each of the rope's swings, he reached out to snatch it but missed.

I grabbed the rope, but no slack remained. Our end was tied to the anchor hook embedded in the wall. I couldn't lower them, and the knot around the anchor looked tight.

I fished the lighter from my pocket, flicked it on, and set the flame to the rope. When it caught, I dropped the lighter and gripped the rope above the burning fibers.

The rope snapped. I lifted into the air while Daryl and Clara dropped. As the rope wheeled through the pulley, I drew closer and closer to Mictar, while Daryl and Clara descended toward the strings.

The second they landed, I let go of the rope. My momentum sent me flying toward Mictar. I crashed into him and slammed him to the stairs. With a bloody fist, I punched him in the face again and again.

Just as I reared back to punch once more, a loud note pulsed from below. The walls quaked. The stairs beneath us cracked and sagged. Mictar shoved me with both hands. As I fell backwards toward the void, the stairway crumbled and collapsed.

CHAPTER TWENTY-TWO

A S I DROPPED, Mictar grabbed my legs. I turned face down and reached for the golden, rope-like strings. Daryl Red and Clara scrambled on all fours toward the ledge. The moment they reached safety, my arms struck and looped around the closest string. My weight combined with Mictar's bent the string down.

I flexed my muscles and held on. When the string recoiled, I shot upward. Still holding the string, I turned a flip. Mictar rode the rotation with me and we slammed into the strings from the top.

As we bounced, mangled notes flew skyward. The chamber rumbled. Glass shattered somewhere above. Pebbles and shards rained down. As they pelted my head, I climbed to a standing position, one foot on the first string and the other on the second. Mictar copied my pose on the third and fourth strings. He faced me, his eyes pulsing red as he fought to keep his balance.

I looked toward the ledge. Daryl Red held Kelly in her lap, whispering into her ear, while Daryl Blue and Francesca lay motionless on the ground. Cerulean and Amber both took a step toward us, but Patar blocked them with an arm. "No. The son of Solomon is the only one who can save us now."

Mictar shot a black streak from his palm, aiming at me, but the recoiling force bent his two strings and sent the streak flying off at an angle. After battling to rebalance, he glared at me, his face bruised and his nose bleeding. "So what's your next step, fiddle boy? One false move, and you will plunge in a forever fall."

"You want to know my next step? Watch closely." I took a deep breath, bent my knees, and leaped toward him. The bounce sent me into the air. As I dropped, I balled my fists. When I got close enough, I landed a heavy blow to his chin, but he caught me, and we fell across the strings in a twanging bounce.

More rumbles shook the chamber. A new shower of glass and pebbles fell. Mictar grabbed my hair and rose to his feet, dragging me upright. Suspending me above the strings, he kneed me in the groin. Pain throttled my senses. I battled to stay conscious. I couldn't lose the fight. Not now.

"Take a last look at your friends," Mictar said as he turned me toward them. "The harlot has merely lost her sight, but you will lose your life and soul. I will breathe you in, and you will die. Forever."

"Patar!" Daryl Red screamed. "Don't just stand there! Help him!"

Patar crossed his arms over his chest. "He has chosen his own path. His sacrifice is noble, and we must let him complete it."

Mictar laughed again. "How delicious to see you finally tasting the fruit of trusting my brother."

I swung a fist at Mictar, but his long arm kept me from landing it. I grabbed his wrist and dug my nails in to no avail.

"When I take this gifted one's life," Mictar said to Patar, "you and ten supplicants will be no match for me." Mictar pulled me into his arms, my back to his chest, and laid a hand over my eyes. "Now suffer and die."

I took in another breath and tensed my muscles. Light flashed through my eyelids, scalding, stinging. Squeezing my eyes shut, I tried to let my body go lax, but searing pain sent stiffening shock waves from head to toe. I heaved in quick breaths and puffed single-word prayers between jolts of agony. "Give … me … strength … to … defeat … this … monster."

Pain overwhelmed every physical sense. Darkness filled my mind. Death stalked new victims — me, Kelly, Daryl Blue, Francesca Yellow, and maybe others. I had failed. At the last moment, when it mattered most. I lost.

Whispers filtered in—Scarlet's voice, gentle, like a breeze cooling the flaming tongs. *Take courage, my beloved. Your faith will bring life everlasting. This test of fire will merely burn away the dross and transform you into the strongest steel. But you must heed what you have been taught. Remember the words Patar spoke to you when you faced doom in a jetliner.*

The voice transformed into that of the stalker, calm and soothing. *Fear not, son of Solomon, and open your eyes. I am bestowing a gift that will, if your heart is prepared, protect you from my brother. When the time comes to use it, the depth of your courage will ignite this power.*

I gasped for air. How could I heed those words? How could I open my eyes and expose them to the flames?

"Nathan," Kelly cried, "I can't see you. I'm back in my nightmare, and I can't wake up. Help me wake up." Sobbing, she added, "Oh, dear God, I want to see Nathan again."

Clenching my teeth, I opened my eyes to the blinding light. Pain flooded my body. I tightened my fists and let out a roar.

"What?" Mictar shouted. "What are you doing?" His hand lifted, and he pushed me away. I fell to my back on the strings. My eyes burned, but I could see. In fact, the chamber blazed with light.

"Nathan!" Daryl Red called. "Laser beams are shooting from your eyes!"

Mictar pressed his palms against his cheeks and screamed, "What did you do to me?"

Patar strode onto the strings and stopped in front of Mictar. "Days ago, I transferred to him my ability to reverse your energy and absorb it. Now your power will continue to leak until you perish."

His eyes bulging, Mictar's face thinned. He clutched Patar's arm. "Brother! You can help me! You can seal the breach! It is within your power."

"Yes," Patar said. "It is within my power." He grabbed Mictar's collar and pulled him toward the ledge. "Come, son of Solomon. We must hurry."

I rose and walked gingerly behind him. With each moment, my vision clarified further, and new energy surged through my body.

"You knew," Daryl said to Patar. "You knew all along that Nathan could ... whatever it is you said."

Patar stopped on the ledge and forced Mictar to sit. "Not all along. Nathan's ability relied on the status of his mind and heart. If he had tried to use it prematurely, it would not have worked, and death would have resulted."

Kelly swung her head back and forth. "What's happening? Is Nathan all right?"

Now feeling unstoppable, I ran the rest of the way and took Kelly into my arms. I held her close and whispered, "I've got you, Kelly. I'm all right."

Casting a faint glow, Amber glided to Mictar and knelt at his side. As she laid a hand on his quivering shoulder, she looked up at Patar. "Father, shall I end his misery?"

I raised my brow. *Father?*

"Yes, child," Patar said. "He is truly a miserable creature."

Pursing her lips, Amber began a wordless song. Filled with rapid shifts in key and abrupt swings from high to low octaves, it seemed fitting—a violent tune, void of melody, void of order.

As she sang, Mictar convulsed, shrinking with every rhythmic thrash. His body twisted. His skin peeled, exposing crumbling flesh that flaked away from gray bones. Then, his bones shattered. A puff of air rose from the heap, taking a stream of dust in its wake as it lifted into the air and disappeared.

Amber scooped a handful of Mictar's remains and let the dust sift between her fingers, leaving a bone fragment in her palm. Clutching it tightly, she rose and looked at Patar. "Let us proceed. My beloved is near death."

"As is Daryl of Earth Blue." Patar nodded toward Cerulean. "You first, my son."

Cerulean embraced Patar, both with tears in their eyes. When they parted, Cerulean knelt at Daryl Blue's side. "In the name of the Father, the Son, and the Holy Ghost, restore the breath of life and renew the spirit within this fragile shell." He pressed his lips against Daryl's and exhaled. As he blew, her chest expanded. When he finished, he lay on his back and folded his hands on his chest. In a bare whisper, he said, "Please tell my beloved that I will see her in her dreams." He closed his eyes and breathed no more.

Daryl Blue's eyes opened. A blue glow surrounded her head as she rose to a sitting position. Daryl Red guided her to the wall and sat with her there.

After hugging Patar, Amber went through the same process with Francesca. When she lay on her back, she looked at me and whispered, "Nathan, are you now ready to dance?" She closed her eyes and released a final breath.

When Francesca recovered, Clara guided her to the two Daryls, and the four of them huddled near the wall.

Still holding Kelly in my arms, I looked at Patar, too choked up to speak. Three beautiful supplicants lay dead. They gave the greatest supplications possible, their lives.

Patar's eyes sparkled with tears. "Son of Solomon, as a gifted one, you must cast their bodies into Sarah's Womb. And do not delay. Convergence will continue taking lives until the healing is complete. Yet, note this warning. Your parents likely survived Convergence because they are from Earth Red, but once the wounds are sealed, all transport to your world will cease."

"So ..." A sudden darkness filled my mind. "So they'll be stranded on Earth Blue."

"Barring a miracle ..." He gave me a solemn nod. "Decide now. Many are falling victim as we speak."

I guided Kelly into Daryl Red's arms and rose to my feet. My legs shaking, I pulled Cerulean's wrists while Patar pushed him from behind. Once we had hoisted him into my grasp, I shuffled to the edge of the hole. As scarlet light rose from the depths, I whispered, "Lord, take this heroic warrior into your embrace and give him blessed rest forever. And if it's possible, please bring my parents home."

Bending my knees, I heaved him into the void. He plunged out of sight. Seconds later, the light below transformed from scarlet to purple.

My shoulders sagging, I turned to Amber. From the wall, Clara, Francesca, and the two Daryls stared at me, their mouths agape. I understood their bewilderment all too well.

Needing no help from Patar, I lifted Amber into my arms. As I walked toward the edge, I whispered, "Amber, I wish we could've danced together."

Her voice breezed through my mind. *When you dance with your beloved, you dance with me. The time is near. Prepare your heart.*

I gazed at her stoic face, so beautiful, so peaceful. Her voice brought a salve of comfort. Somehow she would continue helping people dance for a long time to come.

After heaving a deep sigh, I threw her into Sarah's Womb. Her dress flapping, she fell into the radiance and vanished. My sigh echoed from the depths, and the light shifted once again, this time from purple to white.

My legs ready to collapse from grief, I walked back to Patar and nodded toward Scarlet's body. "Why is she here?"

"I had need of her. For a purpose I will not divulge at this time."

My contempt for this stalker burned. All along he had bullied me to throw the supplicants, his own children, into Sarah's Womb, and now he had gotten his wish. Yes, maybe their sacrifice had saved the worlds, but it felt too costly, and he seemed too callous. "So, what now?"

He leaned closer to me. "I see that you have already been anointed for a return home. That was a wise and forward-thinking move."

I gave him a nod. Even though I held him in low esteem, the rare compliment was welcome.

"Rest for a moment," Patar said, "until I am able to discern if Convergence has ceased. If it is continuing, your vulnerable friends are safer here than at home."

"Rest sounds good." I knelt in front of Clara, Francesca, Daryl Blue, and Daryl Red, who still held Kelly in her arms. Her vacant sockets staring straight ahead stabbed me with twin arrows. I sat and reached out. "Let me hold her."

Once Daryl had transferred her to my lap, I wrapped her in my arms and wept. She buried her face in my sweatshirt and wept with me. In the midst of my sobs, I spoke in a halting cadence. "Kelly, I will always be your friend. You can always count on me."

Kelly broke out with harder sobs, as if my words had punctured her heart. But why? Why would my promise of friendship bring her more grief?

Scarlet's words breezed back to memory. *Nathan, why would a friend stay silent when he purports to convey good news? Would he not speak of it gladly and not hide behind a mask?*

When Scarlet first spoke those words, I misunderstood them. No wonder she said I might need them again. Now was finally the time.

"Kelly?" I whispered.

"Y ... yes?" She kept her face covered.

"I have something to say, and I don't want another moment to pass without saying it." I licked my parched lips. "A little while ago you said something about me not believing in you."

"I ... I didn't ... mean ..."

"No. You were right. I didn't believe in you. Well, I did a little, but I always doubted. Your past, I mean. I couldn't shake it. I imagined you doing terrible things —"

"I did do ... terrible things."

"Well, even if you did, I shouldn't have let that —"

"Nathan ... it's worse ... worse than you think." She continued through another sobbing spasm. "So now ... God's punishing me ... for what I did."

"No, no, Kelly. God's not punishing you." I again swallowed. My brain seemed to melt. No words came to mind, at least nothing that would soothe her torture.

The aroma of roses returned, and Scarlet's voice coursed through my thoughts. *Good news, Nathan. You have good news. Tell her everything. Hold nothing back.*

I took in a deep breath. *All right. Nothing held back.* "Kelly, God doesn't punish a person for what someone else did. You're not who you used to be. Amazing grace changed you."

"Then ... then why ... are my eyes gone? Why am I blind?"

Her question sizzled in the air. Why indeed? Why did so many innocent people suffer while the guilty went unpunished? How could I answer such an impossible question?

"I'm not sure, Kelly. In some ways, I'm blind, too. There's a ton of things I don't know. Like why all of this is happening. The murders. The stalkers. People who want to destroy entire worlds. It makes no sense. We just have to try to survive. We have to trust and believe. It's our only choice."

Kelly sniffed but said nothing.

I hugged her close. "And you're one of the reasons I want to survive. You're the bravest person I know. Your courage and sacrifice already performed a miracle."

"What?" she whispered.

"You helped me roll the stone from my heart. I couldn't have played the key without getting rid of it." I gently pushed her back and set a hand on her cheek. "No matter what you did in the past, it's gone. Forgotten. Cast a million light years away. You're a different person, and you helped me become a different person. Better. Braver. Stronger." As I brushed her hair back, a trickle of blood oozed from each eye socket like scarlet tears. "I love you, Kelly. I will always love you, no matter what."

"Love me?" She pointed at her face. "I don't ... have any eyes. ... I must look ... look hideous. ... I'm a monster."

"You're a beautiful angel."

"No ... I'm not. ... I'm ... I'm ugly. ... Every time you look at me ... you'll cringe. Like ... like you said, you'll be my friend, but you'd never ... never want to be my ... my ... beloved."

"You're wrong." I pulled her close, nearly nose to nose, and whispered, "Kelly, may I kiss you?"

She gasped. "Kiss me? Why?"

"Because you're beautiful, no matter what."

"But ... but ... your first kiss. On your wedding day."

"Just a preference. You're more important."

Her face twisted into a pain-tortured mask. "If ... if you really want to."

"I do." I kissed her with a soft touch — my dry, cracked lips on hers. Although brief, the sensation felt warm, enduring.

When I drew back, she grasped my hand and held it tightly. "Nathan ... I don't ... know what to say."

"You don't have to say anything. I'm the one who was wrong. I needed to make it right. Like I said. I love you. And I always will."

We embraced again. As she cried on, Patar looked at me and said, "Your supplicant has finished her work in a way you will soon learn. Now it is time for her to join her siblings." He slid his arms under Scarlet's body, walked her to the edge of the void, and threw her in. Seconds later, music rose from the hole, a beautiful combination of piano and violin, though the tune was unfamiliar.

When he returned, he stood next to me. "First, I think Convergence has ceased. Second, I retrieved Scarlet's body from the Womb for a special purpose. Now that you have proven your heart in every possible way, I can show you." He withdrew a plastic bag from within his shirt and poured the contents into his hand—two eyeballs with vessels and nerves still attached. "I recovered Scarlet's eyes. I would like to give them to the courageous lamb."

I cleared my aching throat. "Scarlet's eyes?"

"Yes, the gift of sight." Patar knelt next to us and whispered, "This is going to hurt terribly, but the pain will last only for a short while." He drew back Kelly's hair. Her brow stretched upward and forced her lids open. He then inserted the eyeballs, pushing the dangling strands in first.

With each motion, Kelly grunted and bit her lip hard.

After another moment, Patar released Kelly's hair. "Son of Solomon, now we will provide the healing energy. You have already absorbed a great deal from Mictar, but you will also need some from me." He looked at Daryl Red. "Hold the lamb's eyes open while we proceed."

Daryl scooted over and pushed up on Kelly's forehead while pulling down the skin below her eyes. "Ready. I think."

"Now, son of Solomon, lay your hand over the lamb's eyes. Do it immediately, while the energy channels are open."

I looked at my palm, bloodier than ever. Red light emanated from the pores, pulsing in time with my heartbeat. I covered Kelly's eye sockets with the same hand I had used to revive my mother. But what could a mere touch do? "Do I say anything?"

Patar grasped my free hand with both of his. "No need. Just let your love for her pour through. The stone over your heart has rolled away. The music of your soul has been set free, and now nothing can prevent the flood of holy passion from flowing through your gifted touch."

I pressed my hand down. Light flashed around the edges. For so long I had feared such a sight, an eye-covering hand that radiated energy, but now it provided a different kind of shiver — one of hope and anticipation.

Kelly cried out and tried to shake her head, but I kept my hand firmly in place while Daryl did the same with her hands. Kelly's legs stiffened. She gasped and let out a loud groan.

Energy drained from my body, weakening me to the core. Patar's face turned paler than ever. His eyelids fluttered, and he cringed, but he made no sound.

It seemed that my entire body erupted, spilling everything within — love, faith, joy, courage, peace — everything that gave me life, or at least made life worth living.

I cried out but formed no words. My wild groan echoed, filling the chamber. As the light around my hand dimmed, Kelly squirmed in my embrace.

Patar gave me a nod. "The process should be complete."

I pulled one hand away from Patar and the other from Kelly's face. She turned toward me, blinking. "Nathan?" She wrapped her arms around me and held me close. "Oh, Nathan! I can see! I can see!"

I enfolded Kelly in my arms. We wept together again. In the midst of our gentle sobs, the music from below continued.

Patar toppled over. Now on his back, he looked at me, blinking. "I must go to Sarah and join Abodah and our children. Kindly do me this favor. Roll me into the void, and you will finally be rid of me."

"I'll be right back, Kelly." I kissed her cheek, pushed away, and shifted on my knees next to Patar. "I don't want to get rid of you."

"There is no need to pretend." A timid smile made him look more human than ever before. "You were right to resist my demands. I pressed you too hard, too fast. Although your delays were costly, they were needful."

I took his hand and interlocked our thumbs. My blood smeared across his skin. "Is there anything I can do for you?"

"One favor. Allow me to see Amber's wish come true before I die. The music is already playing."

"You mean ... dance?"

"Yes. The music awaits."

"I can do that." I rose and turned to Kelly, my hand extended. "May I have this dance?"

Staring at me with her mouth open, she climbed to her feet and took my hand. "Yes, Nathan. Most definitely, yes."

While the others watched from the wall, I showed Kelly my bloody palm. "I hope you don't mind."

"Of course I don't mind."

I pressed my palm against hers and intertwined our fingers. "Do you know how to dance?"

"If you lead," she said, pulling my arm around her waist, "I'll follow."

I looked into her eyes, now purplish, a blend of hers and Scarlet's. I stepped into a slow waltz to match the rhythm of the music. A voice joined in, humming the violin's melody.

Only a few paces away, Scarlet walked toward me. Semitransparent, her red hair and dress flowed as though she were strolling on a breezy day. She stopped and spread out her arms. A piano materialized on one side, a girl seated on a bench and her fingers on the keys. On Scarlet's other side, a male teenager stood with a violin. Both played their instruments passionately, dipping and swaying with each note.

I turned Kelly so she could see the musicians, Nathan and Kelly Blue. Like Scarlet, they were semitransparent, their eyes restored and flashing with light.

After we danced for a minute or so, the music stopped. I stopped as well, keeping my fingers locked with Kelly's and my arm around her. Scarlet, her smile radiant, leaned toward me and whispered, "I will see you in your dreams, my love. Try to remember me when you rise from your slumber." She disappeared along with Nathan and Kelly Blue.

"Now," Patar said from the ground, "it is time."

I gestured for the others to join Kelly and me. When they did, I set my hands on Patar's side. "I can't roll you in. You're still alive."

"For the moment." He grasped my wrists and kept my hands in place. Radiance in his body coalesced at his side and poured into me from my fingers down to my wrists. My hands burned. Patar grimaced tightly and grunted as if stifling a scream.

After several seconds, he released me and whispered, "Take one more step of faith. Let Sarah enfold you and lead you home." Then he exhaled and breathed no more.

I lifted my hands and flexed them. My palms and fingers, void of any hint of injury, moved without pain. Patar had bestowed another wondrous gift. And I couldn't even thank him.

The white light in the void pulsed, as if asking for his body. "I guess I have no choice." After letting out another sigh, I rolled Patar in. Light exploded from the void and shot into the air like a geyser. It splashed against the ceiling and ripped a wide crack in the stone. The promontory that held the staircase plummeted. Rocks and dirt rained down. Everyone backed away as the debris cascaded into the hole.

Daryl Red set her feet wide apart. "We'd better do what the head paleface told us. I think this place is about to blow."

As the crack above continued to widen and spill more debris, Kelly, Daryl Red, and I helped Clara, Daryl Blue, and Francesca get up.

"Everyone together!" I took Kelly's hand as well as Daryl Red's. When we all had formed a line at the edge of the hole, I shouted, "Jump!"

We leaped in, blinded by the radiance. An upwelling wind met our bodies and shook our tethered hands loose. Instead of falling straight down, we slid through curves as if careening down playground slides. I called out each of my fellow travelers' names, but no one answered.

Seconds later, the light dispersed. I stood upright between Kelly, Daryl Red, and Clara near a large telescope. Daryl Blue and Francesca were gone, likely guided to their worlds by Sarah. Still somewhat blinded, I blinked toward the computer desk. Dr. Gordon rose from the chair and stared at us, his mouth hanging open.

Kelly wrapped her arms around me. "We made it!"

I returned the embrace and looked at Dr. Gordon. "Is this Earth Red?"

He smiled and gave me a tired nod. "Welcome home, Nathan."

Kelly drew back and pointed at her eyes. "I can see perfectly. Even on Earth Red."

I slid my hand into hers. Her infectious joy radiated into my mind, but I couldn't join in her celebration. Not yet. "Dr. Gordon, any word on my parents?"

"Not much. Voice transmissions through the IWART died, but your father figured out how to send a digital message through the data channel. He said he and Francesca were fine, and they'll hike to the Earth Blue observatory. The last I heard, they were only a few miles from it, but even the digital channel conked out. We won't get any further updates."

"So they *are* stranded." My throat tightened once more. "They're not coming back."

"As far as I know. Moments ago, I detected a surge in the cross-world energy flow, but it was short-lived. I wasn't able to connect with them again, though I was able to lock in on the Earth Blue observatory with our mirror. I was hoping I could get a glimpse of them arriving there, but even that channel is dying."

I nodded. "That surge was probably Daryl Blue and Francesca being sent home."

"I *am* home." The voice came from the computer speakers. Above, Daryl Blue appeared in the middle of the ceiling mirror's image, looking tired as she leaned against the telescope in the Earth Blue observatory. She slid the shoulder bag to the floor. "Sorry about making off with Red's bag and Nathan's sweatshirt, but at least it'll remind me of you guys."

I waved. "No problem. I'm sure every time we see Daryl Red, we'll think of you."

She smiled, though it seemed to take a lot of effort. "I don't have Nathan or Kelly to keep me company, but I think a gorgeous, blue-haired hunk might visit me in my dreams once in a while. Things could be worse, you know."

"Good-bye, Daryl." Kelly blew a kiss. "I love you."

Daryl Red raised a fist. "Stay strong, you beautiful angel. You're as awesome as they come."

I scanned the area around Daryl Blue. My parents were nowhere in sight. The screen flashed and went blank, not a good sign.

Dr. Gordon tapped on his computer pad. "I've lost communication. The radio telescope isn't picking up anything."

"Then every channel is dead?" I asked.

"Looks that way. We haven't even had phones or Internet for hours. We're lucky to have electricity." Dr. Gordon eyed the laptop screen, his expression grim. "I'll keep monitoring the channels, but I think our opportunities to reach your parents have run out."

"What about the original Quattro mirror? Did you ever find it?"

He shook his head. "With all that's been going on, I haven't been able to call the person who might have picked it up. It's far more likely that a clean-up crew threw it away, but I'll give my man a call when we get phone service back. In any case, with Scarlet dead, I don't see how it would do you any good."

"Yeah. You're right." A spasm knotted my gut. My parents were gone. They were dead, then alive again, and now lost on another world. And what about Convergence? How far along did it get? Were Nathan and Kelly Yellow alive? Tony? Gunther? Jack? Simon Blue?

I let out a long sigh. Too many unanswered questions.

Dr. Gordon walked toward us, his hands deep in his pockets. "I heard from your father, Daryl. He was about to take off from London. He should arrive in Chicago in ten hours or so."

Daryl clasped her hands and looked skyward. "Come quick, Daddy. I've got some mission impossible stories to tell you." Her smile wrinkled long red marks that striped her cheeks, though they didn't seem as deep as they did before. Maybe they would heal without leaving scars.

I gave Daryl the best return smile I could muster. "That's great, Daryl. Really great."

Clara walked up behind me and set her hands on my shoulders. "Remember, Nathan, everyone here was used by God to save billions of people. You have lost loved ones. You should weep, and we will weep with you. But for now, allow yourself some satisfaction and rejoicing, and let us rejoice with you. Let's celebrate the lives that were saved."

A tear trickling down my cheek, I gave her the same tortured smile and nodded. "You're right, Clara. As always."

"Yeah," Daryl said. "I think the three worlds should give us the biggest honkin' gold medals in history."

I took Daryl's hand, then Kelly's, and gazed into Kelly's sparkling eyes. "What do you want to do to celebrate?"

Daryl pressed a palm against her chest and gave me a dreamy look. "Why, Nathan, don't you know? We simply have to watch a romantic movie. May I suggest *Pride and Prejudice*?"

I linked arms with her and Kelly. "Get me some popcorn, a tall Dr Pepper, and maybe a few Hershey's Kisses, and I'll watch just about anything."

CHAPTER TWENTY-THREE

THE CLARKS' WIDESCREEN television sat against the wall about five steps away, playing yet another movie. Since it was cold and raining outside, the baggy jeans and loose flannel shirts Kelly and I were wearing felt just right, warm enough to ward off a chill but cool enough to allow for close company on the cushy sofa.

Kelly leaned against my right shoulder, sound asleep. Daryl, in her sweats overtop long johns, did the same on my left, snoring lightly. Three pizza boxes lay open on a nearby table, two empty and one with a slice of liver and anchovies still remaining.

Tony slept on a recliner next to the sofa, having fallen asleep after downing several slices. Clara, who rode back to Iowa with us, ate a few slices of her own before excusing herself and going to bed in one of the family's guest rooms.

Our sofa trio enjoyed our share of hero food. A half-empty bag of Hershey Kisses sat on my lap, and dozens of balled-up aluminum wrappers lay strewn on the floor, intermixing with wayward popcorn kernels and three empty Dr. Pepper bottles, each standing upright with a bent straw protruding from the top.

The movie marathon had started with *Pride and Prejudice* and continued through at least three other features Daryl had brought from her house, selected from her collection of what she called "romantic classics."

As *The Princess Bride* played its final scenes, a comical escape from danger driven by the power of "True Love," the screen grew fuzzy, and the stereo speakers droned unintelligibly, as if the characters' voices had blended together to create a new language.

Blinking, I tried to focus. The Sand Man was about to ensnare another victim. And no wonder; after all we had been through, we deserved an entire week of sleep.

As I yawned again, a female form materialized in front of the television, blocking most of my view of the screen. She created a light of her own, a scarlet aura that spread around the room. Within seconds, her features clarified — red hair, crimson dress, and petite frame. "Scarlet?" I whispered.

She nodded. "You seem surprised. I said I would see you in your dreams." She knelt in front of me, took my hand, and stroked my knuckles with her thumb. "You have laid your head to rest, but your mind is still troubled. Tell me, what is disturbing your repose?"

I blinked again, bringing her lovely face into full focus. The movie's credits rolled behind her, and the sound drifted away. "My parents are stranded on Earth Blue. I'll never see them again."

Pain twisted her features. "I heard about that, Nathan. I'm so sorry."

"Yeah. Nothing can be done about it, though."

"I know you hold out hope. I have listened to your heartfelt prayers, and I have added more of my own. Our Father above knows of your plight, and he is aware of your suffering."

"I'm glad he's aware." I blew out a long sigh. "Not that it'll help ease the pain."

Scarlet drew her head back. "Nathan Shepherd! After all the suffering you have survived, do you think God is going to abandon you now?"

I shook my head. "I didn't mean it that way. Of course God's going to help, but I mean ease my pain right now. It's going to take a long time to feel better."

She offered a sympathetic nod. "True. A hole in your heart can take years to mend."

I tried to smile. I succeeded, at least a little. "If you keep visiting me in my dreams, that'll help a lot."

"Oh, I will, my beloved. To be sure. And I know you are concerned about your friends in other worlds. I will learn what I can about them and report to you in future dreams." She tilted her head. "But there is more on your mind. Tell me what it is."

I shrugged. "I'm not sure. We went through so much, suffered so much in a short amount of time, and then it all ended in such a rush. My mind is still a jumble."

She continued caressing my knuckles. "Just talk out your feelings. I will do my best to untangle the knots."

I looked into her eyes, purplish and shining, exactly the same as Kelly's new eyes. "I suppose the biggest questions are, what was it all about? How and why did all of this happen? And who are the stalkers? If your father was one of them, how are you different? I mean, you're a supplicant and not a stalker, so how can you be the daughter of a stalker?"

Scarlet laughed softly. "Such weighty mysteries for a tired mind."

"Are you saying you won't tell me?"

She looked at her thumb as it massaged my hand. "Nathan, it is a blessed wonder that you have been given this view into worlds unseen. You have a special calling, and the wisdom you have gained will illuminate your future path."

She refocused on me. "You see, most humans in your indulgent culture never learn about the battles and dangers that occur in invisible realms every day of their lives. They wake up, go to work or school, come home to rest, enjoy time with friends and family, go to bed in peace and comfort, and then get up to do it all again, never realizing that wars have been waged in spiritual realms while they labored and slept.

"Messages have flown from mind to mind, urgent communiqués undetectable by physical ears. Some of the messengers have engaged in hand-to-hand combat for the sake of those who could not defend against the invisible. As you have heard for yourself, the sacrifices of the heavens create the most beautiful music in the cosmos."

Her smile straightened into a thin line. "You have now seen these invisible truths, though your view into the world of spiritual realities was a skewed perspective. The stalkers were real, though they are quite different from how they appeared to you — musical manifestations you could comprehend. The melodic keys that opened portals were real as well, but they were mere representations of the true keys that open portals of communication between the physical realm and the spiritual. And the supplicants?"

As she paused, tears filled her eyes. "We are very real. We truly love those in our care, far more than you could ever understand. Although your perception of me is also skewed, in a manner of speaking, I am one who guards you, comforts you, and guides you. And you are my beloved, my precious one whom I will never forsake."

"Do you mean you're not a lovely redheaded girl named Scarlet?"

"I am Scarlet, to be sure, but I am a mystery, an illustration of something greater. And I am lovely. In fact, I am far more beautiful than you can imagine. If you were to see me unveiled, you would not be able to behold my glory. Yet, one part of my manifestation has never been skewed." She rose, leaned forward, and kissed my forehead. "My love for you has been completely unveiled, and your love for me is as real as you allow it to be."

"My love for you?" I looked at her hand. Her gentle fingers continued caressing my skin. "How can I love someone I can't really see, someone who isn't what she appears to be?"

"No one is exactly what she appears to be, at least at first. I think you have already learned that."

I nodded. That lesson had been a hard one. Kelly Clark was once the girl with a gray past. Now that past had been wiped away, and a heart of gold beat within her. "I see your point."

"And as you continue sacrificing for someone you *can* see, you will learn to love me more. You are my beloved, but one day someone will bring you the romantic love I cannot, someone who embraces the light that illumines your heart and mind." As Scarlet tightened her grip, red liquid trickled from her wrist and oozed into my palm. "Do you understand?"

I stared at the dripping flow. The moment a drop touched my skin, it evaporated into sparks of crimson. Scarlet's illuminating light was an illustration of the light of the world. "I do."

She smiled. "The days ahead are bright, Nathan. This lover will ride with you on journeys that will knit your hearts as one — melody and harmony intertwined. Although I think we both have already guessed who that companion rider will be, your time to set out on the journey might lie years in the future. So, for now, do not let your bow stray from the composition. The crescendo is yet to come."

"One more question. You once said that you were like a seed. Will something grow from your seed?"

Scarlet nodded. "Earlier you asked how I differ from the stalkers. The full answer is complex, but, simply put, Patar and Abodah combined in a special ceremony that allowed them to give birth to my species."

"You're the first of a new species?"

"Indeed I am." She pointed at herself. "Sancta sum. That is Latin for 'I am a Sancta.' The Sanctae are a special breed of supplicants, and we can appear to our beloveds. I mentioned this before, but since it was in a dream, perhaps you have forgotten."

"I remember now. You said something about helpers dressed in red."

"Yes. After me, more Sanctae will rise to provide aid to your descendants. Because of my death, I am limited to visiting you in your dreams. Those who come after me, however, will take on physical form as I once did, though any mirrors that remain will no longer have the same abilities they had before. Your descendants will benefit from our wisdom, not from mirrors that provide escape from danger."

"My descendants? No one else?"

"Perhaps a few others will be blessed by a Sancta visit, but we are promised to your progeny. Like you, one of your descendants will rise from the ashes of destruction and help his friends save the world. He will need a Sancta's counsel."

"Save the world," I whispered as I gazed into her sincere eyes. "Is that a prophecy?"

"It is a promise." Scarlet blew on my knuckles. "The breath of God has been given to you, Nathan Shepherd. Let it flow forever. And trust. Trust that God will give you the desires of your heart." She faded and vanished, though her caress still tingled.

"Nathan?"

I searched for the source of the call, but Kelly and Daryl were gone. So was Tony. The room warped. My dream was coming to an end.

"Nathan?"

I opened my eyes. A woman wearing a damp trench coat crouched in front of me, blowing on my knuckles. A man stood behind her, shedding his trench coat.

I blinked at them. Although their faces were familiar, my brain couldn't identify them. They were out of place, from another time.

Daryl stepped out from behind the man and plopped down on the sofa beside me. "Hey, Captain Clueless, is your brain so bruised that you don't recognize your own parents?"

Kelly pulled on Daryl's arm. "Speaking of clueless, Miss Buttinsky, maybe we'd better go help make more popcorn before my dad adds Tabasco sauce to it."

"Okay. Okay." Daryl went along with the pull. "It's not like I need to be told twice."

When they exited to the kitchen, I looked into the woman's tear-filled eyes. "Mom?" I shifted my gaze to the man. "Dad? Am I dreaming?"

"No, son." Dad draped his coat over a chair. "But after all you've been through, it's pretty hard to prove, isn't it?"

"Oh, Nathan!" Mom gathered me into her arms. "It's so good to see you again!"

When Dad stepped close, I rose and draped my arms around them both. "But how did you ... I mean ... did the wounds reopen? Is Sarah's Womb still intact?"

"As far as I know, Sarah is in perfect health." Dad drew back and showed me a mirror square. "Dr. Gordon's agent found it at the funeral and brought it to the Earth Red observatory after you left. We saw Daryl Blue at the Earth Blue observatory and learned that she had a mirror in her bag. Your mother played Foundation's Key, and the Earth Blue mirror sent us to the Earth Red mirror. We popped out in the Earth Red observatory right next to Dr. Gordon."

My dream while on the airliner returned to mind. Didn't Scarlet mention that kind of transport possibility?

As often happened, I had forgotten the details of that dream. I whispered, "That's amazing."

"Anyway," Dad continued, "since all communications are down, we couldn't call to tell you we were coming. Dr. Gordon drove us here."

I scanned the room. "Where is Dr. Gordon?"

"Getting some things from the car. He'll be in soon." Dad helped Mom take her trench coat off. "He told us your story on the way over, but we'd love to hear all the details."

Tears of joy welled in my eyes. "Let's do it. I'll wake Clara."

When Kelly, Daryl, and Tony returned with heaping bowls of popcorn, Dr. Gordon joined us with his viola in hand. Wearing a bathrobe, Clara greeted my parents with hugs and kisses. We pulled in extra chairs and sat around, munching popcorn and talking while Dr. Gordon softly played my part of the Vivaldi duet at a lower register. Tony added loud, silly jokes, and we all laughed.

I looked at each face. My loved ones survived, some of them with painful scars, but they were here where I could see them, hear them, hold them. They were all heroes, every single one of them. And so were those who didn't survive. Sometime soon, very soon, we would have to memorialize them with a service, a monument, and a new song.

After a couple of hours, we all began yawning and nodding off. Kelly arranged for beds for everyone, and Mom, Dad, and Dr. Gordon retired for the night. Daryl received a phone call, signaling that some communications had been restored. Her father had arrived safely in Chicago and was on his way home. When the call ended, her grin told me that every moment she had suffered was worth it.

Now alone with Kelly and Daryl, I stood and stretched my arms. "I guess I'll go to bed, too."

Kelly winked. "Same room as before, but no mirror now. No more nightmares, I hope."

"Right. Good dreams would be a great change." Scarlet returned to mind. Maybe she would have news about our other-world friends. If only I could hear that Francesca was all right, then I could sleep in peace.

Daryl brushed my cheek with a thumb. "Is that a tear?"

I nodded. "Just thinking about Francesca Yellow."

Kelly took my hand. "She's alive, Nathan. So are little Nathan and Kelly. And Tony and Gunther. They all survived Convergence. Gunther has a bandage around his head, though. I'm guessing he found a surgeon who could remove the explosive chip. The only sad thing is that Francesca cries a lot, grieving about her husband's death, I suppose, but she's coping. Little Nathan gives her comfort."

"How do you know all this?"

"Remember how I could see into Earth Yellow so well?" She pointed at her eyes. "I still can. When I close these new eyes, and I am resting, calm and still, I sometimes see visions of things on Earth Yellow."

"But those are Scarlet's eyes. She's an Earth Red supplicant. Why would you see Earth Yellow?"

"Just a guess, but maybe because Kelly Yellow is alive there and Amber's sending me updates." Kelly shrugged. "Who knows? But I'm not complaining. I like peeking in to see how they're all getting along."

I stared at her, unable to come up with anything but a whispered, "That's amazing."

"And you ..." She blinked at me. "You saw Scarlet again, didn't you?"

As I gazed into her eyes, I took in the familiar purplish orbs. I would never be able to hide anything from her. "Yes. I saw Scarlet. But I wasn't trying to hide it. I just haven't had a chance to tell you."

"Nathan …" Kelly's voice softened. "You don't have to explain. After all we've been through, I trust you with all my heart. You're my … my …"

"Beloved?" I offered.

She bit her lip and glanced at Daryl before replying. "I hope so."

We stared at each other. A new tear trickled down my cheek, and Kelly's eyes sparkled with wetness.

"Oh boy," Daryl said. "With you two around, who needs romantic movies?"

I winked at her. "Well, get used to it." I reached into the Hershey's bag and withdrew a Kiss. "And it's not just a hope," I whispered as I pressed it into Kelly's palm and enveloped her hand in both of mine. "It's a promise."

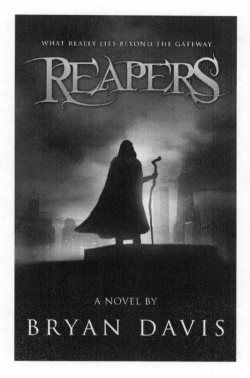

WHAT REALLY LIES BEYOND THE GATEWAY

REAPERS

A NOVEL BY

BRYAN DAVIS

THE REAPERS TRILOGY
THE SEQUEL TO TIME ECHOES

Made in the USA
Middletown, DE
16 December 2024

67391326R00187